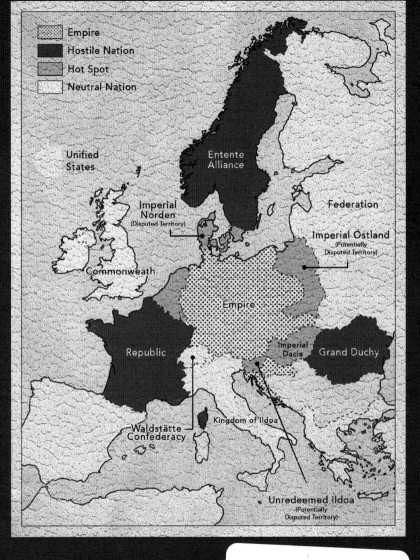

- Empire
- Hostile Nation
- Hot Spot
- Neutral Nation

Unified
States

Entente
Alliance

Federation

Imperial
Norden
(Disputed Territory)

Imperial Östland
(Potentially
Disputed Territory)

Commonweath

Empire

Republic

Imperial
Dacia

Grand Duchy

Waldstätte
Confederacy

Kingdom of Ildoa

Unredeemed Ildoa
(Potentially
Disputed Territory)

D1545636

THE
SAGA of TANYA
THE EVIL

THE SAGA OF TANYA THE EVIL

Plus Ultra

[2]

Carlo Zen

Illustration by Shinobu Shinotsuki

YEN
ON

New York

The Saga of Tanya the Evil, Vol. 2

Carlo Zen

Translation by Emily Balistrieri
Cover art by Shinobu Shinotsuki

This book is a work of fiction. Names, characters, places, and incidents are the product of the author's imagination or are used fictitiously. Any resemblance to actual events, locales, or persons, living or dead, is coincidental.

YOJO SENKI Vol. 2 Plus Ultra
© 2014 Carlo Zen
All rights reserved.
First published in Japan in 2014 by KADOKAWA CORPORATION ENTERBRAIN
English translation rights arranged with KADOKAWA CORPORATION ENTERBRAIN
through TUTTLE-MORI AGENCY, INC., Tokyo.

English translation © 2018 by Yen Press, LLC

Yen Press, LLC supports the right to free expression and the value of copyright. The purpose of copyright is to encourage writers and artists to produce the creative works that enrich our culture.

The scanning, uploading, and distribution of this book without permission is a theft of the author's intellectual property. If you would like permission to use material from the book (other than for review purposes), please contact the publisher. Thank you for your support of the author's rights.

Yen On
1290 Avenue of the Americas
New York, NY 10104

Visit us at yenpress.com
facebook.com/yenpress
twitter.com/yenpress
yenpress.tumblr.com
instagram.com/yenpress

First Yen On Edition: March 2018

Yen On is an imprint of Yen Press, LLC.
The Yen On name and logo are trademarks of Yen Press, LLC.

The publisher is not responsible for websites (or their content) that are not owned by the publisher.

Library of Congress Cataloging-in-Publication Data
Names: Zen, Carlo, author. | Shinotsuki, Shinobu, illustrator. | Balistrieri, Emily, translator. | Steinbach, Kevin, translator.
Title: Saga of Tanya the evil / Carlo Zen; illustration by Shinobu Shinotsuki; translation by Emily Balistrieri, Kevin Steinbach
Other titles: Yōjo Senki. English
Description: First Yen On edition. | New York: Yen ON, 2017-
Identifiers: LCCN 2017044721 | ISBN 9780316512442 (v. 1 : pbk.) | ISBN 9780316512466 (v. 2 : pbk.)
Classification: LCC PL878.E6 Y6513 2017 | DDC 895.63/6—dc23
LC record available at https://lccn.loc.gov/2017044721

ISBNs: 978-0-316-51246-6 (paperback)
978-0-316-51247-3 (ebook)

4 6 8 10 9 7 5 3

LSC-C

Printed in the United States of America

THE SAGA OF TANYA THE EVIL

Plus Ultra

contents

Modern war measures the obvious gap between developed
nations and developing ones—with corpses.

Hans von Zettour, *A Review of the Dacian War*

The first thing Battalion Commander von Degurechaff asks about is the situation in the air.

When the radio operator from Command replies that they have no information about enemy air strength nor any aerial contacts at all, she cocks her head as if she can't believe what she just heard. Her distrust is plain in her next question—whether their communications are in working order.

But the operator assures her that both wired and wireless communications are functioning normally. They're even fully monitoring the Dacian FAC's contact channel.

The next moment, the personnel at Command feel a chill go up their spines. Major von Degurechaff's smiling—an intoxicated smile? An indescribable shock ripples through the room.

No one knew at the time, but if Lergen had seen that expression, he would probably have smiled the same way. It's the smile of a ferocious hunter, and it contains the delight of a starved wolf eyeing its prey.

That's right. She can hardly believe her improbable good luck, but logic tells her it's the truth, enveloping her in a burst of joy. Yes, this is what they mean when they say *filled with emotion*. It's no wonder she can't keep her lips from curling into a grin—the opportunity in front of her is that good.

A battlefield entirely devoid of enemy air cover?

Yes, a battlefield *entirely devoid of enemy air cover*!

The significance of that is so luscious, so terribly seductive. How many officers, how many men, have yearned for relative imperial air superiority in Norden and the Rhine?

Chapter I

Thanks to the complete lack of enemy air forces in Dacia, which is unthinkable in modern warfare, complete supremacy is guaranteed.

No hostile forces in the sky? I have to confess that never in a million years would I have thought the Principality of Dacia's military was this hopeless!

I wanted to avoid the foolish error of underestimating the enemy, but to think I overestimated them to this extent! They say any number of unforeseen incidents can happen on the battlefield, but I heartily welcome any that are this happy.

Has there ever been such a fortuitous turn of heaven's will? Yes, the heavens are literally on our side!

September 24 is only her birthday on paper.

Still, this could be considered her first birthday present ever. Today seems like it's going to be such a wonderful day I'm liable to start skipping around like a giddy little kid. Tanya's cheeks flush, and without thinking, she whispers, "Dear God, thank you for this one-in-a-million chance."

In a normal mental state, she wouldn't even entertain the thought of parting her lips for such an utterance. It must be an expression of her tender feelings toward this command.

The establishment of absolute air supremacy... At least at that moment in time, the only one who understood the significance was Tanya. That's why she shot off running with periodic little skips.

And that entire scene played out where Lieutenant Colonel von Lergen could see it, even as his face was still twitching from the report that six hundred thousand Dacian troops had crossed the border.

Thinking of the dire effects this would have on the front, he wanted to bury his head in his hands. And so, when Tanya ran off with her unit's deployment orders in hand, apparently skipping her briefing, all he and some other personnel from HQ could do was stare after her as if the whole thing wasn't actually happening.

If someone asked what was lacking in the 203rd Aerial Mage Battalion, which had withstood being drop-kicked off a ridge in the Alpen Mountains as part of their extremely authentic training, Tanya would

immediately declare, "Combat experience." Not that the need to further develop esprit de corps and continue training are insignificant issues, but their commander can't stand the fact that her subordinates lack a most critical baptism by fire. No matter how much rookies train at an exercise range, once stationed on a real battlefield they're sure to muck it up.

Not to mention that they've been drilling at the Turao Field Maneuver Area in the southeast—the exact opposite direction from the fighting. She can't deny that they're getting a bit overly comfortable, as everyone does when stationed too long at the rear. It would be a waste if the human resources meant to serve as my shields went soft, so after receiving word to keep an eye out for Dacia, I've been considering it a useful expedient to maintain some degree of tension—and not much more.

Given the disparity of strength between the two nations and the Empire's habit of freely throwing its weight around, I figured Dacia would get the message and mind its own business.

Which is why when the alarm goes off, I'm at a total loss. The Dacians would go to war, risking occupation of their fatherland, in the name of international cooperation? I can't believe idiots like that actually exist! She half expects a stern order to call off combat maneuvers because the warning was a mistake.

But for better or worse, for reasons Tanya can't fathom, they don't seem to care if they really start a war.

"Two hundred and third, to your battle stations, on the double. How's Border Command?"

Command personnel run around shouting requests into radios and telephones to be connected to one post or get information about another.

"Lieutenant Weiss! Reassemble and have someone pass out ammunition!"

"Major, we have a theater report from the Seventh Air Fleet. We've received the Command Post frequency."

"Verify immediately. And get me Lieutenant Serebryakov!"

Efficiently canceling the exercise and giving instructions for their next move, Tanya scowls slightly in the direction of Colonel von Lergen, who seems to have anticipated this. He had dropped her a hint, but if their neighbor Dacia is really planning to oppose them, she would have liked a chance to scope out the area as a military attaché or liaison officer. That way she would have a better grasp of the lay of the land and thus a clearer image of what needs to be blown up.

"...Well, this attack is certainly a bolt from the blue, wouldn't you say, Colonel von Lergen?"

"Spare me the sarcasm, Major. You'll be delaying for us."

As my battalion is under direct command of the General Staff, there's been a constant parade of high-ranking staffers in and out of the garrison. It seems my hunch that they were mainly interested in Dacia was spot-on. That's why when Colonel von Lergen shows up with an urgent update from the border and sealed orders from the General Staff Office, I can only sigh and hold my tongue.

"Huh? Delaying, sir? You mean you want my battalion to stop the Dacian Army?"

"I realize it's unreasonable, but whether we mobilize forces in the east or send reinforcements from Central, war on multiple fronts means we'll need to buy time somewhere..."

Her unit might be newly formed, and she may be an untested commander, but Tanya isn't about to be underestimated. According to the report, it's only six hundred thousand Dacian troops crossing the border. Yes, their infantry is marching through this mountainous region, greener than a bunch of Boy Scouts.

"With all due respect, the Principality's troops are a barely trained rabble of soldiers and farmers, hardly up to modern warfare."

After assuming her post, she'd done a little investigating as part of her Dacian studies and learned that the Principality is a so-called minor nation standing atop an unstable foundation at the moment. It may have a lot of soldiers, but Boy Scouts would probably be better prepared. It's ludicrous if Lergen thinks her battalion can only manage to delay them.

"Mobilize the regional army group? I'm sure four divisions assembled from the surrounding area would be plenty to trample them. My battalion alone would be enough to repulse the vanguard, not just delay."

"...Do you understand what you're saying, Major?"

"I do, sir. I see it as a fully outfitted army driving off a Boy Scout troop. It might even be easier than that."

Chapter **I**

Far from the level of national guard reserves or part-time soldiers, the Dacian forces are half farmers, more like the Korean People's Army. A band of armed robbers would have more discipline than such a riffraff. The imperial troops will crush them in a single blow. If they can't do at least that much, it would be too shameful to call themselves an army. After all, the military of a modern state is a dense conglomeration of precisely managed violence. There's no way such an instrument will find it difficult to scatter an anachronistic mob drawn from whoever happened to be around at the time.

The gap in fighting power between modern and premodern forces is insurmountable.

"All the sealed orders[1] said was to take the most appropriate action to defend the border."

Tanya has been authorized to act at her discretion. In other words, she's been given free rein to do whatever she thinks is best. That's the minimum requirement of a commander as well as the standard for all evaluations. Would a fully outfitted army run from a rough gathering of picnickers? That would be an eternal blot on her record. Tanya would forever be a laughingstock in military history.

Now that the mission has been given to her, the methods are essentially under the umbrella of her discretionary powers. That also means any failure would indicate a lack of resourcefulness. Call me anything but incompetent.

"Colonel, before the Dacian forces crossed the border, was there any artillery fire or struggle for control of the airspace?"

"Well, no."

If these were six hundred thousand Federal or Republican troops with air support, there'd be no shame whatsoever in calling for reinforcements, and that's probably what I would do. But such worries are pointless against an enemy who didn't bother with preparatory bombardment or securing air supremacy. It's quite a pile of soldiers, but they're helpful enough to line up in a row for easy targeting.

---

[1] **sealed orders**   Securely sealed orders. May only be opened in a certain place at a certain time or in a certain war situation. Delivered by an officer.

Experience is a great teacher, and these primitive buffoons are about to learn what a difference modern civilization makes.

"That should tell you something about who we're up against. I'm going to bring the iron hammer of civilization down on these barbarians."

We shall conquer the sky and teach them to fear mages.

"What?"

"My battalion is a fully outfitted and properly trained military force. We'll rout the lot of them."

Modern warfare depends on national strength to a savage degree. Education, training, logistics. There is a world of difference in these areas between countries that are considered great powers and those that are not. History provides eloquent testimony about how undeniable this disparity is. I'm gonna drive these guys off conquistador-style.

"The enemy vanguard alone is three divisions, you realize."

On the map, the Dacian advances are represented by multiple arrows. The one penetrating the farthest into imperial territory is supposedly composed of three divisions—the elite core—from the standing army.

What a joke reality is, seriously. It cracks me up. This vanguard is supposed to be their military's best, and they don't have any armored divisions or mechanized infantry, just plain old foot soldiers. It reflects on their nation's true strength, and it honestly makes me feel sorry for them.

The competition principle, at its core, benefits the strong and crushes the weak. Still, this is the first time I've ever felt guilty that the fight isn't fair.

"This won't even be a battle, just a simple thrashing. I'll teach them what a real army and war look like."

Nothing more than three divisions of amateurs. That's all. The conquistadors had horses and guns, but they still fought it out on level ground. We'll be shooting like mad from our third dimension in the sky, so victory is assured. This is going to be a pseudo-atrocity that can only be described as a live-fire exercise.

"So how far can we go?"

"What?"

"If the enemy's resistance is so fragile that we accidentally overextend, that could be a logistical problem."

"Hold on, Major. What are you saying?"

"Sir, I'm going to give Dacia some educational guidance. I intend to personally drive home for them the high price of the teacher we call experience."

Okay, time for war. No, time for bullying a bunch of weaklings, more like.

How lucky; this pathetic bunch showed up at just the right time. I lick my lips in spite of myself. Unlike the muddy Rhine or freezing Norden, the skies over Dacia in the temperate southeast are sure to have perfect flying weather. It's still September. We'll have any number of opportunities to attack before the sun goes down.

I ponder these things, but all those thoughts disperse when my adjutant comes trotting over.

It's time to work.

"Second Lieutenant Serebryakov reporting in, ma'am. You called?"

"Yes. Lieutenant, what's the battalion's status?"

"Everyone has assembled. Lieutenant Weiss is currently handing out ammunition and explaining the situation."

Their progress is the definition of *smooth*. All according to plan. Tanya even feels her cheeks relaxing into a smile of satisfaction, but she wills them to stay taut. Even elementary schoolers know that the field trip isn't over until they make it home in one piece. It's careless to be so giddy before departing.

But even if I don't like it, it's an undeniable fact that no one at command shares my optimistic view of the situation.

And at the very top, openly anxious, is Colonel von Lergen, watching our preparations in a speechless daze. Well, it seems he's still overestimating these six hundred thousand Dacians from his desk at the General Staff Office. Regrettably, Tanya is forced to confront the reality that though the colonel may be a genius, he's been out of the game for too long. That's why when her adjutant finishes reporting in, she nods in satisfaction and pounds her little fist against her chest as if to tell Colonel von Lergen, *Leave this to me.*

⋆   ⋆   ⋆

Just as described, the unit has speedily assembled and is equipped with their training gear plus the distributed live ammunition. The soldiers are ready to sortie. Apparently, despite being a little winded from the interrupted exercise, it's not enough to affect their combat performance. Very good.

"Attention, battalion! Instructions from our commander!" First Lieutenant Weiss barks orders, his heels angled perfectly at a formal forty-five degrees.

In response, the members of the battalion align their feet and straighten up with movements that are nothing if not brisk. Before she knows it, Tanya finds herself smiling in satisfaction. Surely everyone agrees there is something uniquely charming—dreamy, even—about rigorous discipline.

"Thank you, Lieutenant. Okay, troops, this is war. Well, something resembling war...and it's about to begin."

Perhaps it's even charmed Tanya into taking the dais with unconscious excitement and a smile of pure joy, nearly singing to them how happy this makes her.

"Today is my birthday. Maybe the Principality of Dacia knew that? As you've heard, they've been kind enough to offer the surprise present of targets for a live-fire exercise."

I have been hoping for some. It's so nice of the Dacian men to volunteer themselves.

"You're free to shoot them with bullets or blow them up with spells."

They won't even have a chance as we slaughter them from the sky unopposed. It'll be an even bigger turkey shoot than the one in the Marianas. The only question will be how great a victory we can achieve.

"Troops, we're going to teach these invaders a lesson—with an iron hammer."

Which is why she makes a fist and brings it satisfyingly down on an imaginary Dacian Army as she shouts to crush them. *Beat them into a pulp!* Her enthusiasm makes her intention clear to all present.

It was a savage proclamation that the Imperial Army's advanced forces would literally pulverize the Dacian Army vanguard. The result is a given, so she commands them to go out and make it happen.

"One last thing. I haven't received any confirmation of this, but our target practice should retaliate...in theory. I don't think any of you are stupid enough to get shot down, but keep an eye out. Okay, we're restarting the live-fire exercise. Gentlemen, let the games begin."

This is a manhunt, in a way—literally. A sport.

Or a story to give the legendary knight Don Quixote a run for his money. After all, our enemy is a bunch of anachronistic heroes from a bygone era challenging a terrifying modern monster.

Leaving the rear personnel and the handful of officers visiting from the General Staff Office to man the garrison, Tanya leads the battalion, setting off as the fastest responding unit in the Imperial Army. Their target is the Dacian Army's vanguard, three divisions or so that have crossed the border and started the war. The fact that everyone is flying in perfect strike formation and remembering their training means that Tanya's work is already paying off, to her great satisfaction.

Before long, she manages to make contact with the evacuating Imperial Army Border Patrol units. Receiving the latest about the enemy from them, Tanya is convinced.

Without a doubt, whatever strategy the Dacian Army has in mind is some kind of medieval relic. Moments later, making minute adjustments to their course and preparing for their attack runs as they rush ahead, the battalion sees a writhing mass of humans on the horizon.

How kind of them to wear brightly colored uniforms and pack together in dense formations. Their outdated military doctrine doesn't take magic strikes or aerial bombardment into consideration. They are at once splendid prey and a wasted mountain of human resources. What a pathetic nation. To have so much human capital but be entirely incapable of putting it to good use.

Anyhow, it's the Imperial Army's job to blow these youths away. So I'll leave the condolences for the sorrow of the widows and elderly to the Principality of Dacia's foolish government.

"Aconitum 01 to all hands. This operation is a go! Teach those fools the definition of *war*!"

The battalion is using an incredibly obvious, textbook tactic for aerial mages facing ground forces, where three of the four companies attack from three different directions. That leaves one company leftover, which is a great problem to have. Normally, the enemy would have direct support, and I'd send that company to fight for control of the air, but...if you can believe it, today they are simply extras.

"Company commanders, I'm expecting you to follow your orders and show me good results!"

""""Understood!"""""

I could save them as backup, but things are going so smoothly it hardly seems like I need them. The companies on the attack aren't even attracting any anti–air fire with their tight maneuvers. All the enemy ground troops can seem to do is panic as my mages lay waste to them from the sky. If all I do is watch, people might start saying I get paid to stand around.

"I'm stumped, Lieutenant. There's nothing for us to do."

It's not as if I'm pro-war or a workaholic, but I do worry what other people will think if I'm the only one not being productive while everyone else is working. It has been two months since the battalion was formed, and it's clear to Tanya that the General Staff is keeping a close eye on how they are doing. There's a strong need to take aggressive actions and achieve appropriate results.

"...I was bracing myself for a difficult battle."

"You're nervous about three measly divisions on a reckless, half-baked rampage? That doesn't sound like a veteran of the Rhine front."

"I mean, Major...it's *three divisions*. I don't mean to be presumptuous, but your sense of these things is...a little, er...never mind."

Ahh. I realize that Lieutenant Serebryakov is at least a little bit right. I should use my words properly. This Dacian unit does consider itself to be three divisions.

Is my adjutant's hesitance a sign of her apprehensions regarding my lax use of specialized vocabulary? ...That has to be it, without a doubt. I guess it's my mistake for taking a post-structuralist lightly. It's very dangerous when phenomena are evaluated based on words. I've got to deconstruct this and remedy my error.

"...Sorry, Lieutenant Serebryakov. It seems you're right."

"Er, ma'am?"

"Yes, technically, I should have said it's a fifty-thousand-man mob on a reckless rampage. If you don't properly define your terms, of course you'll invite misunderstanding. Honestly, what was I thinking…?"

It appears Lieutenant Serebryakov and the others were expecting the fight to be a bit tougher. *Their ability to brace themselves for a harrowing battle against a mighty enemy shows good mettle, but it was my mistake to label the enemy forces "divisions."* Tanya can only show remorse for making her subordinates think the Dacian Army is a serious military power.

This conflict will be this world's first world war. For most soldiers, it will be their first experience with many things, including the menace of aerial fighting power. They're so caught up in two-dimensional warfare that they have yet to understand the value of the sky when battles become three-dimensional.

"Okay. We should participate, too. Command Company, follow me. Let's poke at their leaders."

That's why she wonders how this battle against opponents with no presence in the air could be any more one-sided. Lieutenant Serebryakov and the others' worries are starting to seem a little amusing. The point of this battle is simple. All they have to do is reap the heads of the enemy soldiers. Then they'll transition to blowing any remnants of the enemy forces to literal smithereens.

"On me! On me!"

We swoop down and drop formula-fixed anti-surface grenades. The goal with these is to scatter shrapnel, so they explode above the enemy soldiers. The fools aren't even wearing iron helmets, so their heads turn into pincushions. But we don't have time to watch; the company preps formulas, locates optimal locations, then opens fire with full power.

We blow away the tightly packed infantry, and the surface devolves into total chaos as soldiers run in all directions trying to avoid the blasts. There is some sporadic return fire, but for infantry rifles to pierce our defensive shells, they would need to wear them down with a dense barrage.

This battlefield, devoid of the harsh sound of heavy machine-gun fire, is a horrible place for the infantry, forced to use nothing but their basic firearms in rudimentary anti-air tactics, but for those of us who can fly, there's nothing better.

"The Dacian Army is dragging their feet. They're too slow. All companies, give me an update."

"Everything's fine, Major."

"No problems here."

"This really is a live-fire exercise."

"It's weird. I was sure we were the ones being attacked, but…"

This is such a letdown. The scene below is so absurd that I nearly wonder if we mixed up offensive and defensive roles somehow. Those Entente Alliance numbskulls crossed the border without intending to fight, but once battle was joined, they took it seriously and fought almost too passionately.

The Principality, on the other hand, has plenty of motivation and declared war from their end, but they just have no idea what war even is.

"This really is strange. Did they think they could hit us and we wouldn't hit them back?"

"Seriously, these poor half-wits."

Even in a fistfight, you expect some retaliation after punching someone. Of course, when two nations' instruments of violence clash, you should be able to maintain a minimum of dignity, despite the foolish quarrel, with artillery. These guys need to take a tip from Frederick the Great.

I'm stuck waging a war against these idiots, so clearly I'm the one who has it the hardest. Of course, ever since the evil Being X interfered with my ultra-ordinary working adult life, I haven't been optimistic about my fate even once…

"By the way, what's that? What are they doing?"

As Tanya finishes communicating with the companies, she adjusts her altitude to prepare for another attack run when she notices some kind of organized movement beginning on the ground. According to Imperial Army textbook, the expected enemy response to this situation would be to have their soldiers spread out and begin anti–air fire in areas designated by their commanders.

But rather than putting space between one another, they are starting to form densely packed squares.

"Are they panicking?"

True, becoming isolated on a battlefield is a terrifying prospect. My adjutant's understanding of the situation is perhaps the most realistic... but from what I can see, officer-looking types are actually commanding them to form up in those ranks.

"...It doesn't seem to be confusion. I think they're making an infantry square..."

"But that's so stupid...! The age of cavalry is over!"

Yes, just as Lieutenant Serebryakov's astonished remark would suggest, we are conducting not a cavalry charge but magic ground attacks. The correct response is spreading out to minimize casualties, and it's honestly hard to imagine that there are soldiers in this day and age who would form an infantry square under the belief it would achieve anything. Even a civilian should be able to tell that bunching up would be dangerous.

"How far back in time are they living? Is this some kind of mistake?"

Or maybe another power has given them some sort of new doctrine or technology? But as those unlikely scenarios flit across Tanya's mind, the simplest solution is to quit worrying and attack to observe their reaction.

A moment later, however, she instinctively explodes at the scene unfolding in front of her. "Weiss!! Why are you running away?!"

She can't believe her eyes. Confronted with an enemy infantry square, Lieutenant Weiss's company has hastily changed course.

The Dacian troops are all packed together. They're doing nothing but holding their positions and bravely waiting for the moment they get blown up, the poor bastards. The pain of being such a badly misused human resource would have evaporated in an instant.

Conscious that she is practically quaking with anger, Tanya screams, "Hey! Why are you reversing?! Why are you breaking attack formation?!"

"Major!!"

But the scene has made Tanya so furious that Lieutenant Serebryakov's startled shout has no effect.

Weiss's company was in position to make their assault, but then they hastily turned away from the enemy as if they were scared. As far as Tanya could tell, there was no evidence of a counterattack that could warrant such a move.

Her suspicion that they are fleeing before the enemy—the worst explanation possible—rapidly eclipses any other thoughts. Her men are spreading out and pulling back in the face of such flaccid defense? The sheer spinelessness astounds her.

Unaware that her teeth are grinding, she doesn't even hide the fact that she's lost her temper. "Lieutenant, go get the vice commander! If he resists, you can shoot him!"

"Y-yes, ma'am."

I order Serebryakov to grab Lieutenant Weiss by the scruff of his neck and drag him over on the double, but at the same time, a sinking sense of betrayal takes over. I thought he was going to be a good vice commander. I thought he was a great subordinate. So how—HOW?!—could he be deserting now? This is ludicrous. The fact that the vice commander of the 203rd Aerial Mage Battalion fled before this rabble will be a blot on my career that will haunt me for the rest of my life.

I at least want to sublimate my rage rather than waste it on chewing him out, so I seal a compound explosion formula inside a magic bullet. Thanking the archaic mind-set that had the Dacian Army still struggling to maintain ranks, I fire. The shot lands right where I aimed, in the center of the enemy formation, and detonates.

Seriously, this is the easiest fight. It can't even be counted as one of the Lord's trials; it's ridiculous.

"Major, here's Lieutenant Weiss." Lieutenant Serebryakov makes her report as efficiently as possible, as if to avoid conflict.

Tanya proceeds matter-of-factly, not because she interpreted the gesture favorably but more because it simply didn't register. "Thanks. Take my company. Continue the attack."

"Yes, ma'am!"

Even the continuing verbal exchange is irritating. Having rather irresponsibly entrusted her company to Serebryakov, Tanya closes in on Weiss as if she's going to bite him, openly livid. He has no idea why the commander has suddenly called him over.

"All right, Lieutenant, if you have an excuse, you'd better give it to me before I shoot you."

"M-Major von Degurechaff, what exactly do I need an excuse for?"

"You're suspected of fleeing before the enemy, Lieutenant. If you need an explanation, maybe we should grill you in a court-martial!"

Weiss still hasn't figured out why he was called over. Of course he doesn't. After all, he can't recall making any mistakes. But it isn't normal for the battalion commander's adjutant to take a position to shoot him down as if he were an actual enemy and summon him "immediately."

"Major! My men and I would never abandon our duty…"

This is precisely the moment he realizes he's stepped on a huge land mine, despite not understanding why. *What did I do?* Still, he can sincerely swear that he only intended to fulfill his duty. His conscience vis-à-vis God and his fatherland is clean.

And that's why he dares to argue against his superior officer, who looks ghastly enough to be a furious vampire.

"Then tell me, Lieutenant, why you drew back and spread out just moments ago? Why did you turn around?"

"What?"

"Explain why you turned tail and scattered in the face of the enemy!"

But the shouts raining down on him didn't take his defense into account at all; on the contrary, the anger and murderous hostility only increased.

"Ma'am. The enemy infantry assumed an anti–air formation, so I played it by the book and pulled my unit back to the edge of their range and ordered containment fire on the enemy unit."

"Book? What book?"

"*The Twenty-Second Aerial Magic Combat Field Manual.*"

His response is dead serious. From Weiss's perspective, he skillfully acted according to his training in the Eastern Army Group and made the right call. But I want to teach him via actual combat that referring to the manual for every operation is nonsensical. Really, there's a limit to what the manual even covers.

That's why it takes me a minute to remember… Ah, right, it was recommended in the section about anti-surface strikes to avoid anti–air positions…but after recalling it, Tanya's face twists up in disgust.

"Wait a minute. Look over there! That's enemy infantry! Do you not understand that I ordered you to attack immediately?!"

"Yes, they were in a close-ranks firing position, so I ordered my company to avoid them."

It's just— It's just a bunch of infantry standing close together! she wants to scream, but Weiss's explanation was straight out of the textbook.

"Lieutenant, let me make this clear. If we have any mages who would get shot down by *that*, I will kill them before the enemy has a chance."

"But, Major—"

"Listen up, Mr. Common Sense, I'll explain this only once. Do you really think bolt-action infantry rifles firing at the edge of their effective range can pierce a mage's defensive shell?!"

It's not as if you're heavy cavalry about to get dashed against a tercio with their pikes and muskets. The utter stupidity! The lethality of our sidearms alone is enough to render their infantry square defense useless. The point proves itself when you look at the current Rhine front or the amusing nastiness in the Far East between Akitsushima and the Federation.

Hence Tanya's difficulty grasping the notion of her subordinate who had been trained with completely outdated doctrine. If the infantry has gathered together to commit suicide, why not assist them? But apparently, that's difficult to comprehend for someone who has never experienced actual combat. Especially since live ammunition doesn't get used on the exercise range, the sight of all those barrels pointing at them from a dense infantry formation tends to elicit a conditioned reaction to reverse course; the longer someone has been serving and training, the stronger that tendency.

"I'll give you a chance to clear your name. Try shooting a formula straight into the middle of that formation."

"Huh?"

"…After me. I'll give you an example."

With that, Tanya loads a magic bullet into her rifle and maneuvers neatly down to attack the middle of the long formation. If his superior officer is going to rush the enemy, Weiss has no room to argue; all he can do is follow. He's grimly determined as he hastily swoops after her to perform what he's sure is a desperate, reckless charge.

"...You blew them away."

"There are no words. Now do your duty!"

He casts the formula directly in the middle, according to his training. They even have time to watch scraps of flesh scatter in all directions. Whether the enemy could defend or not, surely, they have some way of countering—is what most of the Imperial Army troops think. As Weiss is definitely in that camp, seeing Dacian soldiers, who went to the trouble of bunching up with no plan, get blown apart is an utterly novel sight, even on a battlefield.

"Major...my sincere apologies."

"Lieutenant Weiss, I'll consider your error the result of inappropriate training. I guess it's a good thing we're doing this live-fire exercise."

"Thank you, ma'am."

"Sheesh, I never expected there to be problems during such a simple exercise. The fringes of the Imperial Army are unexpectedly shaky. How sad."

Up above, she breathes a sigh. She even misses what's coming over the radio reports for a split second. Tanya takes a deep breath and suppresses her emotions that threaten to blaze out of control. The reality is that education and training for the new realities of war aren't reaching even the best soldiers. Which means, unfortunately, the army's doctrine[2] is failing to meet real combat situations.

I'm forced to realize that apparently those in the rear don't understand the frontline experience. Or perhaps a better way to put it is that they're failing to acknowledge the paradigm shift?[3] It's almost certain that

---

[2] **doctrine** In a military sense, pertains to beliefs about combat. In other words, the thinking behind employing each army's fighting force and the strategy, operations, and tactics involved. Of these levels, the concept of operations has been nearly forgotten, so be aware of the terrible tendency to discuss war as strategy and tactics. Also, even if you know the difference between strategy, operations, and tactics; the different hierarchy terms; and hierarchy-like terms, it's still so easy to mix them up.

[3] **paradigm shift** When phenomena unexplainable by the current paradigm, the current way of understanding things, pile up and we switch to a new way of understanding. Example: geocentric theory → heliocentric theory

most of the officers in charge of training recruits still fail to understand three-dimensional warfare.

Veterans of the Norden and Rhine fronts have written enough reports on what they learned through combat to make anyone sick, but the people reading them are only interpreting the information through the old models of war. The implications are truly sad. The situation is far worse than I thought, to the point where I feel disgusted—this is just tragic.

The entire Imperial Army is failing to learn from even the instructor whose exorbitant fee can only be paid in blood and iron: experience.

Now I understand why General von Zettour and the other Service Corps authorities assumed the combat accounts couldn't provide enough instruction for the armies in the east and south and wanted to create a unit immediately under the General Staff Office partially just to advise them directly.

The extravagant folly of lowering your guard in combat airspace to sink into thought… This kind of contemplation is only possible because of our overwhelming air supremacy. In a way, it would make sense to be happy we're winning, but there are a few problems on Tanya's mind that make celebrating impossible.

"We've found their command post."

"That's awfully fast. It's not a fake?"

Unbelievable things keep happening one after the other. Even Tanya never imagined there would come a day she would distrust her subordinate's reports this much.

Yes, we have air supremacy, and we're using leadership decapitation tactics…but does that mean the top of the enemy command chain can be exposed so easily?

"There's no mistake, Major."

"Is it the frontline command? Lower than that?"

If they could pick it out in this chaos, it had to be either a division or brigade command post.

"No, it's the headquarters of the invading army."

"What? Are you sure?"

For a moment, the words seem to mean something inconceivable.

Headquarters?

Of the entire invading army?

"We intercepted an unencoded transmission."

Conclusion: It has to be a basic form of disinformation. Even if they are panicking, there's no way even the lowliest radio operator, much less a comms officer from their headquarters, would send information without encoding it.

"Then it has to be a fake message."

"No, I understand why you would say that, but…everything we're picking up in this airspace is clear."

"…Seriously? That's hard to believe."

"But they aren't even limiting the signal strength. It may seem unlikely, but it could be real."

Though the look on his face is half-disbelief, he reports in a voice that can only belong to people who thoroughly understand their job. To put the incomprehensible situation into plain words: Is the Dacian Army attacking with only ground troops and sending unsecured communications from their headquarters…for the benefit of the Imperial Army?

Though Tanya just reprimanded a subordinate for relying too much on rigid common sense, she's plagued by it as well. Of course, her own sense is optimized, raised to a whole other level.

I still doubt what he said, but when I use my orb to listen in to the signals, there is a huge convoy emitting uncoded transmissions in one spot.

"Lieutenant Weiss, bring your unit and support mine. Lieutenant Serebryakov! Round up the company and follow me!"

""Roger!""

Just in case it's a trap, we make sure to secure a route for rapid withdrawal as we approach. I have Lieutenant Weiss's company get into position to support our advance, and with their overwatch covering our backs, I have my company begin aerial maneuvers for reconnaissance in force. Presuming the enemy will fire a volley, I consciously thicken my defensive shell. I enter the enemy's range knowing that in addition to the Type 97, I can boot up my Type 95 in a worst-case scenario.

I'll get shot at.

The possibility was on my mind, so of course I had imagined a number of shots from the ground.

"…Of all the ridiculous—!"

That's why I shout in disbelief. Surely even the sloppiest army can manage to defend their headquarters. In stories, even dictators and corrupt commanding officers diligently make sure their immediate surroundings are guarded.

But…

But no one is shooting at us.

"How disappointing. Gentlemen, are we not at war? Is this lot an actual army?"

It's good that things are going smoothly. There's no doubt about that. But in war, nothing going according to the plan is a given. Even if I thought it would be possible to repulse these invaders, I never dreamed things would go *even better* than anticipated.

To think we can storm the Dacian Army headquarters without even falling out of assault formation and face zero resistance.

"We didn't accidentally attack a tour group visiting the Empire, did we? If so, that would be a major accountability mess." The situation is so unexpected that I murmur something uncharacteristically silly—it wasn't funny enough to be a joke.

"My apologies, ma'am."

"It was an error not to check with immigration first. Next time we'll make sure to consult with them."

The members of the battalion skillfully playing along, hanging their heads to express their regret, must feel something is off, too. If this is all we're dealing with, it'll seem like I subjected them to hellish training for no reason. Seriously, these enemies are so easy I'm going to get mistaken as a sadist.

That's why, when we descend to capture the field HQ, its flag flying prominently despite the danger, Tanya is so confused that she fires off another rare joke.

"…Yes, excuse me. Are you the tour leader? The Empire humbly apologizes for the trouble we've caused. Embarrassingly enough, Imperial Army Border Patrol thought you were an army…" She mimics her subordinates' humorous motions, lowering her head and then bowing slightly in the direction of the pathetically wailing, panic-stricken enemies. A silence falls as everyone in the tent is rendered speechless, but the next moment, she abruptly delivers some stock greetings with a cheerful smile. "Welcome to the Empire! What is the purpose of your visit? May I see your passport?"

The silent Dacians have probably frozen in response to the bizarre circumstances. But as their brains start to reboot, they finally begin to process what is going on. In all the confusion, a fully armed little girl has attacked them before they even realized and is now engaging them in a game of pretend immigration inspection.

"Cu-cut the crap!" The officers were all wearing so many decorations a sniper wouldn't have known who to aim at first. *This girl is toying with us...* Realizing that, one of them leaps at Tanya, but First Lieutenant Weiss steps out of the formation and kicks him to the ground, where he passes out. Problematically, judging from his decorations, he's the most senior officer present. In a way, this is actually the first thing that hasn't gone according to plan.

"How about the rest of you? Would you like to enter the Empire as prisoners?"

If they surrender, Tanya will have no choice but to treat them as regular prisoners of war according to the law. Driving off three divisions is easy, but feeding that many prisoners would be really hard. Just the thought of the additional burden it would put on Logistics is dizzying. Still, as slaughter isn't one of her hobbies, she advises them to surrender...at least, that's what she's doing from her perspective.

"Preposterous! As if the Dacian Army would ever surrender!"

"This is a waste of time. Shoot everyone except that general."

Sadly, they didn't understand, but she's happy to give the order to fire.

The rest is fairly straightforward. Her company of mages conducts a close-quarters battle against a company's worth of command post personnel. Taking on mages at close range with little more than pistols is suicide. Before long, the outcome that will no doubt be printed in Dacian textbooks is reached.

They eliminate their targets without a hitch, and the tent is filled with fresh corpses. Like a gang of burglars, Tanya's company is snatching up every document and apparatus they can find and cramming them into their packs. The papers and high-ranking prisoners, albeit few in number, will be good souvenirs for the General Staff.

"Set a booby trap. Yes, we'll put it by that head."

At the same time, before the disorganized Dacian soldiers realize something is amiss with their headquarters, Tanya has her troops leave a little parting gift for them, too.

"The head of that officer we propped up is going to explode. No doubt it'll be very effective against these guys."

A bit of a crude move but also a classic, and the tactic has been in use for so long because it works: rigging a corpse with a booby trap. It's a huge blow to morale, and we can also inflict casualties on any enemies who come to rescue the HQ personnel. Pretty good return for a low-cost investment of time and effort.

"If only there were a pamphlet about group sightseeing tours..."

"Lieutenant, do you have any paint? I'd like to make an immigration stamp..."

"Hey, don't play with the corpses! Take this war seriously!"

Tanya raises her voice slightly to warn her soldiers, who seemed to have relaxed with the path to victory so clear. This isn't a game for kids. Her troops have to remain vigilant. It's understandable why tension is low, but they had best stay on their toes. If she loses any men in this joke of a fight, it'll be a failure worse than useless Italy getting driven off by Ethiopia; I'd never live it down.

That said, when Tanya flies up to look down on the scene, she's plenty satisfied with what she sees. The Principality's army is still marching in ranks down the road, and the 203rd Aerial Mage Battalion is assaulting them from every direction. The fragility of an army without any aerial or magic support combined with the virtually insurmountable gap between modern and ancient military technology have resulted in excellent achievements for the Imperial Army.

Gaping holes have been blasted into the Dacian Army formations, and personnel who have fallen out of rank litter the ground.

It'll take more than a few hours to reorganize this chaos. After all, we've succeeded in mowing down the command personnel responsible for stepping up and taking charge of this mess. And even if the next in command makes every effort to get the army united again, this is the chaos they'll be up against. There's no way to regain control.

The only way the overwhelmingly inferior Dacian military can hope to hit us hard is by launching a sneak attack with blitzkrieg tactics. Sending unsupported infantry to attack the Empire is incompetent enough to give full-of-shit-guchi in Imphal a run for his money. If any Dacian officers can get this army back on the march by tomorrow, they deserve medals.

"Lieutenant Weiss! Is your unit assembled?"

"Yes, Major. What about the remainder?"

It seems he's about to ask, *Shall we mop them up?* and Tanya just barely manages to control herself and not burst out laughing. All this guy wants is to rack up achievements. Even though he only just wrapped up his first battle, and he played it entirely by the book, he's eager enough to mention the necessity of increasing their success—he is excellent material.

"Our air fleet has been deployed, right?"

That's why she softens up when she poses the question. You could say the key to making things go smoothly is searching for positives. Before, she was critical of his actions but not anymore. That's the trick to managing personnel in the army.

"Yes. The Seventh Air Fleet is under way and should arrive momentarily."

"Then let's leave the cleanup to them. We're advancing."

"Ma'am! Where are we headed?"

Weiss's brisk response is proof that he's at least somewhat soldier material. It seems like he'll perform his duties with more sincerity than I anticipated. If I can use him, I need to use him well.

"The capital."

"The capital, ma'am?"

"Yep." Tanya senses that she's mellowed out quite a bit as she gives him a magnanimous nod. "Have an escort take the injured and prisoners and withdraw. You can choose who to send."

"Yes, ma'am. No one sustained even minor injuries, though, so in that case... What would you like me to do?"

"Oh, right."

When he points it out, I realize that it's hard to imagine sustaining any casualties in that kind of battle. Well, it's not like I assumed there were any. It was more to be considerate. Or force of habit? Though I'll eventually have to admit that I've been just a little intellectually lazy.

Tanya has grown used to the weight of her rifle, so is this just making mountains out of molehills because she's nervous about commanding a battalion for the first time?

If that's the case, I need to compose myself better. A leader shouldn't dampen the mood for no reason.

"All right. Then have the ones who are the most exhausted go. This is going to be a long advance. Yeah, send some of the newer officers who just had their first battle back to base."

"May I send one platoon from Fourth Company?"

"That seems reasonable. I'm leaving it up to you."

Weiss actually makes fairly good calls on things like unit management, and Tanya has come to trust him during their time at the garrison. Peacetime company commanders aren't worth their salt unless they can properly lead their subordinates. Whether he turns out to be a decent wartime company commander or not depends on his experiences going forward. I just hope he grows.

Anyhow, at least one of my hand-selected war maniacs has the right skills and spirit for battle. With his measure of common sense, I have no complaints about making Weiss my right-hand man, and I'm eager to have him contribute to my security. Well, I guess I should just keep using him and see how things go.

"Okay, now we can push farther, Lieutenant!"

"Yes, ma'am."

"Farther! Even farther! Let's see how far we can go! You never know until you try."

But for now, we should enjoy our bonus level. With that thought, Tanya smiles in amusement. It's the smile that chilled Colonel von Lergen to the bone. She grins from ear to ear in celebration of their continuing advance. *Now, onward! Onward, still!*

That is the 203rd Aerial Mage Battalion's raison d'être, and none other. Mysteriously enough, First Lieutenant Weiss is wearing the same smile without realizing it as he salutes.

Every soldier accepts the orders without question, believing that if anyone can forge a path forward, they can.

With the arrival of the Eastern Army Group's strategic reserves, the Seventeenth Army and Air Fleet (which had split up on their way over), the Dacian Army lines were demolished. Two thousand dead and innumerable prisoners. The battle had pitted six hundred thousand against seventy thousand, and the seventy thousand trampled them. The outnumbered side, the 203rd Aerial Mage Battalion, had been the first to strike and held absolute control of the skies over the combat zone. After scoring a victory, they decided to attack the capital ahead of the air fleet. At the time, Battalion Commander von Degurechaff was so confident it veered close to arrogance, boasting, "Who *couldn't* run them over?"

**》》》 SEPTEMBER 25, UNIFIED YEAR 1924, 3:17 AM AIRSPACE ABOVE THE 《《《
OUTSKIRTS OF THE CAPITAL OF THE PRINCIPALITY OF DACIA**

Night fell on the capital of the Principality of Dacia as calmly as any evening since the beginning of time.

The people, roused by a certain excitement that accompanied the start of the war, had chattered boisterously, alcohol in hand, with great and senseless fervor, but by this time at night, every place had quieted down and most had gone to bed.

This could be called a nice, quiet night. Cloud cover is limited; visibility is good. A slight southeasterly breeze is blowing, but it isn't so weak that gunsmoke wouldn't disperse.

The only tiny smudge hidden in the night is the 203rd Aerial Mage Battalion.

"This is the first night attack on a city in this world. That said, the mission actually isn't very difficult."

The one who whispered is the battalion's commander, Major Tanya von Degurechaff, who is leading them from the head of the formation.

If there were a photograph of her to capture the moment where she gazed at the city with a gentle, elegant expression, it would prove the aptness of her alias "White Silver." Soaring peacefully, she enjoys being able to proceed through the starry expanse without trouble. But inside her are thoughts incongruous with the beauty of the night—the upcoming turbulent attack. It will be fun to burn their target down.

A night incursion on the enemy capital that hasn't instituted a blackout—this will be as easy as flying in parade. As expected, though still astounding, there is no aerial or magical interception—not even any anti–air fire. The fact that Tanya can't spot a single artillery battery improves her mood even more.

Of course, although it's only in the realm of possibility, there is a non-zero chance that the whole place is full of hidden gun emplacements. But…if they made such careful preparations, why would they let enemy soldiers into the capital? Ultimately, if the Dacian military takes air combat so lightly, I can't imagine they'd have the wherewithal to construct any elaborate firing positions.

Ultimately, what convinces me is how bright the city is. The electricity and gas are illuminating the place so well that I wonder more than once about the possibility that the lights are decoys. On a battlefield, that nonchalance is a regular occurrence in its own way, but it's abnormal at the same time. When she thinks that she might be able to teach them the concept of a blackout, she even fancies herself a bit enlightened.

I'll teach these fools a lesson through experience. Sometimes I wonder why people would bother teaching the unwise, but now I understand. Behind Tanya's broad grin are pity and contempt. The satisfaction of channeling those emotions into a lesson by means of kicking their ass is ever so unique.

"Education, huh? I see. Becoming the instructor known as experience and collecting a hefty fee isn't such a bad gig."

I guess it's sort of like being one of those Meiji period foreign government advisors.

The job is simple: Give the poor Principality firsthand exposure to the difference between us in modern war, civilization, and national power. Payment will be made in whole by the Imperial Army. This is a sophisticated enterprise where everything, down to each individual round of ammunition, is made possible by the cordial consideration of the Imperial Army General Staff.

Oh, so this is what it's like to understand something once you try it yourself. Bringing the light of civilization to barbarians is clearly my sacred mission. Aha, I see why there are people who confuse differences in culture and civilization with racial superiority. It's far too alluring, and most of all, it provides this horrible sense of omnipotence.

Well, that's not good. Tanya regrets the thought a bit and wisely admonishes herself. If there's one thing I won't resort to, it's interpreting everything through the lens of God. That would interfere with my personal raison d'être, so I definitely can't do that. Well, I guess it's fine to believe in a sacred mission when I shoot Being X…

Anyhow, I pause that train of thought for the moment, like in a video game, and then Tanya flicks her flashlight on and off while whirling it around to call her commanders. It's almost time to move.

The munitions factory is shining so brilliantly it seems to be trying to turn the darkness into day. Even from our distant position, the bustling energy of the workers is apparent in one area where they're putting all their efforts into shell production. We have nearly reached our target.

"You called, Major?"

"We've found our target as planned. You can see it, right, Lieutenant? Over there."

"…I can't believe a weapons factory is unguarded."

"Honestly, neither can I. This might sound arrogant, but…" That's what Tanya says, although she scoffs as she continues. It would probably be more accurate to say that she bursts out laughing at the enemy's foolishness. "Their way of thinking is stuck somewhere about a century in the past. They seem to still be living in two dimensions."

Ignoring the third dimension in the sky, the Dacians only know of an absolutely flat war. What a splendid concept. How stupid can someone be? Thanks to that, I have it easy—their ineptitude really is wonderful. Any enemy of mine is free to let their intelligence atrophy.

Tanya feels she should be genuinely happy about their enemy's stupidity while celebrating the favorable circumstances.

"Actually, we should probably be impressed that their factory is operating twenty-four hours a day."

"Thinkers of the Enlightenment would be delighted to find them so industrious." Though he was wincing a bit as he agreed, First Lieutenant Weiss knew what he had to do as vice commander to clear his name.

Noticing that he's trying his best to restore his honor, Tanya adjusts her evaluation of him and decides he can be trusted with assignments.

"Anyhow, I think it's good that our job will be easy, Major."

Then, not one to betray expectations, Weiss offers his opinion. A vice commander who can make their own calls but also affirm their superior officer's judgment despite their lack of experience is surprisingly hard to come by. Having selected Weiss as her deputy, it's a relief that Tanya seems to have an eye for talent.

"This is a great opportunity to attack. Shall we?"

At the same time, her adjutant, Second Lieutenant Serebryakov, is giving some cause for concern as she's starting to sound a bit impatient, perhaps due to her "opportunities" on the Rhine front. I've been teaching her how to wage war but not how to navigate its rules… Tanya has only received short, intensive officer training, so even if there are no issues with the way she led her subordinates, it may be necessary to pay more attention to the legal side of things.

"Lieutenant Serebryakov, we're not such brutes that we would ignore the law of war."

Yes, established by humanitarians and people with legislative experience, these statutes stipulate the sanctioned way of waging war on cities.

It's a parade of arguments no one could reasonably disagree with: You mustn't attack facilities that would interfere with people's daily lives, attacking civilians is prohibited, indiscriminate bombing is inhumane, and so on. Oh, how great are laws that try to bring some sense into the mad realm of war! They are worthy of respect. If we can do this sanely instead of like maniacs, humans are honestly wonderful. Long live humans. If there's a problem, it's that many of the laws are just slightly impractical. But poorly conceived laws are still laws.

In reality, though, we don't have any issues operating within them. What with murky scopes of application and interpretation difficulties, most laws can be handled simply. At least, we don't have any problems this time.

"Please excuse the error, ma'am."

"Let all units know that we're only destroying the arms factory. Hey, put out an evacuation notice—broadcast on the international distress channel according to regulations."

The enemy manufactory is obviously a military facility. It isn't baking bread or generating electricity to assist people in their daily lives—nothing like that. Even if someone wanted to insist to the contrary, there's no such thing as a peaceful purpose for ammunition. Well, maybe the warm-hearted humanitarian Mr. Molotov[4] would be making bread baskets. Still, that's no problem. It would be their fault for making bread baskets in a facility so easily mistaken as an arms factory.

"But, Major, if we do that, we'll lose the element of surprise!"

"Lieutenant Weiss, common sense says that fear is justified, but you're thinking a bit too straightforward."

It seems Tanya's suggestion that they conduct their attack in line with the rules dictated by international law is completely lost on her subordinate officers.

"We came this far in secret only to reveal ourselves…?"

The same questioning look is on all their faces.

Their expressions share a common type of soldierly doubt. They don't have any question when it comes to carrying out their military objectives.

---

[4] **Molotov** A Soviet diplomat. Stalin's minister of foreign affairs. He once proclaimed that even in wartime, noncombatants should be protected and that they had the right to be free of starvation. In retaliation for dropping "bread" from heavy bombers on Finns in war against Finland, Soviet soldiers got to taste special Molotov "cocktails." Now that is a friendly, well-mannered relationship between two civilized nations.

Of course, the one who was selected for that character was the battalion commander, Major Tanya von Degurechaff—in other words, me. Even if I try to put the blame on someone else, I'm the one responsible in the end.

For a split second, I wonder if I made an error in gathering these particular subordinates, but I console myself with the thought that they are magnificent imperial soldiers who obey orders even when reluctant. Tanya opens her mouth to instruct them in a stately manner.

"Lieutenant Serebryakov! Issue the warning. Order an evacuation according to regulations."

"You want *me* to do that?"

But in the next moment, Serebryakov asks a question, without any deep meaning, that unintentionally highlights Major von Degurechaff's acumen as a specialist. It's enough to make her sick.

Yes, the warning is only a formality, so less believable is more desirable. In that case, the cruel reality is that Tanya figured Lieutenant Serebryakov's slightly unsophisticated voice would sound less reliable than the hard, soldierly tone of Lieutenant Weiss's.

Of course, Tanya is quietly exempting from consideration the youngest member of the unit—herself.

But now that it has been mentioned, I have to admit Serebryakov has a point. If someone were to ask Tanya afterward why Lieutenant Serebryakov made the announcement, I was planning to say, "My assumption was that if a girl made the warning, they would drop their guard," but the worst thing that could happen is someone asks, "Don't you think the commander should have issued it?"

I have to do it. I don't want to, but…

"…Mm, okay. You're right, I should do it. I'll make it really sound like a little kid."

Agh! Nothing for it. At this point, all I can do is think about increasing our chances of success. Argh, these shitty international laws—what a pain. Can't they hurry up and meet their de facto death? What genius got on a high horse and suggested upholding rules of war?

Having partially given up, she shouts into the receiver a subordinate handed her, leaning heavily on the infantile sound of her voice. "Thish is a warning."

And so the warning that day echoed grandly throughout the Dacian capital... Except it didn't.

It's true that she is following the law to the letter and broadcasting it over the international distress channel.

"We, the Imperial Army, are now commenshing an attack on a military supply facility!"

However, I suppose would be the appropriate word...only a very tiny number of people will hear the announcement. For starters, radio penetration in Dacia isn't high enough that every house has a set. Furthermore, households who leave their radio on in the middle of the night are no doubt an extreme minority.

"We will begin maneuvers thirty minutes from now."

Most of all, would anyone take a threat from someone who is obviously a child at face value? Not really. If someone with a more rigid tone, voice, and manner of speech that practically shouted their identity as a soldier—someone like Rudersdorf or Zettour, with that undeniable military air about them—gave the warning, it would be a different story. But with Tanya as the announcer, objectively speaking...aside from the content, the announcement is awfully heartwarming.

Many people will consider it at most an elaborate prank and think little more of it, going back to sleep with a critical frown.

"We solemnly pwedge—errybody swears to fight fair and square, according to international law."

On the other hand, there remains the goal of playing the part properly despite the ridiculous voice, so Tanya lets all the emotion drain out of her words. In a way, this performance is a mortification of Tanya's mind comparable to using Type 95 at full power. Praising God and affirming Being X is bad enough, but I still see my duty through to the end.

Naturally, she is openly indignant as she scowls at their target and shouts that she will crush it. Visha's emotions as she looks on next to her are probably shared with the rest of the battalion—unshakable solidarity.

...No, her thought is, *That's so low, Major.*

Tanya finishes reading the warning in a voice appropriate for a child her age. No matter how you think about it, the only appropriate explanation would be some kid's prank; anyone would think so. Even we feel like we've caught a glance of some gruesome sight.

"Major, do you have experience in acting?"

"Acting? I'm not sure I understand what you mean. I'm just hoping they lower their guard."

Though the tone matches her age, Tanya murmurs her dissatisfaction in her usual cold voice. It must be a sign of complex internal feelings. Weiss has only known her for a short time, but even he can pick up the displeasure his superior doesn't bother hiding. Her mood is as dangerous as nitroglycerin.

When Weiss quietly takes a step back, everyone discreetly follows suit. Nobody wants to be so close to Major von Degurechaff when she's irritated.

"…Okay, troops. It appears shaming myself was worth it."

Still, something has been beaten into them during their training as soldiers.

And that's why they understand that their superior will vent her feelings on the enemy as they ready themselves for the attack, grabbing their orbs and rifles with as much as a measure of sympathy.

"This munitions factory has been receiving Republican assistance. It's probably full of flammable materials." Tanya's tone contains a clear determination to blow the target sky-high. Normally her inner thoughts are inscrutable, but today, at this very moment, every mage in the 203rd Aerial Mage Battalion can understand exactly what's on her mind. There's no mistaking it.

She's motivated.

"I issued the warning. Our obligation has been fulfilled. Now let's watch the fireworks."

I'm openly indignant—blowing off steam or maybe taking it out on them.

The expression on Major von Degurechaff's face while she casts an extra-large yet precise formula and conjures a long-range projection formula is a mixture of intoxication and anger, all indicating very real danger. *Let sleeping dogs lie.* Since no one has interfered, she's able to turn her undiluted fury on the enemy.

"Let's educate them in the name of God."

That murmured remark informs her unit how serious she is.

"I will manifest the power of God on this earth!"

Their commander continues constructing an extra-large disaster.

"Deploy formulas! Look sharp, observers!"

"Deploy formulas! Target: Carberius Arms Foundry!"

"All companies, match your timing to Major von Degurechaff!"

Not wanting to fall behind, the commander of each unit shouts, and several long-range attack formulas are cast.

Normally, any attacker leisurely launching this slow formula in the middle of a battlefield would end up pummeled by anti-magic artillery or picked off by enemy mages on patrol.

But if the enemy's even slower, then it's a different story.

"Deploy formulas!"

"Fire!"

We loose a volley of long-range explosion formulas cast by a forty-eight-man augmented mage battalion. That power and range requires more magic than usual, but this time at least, it's the optimal solution.

No one interrupts—no one even notices.

The formulas rain down on the target so easily the mages are almost disappointed, and the spells explode on impact with the factory literally filled with ammunition.

"Sixteen direct hits! The rest are close!"

"If we can do that with long-range formulas, then I can't complain." Tanya nods in satisfaction.

Then, just as Weiss is about to say something to her, it blows up.

The flare is so dazzling, even the mages are blinded, despite having anticipated the blast. The light fills the quiet night with naked hostility.

The roof of the factory, blown skyward, seems to fall in slow motion, and the Dacian capital has been jolted awake by a glare that lights up everything for miles around.

"There go the secondary explosions."

Then a quiet, satisfied remark sums it all up.

"Tamayaaa!"

"Huh?"

"It's just an exclamation. Don't worry about it."

She turns around and appraises the scene with a deflecting remark about the fantastic sight.

"I gotta hand it to Dacia. Not only did they help us out with our live-fire exercise, they even arranged for a post-training fireworks show."

She cackles in amusement, her expression exuberant. If she had to sum it up, the gigantic sunlike explosion below feels just like a fireworks show in honor of her service.

"Anyhow, we achieved our objective. We're returning to base, troops."

》》》   OCTOBER 23, UNIFIED YEAR 1924, IMPERIAL ARMY GENERAL   **《《《**
STAFF OFFICE, DINING ROOM 1 (ARMY)

"That captain did say it lets you experience war rations."

An officer who worked in Personnel was reported to have said it. The General Staff Office dining hall was a "perpetual battlefield café" that didn't let soldiers forget their combat experiences, even in the rear.

Major General von Rudersdorf had no words to deny that. In fact, he secretly agreed with his junior colleagues' opinion that the dining room and its "unique" cuisine seemed to be engaging with the Commonwealth in a fierce competition no normal person could comprehend.

And likewise, as far as Major General von Zettour knew, there were no General Staffers who actually liked the food. So perhaps it was ironic that although discussing confidential matters in a cafeteria was generally considered a poor idea, this particular place was actually the optimal venue for strategy meetings if secrecy was desirable.

It was Zettour's and Rudersdorf's natures to use whatever they could, together, to the fullest, and when it occurred to them that the dining hall was the best place for keeping things confidential, they reluctantly began taking at least one of their three daily meals there.

"…Time is not necessarily on the Empire's side, though it isn't exactly on our enemy's, either," Rudersdorf grumbled, sounding absolutely fed up. Irritated, he washed down some bread-like foodstuff with pseudo-coffee. Among all the ersatz items on the table, he could tell from the feel and luster that only the Meissen cup in his hand, and only that, could be called genuine.

"Taking our current situation into consideration, it's not a good idea for the Empire to deal with two fronts for too long, but you still think time might be with us, Rudersdorf?"

Zettour looked dissatisfied with the food but smiled, somewhat amused, as he replied. He was in charge of logistics. Of course, as a General Staff officer, he could stick his fingers into strategy or operations just as much as Rudersdorf, who had long been involved in operational theory research and development.

The General Staff had simply seen what these two were capable of, so they put energetic, dynamic Rudersdorf in charge of war operations—mainly mobile—while expecting Zettour's wise, scholarly precision to keep the military organization running smoothly.

And in Dacia, all expectations had been met. Rudersdorf set a perfect example of how to conduct maneuver warfare with his astuteness, whereas Zettour made arrangements for the efficient deployment of troops, even organizing the dispatch of an advance unit. Both of their talents achieved everything the General Staff had hoped for.

"Of course, more time spent will mean more waste. But that's exactly why our basic strategy of knocking out the weakest enemies first, like we did in Dacia, shouldn't change."

"In other words, what you mean to say is, 'I'll give you time, so handle the logistics?' Rudersdorf, I have to warn you, the Anluk E. Kahteijanen as well as the port facilities are already at their limits with the construction jobs and expansion work in Norden. Transporting enough matériel for a winter offensive will be much too large a burden."

"If you say it can't be done, then I guess it can't. But I've known you long enough. You say it's impossible, but you won't convince me you don't have an alternative plan."

An ideal mutual understanding between the front lines and the rear. In a way, this was made possible by the rare cooperative relationship the two men had been able to build where they completely trusted in each other's exceptional abilities.

"I'm sorry, General von Rudersdorf, but as far as I've heard from the managers of rolling stock in the Service Corps, the logistics situation in Norden isn't going to improve anytime soon."

"General von Zettour, do I need to explain to you about the possibility of a maritime supply route?"

Relaxing both his expression and the mood just a little bit, Zettour dropped all pretenses. "All right, all right. As you say, since the war began we've had our sea routes cut off, so there are all kinds of trade vessels anchored in the port that we could requisition." It was a plan he had considered many times. "If necessary, I can send a nearly three-hundred-thousand-ton ship to a port facility somewhere in the north for a landing operation."

"So it's decided, then? I wish you would just say that from the beginning."

"I have to warn you, this discussion is only valid assuming we have control of the sea. I'll put up with a skirmish or two, but I'm not keen on the idea of losing a unit and a ship for the chance to gamble on an amphibious operation far behind enemy lines."

Zettour frowned slightly. He was more worried about the possible losses than he was about the potential success of the operation.

It was true that the Empire currently had a glut of ships because the sea-lanes had been tenuous since the war started. There was a chance they could solve their supply and operational issues with them. But put another way, the Imperial Navy had nothing but vulnerable sea-lanes, so would they really be able to protect supply lines? That was the risk they faced.

As long as that was the case, maybe they could use the narrow straits near the Empire, but they had no choice but to be pessimistic about the idea of establishing a major supply route.

"You worry too much about supposed losses. Even if it's a bit of a risk, getting behind Entente Alliance lines and cutting off their communications would crush them."

Rudersdorf's reply was almost carelessly optimistic compared to Zettour's strategic concerns.

Despite the deadlocked front lines, the substantial gap in national power left the Entente Alliance on the brink of collapse just like Dacia. In other words, Rudersdorf's take on the situation could be criticized as an oversimplification, but if the Imperial Army could seize a region in the rear the same way their soldiers had trampled Dacia, even the Entente Alliance would collapse on its own.

"I can't deny it, but frankly, I don't think they are much of a threat anymore even if we leave them as they are. Shouldn't we forget about them and finish off the Republic?"

"There's nothing better than having fewer fronts, but…"

On the point of whether it was actually necessary to force the Entente Alliance to completely collapse, a slight disagreement between Operations and the Service Corps began creeping into their remarks. Zettour didn't think advancing north would do anything to ameliorate the logistical strain. On the other hand, from Operations' point of view, cleaning up that front would make things much easier strategically.

"From the logistics standpoint, the burden of maintaining the amount of troops necessary to hold against the Entente Alliance is not a light one. Even without firing a single round of ammunition, soldiers starve to death if they don't eat, you know."

"I'm aware of that. But it's true that compared to the Republic, it would be easier to take out."

"Fine."

In the end, both men had clear criteria for how to optimize the instrument of violence known as state warfare while not losing sight of their greater objective. An operation could be undertaken if it didn't strain logistics too greatly and if it gave them a chance to shrink their active fronts.

Given the fact that in those operational terms there were no issues with gaining control of the rear in the north, Zettour agreed to draw up an attack plan.

"If we're going to attack, I'd like us to consider the Osfjord."

"The Osfjord? It's too heavily defended. It's situated inside that narrow bay, but I'm pretty sure they have a few coastal guns."

"The city of Os is the main railroad hub. If we take that, all the Entente Alliance's trains should be out of commission. Then we can stroll in and keep our troops' supplies using their rails."

The city Zettour pointed out was significant because of its role as a transportation center—presenting an opportunity to knock out enemy logistics in one fell swoop. It would be difficult, but if they could cut the enemy's supply lines... When the thought crossed Rudersdorf's mind, he could no longer hold back a savage smile.

"Got it. You come up with some really nasty plans, don't you...? But it does make sense. So you want us to capture Os..."

If the Entente Alliance was crippled like that, their army would die like dogs even if their frontline forces put up a heroic resistance. A military with no head or limbs was just a mob that used to be called an army. Assuming things went as Northern Command hoped, victory could then be achieved with a short frontal assault... It could be so easy that they might want to consider how to achieve an even better outcome.

"Say you can do it and I'll give you a unit. If it doesn't work, I'll just deal with Norden in a less sneaky way."

"No, let's give it a shot." With that same grin on his face, Rudersdorf decisively met the challenge. He would try to take them down. It was the dream of every General Staff officer to dramatically shift the tides of war on the operational level with one large-scale battle. He nodded at Zettour as if to say he would even drink down this dirty-water coffee with a smile.

"Very good. If you need anything, let me know."

"Oh, then lend me a mage unit."

Rudersdorf was merciless in asking for what he wanted.

"A mage unit? Sure, but which one?"

"The pet in your pocket, the 203rd. I want you to let me use the troops that performed so well in Dacia."

"That battalion's a handful. Are you okay with that?"

The pet in Zettour's pocket... They were a dauntless combat unit that had waged impeccable maneuver warfare in Dacia and had even bombed a weapons factory. Not only that, but they were an augmented unit equipped with cutting-edge gear from the Technical Arsenal. When Lieutenant Colonel von Lergen had reported on their training progress, he insisted, with undisguised shock, that there was no unit in the Empire that could match them.

"That's fine. Besides, I believe the commander has combat experience in Norden. It's reassuring to have someone who is even a little familiar with the lay of the land."

The 203rd's commander was said to have a distinctive personality, but if she had to be sorted into the groups "useful" or "not," she was certainly a part of the former. That made her just the type that he could afford to push hard as a game piece.

"All right. I'll make the arrangements right away."

"Thanks. Here's to the hope that we win."

A glass was raised.

"Then here's to the hope the food here improves."

The return toast made them both wince.

"I think the war'll end first."

"You're probably right."

Though grimacing, they stayed faithful to the basic soldiering principle of eating whenever a chance presented itself. That said, neither hid the fact that they would rather dine elsewhere.

If the youth are going calmly to the killing fields, an adult should at the very least go along to lead them.

Anson Sue, *O Fatherland, Long May You Live*

A man in the Entente Alliance Army's type II dress uniform was receiving a new rank insignia from his superior officer in the Army Personnel Division, who wore a smile plastered over his face like a mask.

"You've been promoted. Congratulations, Colonel Anson Sue."

"If I'm getting promoted after suffering such a loss, our country must be at its end." He didn't fly into a rage at the state of things, but neither did he bother to hide his murmurings. He simply expressed his sentiment before he realized what he was saying.

Normally, an officer of his rank shouldn't have talked like that. But the miserable situation of the Entente Alliance created a peculiar atmosphere in which Sue's bitter comments could be excused.

Their defeat was all too clear. The kind of fall that was guaranteed to come. Of course, there was still some hope.

But in a room full of people who understood their circumstances and could see where they were headed, optimism was in laughably short supply.

"Now then, here's your new insignia. We expect a lot out of you, Colonel."

And that was why the people who fully comprehended the gravity of the situation were already exhausted. Their hearts were long spent from the intense rage they felt.

"The fatherland is in crisis. I have to hope you'll do your duty as best you can. That's all."

"There is no greater happiness than to be entrusted with the fatherland."

"Excellent."

They did nothing but exchange set phrases. Probably the only thing on Sue's mind as he delivered his stirring lines in monotone, like a sutra, was simple contempt for formalities. *Since the leadership's choices have been so grievously bad, aren't the duties we soldiers can actually fulfill rather limited?*

It was for that reason that Sue was miserable. His only reaction to the impassioned commotion caused by mobs of citizens frantic to save the nation was the extreme fatigue on his face.

He saluted according to protocol and left the room with a gait that grew even heavier when he saw the excited young volunteers, brimming with love for their country, forming up before marching out. *They're so innocent... Eager to go to battle, but what can they even do when they finally arrive?*

"How disappointing. What awful luck to have been born in a country that can only ask its youths to die for it."

A patriot would cry. They were supposed to protect their fatherland; they should have been proud of it. Instead, their nation had committed a grave mistake, and now it was ushering young people down a path that promised death. Though he could have sworn he was emotionally spent, he found tears blurring his vision.

"Colonel Sue?"

While trying his best to keep up appearances in response to concerned voices, in his heart, with a hint of resignation, he made a vow. *If I'm going to send them to their deaths, then the least I can do is fulfill my duty as best I can, too.* The commitment to self-sacrifice stemmed from his sense of responsibility and fate as a leader.

If the youth are going to sacrifice themselves for the fatherland, then there at least has to be someone to accompany them down that path, an adult who will fall beside them. He was grimly determined. *How could I let them die alone?*

Even so, as the young men paraded proudly down the road, he couldn't stand the sight of the anxious-looking women carrying children in the crowd of people bidding them farewell. Thinking of those who were left behind, he prayed for salvation and nearly cried out. *Anyone, anyone at all, please end this nightmare...*

If there was a hope he could cling to, it was that the Republic or some other great power would maybe, just maybe, show up in the nick of time to save them. Then the Entente Alliance might have a chance to escape total collapse. *But can it really?* Having thought that far, Sue sneered at the futility of clinging to a wish that couldn't even convince him.

He knew they were well and truly cornered, with no way out.

They were supposed to protect their fatherland, but it was already ticking down its final days little by little, like an hourglass. In the future lay inevitable ruin.

Facing downfall, he could only stand still, tormented by a sense of helplessness. His resolve to share the fate of the fatherland was unwavering. Nonetheless, when he thought of what hardships would befall the people when they lost their home country, he could only shed tears of grief.

Wait. It must have been the workings of fate that made him realize something at that moment: Just because a country was destroyed didn't mean its people had to be. If they couldn't protect their homeland, they at least had to let its citizens escape. Even after the state was broken, mountains and rivers would remain. Yes, countries fell, but they were made up of people. Perhaps they would have a chance to rebuild their broken home. If they saved the people who would become the seeds, they could dream of a day when the field of the fatherland would bloom once more. It would be a difficult journey. Times would be hard. But this wouldn't be the end. There was the hope of rebirth.

A homeland is more than territory; as long as home existed in the hearts of its people, this wasn't the end.

He had to help as many fellow citizens escape as possible. Surely that was the great cause worthy of dedication for a soldier of a failing nation. No, it was the one and only way of sacrificing oneself that a soldier who had sworn to protect the fatherland could be proud of.

"Here it is. Yes, I found it!"

With a shout so full of hope and purpose you would never have thought the speaker had been on the brink of despair just moments earlier, Colonel Sue made a vow. *I'll never let anyone destroy thee, O Fatherland.*

This country was his family's home. He was a father, even if he hadn't been around his child much. Though he regretted that, and it was a bit late to start caring, he swore to leave his wife and daughter a future. Though it was immodest, he wanted to be glad he could use the military connections he hadn't paid much attention to until that moment.

Meanwhile, the new Entente Alliance councilors, with traces of difficult-to-conceal resignation and contrition in their gloomy expressions, groped for a way to flip the hourglass back over as time slipped away.

Nobody had foreseen the start of open hostilities with the Empire. Everyone present had been appalled upon hearing the news. "Why has the fatherland done something so reckless?" When they came to grips with reality and left by the wayside ideologies and the illusion that this was the way things should be, it was clear that the Empire was going to pulverize the cheeky little contender snapping at it.

Though the gears of destruction had ground to a halt briefly due to the Republic's surprise attack, the situation had definitely not improved for the Entente Alliance. On the contrary, the Principality of Dacia, after their warrior's fanfare that sounded like music to the councilors' ears, had been wiped off the map in the span of a few months.

The overwhelming military might of the Empire and the pathetic final days of the upstart challenger... To anyone with a heart, this was a nightmare come to life for the Entente Alliance.

In the midst of all that, the new councilors, despite their fear, were doing everything they could think of to maintain the front and continue the resistance.

"Now then, I've got some good news for you, gentlemen. It's only a stopgap solution, but we've begun coordinating with our allies."

As he read the announcement to the other nine councilors in the meeting room, Foreign Affairs Councilor Abensoll was a little excited by the first good news in a long while.

Diplomacy had fallen into chaos ever since the war started, but he finally received a favorable reply. Ever since the Republic had entered the war, he had been going around apologizing to all their allies and begging for assistance, and finally someone replied. The Republic had stepped in, fearing the collapse of the Empire's encirclement following the Entente Alliance's reckless move, but between the stalemated front and a huge number of casualties, its attitude rapidly soured to the point that the Republic barely even gave the Entente Alliance the time of day after Dacia got involved, addressing them with openly cold contempt.

What the nation wanted to say was clear: "Your heedlessness is the cause of this catastrophe." A Republican diplomat had made that remark to Abensoll under the influence of alcohol, but those words said it all.

"That's fine, but all the Republic really hopes for is someone to lessen their burden on the Rhine front, no?"

Because they knew exactly what the Republic was truly after, what should have been good news instead left the ten councilors in a hollow mood with low expectations. *At most, the Republic hopes to take some of the heat off themselves by having us continue fighting on a second front*, they thought.

"Councilor Cazor, your apprehension is reasonable, but the Republic is worried about a repeat of Dacia."

"You mean they're worried that if we fall, the Empire will turn its full energy on them? I see. Well, isn't that a wretched thing to hear." Army Councilor Cazor shrugged, seeming offended at being treated like a second Dacia, but his arguments weren't very persuasive given how much he had hoped the Grand Duchy's entry in the war would lessen the Entente Alliance's own burden.

"Councilor Abensoll, surely that isn't all?"

"No, excuse me. In addition to the Republic, it appears the Commonwealth will send over some manner of assistance. At least, there is consensus among the great powers that they would like to stop us from being completely annihilated."

Foreign Affairs Councilor Abensoll had trailed off, but at the urging of an older councilor, he presented some good news about a sympathetic neutral power's foreign policy.

The Entente Alliance would receive a helping hand from another nation, in addition to the Republic, that wasn't happy with the prospect of the Empire expanding its influence. The Commonwealth, known for its excellent naval forces, was concerned by the Empire's sudden expansion on the continent, so it had decided to take the first step toward joining the battle. Its plan was to maintain the balance of power—not much more than an excuse, but that was why they could be trusted from a realpolitik standpoint.

"Ohh, the friendly Treaty of Londinium again? Though we're the ones who broke it..."

Despite thinking it was probably a good thing, there was no way anyone present could be genuinely happy to accept the help. Any member of the Entente Alliance leadership who was familiar with how the other powers felt about them, given that they had broken the treaty, could understand that the Commonwealth had offered half as an insult.

"So what are our options?"

"After analyzing the Dacian War, the Republic told us they worry our rear regions are under-protected."

Unlike the Republic, forced into a head-on clash with the Empire, the Entente Alliance was using its topography and climate to maintain its front. But in reality, what allowed the Entente Alliance to just barely hold was that the Empire didn't consider it a serious threat and was treating it as a side project.

"...I'm envious of countries that have power to spare. We've got nothing left." The interior councilor commented on the disparity in national strength, which was truly massive.

In fact, simply going at it with just one of the Empire's army groups required the majority of the Entente Alliance's resources to maintain the troops on the front lines.

"For now, we have mage units stationed to fend off any attempts at incursions in the rear. They should at least be able to handle most things before it becomes a serious problem."

The Entente Alliance was on guard against surprise raids deep in their territory, but so far nothing major had come up—one of the leadership's few comforts. The most they expected was a gamble by an imperial cavalry brigade to destroy Entente Alliance railways or an airborne operation by a handful of aerial mages. The Entente Alliance's quick response division had been successful in repulsing everything that had come before with their mages, so they were fairly confident they could fend off most invasion attempts.

"The Commonwealth says they're anxious about an imperial naval assault."

"A seaborne invasion? I don't mean to be master of the obvious, but couldn't we just attack them once they make landfall?"

Foreign Affairs Councilor Abensoll himself was dubious, but the Commonwealth was seriously concerned the Empire would try an amphibious assault, and its officers were unanimous in voicing the warning. "I understand your country's situation, but your coasts are wide open."

"If our main forces are all tied up, even a small amphibious landing force could prove catastrophic."

Abensoll had no choice but to warn his colleagues with a measure of anxiety that if invaders met no resistance when they made landfall, then it would open up the Entente Alliance to a thrust from behind and bring their whole country down.

"Councilor Abensoll, the Republican Navy doesn't have the power to put a stop to that. And might I remind you we only have two capital ships ourselves?"

But he still managed to feel hopeful.

"That's no problem. This is confidential, but the Commonwealth is already monitoring the Empire's navy. The Republican fleet is apparently ready to deploy if need be."

Which means...

"Gentlemen, time is key. We need to buy time."

"We must ask the other powers to intervene. It's utterly shameful, but we have no choice. In the meantime, let's do our best."

>>> NOVEMBER 5, UNIFIED YEAR 1924, IMPERIAL CAPITAL GARRISON 14, <<<
AUDITORIUM

"Battalion Commander!"

In the auditorium where all the unit members have already gathered, the commander of Second Company, First Lieutenant Weiss, stands and salutes the battalion commander as she enters. The troops follow suit, saluting and voicing their greetings as Tanya gestures for everyone to be at ease. She takes the dais in the center and nods in satisfaction after glancing around at her men.

"I think you've already heard, but the 203rd Aerial Mage Battalion has been given transfer orders. We're going to Norden."

Man, that's exactly what I don't want to do, but I don't let my opinion on this injustice show on Tanya's face. Right now, it's all hidden with that particular tone officers use to keep their emotions unreadable, but I sent a dozen complaints in writing to Lieutenant Colonel von Lergen about how much the military has been overworking Tanya. Rest and joint training for four months, plus two months of basic training to improve the recruits' skills. The unit should have had six months of deferment. It was no small shock to have the unit declared trained and ready for deployment after their combat exercise in Dacia.

Running my gaze over the troops from the platform, I can understand how it was possible to see them as a disciplined unit brimming with confidence. With their field gear perfectly polished and their feet all lined up as if they were toeing a ruled edge, they do seem elite.

But the 203rd Aerial Mage Battalion isn't as ready as the General Staff might want to believe. They have so many weak points remaining that it's enough to give Tanya a headache as their commander. First, as exemplified by Lieutenant Weiss's misstep in Dacia, most of them are still operating on an obsolete version of common sense, even if only partially. Of course, it's true that after their baptism by fire, their understanding had changed so dramatically it wouldn't be an exaggeration to call it a Copernican-level revolution. It was almost like Paul's conversion—Tanya could practically bless them and inform all that they were on the right path. But that's still nowhere near good enough.

"Naturally, the General Staff expects us to bring to Norden the same skills and quick thinking that we showed off in Dacia, so we need to be ready." On Tanya's face is a smile of anticipation, but it feels so forced. Well, that makes sense. This unit has never been through a tough fight. There are too many examples from history of game dogs who only just learned the sweet taste of victory and turned into a pack of cowed mongrels with a single loss. No one is weaker in the face of adversity than purebred elites, which applies to Tanya as well.

"Gentlemen, be proud that you've finally been given a chance to overcome a trial of fire and iron."

No army can win forever. Even the USA, despite boasting that it would bomb its enemy back to the Stone Age, was long traumatized by the nightmare of guerrilla warfare. It dispelled the trauma momentarily in the Gulf, but when it got overconfident, the result was Iraq.

I recall that even the great Empire, one of the leading world powers, hasn't achieved military strength on par with the USA's dominance. I really need to cultivate subordinates who can withstand hardship.

Not only will I be branded as incompetent if I handle it poorly, it could literally mean death for me. After all, once a bunch of numbskulls who've never lost a battle collapse, they're extremely fragile. An army with a broken spirit is simply a mob. Even with magic technology, it's not as if soldiers can be miraculously imbued with an iron will to fight—although somewhere in my heart, I'm sure that's what a certain mad scientist and his cohorts are trying to accomplish.

That said, at present, all I can do is manage as best I can with the cards I've been dealt. My salary is looking better, and considering my raises on top of that, I need to work at least as hard as I'm getting paid.

"Gentlemen, Dacia was nothing but a live-fire exercise. Now it's time for the real war you've all been thirsting for."

The best part is probably that a whiff of war fever is coming off most of her handpicked subordinates. Under normal circumstances, of course, there would be nothing good about that at all, but the moment a unit has to go into battle, that trait becomes more than welcome.

"Give your all for His Imperial Majesty the Emperor and your fatherland. Never forget your duty."

"""""Yes, ma'am!"""""

Their magnificent reply satisfies her for now.

In terms of personnel management, it can be necessary to remind them that their duty is commensurate with what they receive, but this time, given their reactions, there doesn't seem to be any need. Of course, I can't let my guard down.

It's for the Empire that everyone seems so attached to and for myself. Yes, I'll have them properly serve the apparently beautiful and respectable

Chapter **II**

emperor as well as the fatherland… Luckily, my subordinates are strong, so in a worst-case scenario, they can be my shield, too.

It's too bad they're so obsessed with fighting, but for the most part, they're still talented enough mages that I want to work with them.

"Good. Now we'll hear the notice from the General Staff. Lieutenant Weiss."

Of course, I'll have my deputy explain the details. After all, that's why the Empire and every other country established a system with adjutants and vice commanders.

"Ma'am. As you've already heard from our commander, this unit will serve as a mobile battalion."

According to the notice from the General Staff, the 203rd Aerial Mage Battalion will be deployed in an entirely different way than being assigned to one of the army groups, as would be standard. We are the first unit created specifically as a mobile battalion.

Naturally, it's safe to assume that there will be plenty of experimenting and that we'll be expected to bring back a lot of informative reports. Due to our status as a unit the General Staff can deploy without coordinating heavily with an army group first, we won't be picked on much as long as we can live up to their expectations. In other words, be an easy-to-use independent unit that promptly tackles any mission entrusted to us and we'll have no problems. Yes, though it hasn't been explicitly stated, we've been given de facto autonomy.

"To put it another way, we'll be constantly shuttling around via interior lines."

In other words, it's an even exchange of authority and responsibility. If there is ever a problem on the front, we'll be sent over and expected to resolve it immediately. To explain it simply, Tanya employs a simile.

"The General Staff's working us like a team of harnessed draft horses. Rejoice. Apparently, they've prepared some carrots for us."

I don't know what the exact perks will be, but I predict the General Staff will do all they can in terms of salary increases and chances for promotions. Whether it will be enough for her men is another question.

"""Wa-ha-ha-ha-ha!"""

Well, laughing was probably all the troops could do. Who would happily go to war for a perk or two? The officers and generals might see a modest raise, but the rank-and-file soldiers don't get much in terms of special rewards. It honestly isn't a very good proposition considering they're putting their lives in danger. Of course, if a free market system were in place, it would be up to each individual to decide whether it was worth it.

In that sense, the conscription system is outrageous. The Empire drafts people like Serebryakov who might be even slightly useful because the nation doesn't have the resources to fully attend to its citizens' rights... Tanya herself had no other option than to volunteer for the military for much the same reason.

I would prefer it if they switched to a system of voluntary military service as soon as possible. Or let me resign this very instant. Of course, only if I can still collect on my civil servant and commissioned officer pensions.

Tanya shakes her head slightly to clear out the extraneous thoughts, then gestures to Weiss, who was looking at her questioningly. She indicates that there's nothing to worry about and has him continue.

"Battalion! Attention!"

The way the room quiets down the moment he shouts is extremely satisfying. At least they're disciplined enough to follow instructions properly. Then again, of course soldiers should be able to do that much...

"Carrots or not, even horses aren't lucky enough to eat for free."

Lieutenant Weiss almost seems like he's lecturing the soldiers as he insinuates that the unit is expected to produce results. Watching him talk to the troops is gratifying. I adjust my evaluation of him upward in a mental grade book. My vice commander isn't half-bad.

No one likes meaningless expenditure. A racehorse is expected to win; a farm horse, to plow; a stud, to pass on his genes; and the workhorse earns its keep through pure labor. If the vice commander can understand that and explain it to others, he's a keeper.

"Of course, we need to prove that we're capable of handling a bit of work."

I've never particularly wanted to be a horse. And I wouldn't want to risk my human dignity by thinking I'd want to be "cultivated." But if they're going to wedge the carrot into my mouth, I'm not opposed to biting it—although it would be unfair if afterward they said, *See? We're supporting you, so get to it!*

"We'll be assigned to a mixed group drawn from the Eastern Army Group and the Southern Army Group, but we're going to be under Northern Command as a unit dispatched from Central."

Political dignity as a concept is honestly ridiculous. Perhaps political decisions that are considered without looking at the issues logically show its limitations. Then again, the dictatorship of an emperor or nobles can be just as terrible. Even democratic forms of government falling into the hands of mob rule may be due to latent defects within the system. Humans truly are political animals.

It's possible that animals that have no honor are far more rational than any human. Of course, this might just be a misunderstanding, since we haven't yet confirmed whether animals understand the concept or not.

"The General Staff wants us to test new combat tactics in the north."

While listening to Lieutenant Weiss's explanation, the essence of the message echoes in Tanya's mind.

This is a test. In any case, we belong to the General Staff, and no army group on the front can order us around directly. Basically, we're a unit the General Staff can send on missions without interference from the regional armies. I suppose all we can do is reconcile ourselves to our duty and follow our orders to put on a show.

I feel like a circus monkey being forced to perform for other monkeys. You could call it a species of abuse.

The only difference between me and the monkey is that there are countless protection groups dedicated to preventing animal cruelty. There is no organization that would shout *That's abuse!* when it comes to imperial soldiers. I'd like the people who cry *Animals are not your food!*[5] to spare a thought for us, too; people may be political animals, but we're still animals.

I guess this is better than the pity of paternalists, though…

---

[5] **Animals are not your food!** From an NPO's sign.

"...And so we've got to show them that we can work well enough in a group to go picnicking."

We're stuck with orders to go up north to try some new stratagem for the General Staff's Operations Division. This isn't really a mission that I want. It's the same as being sent on a pointless business trip due to company hierarchy.

And talk about wasting time and resources. New tactics or whatever are generally just novelties; they can't be trusted. And on the off chance there is an element that turns out to be something we could implement, how much trial and error will we be forced to do before it's usable? Tanya hasn't said much about it to anyone, but I can only think that someone thought this up after noticing her service with Technology and the instructor unit.

Anyway, putting that irritation on display won't get her anywhere. She nods benevolently at Lieutenant Weiss, who was looking at her for permission.

"Today at 1800 hours[6] we'll begin a long-range maneuver toward the supply depot. Company commanders, after everyone is dismissed, we're having a meeting to decide the flight plan."

While watching them trying to get down to business in the meeting, I decide to throw out a few words—instructions, I guess. Soldiers love these kinds of formalized interactions.

Let's just say that not only do I disapprove of this waste of time, I can't sincerely appreciate this prioritizing mental intoxication. Of course, as a member of the organization there's no good reason for me not to participate.

That's where Tanya endeavors to string together some sort of advice.

"Sorry to interrupt while you're enjoying your chat, but I have some quick news."

It was a truth that people at company commander–level should have already picked up on. Though it was only an unspoken doubt at this point, if they knew it, their units would have a different outlook. It wasn't a particularly confidential matter.

---

[6] **1800 hours**   Six PM in military time.

"The Great Army may have pulled out, but it's strange that the fighting in the north hasn't settled down yet."

According to military standards, the Entente Alliance isn't considered a major world power. The fact that it's able to qualitatively compete with the Empire, on any level, implies that they're receiving aid from somewhere.

Needless to say, its ally the Republic has already given it a formidable helping hand, so there is no doubt that the majority of the support is from there as well.

The real crux of the problem is whether those that claim neutrality are intervening. Of course, these bystander countries deny any participation on a national scale, but they are silent whenever the possible existence of voluntary armies comes up. The participation of at least a few countries like the Federation and the Commonwealth is certain.

To begin with, the Entente Alliance is dramatically less capable than the Empire when it comes to the national strength that can be devoted toward total war; Entente Alliance mages alone shouldn't be able to put up such stiff resistance. Its troops' ability to fend off the Great Army while holding steady against the pressure of the regional Imperial Army group speaks volumes to the amount of aid they must be receiving. That's the reason why even Tanya's battalion is stuck going on a picnic despite the Dacia situation not being quite settled yet.

"So there has to be something going on—in other words, someone is poking their nose where it doesn't belong."

"Commander?!"

Lieutenant Weiss was on his way out of the room when he changed color. He must have had some idea what she was saying. It annoys me, but he's right that there are things that can be said aloud and some that can't. But considering the situation, it's better to have Tanya's subordinates in on this from the beginning.

"Lieutenant Weiss, this is just my guess. A personal take on things."

Well, for now, I'll stay quiet about the supposedly neutral Federation. I don't mean to stir up unnecessary trouble. It could affect my career, and I wouldn't want to invite the fatal misunderstanding that I can't be discreet. Still, the troops are relaxed from their easy win in Dacia, so it feels like Tanya has to brace them for what's coming.

"Well, gentlemen, I just mean to say that I don't know if it's the Republic, the Commonwealth, or some other nation, but someone is definitely interfering."

It really pisses me off that some other party is joining in. It's faithful enough to the principle of raison d'état that it makes me sick—simply put, it's actually a very rational decision. From the point of view of the other powers, it's a standard move to protect their national interests. Surely the people of the Commonwealth and the Republic can rest easy knowing they have heads of state who take security seriously. So compared to the Commonwealth and the Republic, which conduct themselves as proper political animals, the Entente Alliance, which starts a war on an impulse, is even more irritating. What in the world is so fun about picking a fight with the Empire?

Are its leaders just addicted to war and love it soooo much that they can't help it? Well, if that's the case, maybe that's why the Republic has to help out its game dog after pitting it against the Empire.

Still, it's a surprise world-class players even pay attention to such a remote nation. Usually territories short on resources and potential concessions don't even show up as blips on the radar of powerful leaders.

"In other words, we're going on a nice hiking trip with the whole world watching."

It's significant that we're heading to a battlefield that has every nation's attention. The General Staff are wagering the nation's dignity on a swift victory, so they must want a win badly. We also have to bear in mind Supreme Command's desire for an outcome that demonstrates the Empire's superiority as much as possible.

In any case, failure will not be tolerated in the slightest. We can probably expect some sort of disciplinary reprisal if that happens. In order to avoid falling into ruin, we have to be model imperial mages.

So despite my deep reluctance, to the battlefield I must merrily go. Otherwise it'll be interpreted as lacking the will to fight. In reality, I have no love whatsoever for war, so I have to do everything in my power not to be suspect.

"So? Great news, right?"

You guys get it, too, don't you? They seem to pick up on my look.

Chapter **II**

"This is the best. To think the General Staff would provide us with an opportunity to shine so soon."

"I was just feeling like a skiing trip. What thoughtful orders!"

"I thought the General Staff only asked for the impossible. Are the orders really from them?"

Luckily, everyone goes along. These guys have more tact than I expected.

They understand both respect for a superior officer and what is being asked of them. Maybe I don't have to worry too much.

"Good. Well, that's where we're at, troops. We've been given the opportunity, so we're off on a trip up north."

Am I pulling off the *I can't wait for combat* look? I manage to avoid spewing expletives by smiling.

"You're excused."

》》》》 NOVEMBER 6, UNIFIED YEAR 1924, NORTHERN DISTRICT, KRAGGANA **《《《《**
DEPOT, ADVANCE GUARD

For the Imperial Viper Battalion, the words *the worst* described everything about their day. Certainly, there was no other way to explain the circumstances after they sortied.

The bulk of the Empire's proudest force, the Great Army, had been abruptly redeployed, which caused massive confusion. By the time the Imperial Army's Northern Command managed to get everything under control again, the Entente Alliance had taken the chance to recuperate and rebuilt their lines. As a result, the imperial units that had been sent out to pursue and mop up the enemy had to be reorganized, and the Northern Army Group's logistical network was overextended.

That meant opportunities for continuous Entente Alliance Army strikes on imperial supply depots. Once the Northern Army Group had been forced to spread their manpower thin to fend off the Entente Alliance commando attacks, the enemy aerial mages would strike.

The Northern Army Group had already been hit with this tactic twice. They were just barely managing to keep the front supplied, but they couldn't afford another major disruption. The depot raids had to be stopped. That was the gist of the Viper Battalion's mission to guard the supply lines.

The brass had made it sound simple, but for those actually tasked with the assignment, it might as well have been impossible. Although the Entente Alliance's total mage strength was less in absolute terms, it had total freedom in deciding when and where to attack. Meanwhile, the Viper Battalion had to allot troops to multiple points and communication lines because they were committed to defense.

It was a huge bother that the enemy had made remarkable qualitative improvements. Most of the remaining Entente Alliance mages in this commando unit had been in service since the war started. Furthermore, these tenacious soldiers had been equipped with the latest model of orbs that, though officially unmarked, were actually supplied by interested world powers such as the Republic, the Commonwealth, the Unified States, and the Federation. With this, the quality of their gear and combat capabilities rose dramatically. The Entente Alliance mage commando unit had transformed into a threat even imperial mages couldn't take lightly.

On top of all that, the fact that imperial forces couldn't let their guard down against even new units on the front made it difficult for imperial commanders to station troops. Sometimes the Entente Alliance sent in fresh soldiers. If they were new mages rushed through training, they could be immediately slaughtered, but sometimes there were "voluntary mages" of unknown nationality mixed in; it was hard to know how to deal with those.

"Fucking hell. Entente Alliance mages again?!"

As a result, despite outnumbering their opponents on paper, the imperial mage units on the defensive were suffering from local numerical inferiority.

The Viper Battalion's skill was fairly standard for an Imperial Army unit. Compared to others in the district, they were veterans with a good amount of combat experience, and as usual in the Imperial Army, they were well trained. There was no reason not to label them as a first-rate combat unit.

Chapter II

So the fact that they were outnumbered by a fearsomely powerful enemy unit could only mean the situation was terrible.

"This is sooner than we thought! Why did Intel say we had nothing to worry about?!"

Information regarding the skill level and equipment possessed by the average Entente Alliance mage had been passed on to Viper Battalion so they were ready for the qualitative improvements, the disciplined fire, and other tactical measures their opponents had taken that made them a greater threat than before. But despite the force's upgrades, according to their data, the imperial mages should still have been superior on an individual level.

That's why they were confident they could defend to some extent, even if they were outnumbered. They figured with Airspace Control holding the sky they could overwhelm the enemy with their individual abilities; a little numerical disadvantage wouldn't beat them.

So they wanted to curse Intelligence as the ones responsible for the phoned-in report. They could explain it away as the fog of war, but the ones who suffer are always the troops on the front lines. When everything was predicated on different information, it made them want to be mean.

"—Commander!"

He blossomed red upon shielding a subordinate who had carelessly maneuvered into the enemy line of fire.

Luckily, his flight was only momentarily disrupted, and he soared across the sky in an evasive maneuver; he must have managed not to black out. There was no immediate threat to his life, but as far as the soldier could tell, it was a serious wound.

As his buddies covered for him, maintaining coordination, what crossed their minds was the notion that output strong enough to penetrate an imperial mage's defensive shell didn't come from standard Entente Alliance equipment. In spite of their grim suspicions, they cast formulas one after the other. Even when the Entente Alliance unexpectedly made it a three-way fight, the mages of the Viper Battalion were fulfilling their duty thoroughly.

"...I messed up. Sorry, 02, the rest is up to you."

"Understood, Commander! 07 and 13, you two have reached your limits. Fall back with him!"

02 had taken command, so he quickly shifted mental gears. Their commander wouldn't be able to continue fighting, but he needed an escort to retreat, so the only option was to assign soldiers who were exhausted or heavily injured to go with him. They hadn't expected this to be such a tough fight, but the enemy was also wearing down. *All we have to do is defend,* he encouraged himself, but it pained him that their battalion was down to half its original strength. A company's worth of mages had already retreated. Another half a company's worth had been shot down and were still lying on the ground below. Down to half strength, and their enemy was still raiding their supply depots, though the fight should have been wearing them down, too. Their determination was extraordinary.

"CP,[7] do you read me? This is 01. Command of the Viper Battalion has changed hands."

"CP, roger. Viper 02, do you read me?"

Of course, there was tension in the CP radio operator's voice. The company they'd sent ahead was already combat ineffective. Almost all their anti–air gunners who were supposed to be a powerful deterrent against mages had already been evaded. Behind those, the only defense the supply depot had was the temporary anti–air gun emplacements established to provide direct support fire. Maybe they could do a little intercepting, but there was no way they could handle a large-scale assault.

"No problem. This is Viper 02. The commander has been seriously wounded, so I'm taking over."

Agh, what should I do? I want to take my time to think of a way to handle this. If God exists, he's a real asshole.

"CP, roger... Got some bad news for you. The surface observer squad

---

[7] **CP**   Command Post. It's one step down the hierarchy from HQ.

spotted two company-sized groups approaching from the northeast. Seems like they're definitely headed your way."

"Reinforcements? How the hell do they have any left?" Viper 02 took off his receiver and screamed. *They're chipping away at my friends in this bloody battle, but we've downed way more than a company's worth of these bastards.* And yet, two more companies were closing in on them. A little math was all it took to see that the Entente Alliance was pitting a regiment's worth of mages against a single supply depot. *Why?*

This is a bigger problem than our intelligence agency being incompetent. The Entente Alliance obviously has way more troops than we thought.

"Viper 02 to CP. If I may share my thoughts on the matter..."

We won't be able to continue interception missions like this. Our only choice is to use the supply depot we're supposed to protect as a shield, even if it sustains some damage, and commit to a defensive battle. If we take any more casualties, our unit will be wiped out, and the supply depot will be overrun. Having made his decision, 02 had to tell CP.

"This is an emergency. Please make handling this top priority. The battalion has sustained serious casualties. I don't think we can take much more. Requesting immediate permission to retreat. I want to take us back to the depot."

Even the exhausted Viper Battalion could fight their hardest in a tough battle if they joined up with the depot's defenses and the mages who had retreated. It would increase the likelihood of the depot getting damaged, but there was no other way to intercept at this point.

If the battalion fought with only the remaining mages, they would just be picked off one by one. It would be better to at least join up with the remnants of the units that could still fight and get support. They might get cut, but they would be able to put up a better resistance that way than with broken bones.

"CP, roger. I hear what you're saying. I'll consider it with high command. Wait five minutes."

Under normal circumstances, five minutes would be wonderfully efficient. It was proof that the bureaucratic CP understood the gravity of the situation. But even if he should have been happy for the prompt assistance, as someone on the front lines, he had to think, *Five whole minutes?*

Three hundred seconds. How many times would they have to evade and counter while waiting them out?

"Please respond as fast as you can. The vanguard is already beat up!"

In a brawl like this, the vanguard always had to face the enemy the longest. They were already so worn down they could barely fend for themselves as individuals, much less perform as a unit. Even if they set up for a protracted defense, they wouldn't last long. Just staying in the air was a huge burden for them now. Only someone who had experience knew how hard it was to dodge formulas. Anyhow, they had no choice but to hold out until they got permission to retreat.

...That was the right mind-set, but it wouldn't be that easy.

"Lieutenant, multiple aircraft at two o'clock—bombers," came the half-screamed report from his subordinate on guard. *Agh, the worst guys show up at the worst times.* Mechanical birds that were comfortable flying at high altitudes and could carry a huge amount of explosives a human could never manage. They had almost never been spotted on the northern front: bombers.

"H-how high?!"

"They're at 9,500."

His question contained a sliver of hope, but the response was cruel. It sent a chill up his spine.

Nine thousand five hundred feet. That was too high for a mage but low for a bomber. At that altitude, they could also bomb targets to some extent.

Naturally, they had sturdy armor. And a bomber unit under pursuit from mages could shake them off with no trouble by leisurely climbing to a higher altitude. Between the huge altitude gap and their armor, intercepting bombers was too hard a mission for mages. That was why the aerial units that specialized in interception always fought the air supremacy battles.

But with a mere mage battalion, they didn't know what to do. Intercept the bombers while fighting two battalions? That was the definition of an impossible order.

"Viper 02 to CP! It's urgent!"

"This is CP. Viper Battalion, what is—?"

"We've spotted multiple bombers! Altitude is just an eyeball estimate, but they're at 9,500 feet! Intercepting is impossible. Deploy all the marshaled troops immediately."

What the heck? CP was taking too long asking the question, and he furiously interrupted.

Bombers don't have great mobility, but they are fast. If fighters go around 250, then bombers go 200 to 210. Mages usually go around 230. If they really worked, they could tolerate 250, but at that point they could only really fly in a straight line.

The enemy was going for a one-two punch of bombs and mages. The methods to deal with that were certainly limited. This enemy was awfully crafty and capable.

"Bombers? Tell me how many and what direction."

"Two o'clock from our perspective. About twenty."

It was only twenty planes, but getting bombed in this state would entail more than a little damage. It would be a disaster if they lost the winter fuel stockpile. The troops on the front would have a cold time.

Surely their opponent knew that. That's why they'd brought out not only mages but bombers as well. This was what it meant for worse to come to worst.

"CP, roger. Can you intercept them?"

He suppressed the urge to shout, *How?!* "They're too high, and we still haven't eliminated the enemy mages. We can't really use long-range sniping formulas right now."

Basically, *It's obviously impossible.* It would be difficult even under normal circumstances to eliminate bombers with a 3,500-foot gap in altitudes. If they were operating fully manned and employed disciplined fire, maybe, but that was about as much of a chance as they had. Intercepting them while dogfighting enemy mages was unfeasible.

"…We definitely want to avoid Kraggana Depot getting bombed."

"We can't put up a fight if we're all dead."

CP seems to want to rely on us, but the impossible is impossible. There are things that can and can't be done, and we are doing our absolute utmost.

The voice of the Viper Battalion leader couldn't help but become sarcastic and even a bit resigned as he replied with pride. It seemed like no matter what they did, they would be wiped out.

So are they going to tell us to brace for annihilation and resist? My interest is purely sarcastic, but boy, even I'm getting pretty philosophical. Maybe I should get ready to die.

It happened just as he thought that.

"Roger... What? Really?"

A whisper, then a shout. Then a flurry of voices. Something was happening at the command post.

"CP? What's going on, CP?"

"CP to Viper Battalion. Fall back immediately."

The awaited retreat orders came down in a tone that brooked no argument, but he never imagined they'd get them like this. *What the hell happened?*

"We have permission to retreat? I appreciate it, but is everything all right?"

"Rejoice—you have reinforcements. A battalion is rushing over from Sector B-3. Once you join up with them, you'll be under their command."

Reinforcements? What woodwork did they suddenly come out of this late in the game? If we had reserves, why did we end up in this struggle?

"Reinforcements? That's news to me. If we had extra troops, what were we waiting for?"

"They were dispatched from Central. Call sign Pixie."

The operator ignored his attitude and simply conveyed the information. If it was a unit from the central forces, they must be getting caught up in the fighting as soon as they arrived. It was likely they had shown up ahead of schedule and Command thought, *Great!* before throwing them right in.

"And you should be happy. Their commander is Named."

He forgot his grudge in spite of himself and nearly whistled in amazement.

Wonderful. That's absolutely fantastic. A battalion of reinforcements and a Named. It's like the harvest festival and Christmas both arrived at once, and we got this terrific present. If I could, I'd open a bottle of champagne and welcome them with a toast.

"Viper 02, roger. Those are some fancy reinforcements."

If we're getting that kind of quality backup, then…yes, I see why we were granted permission to retreat. I want to shout hooray, but I do wish they could have come a little sooner.

At that last thought, he realized humans rescued from hopeless situations tend to expect an awful lot, and he winced. Well, he knew it was completely unreasonable, but he still had the nerve to think that if the reinforcements had come earlier, his battalion wouldn't have had to suffer so much.

Add some fighters, and it'll be perfect. There probably wouldn't be many, but he was sure they would scramble some to intercept before too long. His mouth naturally relaxed into a grin at the prospect. It was such a load off to know that the enemy would be crushed one way or another.

"When will the fighters be taking off?"

"…They were judged to be unnecessary."

The unexpected response stunned him.

Fighters? Unnecessary?

"Huh?" He wanted to ask what the radio operator was talking about.

"Don't worry about it. Just hurry and meet up with your reinforcements."

"…Roger."

〉〉〉 AT THE SAME TIME, NORTHERN ARMY GROUP HQ 〈〈〈

The staff at Northern Army Group Headquarters were staring at the map of the war at a loss, and that was when they got news they didn't really want to hear. The deputy director of Operations in the central General Staff had gone out of his way to come and deliver the notice in person. It might have been central interference, but the wording was simple: "We've dispatched reinforcements. Don't touch them."

"The damned General Staff. Why do they think they can go around meddling in frontline business?"

The complaints of the high-ranking officers of the northern forces that it was insulting were unsurprising. After all, they finally thought they were getting support from Central, but the moment they had managed to accommodate the hastily deployed Great Army, most of it was transferred abruptly to the western front, and they were left in disarray. It was only human nature that anyone stuck enduring unnecessary hardships in that chaos would want to give Central a piece or two of their mind.

According to the report from the observation post, a battalion-sized group of aerial mages was indeed rapidly approaching.

Aha, well that certainly is a nice batch of reinforcements. Seeing as they were sent immediately after we requested them, they're apparently serious about being a response team. But Central giving us reinforcements and then telling us not to touch them is overstepping their bounds.

"Well, maybe they gave us really elite troops?"

Even so, from another perspective, this is an opportunity for the Central Army to pay us back. It pulled out the Great Army before the battle was completely decided. Those guys are proud—they won't come bowing in apology. Although he wouldn't go as far as to accuse them of taking advantage of Northern Command's current issues, they were probably thinking to cancel out the debt.

"Are they trying to make us feel indebted to them...?"

"But 'Don't touch them'? That takes some nerve."

Yeah, I can't believe they said that. And if they were trying to make us feel indebted...the northern supply depots are in trouble! Do they realize that the already poor logistics framework for the Northern Army Group could completely collapse?

"They're talking pretty big considering the northern supply lines are in crisis. I wish I were that confident." *You could even call that warning arrogant.* He made his spiteful remarks without thinking, but from someone in the thick of it, it was the natural response. Then came even more dumbfounding news.

"We just got a telegram from the 203rd Aerial Mage Battalion. 'This is the Pixie Battalion.' Uhh..."

A telegram from an incoming battalion of reinforcements? Normally, they would report their call sign, and that would be all, but for some reason the radio operator was hesitating.

"It's fine—read it."

A suspicious staff officer urged him on, and he finally continued.

"It says, 'We don't require assistance. Have the Viper Battalion retreat immediately.'"

"We don't require assistance"? The Viper Battalion has been intercepting up until now, but they want it to fall back? This went past *impressively* confident to *overly* confident.

There were two mage battalions and bombers out there reinforcing the enemy side. It definitely didn't seem like an attacking battalion fresh off a forced march could handle it on their own.

They were supposed to put their units under a commander who didn't understand that? That was simply out of the question.

"...We can scramble fighters to intercept at any time, right?"

"Every hangar is on standby. One word and we can send them out."

A few staff officers began quickly developing their own interception plans. Even if the time they had to climb was limited, fighters scrambled from the surface should be able to contain the bombers.

Originally, they were outnumbered and needed a way to deal with the mages, so they were grateful for reinforcements, but...perhaps it would be smart to stop the bombers on their own?

"Shouldn't we use them? This situation is plain bad."

"Well, it's an order, though. Doing anything more would be..." He swallowed the words *acting without permission*, but they embodied the worried staff officer's fears.

Staff members' authority did not extend to acting without orders. Their job was to plan operations, not make decisions. That was one of the hard things about being a staffer. What freed them from that agony was ironically the source of their current headache, the Pixies.

"The control unit got a read on the Pixies. Forty-eight signals. Speed 250, altitude..." The control unit on watch detected the incoming Pixie Battalion.

The reported speed of 250 kilometers per hour was virtually the maximum. If they could fly that fast and still maintain formation, it indicated they were highly trained.

"That's awfully fast. Hmm? What about the altitude?"

The staff officers were starting to feel like maybe they could count on this backup and asked for the altitude data.

"They're at...7,500? No...they're still climbing."

"What?"

"Are you sure? They aren't fighter planes, you know."

Lessons learned in combat made six thousand feet the commonsense limit. Maybe the data said the record was eight thousand, but it was hard to trust that until they saw it in an actual battle.

The theoretical values the engineers talked about and the values a frontline unit could achieve were of completely different importance. The members of the class known as soldiers were always suspicious of new frameworks, weapons, and technology. It was healthy skepticism given their lives depended on whether the things were usable or not.

And that was why, in one sense, they had no choice but to be humbled by what they were witnessing now. That was the weight of proof in combat.

"No mistakes. The Pixie Battalion is currently at eight thousand feet!"

"They're accelerating! Three hundred?!"

Just as unbelievable was the jump in speed.

A unit flying in formation toward combat on the front lines was at virtually the same speed and altitude that the tech tests had achieved. If the data was real, it would indicate skills on a whole new level.

Is it true? If it was, this battalion's performance was in such a realm of its own that it would render all the existing units obsolete.

"Are those control unit readings accurate?"

"I don't see any other abnormalities... Everything's operating normally."

The same unbelieving expression rose to all the staff officers' faces.

"It seems the central General Staff has a deviation as their trump card."

"Seriously. Deviation is right."

The only thing they could say was that they were glad this battalion was on their side.

>>> COMMONWEALTH VOLUNTARY ARMY FRONTLINE COMMAND <<<

"It's Named! It's a Named who was spotted in the west! We've got an individual match—it's the Devil of the Rhine!" the observer cried out in surprise, and the entire HQ focused on him for a moment. The Named they weren't even sure existed had appeared.

The one who flew casually through the death zone.

The one who single-handedly slaughtered a company.

The one could use interference formulas so powerful they distort space.

When their contact in the Republican Army had given them the intelligence, they'd laughed it off thinking it was too early for April Fool's, plus he'd been drinking.

It was true the Empire had superior technology and tactics, but they'd thought this was beyond impossible. Their analysts had said she was a sort of battlefield legend. Though they respected the Republicans and wanted to avoid outright denying the claim, they figured she was at most a phantom generated by the chaos of the battlefield. The gossipy officers had whispered that sort of thing, questioning whether this Named even existed.

But now if their own observer was detecting her in real time, they needed to reevaluate the data they had tried to forget like a bad joke over a nice cup of tea.

"She's real? I thought the Republicans were just daydreaming."

Misunderstandings weren't uncommon. If you took every confused soldier's report at face value, you'd join the ranks of the insane from the paranoia. Thus, the Commonwealth officers who had realistically deemed her either a false report or, at worst, some kind of mass hallucination had to leap for their machines.

Some jumped for receivers to wake up the analyst squad. Others promptly notified high command.

"We've identified the signature. There's no mistake. She's heading this way."

Then multiple observers succeeded in identifying her. They had input the pattern half wondering if it was even real, but now they had a match. An individual might misreport, but the conclusion reached by multiple precise observations made by several observers wasn't likely to be wrong. At this point, they had to acknowledge that she was real.

"The enemy reinforcements are a battalion-sized group. We have no record of this unit."

Add to that the signal of a group containing numerous unknown signals. Judging from the scale, it had to be a battalion—maybe even an augmented battalion. If the mana inclination didn't resemble any existing records, that meant the Empire had deployed new mages.

The fact that there was almost no overlap with the Republic's library from the Rhine front had to indicate that the Empire had as many reserves as ever. Apparently, despite the muddle, they could still produce a new unit led by a Named.

"...I'm surprised they're sending out a new unit when they already have so much pressure on the Entente Alliance."

"You think it's the unit from Dacia? Most of the fighting is over there, so they could probably afford to transfer them."

Aha. He didn't know who, but someone had said the Dacians couldn't even stand up to Boy Scouts, so certainly an Imperial Army Named would have no trouble blowing them away. And it made sense to think that if they were free, they would be sent to take care of the impudent Entente Alliance command team and its rampage.

"We'll take data. You got the recorders running?"

"If it's true, he's a monster who can take out a whole company on his own. Don't miss a thing."

The intelligence officer may have been chatting, but he was staring at the data the whole time. This unit had a mana inclination he'd never seen before. And more than anything, he couldn't ignore the actual existence of the rumored Named from the unconfirmed reports in the west. If they had so little info on a battalion led by a monster of that caliber, it had to be a failure of their espionage in the Empire. So he realized, even if he didn't want to, how important objective observation of this new enemy was.

"Picking up any transmissions?"

"It's no good. They're using an unknown code and protocol. At least, it's not in the library."

That was the answer he had expected. Even if they couldn't decipher them, by intercepting and recording wavelengths, they would be able to grasp enemy unit hierarchy and movement.

But if all the records they had didn't contain this code or protocol, who was this new enemy? He was keenly disappointed that Dacia had fallen so quickly. They had gone so fast it was no wonder they weren't able to get any data out of the conflict, but he still wished for the impossible.

"Commander, it's nearly certain they're a new unit with the Empire. There are almost no similarities with existing records of the Northern and Western Army Groups."

"All right. Well, gosh, I'd really like to send up a control unit."

Everyone grinned. Even deployed in the frozen north, they hadn't lost their sacred sense of black humor. All of them understood. They didn't need to be told that they were under too much pressure in this war. It was evident that the Commonwealth was wrestling with political restraints at home, which limited its military in ways individual soldiers could do nothing about. God and the devil seemed to be involved somehow, so after a round of curses for each, the officers on-site reluctantly accepted their circumstances, resigning themselves to their fate.

"Yeah, we can't send a plane in."

"Right… We should probably be more worried about whether we'll be able to withdraw with our gear in one piece."

Pressure on the Entente Alliance Army was gradually increasing. They weren't completely falling apart yet, but that was just it—the only way to describe the current situation was *not fallen apart yet.*

The calmer third-party observer could see that the Empire, without even making this front its main focus, was driving the Entente Alliance to collapse. The Entente Alliance was like a bedridden patient with a serious illness, just barely hanging on. If the situation changed even slightly, it would have a seizure and breathe its last.

"Ngh. Well, for now, alert the front lines."

"Roger."

But the CP officers consciously cleared those thoughts from their minds and focused on the tasks before them, shouting instructions into receivers.

Determining the enemy's status was a task that involved many difficult elements, but at least the team on the scene was a group of intelligence-gathering veterans. They had been sent out with an eye on future fighting with the Empire.

Since the Commonwealth hoped they would gain all sorts of experience and learn a lot in combat, from a national defense standpoint, it was very considerate toward its personnel and had outfitted them well.

"But I'm surprised. Who'd have thought a battalion could come flying over at three hundred kilometers per hour?"

"That's far from what you'd expect. Maybe the apparatus needs tuning after all?"

So these men chosen from across the Commonwealth's armies were expected to learn from the Imperial Army and master their tactics. But even these most promising soldiers hadn't had much combat experience, and on top of that, the assumptions that had been pounded into them were all prewar doctrine. The reality of the battlefield was far removed from the experiences and techniques they had accumulated during peacetime.

Thus, if they didn't learn a thing or two before their country was enveloped in war, they would pay for it with their own flesh and blood.

Most of the staff officers had thought this Named couldn't exist, but she did. In other words, she wasn't an illusion of the battlefield but a real nightmare. It was no laughing matter, but the predictions made far from the actual fighting had already missed their mark.

Ironically, the fruit of the Commonwealth's diplomatic victories was a vexing dearth of combat experience. Only specialists can do the analysis necessary to distinguish subtle changes in the war situation. Their failure to read the situation was irritating.

In intelligence work, there wasn't anyone who could teach that essential sense—you had to develop it through your own experience. Of course, there were no specialist textbooks, and even if there were, they wouldn't be of much use.

"…We should probably be ready for about half of what we heard."

For that reason, most of the officers dispatched were chosen so that they would gain experience. Of course, most of them weren't told they had been selected for purely educational purposes, but the ones who couldn't figure it out were forcibly sent home as wastes of time and resources. That being the case, the remainder went about performing well-focused, objective analysis.

It was precisely for that reason, due to their quick sagacity, that they sensed they were facing a crisis. Even if all the stories had been exaggerated, this was an imperial Named. And the reinforcements consisted of a battalion—very likely an augmented battalion. Even taking the simplest view, it was a battalion-scale attack. There was no cause for optimism.

"So what if that Named can blow up a whole company instantaneously? There's no way the bastard can take two battalions, right?"

Still, a wishful hope existed somewhere in their minds. Let's just say, hypothetically, that there was a Named who could fight against a company. Even so, numbers can overwhelm strength—so they still had a chance. If she had been alone, she probably wouldn't have been such a problem.

"But we can't ignore the battalion. They must be highly trained if they're coming in that fast."

"Meanwhile, we have numbers, but we're a composite unit… Could be tough."

Purely from a numbers standpoint, the new enemy battalion was a grave threat. There was no doubting the fact that a fresh battalion would be a hard fight for two tired battalions. Conversely, you could say *a hard fight* was as difficult as it would get. That was what they were thinking.

"So the Republic, the Commonwealth, and the Entente Alliance all have different combat doctrines, huh?"

What the Commonwealth men were most worried about was the possibility that even if they all joined forces, they wouldn't be able to cooperate well. The Republic and the Commonwealth were secretly fighting together, but as long as there was intelligence they couldn't share, there would be major losses.

The Republic (to whom the Entente Alliance had cried and who was now asking for help itself) and the Commonwealth (which was gathering intelligence for war with the Empire on its mind) had gotten very out of step. Today they were extra conscious of that fact.

"If our coordination gets disrupted, we might have to split up."

No matter what the Republic and Entente Alliance did, the Commonwealth was loath to give up its neutral status; even when it did join a war, it did so with caution.

The Republic and Entente Alliance would bad-mouth the Commonwealth, saying it had a tendency to conserve power or that it only fought to test a new weapon in actual combat. But were those really insults? The officers had to wonder. The state wanted to keep casualties to a minimum.

"It will take some time, but a reorganized battalion might be able to come help."

Naturally, the Commonwealth's voluntary army—full of soldiers who signed themselves up—didn't want to break through if it meant a high number of casualties. After all, they had to buy the indispensable time for their home country to switch over to the wartime system. Though they had numerical superiority, never for a moment did they want to fight head-to-head on a battlefield where a Named was coming to meet them.

And when she had an Imperial Army unit as backup, it was time to start considering withdrawal, but they couldn't ignore the fact that they had sacrificed so much to disrupt enemy logistics.

"I guess in the worst case, we'll smash the position using just the bombers?"

So accomplishing the minimum goal would depend on the bombers.

They were bombing a fuel depot. Even a small number of successful attacks could get them great results. And if they failed, the planes they were leasing to the Entente Alliance were old models that the Commonwealth wouldn't use anyway—something they thought but couldn't say.

"I'm against that. If fighter planes intercepted, we're liable to sustain more damage than we can brush off."

"Can't high-speed bombers shake them off?"

"The Republic already tried it and got burned, so I'm against it."

"In that case, we need to eliminate the enemy mages somehow."

"We stand a lot to gain from that. I guess we have no choice."

They pretended to worry about the bombers for appearances. Really, they just had to make remarks for the record. After all, everyone knew the "high-speed" bombers they had provided moved dirt slow.

"The issue is the ability of the Named and the unknown battalion. It would be great if the bombers could take care of them…"

Those were their true feelings on the matter, a boorish hope that the enemy would overexert themselves attending to the bombers.

At that moment, fate played a trick on them.

They had taken over a simple, hidden Entente Alliance Army control center used for observing the front line over twenty kilometers ahead and giving direction. But they had forgotten something. They had forgotten that twenty kilometers was not much distance at all to a mage.

"What? For real?! There's no mistake?!"

Suddenly the CP officer on control duty jumped up, turned pale, and shouted into the radio. A moment later, a number of other officers stood with equally bloodless faces.

"This is α Battalion! This is urgent! What the—?! Recommend taking shelter!"

"Kill the power! We're getting traced!"

Everyone was shouting at practically the same time.

"I'm getting a strong mana signal from the Named! She's rapidly deploying a magic bombardment formula!" Then the controller started shrieking, and the panic escalated.

We're getting traced? A warning to take shelter from α Battalion…? A strong mana signal?

"What? She can't hit us from there!"

"Take shelter! Take shelter!"

A few of the officers kicked aside the idiots who instinctively denied the necessity of the warning, ran for the dugout, and were blown away a moment later.

)))) ALTITUDE 9,500, IN THE WAR ZONE AHEAD OF THE SUPPLY DEPOT ((((

"With his glory like the morning sun, he illuminates the darkness. He is born! Praise the Lord!"

A converging magic bombardment formula.

Magic bombardment has the penetration and destructive power of a 28 cm gun. The seven-layer control equation that created it scatters and disappears. For an instant, the battlefield shines with a great light, and then the sound of impact roars through the air.

"Collapse of surveillance waves confirmed. Elimination of enemy observation unit complete." At the same time, a noise-heavy report of the effects comes in from her observer, Lieutenant Serebryakov. "Splendid, Major," she adds, and Tanya has to agree.

She rarely registers the satisfaction of an attack, but this time she feels it. It goes without saying that she hit her target. And it had to be quite a blow to them. In any case, this fundamental part of any mage battle, eliminating the enemy observation personnel, had gone quite smoothly.

The victims were either amateurs, or they were awfully confident in their dugouts, but they had been putting out powerful surveillance waves like crazy, so they had been discovered right away. Compared to the Republican Army, which was mainly a passive receiver of waves, they were quite easy to find.

Apparently, the Entente Alliance's army continues to be qualitatively inferior. You wouldn't normally actively emit surveillance waves unless you were at a distance in a control unit where you could easily escape, or at least a surface surveillance train.

How dumb are they to blithely observe from a fixed position?

That's Tanya's judgment coming from experience. It seems luck is with her. She balls her little hands up and enjoys it.

Chapter **II**

"Enemy transmissions dramatically increased. Multiple calls from mages confirmed. You must have hit their Combat Direction Center."

The report from her subordinate observer only deepens her belief. She has definitely, without a doubt, blown away the enemy controllers. Knowing the implications of that, she triumphantly raises her rifle and crows.

Even just looking from a distance, she is satisfied to see the enemy formations begin to waver—an indication of the shock they just received.

"Okay, we definitely got them, right? Then let's move in."

Normally, engaging the enemy in an airspace of their choosing with a numerically inferior force is out of the question. I would stubbornly refuse. But once the enemy's head is blown off, that's a different story. A conservative description of the units fighting in the air would be *chaos*. The job of maintaining discipline and turning this into organized combat is too big for their frontline commander to handle.

No matter how outstanding the commander, once combat devolves into a brawl, it's impossible to keep an eye on the entire situation. There are limits to how much a commander can monitor their unit while engaged in dogfighting. On that point, Tanya is thankful for the Imperial Army's combat doctrine. Its mission-oriented beliefs mean that if an officer has good subordinates, they don't need to hold their hands and show them how to shoot.

Of course, the 203rd Aerial Mage Battalion is receiving a minimum of direction, including navigation support, from Norden Control. A war without Control is just a crude dogfight between isolated mages.

After all, without Control to keep the necessary order, you're left with individual mages flying around. Power that can't be harnessed isn't much of a threat.

"Pixie 01 to all hands. Enemy Control has been eliminated."

We are lucky the linchpin of the enemy command scheme gave away its position. You never know till you try, so she had thrown out the bombardment and blown them away with ease…apparently.

Now the enemy is no longer units but a mob of individuals. Mages without their CP are like a pack of Don Quixotes each fighting their own battles.

"Pixie 01 to CP. Send the status of the enemies you spotted."

"CP, roger. The remaining enemies are flying at 6,500 feet. Looks like the vanguard is about a reserve regiment's worth. Two companies guarding them. They also have bombers. No sign of reinforcements."

The situation is exactly what it looks like. The only enemies who can engage with us right now are the disheveled troops directly before us. Normally, enemy control would have any number of options how to proceed, like sending the escorts ahead to shore up the disordered vanguard.

But now none of them know what to do—they're panicking. Entente Alliance and Republican mages, I've noticed, have a tendency to be overly specialized in group combat.

The mages of our Imperial Army's pride, the 203rd Aerial Mage Battalion, who somehow cheerfully survived their hellish training, should be able to overpower them. At the very least, they probably won't hold me back, so I can use them as a shield with no problems.

And this time we also have the wonderful addition of enemy bombers. If I take them down, I can expect a raise and other perks, according to air force regulations.

Ah, this really is great. Tanya unconsciously gives her lips a vulgar lick.

For once, she's in a situation that is virtually blue ocean. It has to be her efforts day after day that have created such a blessed environment. As in Dacia, fate, or the law of cause and effect or whatever, is finally on my side. I'm willing to stick with the hypothesis that Being X is evil, but I'm in a good enough mood to argue that a benevolent entity might exist.

"First, Second, and Third Companies, hunt the two enemy vanguard battalions. Fourth Company, with me."

We aren't lacking a necessary cause to act. I'm the commander of the battalion, the one who leads.

To put it bluntly, my attitude is more or less *Maybe I'll end up fighting myself at some point.* I can push the annoying job of dealing with enemy units onto my underlings.

Or rather, that's what they're there for. I want my subordinates to give it their all so I can think about more important things.

The Imperial Army General Staff has invested a lot in these guys. It's not my money, but it is taxpayers' money, so I've done my best to put it to wise use. I don't want to do anything that would make me look inept, and though taxes are a sort of evil, I'd like to atone for it by using the funds in a meaningful way.

For that reason, I need to show that the investment was worth their while. Most of all, I don't want to be branded all talk and sent to the front lines as punishment. So I'll leverage my position and make my subordinates do the tough stuff.

There's a right man for every job, you know. Since they like war so much, I'm sure they'll be happy to do it. I intend to make my way to the rear with a record of discovering and recommending talent. This is the ideal win-win scenario. It's fair to call it truly wonderful.

"Fourth Company, we're going to strike the escorts and the bombers. After that, we'll go around the back of the other fight and pincer those two battalions."

For the time being, I take Fourth Company as my escort and initiate maneuvers to take the rear. I want to avoid any danger spots, so under the pretense of a detour, I put off some fighting. First, I want to see how they do against my subordinates. If the enemy seems stronger than expected, I'll abort the roundabout sneak attack and head back to assist the rest of the troops. My insurance is all in place.

"That's it for the battle plan. That said, gentlemen..."

The Northern Army Group is watching, so I need to show them this frontline commander's fighting spirit.

This'll make us look like an army.

A resolute commander with a loud voice and an offensive mind-set will silence any meaningless criticism.

Just look at the loudmouth Tsuji. He indiscriminately ground down talent, caused a catastrophe, and still got promoted.

"Though your job is to stop them, you don't have to wait for me by any means. I don't mind at all if you defeat them."

If things get bad, I'll use the Tsuji doctrine to protect myself. For better or worse, after World War II, that guy brilliantly managed to avoid war crime prosecution. Even if I can't imitate his shameless nerve, there are still things I can learn from him.

He could have been a corporate warrior who would have forever been waging internal company battles with his demonic drive for promotion. Well, I don't actually want to be that kind of person. This world is rather impossible for good citizens like me—I have shame and a conscience.

"Also, when we get back, whichever company gets the worst results will have their commander treat the rest of us to a party. I ordered some twenty-five-year-old wine, so fight hard if you don't want to go bankrupt!"

Thus, I came up with an elegant way to get around socialization expenditures. Associating with one's subordinates is part of a boss's job, but I hate getting my expenses audited for no reason. Take that guy, for example. Tsuji was really picky about inspecting for improper spending. He would find people's weaknesses that way.

What you can learn from that is that armies and companies aren't so different from one another. Improper spending on entertainment will affect your future career. So I'll use my subordinates' money—just below the threshold of power harassment.

Furthermore, though in society it's generally accepted that children aren't allowed to drink wine, if one of my brothers-in-arms offered me some, and I can't refuse, perhaps the army would look the other way. The thought that I might finally get to have wine brings tears to my eyes.

""""""Understood!""""""

"Good. Now then, gentlemen. Do your duty for the emperor and the fatherland."

I don't have a lick of love or respect for the emperor, and as for the fatherland, I just hope I get benefits commensurate with the taxes I pay. But the state does give me my soldier's pension and other various allowances. Then again, this place sadly seems to be in the strategic position Germany was in during the First World War...

Ahh, what a tragedy. I feel like I'm at a company guaranteed to go bankrupt. Or like an employee who is going to be worn down to nothing at an office with abhorrent working conditions. There's no way to win here.

I'd like to submit my voluntary resignation and transfer to a better company. In the worst case, I would even be ready to bring a labor suit.

But betraying the army during a war would come with all sorts of troublesome issues. Who would trust a whistle-blower like that? Even if they promise freedom of belief, nobody would want to take on a hard-core leftist activist in a million years.

Thinking logically, only an idiot would risk betrayal if the returns aren't guaranteed to be worth it. What's more, it would be difficult to protect myself when I've already done so much killing in this war.

My position is somewhat like a sniper's. If the war ends and I can be safely demobilized, that's great, but on the off chance I find myself having to surrender, there's a good chance I'd be shot on the spot. In a word, I'm buying my enemy's enmity at limit up.

"Let's teach those Entente Alliance mopes and the rest of them a lesson. They don't get it when you only put it in words."

Actually, I tried to get them to surrender once, and I couldn't get through to them at all. Hideously enough, they're people without a shred of economic sense. If they like war so much, they should just split their country in half and fight among themselves.

But apparently, the Republic and the Entente Alliance are really into involving others. Talk about a pain in the neck. They're beyond saving if they ignore the balance between public matters and personal freedom by causing other folks trouble. I'd like them to think a bit about what a nuisance they are to the average person.

"We're gonna bring an iron hammer down on them from the heavens. They're about to learn how powerless they really are." If we can't leisurely attack them from high in the sky, I won't be able to take this.

For now, we have the bandwidth to spare, but this really isn't good for my heart.

The only time I'm thankful for this little body is when the enemy is aiming at it and having trouble hitting. A wise man once said, "They call bullets slugs because they pack a punch." Well, I don't want to get shot.

"First, Second, and Third Companies, go on ahead. We'll go around and strike from behind."

That's why into the most risky situations—with the greatest potential for achievement—I send the volunteers.

"""Roger! Glory to the fatherland and our commander!"""

"I wish you all luck."

Well! It seems my subordinates are really starved for war since we walloped the Dacians. They're more fired up than I imagined they would be—it's a bit moving. They have a consummate service spirit.

They're so wonderful that if they weren't so dedicated to the pursuit of the unproductive enterprise of war, I would definitely want to recruit them. It's really too bad. It's this kind of thing that proves the devil's existence.

If God existed, resources wouldn't be allotted so improperly. The market principle is the one truth path. Only the market has an invisible hand.

Honestly, it's so unfortunate. The world really is made to be difficult. It seems like it'll be a long time before economics works everything out.

"Fourth Company, we're climbing. We're going to go around and attack those two companies that seem like reinforcements."

Anyhow, this job is fine—I'll just do what needs to be done. We're an augmented battalion—four companies. What that means is we're a battalion plus an extra company. Our battalion will intercept the two battalions, and the extra company will take on the two companies. What simple proportions. As for where to employ my personal strength, the latter situation is easier. And I want to make it easy on myself, so I'm going with the latter group.

There is no greater aim on the battlefield than to defeat the enemy with as little effort as possible. It's all about how comfortable you can make your life.

The idea that struggling while you're young builds character must have as much truth to it as a hedge fund advertisement. I think I'll go ahead and build other people's character.

"Understood. What will you do about the bombers?"

"They're mine. Don't hate me! I'd just like to be an air force ace as well as an army one."

"Ha-ha-ha. Good one."

He asked something important, so I made myself clear. I replied casually enough, but I meant it. Though it was a sort of snobby motivation, I read somewhere that it's not bad to show a human side once in a while. Of course, I also read that if you're too snobby, people won't like you. Why is a good person like me so unreasonably tormented by Being X and made to fight in this war in the first place? I can't help but lament my fate.

But now my subordinates have started to laugh like they've heard a great joke. Finding that suspect, I glare at them and ask what in the world is so funny.

"You know you have to do it with fighter planes, right?"

But the answer is simple. Vexingly enough, it seems I've misunderstood the rules. How regrettable that I should expose my ignorance in front of my men like this. What indescribable shame.

"Really? That's too bad. We should have borrowed fighter planes. I'd almost like to go back and get them."

"Why don't you? Although, if I go with you, I think I'll end up having to treat the battalion."

They must be having a great laugh at my expense. Going back to borrow fighter planes from the air force? I can't do that.

If I did, it'd be treated as fleeing before the enemy. Death by firing squad! Death by firing squad would be waiting for me. And on top of that, it's not like I can pilot a fighter plane anyhow, so I wouldn't even have an excuse. I have no doubt this bureaucratic system would execute even a young child like me. Isn't there some kind of interest or rights group, or even a group with vested interests, that would protect me?

"I couldn't possibly turn my back on the enemy."

"Well, that's that, I suppose. Let's just finish this up as fast as we can."

And then messages from the other units come in. There's nothing better than good timing.

I love that my men can read a situation. I'm sure they'll be a great help in getting promoted. This is very good.

"Sorry, you're definitely going to be treating us. Engage!"

"Twenty-five years... I'll be drinking my fill. Company, forward!"

"Nothing better than having good brothers-in-arms. Well then, 'scuse us, Commander."

"A-argh! Those guys! My apologies, Commander."

The atmosphere had completely changed. They were great backup.

Even though I had been in human resources, where I didn't have to deal with too many nights out drinking or entertaining clients, when someone is this good, I know in a glance. These guys are definitely cut out to be in sales. I'm sure they have what it takes to handle strategy.

What a waste. It really is a shame. The fact that they love war instead of business is just too bad. I have to respect their free will, yet I still find it unfortunate.

"Okay. Don't worry about me. Go on ahead."

"Thank you. Fourth Company, we're going out in front!"

Apparently, all my company commanders are full of fight. They're raring to go like Dobermans before their prey, so when I let go of their leashes, they're off.

They immediately get into a spindle-shaped assault formation and zoom out of the sky to put pressure on the enemy from above. It's a truly beautiful maneuver. The instantaneous charge is performed in perfect unity, but their desire for battle is so intense they get a bit too daring.

Really, I had intended to have Fourth Company be my direct support, but if they like fighting so much, maybe it's safer to keep my distance. They might be too aggressive to use as my shield; enemies might actually be attracted to them.

"Sheesh, so I'm up against the slowpoke bombers? Doesn't seem like we'll be able to dance."

My own lonely interception battle. Against bombers, I probably won't get to perform any elegant maneuvers. It'll be the simple labor of turning into a fixed battery and blasting them out of the sky. If I miss, I'll just be a laughingstock, so although it's a safe job, I can't take it too easy.

"I'm not really in the mood, but this is work. Let's just get it done one step at a time."

Maybe it's good not to stick out, but you can't show people what you can do that way. Besides, I'm up against bombers. I have to aim very precisely to take them out.

Since I can't sense magic and use that for guidance, I have to employ either heat detection or radar. I may be a mage, but I don't come with radar, and building in a heat detection formula is a pain. Considering it's going to basically be a sniper attack in the end, it doesn't seem worth the time and effort.

Frankly, it's no wonder that puts me in a foul mood. At least if I down the things my score will go up.

"Major von Degurechaff, how copy?"

"This is Pixie 01, solid copy. Since when have you forgotten we use call signs?"

And that's why I gave a cranky response to the message that suddenly came in.

Perhaps not being able to control my emotions disqualifies me as an adult member of society, but nobody would be happy to have a difficult job interrupted with a flagrant violation of regulations. Honestly what does everyone think rules and regulations are for? There are too many careless people in the world.

"M-my apologies."

"What do you think the military discipline and regulations are for?"

You can't just fix this kind of thing by saying sorry. Regulation violations lead to accidents. Don't you know Heinrich's Law, the rule of thumb an insurance worker discovered taking statistics? Accumulating small mistakes is the first step to a serious accident. Mistakes must be eradicated.

"Please leave it at that. This is Hotel 03, Hotel 03. Do you copy?"

Someone who sounds important got on the line, so I decide to adjust my attitude. Sometimes swallowing your pride is the right choice. As a member of an organization, what you need to do is simple: Don't bite the hand that feeds you.

"This is Pixie 01. Loud and clear. What can I do for you?"

"The reorganization of the Viper Battalion and the units that retreated is complete. Shall we have them act as a rear guard?"

This time instead of scolding, Tanya breaks into a smile at what a well-made address it was. The Viper Battalion is worn down, and she figured they would be more like deadweight than reinforcements, but it seems their reorganization has gone well. Perhaps the Northern Army Group is more efficient than she gave them credit for.

"Wow, what a speedy reorganization! Very well, please do."

Anything useful is welcome. Deadweight that can't even serve as a shield is annoying, but she is always happy to accept pawns.

She has more luck than she thought this time. People shouldn't rely on fortune, but neither should they be too narrow-minded to seize a good chance.

"What? Oh, understood. I'll get them on their way."

"You have my thanks. Now watch us work. Over."

While I'm at it, I want to share the news with my unit. Even for a bunch of war aficionados, there shouldn't be anything better than getting more friends. Frankly, Tanya is ready to welcome reinforcements right away.

The truth of the matter is that they were outnumbered, so she couldn't wait for the reorganized battalion to arrive.

"Battalion, this is your commander."

Yeah, they'll probably be happy. They'll be able to fight without worrying about their rear. I live by the creed "safety first," and even I'm not against realizing a few achievements in this battle.

"Rejoice. We're getting backup. Some reinforcements are coming all the way out here to help us."

I'm surprised a unit that withdrew could be reorganized so efficiently. *Wonderful.* That's the word to express how moved I am. Granted, it's dangerous to judge a whole situation by looking at only a couple events. Still, even if the radio operator is inept, this shows his superior officer is on point.

The reinforcements will probably be here any minute.

"Do you understand what I'm saying?"

Why don't we just take our time and wait for our backup? I can't say that because my will to fight would be suspect, but if I can get them to understand as much indirectly, there would be no problem. Tanya's real intention as she informs them of the reinforcements is to change the plan in a big way, from an offensive tactical formation to a defensive one, just like in *Dragon Quest.*

""""Yes, ma'am!""""

The clipped reply surely means they grasp her intentions. Tanya nods in satisfaction.

"Now, let's do as much work as we get paid for!"

Chapter II

"The bombers are done for! No support yet?!"

"The light—the light!! Uwaaaagh!"

"We lost the formation leader's signal?!"

"Break! They're fast! Put up a wall of bullets! Don't get anywhere near them!"

"Pixie 02 to all companies. Charge!"

"Ngh! They're past the vanguard?! Stop shooting and be ready for a close-quarters fight!"

"Mayday! Mayday! No rescue yet?!"

"Norland Control to all units. Abort the operation! Abort the operation! As of this moment, abort the operation!"

"The bomber unit—!"

"Fucking hell! The vanguard got savaged! Who are those guys?!"

"The recon company has been wiped out! At this rate, we'll be surrounded!"

"They got past our close support?!"

"Viper 02 to Pixie 01. We're on our way now."

"Roger. No sign of enemy reinforcements. Expect a hot pursuit."

"Viper 02, roger."

"Detecting enemy reinforcements! They're the size of a battalion."

"Reinforcements? What about ours?!"

"Norland Control to all units. Retreat immediately to marshaling point two. I say again, retreat immediately to marshaling point two."

"It's no good! I can't lose them!"

"Damn it, damn it, damn it!"

"Pixie 01 to all hands. Transition to cleanup."

"Viper 02 to Pixie Battalion. We have visual."

"We see you, too. Can we leave the pursuit to you? I want my team to mop up the stragglers."

"Enemy reinforcements have arrived!"

"Fucking hell! Don't stop! Run! Hurry!"

"Roger. Thanks."

"For fuck's sake, this is hell!"

"My intestines… Someone pick up my intestines!"

"They're your sworn enemy. No need to hold back. Over."

What the hell did I drink last night?

The first question that entered his mind was absurd.

He could tell someone was shaking him, but it took a long time for his brain to start working.

First Lieutenant Gunning wondered why his whole body felt so heavy.

Someone is…calling me?

"Nn…!"

His consciousness returned, though it was hazy, and outlines began to appear.

"Lieutenant! Lieutenant!"

…Well, this is no good. If they're not using my name, it's either my boss or the military police.

But I'm still out of it. I'm so dizzy I can't take it.

Seriously, what did I drink? I'm fit as a fiddle after a bottle of Scotch, so why…? Did someone slip me vodka?

He only cracked his eyes open, as was his habit.

A blinding white space. Something was blinking. *No, maybe some kind of machine?*

The brightness still bothered him, but a strange sense that his body wasn't his own confused him. He was so weary that try as he might he couldn't move.

As he stared up at the ceiling, his brain finally woke up, and as it got up to speed, he started to grasp his surroundings. At a glance, it didn't seem to be his room. *So what's going on?*

He had no recollection of this. A pure white field. *Hmm? A room? I think I know this place. I have some memory of it. So where am I?*

"…Uhhhgh. Where…?"

He wasn't particularly looking for a reply with the groan, but it seemed the person who had been calling out to him had heard. It caught the attention of everyone in the vicinity, apparently, and suddenly he was

Chapter **II**

engulfed in a huge commotion. For whatever reason, he tried to sit up, but he nearly tipped over instead. His body wouldn't move the way he wanted. It seemed like someone propped him up, and he vaguely understood he was being held.

"Lieutenant! Okay, you're conscious, right? Medic! Bring a surgeon, quick!"

"What...?"

Just voicing the question exhausted him completely. *Something weird is going on.* He couldn't find the words for it, but something was different. *What the heck happened to me?*

He wasn't half-asleep, but though his awareness kept increasing, the foggy light before his eyes failed to dissipate. Not only would his eyes not focus, he couldn't hold them steady.

If I were hungover, I'd feel sick and have a headache...and I don't. As reality slowly returned to him, it started to dawn on him what a strange situation he was in.

"Relax. How much do you remember?"

"...What? What are you saying?"

No. I don't want to remember any more than that.

I must not remember.

I can't... What?

"Captain, it's no good. He's totally minced."

"Here, too. The log's been destroyed. We recovered it, but I don't think any of this will be useful."

Minced?

Destroyed?

My...

What about my mates...?

"Welcome to the Empire. Do you have a passport?"

"Ha-ha-ha, Commander. We didn't bring a welcome bouquet. Now what?"

"Oof, what will I do with you guys? But you brought the fireworks, right?"

"Oh, that's right. Those look kinda like flowers, right?"

"Great. Then maybe I'll sing a welcome song."
"Hmm? You know a song?"
"Yeah, a good one."

"Do you need me to sew your mouths closed?" the captain snapped.
Somewhere, someone hastily shut their mouth, but it was too late.

Red, red flowers. My brothers. My superiors. My men.
"…Ahhaahhhhhhhhhhhhggghh!"
"Medic! A sedative! Quick!"
"You idiots! You can expect disciplinary action for this!"
They're meat now.
Bright red, bloody blossoms.
Burst.
Blooming.
All over.

| chapter |

III

Norden II

In a crisis, there are two types of people: those who run and those who get left behind. I've never despised the former. But it was only later I learned that the latter deserve respect.

———————— **Donald Habergram, Memoirs** ————————

The chill of Norden naturally urges people to prepare for it obsessively. That said, it's a pleasant fixation. A fire blazing in the hearth, its warmth filling the room, is an indispensable feature of a quiet Norden winter.

"Welcome to Norden. Or I suppose I should say, 'Welcome back'? We're happy to have you, Major von Degurechaff."

"Yes, returning to this battlefield does bring back memories. I'm eager to serve under you, General von Rudersdorf."

There is something off about the General Staff officers and their extremely serious expressions while they are having that utterly out-of-place exchange. Of course, Major General von Rudersdorf and Major von Degurechaff have simply both judged that it is easier to speak pragmatically with each other, so they hit it off relatively quickly.

"…Now then, let me tell you what a wonderful job I think you're doing right out of the gate. I heard from Colonel von Lergen—it's quite the achievement."

"I'm honored, sir."

"Ah, but I expected nothing less. I knew having Zettour send you here was the right move."

The cooperative relationship between these two geniuses within the General Staff really is something. For better or worse, the only one who can get their way with the deputy director of the Service Corps is his cohort or his boss. Since Zettour had to be persuaded for her to be dispatched, she inwardly braces herself to be worked to the bone by the deputy director of Operations.

"We'd like you to cut loose up here, too."

"I'll do all I can, though it may not be much."

"That's fine. Then let's get down to brass tacks."

"Yes, sir."

"Does your unit have experience conducting attack missions on enemy positions?"

"A handful of our core members have some experience from the Rhine front, but that's it. In Dacia, we mainly did air raids, and even then it wasn't many."

"So it's more or less as I feared… But you at least understand how it's done in theory, right?"

"Yes, sir. I learned with 205th Company on the Rhine front."

"All right, then I'll be frank. I want you to think of this as an airborne operation. Major, we're probably going to have your unit seize the enemy defense line."

"You mean push them back? Whatever your orders, I'd like to get started right away."

"That's very thoughtful of you, but I imagine you'll need to make careful preparations. I'd like you to focus on training for a while."

"Thank you! But are you sure that's all right?"

"It's fine—I'll work you hard when the time comes."

"Yes, sir. I promise you we'll be ready in every possible way."

》》》   THE PRESENT: ON PAPER   《《《

Londinium Times special correspondent Jeffrey told us about a theory he had regarding the Eleventh Goddess.

In general, he thought the notion of its existence had some truth to it. Although it wasn't a very pleasant prospect, he considered the possibility to be reasonably high.

Today I wanted to see whether it was nothing more than a battlefield rumor or if it had any basis in reality.

All the people we asked related to the Eleventh Goddess refused to comment on its existence.

Normally, most people would deny or confirm, but no one wanted to talk about it at all.

The refusals were so firm.

"Is it something the army is ashamed of?"

When we asked that question, a retired general who had been silent up until then pounded the table almost hard enough to break it.

He leaped to his feet, and the grimace on his face made him look just like an ogre.

We shrank back in spite of ourselves; the retired general's rage was that terrible.

"There's a world that people like you can't understand! You weren't on that battlefield!" he barked, kicking his chair away as if even talking to us was offensive.

Strangely enough, the other retired officers present also all stood up at the same time.

It was as if they were all communicating their unanimous agreement by way of their silence. I confess things got pretty awkward then.

So this much is true.

But if we rely solely on what we've seen in person to talk about the truth, we won't learn anything new. That's why I'd like to discuss the data and theory Jeffrey brought us.

Jeffrey says the first time the Eleventh Goddess was spotted by the Commonwealth wasn't in the west but in the north.

How?

Up until the big counterattack operation in the north at the end of the war, the Commonwealth had concentrated their efforts on the western lines.

So how did the Commonwealth see the Eleventh Goddess up north when she should have been in the west?

The answer, according to Jeffrey, is simple.

Before the Commonwealth officially joined the war, they sent an expeditionary unit to the Regadonia Entente Alliance in utmost secret.

Yes, the Commonwealth assisted in combat before formally declaring war.

People have always whispered rumors, but apparently it's true. We have the documentation to prove it. The national archives were a formidable opponent, but they've already agreed to release the materials.

Chapter **III**

What was going on back then? We discovered this truth while in pursuit of an answer to that question. Apparently, the Commonwealth had decided to intervene while the Republic and Empire were busy clashing. The national defense committee recommended gathering intelligence in actual combat in order to better understand a future enemy.

In response, a "volunteer army" consisting mainly of a small number of mage units was dispatched to Regadonia. In order to dodge accusations of violating international law, the force consisted mostly of retired officers and soldiers who "independently" volunteered and had gathered "on their own authority." The archives still refuse to release the details. Right now, what we know from speaking with those involved is that a regiment-sized group of mages was deployed. So maybe this had something to do with it.

At the time, the Commonwealth was a neutral country. Even if the growing mage shortage had yet to become a major consideration the way it did during the middle of the war, the fact that so many went was surprising. This "volunteer army" was big by any measure.

Naturally, we can see there were political quarrels. And apparently, the volunteers were brutally annihilated. That was the worst part. After suffering the loss of precious combat mages, they had to bury the clandestine intervention.

This is where we start to see references to the Eleventh Goddess. In his report, the commander of the volunteer army says that's what got them. So we started to wonder: Is the Eleventh Goddess a person? Or is it some specialized term?

Jeffrey's take on this point is simple.

"Supply hell" is exactly eleven characters when you include the space. In other words, it was a euphemistic way to complain about the leadership's management in a situation where a more open comment wouldn't have been tolerated. That would definitely be something for the army to be ashamed of, right? Then again, "mass mutiny" would also work. In any case, they must want to hide some sort of organizational failure.

In short, Jeffrey posits that the Eleventh Goddess was not a person but a phenomenon.

Honestly, I simply can't agree. I was embedded on the western front, and from what I remember, supplies were coming in as well as could be expected. And discipline seemed fine from what I could see. Of course, I'm only one reporter, but I've been at it a long time, so I should be able to tell.

More than anything, there was an abnormal number of casualties on the western front. No, you could say that abnormal became the norm; it was like another dimension out there. It wouldn't be surprising to find out a devil had been on the rampage. And so our debate has gotten nowhere.

Well, the *Londinium Times* sort of serves as a watchdog keeping an eye on the government. *WTN* specializes in offering news from abroad, so maybe we just have different viewpoints.

Anyhow, I'd like us to keep investigating this. Lastly, I'd also like to say how blessed I am to have such an understanding wife.

Well then, until next week.

*Andrew, *WTN* special correspondent

>>> NOVEMBER 16, UNIFIED YEAR 1924, NORTHERN ARMY GROUP <<<
COMMAND, STAFF MEETING ROOM

I don't know what era he was from, but some great man once warned us: "Victory is like a drug."

Military triumph brings radiant glory and a most splendid intoxication to a nation. For that reason, when people are drunk on victory, they think only of getting more. Soon, no one is allowed to ask what the victory is for. Military romanticism has a violent effect on countries.

That's why no one likes pragmatic soldiers. They're lucky to get off with being called cowards.

"Thus, I think avoiding losses and keeping casualties to a minimum is desirable."

Drawn on the map is the Imperial Army pulling back. Mounting a predictable pursuit is, naturally, the enemy army. It's a proposal to retreat so as not to put too great a strain on the supply lines. If a normal

Chapter **III**

officer were to suggest this plan, they would have to be prepared for an immediate string of names worse than *coward*.

And the meeting room did freeze for a moment. With no idea when Colonel General von Wragell might explode in his seat at the head of the table, Lieutenant General and Chief of Staff von Schreise was inwardly annoyed, but at the same time, the atmosphere was so tense he wanted to bury his head in his hands.

"By moving the lines back, I believe we can lessen the inevitable burden of distance on logistics as well as simplify plans for a spring offensive."

But Tanya, who had purposely ignored the atmosphere and stated her thoughts on the matter, quietly takes her seat. Acting like she has finished her report, her impassive Noh-mask face is unreadable while she completely ignores the staffers' stares.

Actually, no matter how stormy it gets in the Northern Army Group meeting room, I simply can't seriously see it as something that has anything to do with Tanya. Her battalion has carried out its mission and has already returned to its garrison for the moment. She's only present because Major General von Rudersdorf ordered her to attend since she had time.

When it comes down to it, Tanya is a part of the Central Army, serving directly under the General Staff, so she doesn't have a place in the Northern Army Group chain of command. And that's precisely why she proposed, as a bit of advice, that they use this time to shorten and consolidate their lines.

Really, I didn't mean to interfere so much at first. Rudersdorf was there from the Operations Division of the General Staff—I figured being pushy was his job.

A major general in the General Staff serving as section chief has far more influence than the rank indicates, so I thought I would politely listen to him speak. But then, ahead of the meeting, he declared he would like to hear the opinions of officers from the field, and several brigade commanders were selected to comment. Perhaps their reports didn't satisfy him? Even though it would be easier to count up to her rank from the bottom, the ball had been passed to her.

In that case, I felt I should probably show these hemming and hawing numbskulls, who can't offer a straight remark, how it's done. The only ones who don't give their opinions at meetings are the inept or idiots too worried about what everyone else thinks. That said, there are also times where someone has to stand up and bear the brunt of the silent majority's pent-up frustration. The fact that someone has to be forced into this role, reminiscent of the ship that draws fire away from the rest of the fleet, is a problem that will no doubt plague all organizations forever.

And if the boss of the group dispatched from Central is going to keep his mouth shut, then the role of the scapegoat falls to me, another person who hails from Central, with field achievements to boot. It's aggravating but true.

First of all, I repulsed a regiment-sized assault. That's a solid feat no one can deny. In addition, my considerable accomplishments in Dacia as a mobile strike specialist ought to lend some weight to my comment.

My battalion did its best. They're a real bunch of war nuts, but they gave their all. We turned back a regiment and shot down their bombers. We can be proud of the serious blow we dealt to the enemy.

"Hmm, Major von Degurechaff's proposal is quite novel... What is the Northern Army Group's take on the logistics involved?"

"Quite novel?" He has thicker skin than I thought.

But I suppose Central can't come out and say that the supply lines are dangerously overextended. Our now-dismissed predecessors, dreaming of smashing the encirclement, mobilized the Great Army with gear appropriate for fighting in the north, only for them to hastily deploy to the Rhine front. It's not just General von Rudersdorf—no one could ask whose fault the messy supply lines were, because the blame lay with their predecessors' blunders.

On the other hand, if it was simply an organizational failure, the problem shouldn't require Central to handle it so delicately. The issue at hand is that the Empire is panicking, and the enemy is taking advantage of that. Winter is already on its way, and partially because the Imperial Army's Northern Army Group is lacking supplies it needs to weather Norden's cold, the Empire's movements are becoming severely limited. The Entente Alliance, of course, is on its home turf, so its commandos are dominating and constantly conducting guerrilla attacks on the

Empire's supply bases. Security at small depots is already in shambles and growing difficult to maintain. But the soldiers still need bread if they are going to march on the enemy logistics base.

If it were a tactical disadvantage we needed to fix, commanders would still have room to work. Or if simply fighting hard could solve things. But the supplies in a burned-down depot can't be recovered. The conclusion I reached is simple. It isn't clear if the Imperial Army has enough supplies to survive the winter. The supplies exist, but they need to be carefully managed.

And that time could be used to reorganize the lines. Aha, so that's why he suggested I make careful preparations before the airborne assault on the enemy. If you want to buy time with harassing attacks,[8] airborne operations are an effective option.

But Tanya is (I am) not very well-informed when it comes to the average human psyche. Of course, she would come at this from the perspective of her own unit's airborne assault in the spring offensive.

But that's why if I'm here, I have to sound the alarm about the danger regarding our winter supply preparations—and declare that aiming for a swift end to the war is too great a risk.

General Jekof von Schreise just barely keeps himself from losing his temper as he thoroughly reviews the plan as chief of staff for the Northern Army Group. At the same time, the part of him that remains cool and rational screams in his mind about how bad this is.

Really, this proposal is only that and nothing more. In other words, it's simply one possible option. General von Schreise is a veteran who has worked his way up in the Imperial Army's meritocracy. He can see that despite having its main force, the Great Army, pulled out and the local numerical inferiority of its mages, the Empire still has a clear advantage over the Entente Alliance.

Certainly, he understands that the burning of bases supplying the front lines, including small depots, was a thorn in his side. He's relieved

---

[8] **harassing attacks**   In a nutshell, attacks with the intent to cause disturbance and confusion—e.g., the Doolittle Raid or saying hello to Berlin with Mosquitoes on January 31, 1943, during Göering's speech celebrating the tenth anniversary of the Nazis gaining power.

that after they shed some enemy mage blood, the raids should stop. But at the same time, he's equally worried about the supply issues on the front lines. No, it's not as if he isn't already aware of the problems.

But to have it smugly pointed out by Major von Degurechaff, dispatched from Central, is another issue.

"Major von Degurechaff, I'd like to confirm something." After a moment, a Logistics officer speaks. "Are you envisioning us digging in, then waiting out winter?"

"Yes," she replies calmly. Her tone is rather matter-of-fact. "At present, we can't maintain the supply lines. We're under no obligation to please the enemy by wasting matériel and men in a futile offensive."

Schreise looked at the Logistics and Operations staffers. As he expected, Logistics was resisting the urge to shout her down with obvious displeasure and expressions that seemed to say they weren't buying her plan.

After all, even the lowliest private knew there weren't enough supplies—you didn't even need security clearance to realize that.

It wasn't as if this Logistics staff was extraordinarily skilled, but they were capable of approaching supplies with common sense. They understood quite well that they didn't have enough matériel. They also knew that even if the chaos was due to an error on Central's part, the ones who made the error in the first place had already been dismissed. Their continued dissatisfaction had to mean that Degurechaff's appearance was affecting their judgment. Nobody wanted to be the kind of adult who whaled on a little kid. If Rudersdorf knew that and was having Tanya speak up for that reason, he was quite the crafty fellow.

But though the Operations staff were restraining themselves, their masks were beginning to crack, showing the limits of their tolerance. This would surprise no one, but their purpose was different from that of Logistics. Every day the other army groups would pressure them, asking how much longer they were going to drag out the conflict. After all, Dacia, with about the same number of troops committed to the theater, had fallen in six weeks. The criticism of the Northern Army Group *still* fighting up there" was growing sharper with every passing day.

"Major von Degurechaff, if we did that, we'd be losing time."

"Huh?"

There were all manner of expressions around the table, but on the whole, everyone was waiting to see what would happen.

The Operations staff especially were looking to Schreise so as to understand their boss's intention.

Schreise nodded and pressed his point. "It'll be a new year soon. We don't want a long war. And we don't want to exhaust supplies, nor can we continue tying up troops here."

Operations continued, imparting internal details of the northern forces' struggles. Commander Ragheno of the Northern Army Group expressed his agreement with a nod, and Schreise felt some of the tension go out of his shoulders. Apparently, the desire to put a swift end to the war wasn't only the wish of Operations but a view shared by high command as well. That must have meant that the northern forces agreed on time being the primary concern, at least. And that's why he glared at Rudersdorf, shameless and cheerfully listening to their debate with a smile plastered on his face; he wanted to figure out what the man was really after.

"The enemy faces the same conditions." Operations had raised their objections in a near panic, but her reply was cool and calm. Degurechaff, completely unfazed by all the eyes on her, gave a deadpan counterargument.

"Rather than wasting our resources in enemy territory, we should wait for a chance to settle it in one decisive strike."

"Logistics can't take it." Her suggestion was made with their circumstances in mind. Of course, that's why she proposed shrinking their lines. But she hadn't arrived at this solution by groping around in the dark; her attitude said that she fully believed it was their only option. She couldn't so much as lend an ear to the suggestions of the Operations officers who wanted to escape this phase of the war by bringing it to a swift end. No, the expression on her delicate face said she thought their plan was stupid.

"The minute you sally forth, you'll already have gone as far as you can go."

Pressing lightly on his right temple, Schreise glared at the Logistics staff.

They had guaranteed the supplies would cover a short offensive. The problem was that the guarantee was for *availability*, and that was it. Nobody had presented him with a foolproof plan for actually delivering those supplies to the units that would be advancing at the edge of the front lines.

"We can cover a short offensive without issue. We've secured almost all the provisions we need for the front."

Catching his glance, the Logistics officers mentioned they had enough standard ammunition for two battles and rations for three weeks. They had baseline levels of aviation and general-purpose fuel. Their numbers showed the army group could fight for three weeks. Three weeks. Now that the northern front had been reorganized and the units were preparing for an offensive, if they launched a big push, they could wrap it up within that time. The enemy's reserve forces had already run dry, so if they could just take care of the rest on the front with a large offensive...

But Degurechaff replied without even furrowing her brow at their reports. "I'm against it. The enemy is putting up stiff resistance. I really don't think we'll be able to break through in such a short time." She flatly rejected the idea, as if she thought it was simply unreasonable. "Once the troops get more than twenty kilometers from the light-rail, we'll be forced to maintain the supply lines with sheer manpower. A steady winter advance is practically out of the question." She heaved a pointed sigh.

A few of the officers winced, but Schreise stood his ground even under her scathing critique.

He was sure that mopping up enemy remnants would take a week at most. Even in the worst case, he didn't think the enemy could hold out against a major offensive for three weeks. The one worrisome element, the enemy mage commandos, had been mostly neutralized. Ironically, the one who had played a major part in taking them out was the one stubbornly disagreeing with him, Major von Degurechaff.

Even the logistics situation could be ameliorated if field engineers performed road maintenance and laid down more light-rail. Frankly, the staunch objection from the Central officers was just a pain in the neck at this point. If he could find a way to get rid of them, he would keep holding out.

"You have a point, but the enemy is too worn down to put up a fight. You're the one who achieved a victory despite being outnumbered two to one. Do you really think you need to be so scared of the Entente Alliance?"

After all, in terms of mage casualties, too, the enemy army had long exceeded their limits. Even if the other powers were intervening to some extent, when a newly formed imperial mage battalion could drive off a whole Entente Alliance regiment, it said something about the state of their opponent's affairs.

The enemy's major line of defense only mounted sporadic attacks. Capturing the entirety of the Entente Alliance was only a matter of time. A few intelligence staffers tried to coax Tanya.

"We're winning on the strength and quality of our troops. We should make our move now instead of burning through our limited supplies doing nothing."

The intelligence they'd gathered from enemy prisoners indicated that their opponents were hard up for not only weapons and ammunition but even food. Intelligence had already decided that the enemy army had lost the ability to fight as a cohesive whole.

Rather than camp out across the way, the Northern Army Group wanted to decisively end the conflict before the winter set in, but because of one stubborn major, the debate had been dragged out. What an enormous waste of time.

Schreise couldn't be the only one thinking that he would have thrown her out immediately if she weren't a representative of the Central Army's view.

"Really? Personally, I can only recall two battalions worn out by our fellow soldiers' efforts and an unsupported group about the size of an augmented company."

Intelligence's coaxing only earned them a reply that ruined their schemes.

If she hadn't achieved anything, then they could kick her out for clearly being a brat who knew nothing of the battlefield. Beneath Schreise's dignified exterior, he was gnashing his teeth. Her achievements were extraordinary.

This was always how it went. The Central Army Group was constantly pushing the regional army groups around with orders that weren't appropriate to their actual circumstances. But Rudersdorf, Schreise's junior at war college, had been whispering in his ear how futile it was to refuse to cooperate with Central. The delicate issue was that Schreise's superior officer—commander of the Northern Army Group, Colonel General von Wragell—was very angry.

Though he was getting on in years, the veteran who had long been defending the north was furious that the Entente Alliance was trying to trample his home, his fatherland, but he flung curses at the General Staff in equal measure for their repeated errors. So whenever Schreise thought of his boss, who wanted so much to crush this threat with his own hands, he felt depressed.

"That doesn't change the fact that you overcame an enemy that outnumbered you. You slaughtered a group double your size."

"The only confirmed kills were less than the company's worth. It was less defeating them and more just barely driving them off."

The magic staffers frowned as Degurechaff indirectly emphasized that her battalion had driven the enemy off. After that, the Northern Army Group had pursued and achieved as good as nothing. They were to the point of counting anyone they injured even slightly as a confirmed kill, whereas the Central Army was underreporting.

They'd been granted a concession. He knew they were on the receiving end of some kind consideration for their reputation. They were listed as having downed a battalion, but the score mostly belonged to the Central Army troops. Only a few people were aware of the behind-the-scenes dealings.

That's why, as most of those present looked perplexed, Schreise shot the mage staffers a look. *You owe them, so shut her up!*

A staff officer's job is to come up with a concrete plan to actualize the higher-ranking officers' intentions. So he tried to persuade Degurechaff

again. *Please just understand your superiors' wishes and relax your stance!*
"You can say that, but in our battle together, the truth is that you
achieved the most with your fierce fighting." Hadn't her dedicated struggle changed the tides of the war? "You say it was only a company, but
that company was the core of the enemy's only mage commando unit.
That's the same as taking out the supporting pillar of the whole regiment!" Hadn't she admirably defeated them? "Major von Degurechaff,
I welcome your prudence, but I think you and your battalion would be
able to guard the supply lines." If anyone could do it, surely the 203rd
Aerial Mage Battalion could!

He obliquely implied that the contributions of her and her battalion
were very highly regarded. *Even if I'm ignoring your cautionary arguments, I'm not failing to appreciate the 203rd Aerial Mage Battalion.* A
high-ranking field officer wearing the staff braid was, strangely enough,
flattering someone who was still only a major, though wearing the staff
badge.

Work with me here, please.

He stared at Major von Degurechaff with the same silent wish as
everyone else, careful not to let her suspect how much pressure he was
trying to put on her. She asked permission to speak, as if nothing was
out of the ordinary, and stood casually.

"I don't even know what to say in response to such undeserved praise."

Does she get it?

Yes, it was just as everyone was sighing in relief and the tense atmosphere began to relax that…

"But as far as I can tell, Entente Alliance Army command units are a
mixture of infantry and mages, so I don't think downing a single company will hinder their activities very much."

"…What do you mean, Major von Degurechaff?"

"Sir, it's true that in local skirmishes my battalion has emerged victorious. But that group was the same one our troops fought hard to exhaust
and isolate. We drove off an enemy weakened by consecutive battles, so
I hardly think you can say my battalion took the brunt of their attack."

Can't you even drive off a weakened enemy? she seemed to say with a
hint of nastiness. Probably not on purpose.

"…You're very humble, aren't you?" one of the staff officers murmured, curling the corners of his mouth into a smile that was more of a sneer.

Normally, they would scold her. That's what everyone was thinking, but they all hesitated. Scold her for what? Disturbing the harmony of the officer group? But all she had done was share her opinion on a military situation. Silencing her would go against the staff officer traditions that the Empire, the Reich, was so proud of.

The one who broke the silence in that awkward atmosphere was the very person who had created the tense mood. "No, Colonel. I'm just answering based on the facts." Major von Degurechaff glared at the high-ranking staffers. Well, it was proper etiquette to look a superior in the eye when addressing them.

But when a mage who had been steeping in gunsmoke and blood on the battlefield until just recently began staring you down, that was a different story.

A few rash magic officers—no doubt unconsciously—reached for their computation orbs.

"That's about enough of that." *Any more is too much*, Schreise decided and interrupted. Piercing his subordinate with his gaze, he continued as a mediator between the two. "We understand Major von Degurechaff's opinion now. And her fears are worth listening to, in part, but our pressing topic right now is bringing the war to a swift end."

They'd already let her yap this much. They understood the Central Army's position so well it made them sick. Honestly, it bothered him more than anything in the world, but he could understand where she was coming from. For a mere major to protest so stubbornly in a room full of superior officers, she must have been under some strict orders. Schreise had never seen a major with such a big head without making light of him.

So the little messenger needs to pipe down. He gave her a resolute stare.

"It is my duty to firmly object. The goal of lessening the load for each regional army group could backfire and result in a larger burden."

But surprisingly, it had no effect on her. Without hesitating even a little, she—a mere battalion commander—matter-of-factly gave her opinion to the staff and even had the audacity to disagree with them.

Chapter **III**

Even with the sacred, inviolable General Staff's power behind her, she was nearing an inexcusable challenge to authority.

A head could be allowed to swell only so far. *There's a limit to what can be tolerated, even for recipients of the Silver Wings Assault Badge!* Though he wanted to scream at her and chew her out, he suppressed his fury and said, "Our intention is to lessen the load on the troops. Major, please refrain from rash remarks."

The major, though still rather new, was readily crossing a line of which all graduates from the war college should have been aware. She was protesting too much. If they weren't in a war zone, it would most certainly not be allowed to stand.

This sort of behavior could only escape rebuke on a battlefield. It was practically an outrage, wasn't it? Indignant, the officers turned their anger on her with violent glares.

But even under such silent censure, Degurechaff made a bold move. She lifted the coffee cup she had been served for the staff meeting, eyed the milk and sugar on the table, and murmured, "...In the west, our troops are drinking dirty water, starving and suffering in the mud. The north is so blessed..."

To the officers watching her, hanging on her every word, the smile on her lips was both offensive and profoundly meaningful. At the same time, she scanned the room with an expression that seemed to ask what exactly they were all trying to say from their seats in this comfortable office. Her face did the talking.

"Naturally, I don't think that affects how much you care about the troops..."

That comment was the last straw for Schreise.

The Central Army was always making unreasonable demands on the regional army groups. He couldn't take any more of this interference.

Without realizing it, he had kicked his chair away and stood up. He wouldn't listen to any more of her mouthing off.

"...Major! If you're going to talk like that, then go back to the west! We don't need any cowards in the north."

"Is that the will of the Northern Army Group?"

"That's enough!"

He realized he was shouting at an officer. He was seized by the urge to kick her out. Most of the others in the momentarily silent room held their tongues, but they felt the same way.

Then, with a despicable calm, Degurechaff snapped off a splendid salute.

"Then if you'll excuse me."

With that, she straightened up smoothly and bowed. They could hardly believe it, but she approached the door with fluid motions and exited the room. No one tried to stop her.

>>>   NORDEN HQ, MAJOR GENERAL VON RUDERSDORF'S OFFICE   <<<

It was after Major von Degurechaff had politely thrown down her gauntlet and left the meeting with no way to vent her rage. Hearing that she had asked to see him with utmost urgency, Major General von Rudersdorf nodded. *Just as I thought.* She never disappointed, so he was fond of her.

That's what she had to do.

"I know what you're going to say."

That's why he implicitly stated they would get right to the point. *Do away with the empty formalities and spit it out.*

"Sir, frankly, considering the situation we're in, an offensive is reckless! Why don't you stop it?"

"Major, I want you to tell me what you really think."

She raises these indirect objections.

Yes, it was amusing to watch her maintain composure and deliver her opinion with all the correct etiquette despite the anger seething in her eyes. But he didn't want to hear tactful, formulaic thoughts.

"Respectfully, sir, I'm a staff officer. I don't believe I'm in a position to say any more."

"I see. You're very easy to understand. Speak freely."

"Thank you, sir."

He'd urged her to speak her mind, but he accepted her polite yet also sharp response.

Aha, so her criticism is so intense that it would be inexcusable for a staff officer to give it voice? That's an interesting way to get your point across.

Though she didn't say exactly what was on her mind, she'd conveyed her thoughts with a single indirect remark.

"So this is why Zettour thinks so highly of you, Major. Splendid. Now let's get down to business."

Zettour would be thrilled. I see. Work goes smoothly with a mage who has strategy on her radar and is also an outstanding battalion commander.

"What would you think about this offensive if you considered it as a distraction, Major?"

"It'd be an almost perfectly timed supporting attack... Ah, but do you mean as a decoy, assuming another main attack?"

She's got a decent head on her shoulders. She's quick, and more importantly, she has the smarts to put what I'm trying to say together with what she already knows. She's one of the rare talents who has the steady composure of a staff officer plus the courage of a commander.

"Evaluate the effects it will have on the various fronts."

"At the very least, the Republic and its supporting countries will keep an eye on the exchange in Norden, but being able to distract them from offensive preparations doesn't give us a very large benefit... So then, is there a real operation in Norden? No, the supply lines couldn't possibly..."

The way she lost herself in thought, as if she had forgotten her rage of a moment ago, displayed the calm sensibility that was a quality greatly desired in staff officers. Not many people could think on command under the cool eyes of a third party. And that's why those few exceptional individuals were always welcome in the Imperial Army.

"And if it goes well, we might even be able to tie up the enemy reinforcements."

"With all due respect, sir...I don't see how launching an offensive with the objective of tying up enemy reinforcements would help other fronts. I don't think the forces involved on this front would send out enough reinforcements to affect the Rhine front...which means the offensive should be a feint with some strategic goal in Norden."

When he told her to work out the meaning of the Northern Group

Army's offensive, to which they were opposed, she arrived calmly at the idea of a feint in Norden. *Impressive,* Rudersdorf thought and inwardly raised his opinion of her.

"Hmm, continue."

"To be blunt, are you thinking of occupying territory behind enemy lines? I was ordered to prepare for an airborne assault...so we'd need some sort of diversion and then we'd... In the rear? Is it the rear?"

But a conversation is a two-way street. At the same time Rudersdorf is reading between the lines, so is Tanya. She's thinking that she's seen and heard something like this before, and she finally manages to salvage the memory from the deepest corners of her mind.

"What is it, Major?"

Letting Rudersdorf's question slip by at the outer edges of her consciousness, Tanya assembles the fragments of the memory she's seized.

Tying up enemy forces on the front lines. A feint. An assault on the rear. Remember. I know I've heard something like this somewhere before. And it was the kind of news I really like to hear...

Where? Where did I hear it? No, I could have heard it or read it. But I know I've encountered it before.

"Behind, back... Supply lines? Yes, their supply. Cutting it off?" As the pieces come together, she mumbles without realizing it. She shuts out even the way Rudersdorf's face stiffens in shock as she speaks and focuses her thoughts.

The back, yes, something from behind? It was— Right, a thoroughly delightful kick from the rear.

Suddenly, a word appears in her mind.

Inchon? Yes, Inchon.

...That's it. That immensely pleasurable commie ass kicking. MacArthur pulled off a miracle with his meager talent: the Battle of Inchon. They made a large-scale encirclement and cut off the enemy from behind. It was a decisive strike that caused the North Korean army to collapse.

A great reversal from the annals of world history, where capitalism smote evil communism!

"Sir, if the main enemy forces are concentrated along the front lines, then wouldn't a land operation in the rear be one way to end this?"

It seems as though she has just now remembered Rudersdorf's existence, but her sudden query and calm tone appear contrary to her overflowing confidence.

Thinking of the Battle of Inchon, she realizes the invigorating, admirable strategy of kicking numbskull commie asses from behind could be employed against enemies other than communists. After all, it's a way to completely encircle the enemy and get their own logistics organized. If there's anything wrong with the plan, it's that it requires absolute control of the sea and the absence of the enemy's main force...

"A large-scale amphibious operation in the rear followed by encirclement to sever their supply chain. So the offensive would be a diversion for the landing operation?"

To Tanya, all she has done is rediscover historical fact, which is why she forgot that in this world, it's merely a concept; it hasn't turned into history yet.

So Rudersdorf felt unfathomable shock as Degurechaff mentioned it with such calm nonchalance, as if it were already a foregone conclusion. But Tanya completely missed that.

After all, from Rudersdorf's point of view, the amphibious landing was a secret plan he'd only mentioned to a select few, and now a staff officer on the lower end of the middle ranks was suggesting it to him as if it were a simple answer. He stopped the muscles in his face from twitching through sheer power of will. Still wondering where she'd gotten that idea, he cautiously asked, "Did you hear that from General von Zettour?"

"Hmm? I'm not sure I understand what you mean, sir."

But Degurechaff gave a puzzled response. It wasn't as if Rudersdorf could read all the emotions and thoughts of his subordinates, but going by his experience, he judged this was a genuine reaction and was immediately aware of his misunderstanding. The officer in front of him hadn't heard it from Zettour.

So then, could it be?

Chapter **III**

No, he thought…but the question welled up inside him: *Did she come up with the idea to do a large-scale landing operation in the rear on her own?*

"Did you come up with that yourself?"

"Yes, sir. Considering our situation, I thought it seemed like an effective option."

"…I suppose I should say that's a very interesting idea."

She confirmed it so readily. It was all Rudersdorf could do to conceal his emotions. As he worked to maintain his facade, he was astonished that she had come up with it, but at the same time, he could now understand how she had been able to make a convincing strategic argument regarding transportation even back at the academy.

So that's why, he understood. *You can see that much?* He was flabbergasted. Either way, she was a terribly promising officer.

"All right. Yes, we're going to use your unit. Major, transfer orders. Your battalion is to stand by at the naval base."

"Yes, sir. Understood."

He watched Degurechaff as she calmly nodded in acceptance of her orders; she seemed just like a child happy to be sent on a little errand. *And I gave this child the orders as easily as if I were sending her to do just that…*

…Ahh, you never know what will happen in a war.

"You'll drop in ahead of the landing party and be the vanguard for the army. I'm expecting great things from you, Major."

Having someone this smart head up the vanguard… Not too shabby. We should be able to expect a lot from the tip of this spear.

"But may I ask something, sir?"

"What is it, Major?"

"If this was your plan all along, then you didn't really need to suggest I put a check on the Northern Army Group's offensive, did you?"

Hmm, she's right. Not that he hadn't thought of that. He didn't really want to call for a halt on the Northern Army Group's offensive and create ill will, especially when he had heard from Lieutenant General von Schreise that Colonel General von Wragell was about to explode.

But as Zettour had told him, there were pros and cons to both bending over backward to attack and bending over backward to avoid attacking. For Operations, fewer fronts would give them an easier time, but the Service Corps had to worry about supplying the troops regardless.

"Well, it was General von Zettour's condition."

"What?"

He didn't particularly think he needed to hide the fact. Or rather, he figured she would find out anyway, and telling her now would be an act of goodwill toward a fellow member of the General Staff.

"He said we should forget about the Entente Alliance and focus on domestic defense. Either way has its logic, and if the Northern Army Group had agreed, I would have sent you to the Rhine and been preparing to survive the winter."

"Understood. If you'll excuse me, I'll be on my way."

》》》　NORTHERN ARMY GROUP BARRACK 7 (WHERE THE BATTALION　《《《
HAD BEEN GARRISONED)

"Major?"

The one who meets Major von Degurechaff when she returns to the barrack to notify the troops of their reassignment is Officer of the Week, her vice commander, First Lieutenant Weiss. How considerate of him to have an orderly ready an extra coat and coffee—that efficiency is skill and experience. He really is excellent material.

The best part is that he doesn't smoke. Tanya's nose is sensitive to tobacco. And the staff meeting is always smoky. No, I wouldn't deny anyone cigarettes on the battlefield, but I'd like separate smoking and nonsmoking areas. Or just tell them, *Don't blow smoke in my face.* It makes my eyes sting and my nose itch. I resent this assault on my tear ducts.

Limitations on individual rights are obviously oppression and, as such, difficult for people to stomach. Still, it should be fine if I murder the senior officers who refuse to stop obnoxiously huffing their smoke in my face, right?

They don't even do any work, but the cigars they light up are luxury items. Tanya can't help but be disgusted. The gall they must have to voice nonexistent concern for the troops. *Even when I have to spout some wholesome crap, I keep up appearances better than that.*

"That was truly pointless. What an utter waste of time and budget."

We could have a phony war,[9] but instead these nutcases want to fight for real. You don't even need a consultant to point out how little can be done with scant, poor managerial resources.

Lost in thought, Tanya sets her staff officer's bag on the desk and begins scribbling notes about the state of the war on a map. Her cover of staying in the north can't keep her from the front lines anymore now that a mobile defense unit was no longer necessary to protect pulling supply lines back.

Not only that, but the Northern Army Group is planning an offensive that reeks of a death march. Meanwhile, the General Staff, for its part, is planning a top secret landing operation around the rear.

"These guys are too into war."

From the bottom of my heart, I advise you to think twice about surrounding yourself with people who are overly fond of war. I can't keep up with their notion of fighting with barely any matériel.

I can't believe they don't want to leisurely build fortifications while we wait for supplies and leave the fierce fighting to the others.

I'd like to suspect them of being too steeped in the romance of achievement and militarism, but now that the General Staff is planning a major amphibious operation in the rear, they, too, seem way more into the idea of fighting than I thought.

"I can't understand this world."

I didn't want to confess my incompetence, but I decided there was nothing else to do.

That said, if it's a winnable battle, then it should be fine to advocate loudly for the advance. And if we're air-dropping in, we can just fly right back out if things get rough. Considering how uniquely mobile aerial

---

[9] **phony war**   The France-Germany border during the beginning of World War II was the very picture of peace. This phrase describes a strange state of conflict in which parties are at war but not fighting.

mages are, she estimates the risk to be low and grows fairly enthusiastic about the strike on the rear.

Even MacArthur managed it. The Empire's General Staff is way more serious about war than that guy was, so I'm sure they'll come up with an ultraprecise plan for us. It will be my first time to fight according to an operation plan by General von Rudersdorf, but when I tried talking to him, he seemed unexpectedly easy to work with. *This might just pan out,* thinks Tanya, genuinely looking forward to it.

"Get me an extra map."

"Here you go, ma'am."

But that doesn't mean there aren't any problems.

She takes the map of the entire northern theater from her subordinate and compares it to her annotated situation map.

She buries her head in her hands and racks her brain, but fjords really have an optimal shape for coastal defense. You could bombard the narrow bodies of water all you liked, so if you placed as many batteries as you had along them, they would be impenetrable.

The only thing that saves Tanya is the lesson from history that sometimes a fortress built against the water is terribly vulnerable to an invasion by land, like Singapore. Having had that thought, Tanya tries moving the pawns according to the scenario she envisions.

The batteries guarding the fjords are certainly a threat to a fleet of warships. Yes, a threat—but to warships… If they all face the sea, they could probably be blown up fairly easily from behind with explosives or what have you. And coastal guns are usually positioned facing the mouth of a bay. They aren't built with the expectation of bombardment from behind.

Can we win? To Tanya, even if their opponents were spirits who strayed from Moominvalley, the deciding factor is that their defensive shells could be shattered.

"An attack from behind… I suppose our chances of success are decent enough."

Farewell from a sinking ship. It's the most obvious, commonsense thing to do. But in extremely rare cases, the ship doesn't sink, and sometimes you can even make a fortune. If that possibility exists, we should happily count it as a winning battle. With that thought, Tanya rolls up the map with the war forecast and mixes it in with the reports for the General Staff.

After all, the General Staff is planning an operation on such a large scale. You can only call them stupid if they get so far without a contingency plan in case of failure. It's worrisome that the Operations Division of the General Staff—section chief–rank officers—are planning the operation on the assumption that the northern forces will ignore the General Staff's "advice" and march north. Is the cooperation between the regional armies and the General Staff even shakier than I thought? This anxious thought crosses my mind.

Then again, if I think of the ill will as a legacy of their predecessors, who committed the Great Army to Norden and then pulled it out the next instant, it makes sense. Ludwig really mucked it up. Technically, of course, the General Staff is nothing more than one of His Imperial Majesty the Emperor's advisory committees—even if the supreme authority is simply rubber-stamping things for them. Each regional army group may be nominally loyal to that committee, but if everyone isn't cooperating well, that's a problem.

But no, that's exactly the point. After that realization, Tanya practically sighs. I should probably be thinking that if the northern forces' little adventure fails, the General Staff will take advantage of the fact that the world is watching the foray by attempting a major operation of their own in Norden. And if that works, the General Staff will have taken the initiative to lead the war.

Currently, the Entente Alliance can repel the Empire's advance with guerrilla-style interception, but they don't have the available force to counterattack. Until some obstacle to defense in Norden appears, it's practically a political issue to consider something that isn't in accordance with the Imperial Army elites' wishes.

In other words, it's a Vitamin P problem.

"I don't want to get mixed up in this…"

No, wait. Let's chill for a minute. At least Tanya has a lot of experience. She won't make the same mistake over and over.

My common sense is not always common. Might there not be some sort of religion that teaches people to love war and recommends suicide?

"Lieutenant Weiss, do you want to kill yourself?"

"Huh? Er, why do you ask that all of a sudden?" He replies with a question to confirm her intention. Well, judging from his reaction, I'm worrying over nothing.

I guess that makes sense. After that thought, Tanya reaches for the coffee Second Lieutenant Serebryakov brought. It's cold up north. There's no way I could stand it without drinking hot coffee. The only thing is, Northern Command has a tendency to treat me like a kid and load up every cup with milk and sugar... I hate that.

"It's hard to believe, but apparently there will be an all-out offensive. What a waste of soldiers."

Until the appointed hour arrives for Tanya to open her sealed orders, she tells her trusty vice commander, Lieutenant Weiss, only as much as she can. She can't let anything slip.

In other words, to summarize what she can explain now: There will be a big offensive this winter. And with only that context, she can't get rid of the impression that the Northern Army Group is rushing things with their sights set on an easy advance like what happened in the war with Dacia.

It's like making a huge gamble when you don't have much cash on hand—although since the stakes are actually soldiers' lives, it won't hurt the high-ranking officers' pockets at all. If the Chicago school were to analyze it, they would diagnose a severe lack of proper incentives.

"...Is there money for logistics?"

I'm guessing Lieutenant Weiss's incredulous reaction is an average person's response. Unless the Northern Army Group's commanders have some strange concept of supply lines, I don't know what they're thinking. Do they have a secret stash of cash somewhere?

If so, those are off-the-books resources. We'd have to dismiss the inspectors. Talk about lazy. This is why they say we can't prevent bubble economies. Proper audits are indispensable for a market to function normally!

"How would there be? Once winter hits, the trains will stop running, too. I have no idea where they're planning on bringing in supplies from."

Well, in any age, there are also markets that only officials who come to collect taxes do well in. To prove it, not even believers in the free market system call for the privatization of tax collection.

Meanwhile, there's a fountain of diverse critiques and plans regarding expenditures.

Look, even the Chicago school is against privatizing tax collection!

With that thought, however, I suddenly feel like something is off.

"So what about us?"

"When I pointed out the risk of an offensive, we were ordered to the naval base. So I don't think we can expect funds for a victory celebration."

And this is an absolutely miserable misunderstanding created in the name of confidentiality. Even if my intention is to be transferred according to the will of the Central Army, a Northern Army Group administrator won't see it that way, so I'm sure the Budget section will reject the fund requisition. They'll make the excuse that it's not under their jurisdiction and refuse to pay out what they promised us just the other day.

I can only see it as bullying. Even if I accept the reshuffle, we have made contributions here and should have the right to commensurate compensation. Anyhow, we'll just have to secure celebration funds by "borrowing" from the Northern Army Group somehow. *Hmm...? Finding funds somehow?*

"As such, Lieutenant Serebryakov, we need to dip into the battalion's treasury, so draw up a budget."

"Understood. Umm, how much should I use?"

I could take funds for a little party from the battalion treasury, but maybe we should avoid having a big bash in this war situation...? When she considers this, Tanya figures she is thinking too hard and shrugs. She has worked her troops hard in this freezing cold. Rather than developing a cruel reputation, it would be better to have a heart and convince them she was kind, even if they got a little wild.

"Hmm, let's have a grand old time and not set an upper limit for alcohol spending."

Just as she is about to tell her to get it done—

"Major, sorry to intrude, but we have enough free alcohol to swim in."

It was Lieutenant Weiss who interrupted with a triumphant look on his face.

After inadvertently starting to ask where he'd snatched the liquor from, Tanya wills her mouth shut, somehow successfully communicating with her expression of disbelief instead.

"Umm, excuse me for butting in, but we were able to get this full complement of canteen alcohol due to the kindness of a local unit."

Lieutenant Serebryakov jumps in to respond to my suspicious look. Partly because we've been together for a while now, she's getting good at knowing what types of things I worry about.

"Oh, don't worry. The Viper Battalion bought it with their own money as a gesture of goodwill, I guess you could say."

Very good. Tanya nods in satisfaction. Someone is treating us because they're pleased with our work. That's wonderful. The only problem is that due to military regulations and my age, I can't drink a drop even if I want to.

"Great. Go and buy some chicken or something, Lieutenant." I'd like to sink my teeth into some roast chicken, at least. "We'll have to toast the Viper Battalion. Thanks to them, I can treat my battalion."

"Yeah, we can't really thank them enough."

Well, they're mages. They're well-paid. After all, there are deployment allowances, transfer allowances, hazard pay, etc. They each make enough to build a small house, so if you count the entire battalion's funds, it adds up to quite a lot.

"Indeed. Well, this is a good opportunity. Let's send them a message inviting them to the party."

That's what we'll do. It's not so bad to bond with our kind allies who weakened our prey for us before we arrived. More than anything, I want to clear up the misunderstanding that must have arisen due to that repugnant confession of faith.

I'm normal.

I have to prevent weird rumors from damaging my reputation.

Chapter **III**

Along the strait, it's nearly time for the decisive battle. A high-strung excitement runs through the air at the Imperial Army base. Usually the atmosphere feels almost heavy, but for the moment, it's so lively it keeps the cold at bay. The officers and men running here and there are visibly tense—no one is relaxed.

It's the excitement that occurs immediately before a large-scale operation. Humans are a pain in the neck; though wise enough to fear fighting, they are also easily intoxicated by the romance of the military. This has to be the concentrated effect of everyone's wish to taste sweet victory.

Those who can't share in this festive atmosphere appear to be in the minority. Resigning herself to the fact, Tanya goes to the designated flagship command meeting room. As far as she can tell from a glance at the soldiers coming and going in the halls on her way, the entire Northern Sea Fleet crew seems full of fighting spirit. Even the vessels that would be left behind seem to be longing to sortie enough to rush out of there at any moment.

And the operational factors necessary for taking advantage of that spirit appear to have been given the necessary consideration. A large number of transport ships are anchored in the bay, and among them are some that could qualify as landing crafts after being outfitted for the amphibious assault. They probably have landing crafts requisitioned as high-speed transports ready to go as well. As far as she can see, traffic in the bay is orderly, and ships are in a position to begin operations at any time, thanks to the controlling performed with the Empire's usual efficiency.

Tanya is conscious again of the weight of her responsibility; a lot is expected of her unit as the vanguard. It's better for people to expect greatness of you than not, but it comes with a lot of annoyances.

That said, she conceals any determination to live up to those expectations and calmly takes her assigned seat in the meeting room. She ignores the attention she is getting by nonchalantly looking over the pre-meeting handouts once again. Of course, in part, she wants to reread them to circumvent any avoidable problems during the operation.

Just as she's already read many times, it seems like her unit's role is fairly large. Having their performance determine whether the operation would work or not is a big responsibility. Drop in, capture the coastal guns. It'll be glorious but a challenge. If we fail, the whole army will be stuck in the fjords.

"It's time, so I'd like to begin."

Even while she is lost in thought, the hands on the clock keep ticking. Then, when they reach the appointed hour, an Imperial Navy staff member announces the beginning of the meeting in a solemn voice, and everyone turns toward the commander of the operation, the fleet commander, in unison.

"All right, I'll explain the situation."

Tanya listens to the commander as he briefs everyone, unaware of her feelings on the topic and with a sober expression, but the gripes in her head threaten to overflow. Internally, she complains up a storm, whining over and over that it sure would have been nice if the drop team had been given a few more men.

"We'll be performing a mission in support of the Northern Army Group's operation."

...In support of the Northern Army Group? Tanya starts to think, but then it makes sense to her. Yes, the Central Army is nominally giving credit for the operation to the Northern Army Group. I guess it's a show of the General Staff's intentions or kindness, you could say. After the awkwardness between them over the Great Army mobilization issues, this'll be a heartwarming reconciliation.

In other words, this is a lousy plan, a military operation loaded with the higher-ups' motives. But you could also say that they'd managed it in a nominal way that wouldn't come back to bite the troops on the ground; instead of a political compromise, they had pulled off a splendid handshake.

After all, the Northern Army Group is going on the offensive, and as a bonus they get the honor of leading the operation. Even if they fail, no one in the Northern Army Group will be harmed if the General Staff take responsibility for implementing the action plan. Then again, if it goes well, the war situation improves, so it's worth it for the General Staff.

Major General von Rudersdorf came out to make an inspection—it's probably his evil scheming. On the one hand, I'm impressed with the move, but on the other, I want to lament just a little bit that when you belong directly to Central, this is how you get used as a tool.

"As you all know, we currently have both the Northern Sea Fleet and the High Seas Fleet deployed on a northern support mission."

Then there's the situation being described. The main force of the Northern Sea Fleet is a support unit that acts as a sort of check on the Entente Alliance. Their mission is to prevent the Entente Alliance's warships from escaping to Republic waters while simultaneously supporting the army maneuvers on land.

So ignoring those ships to perform the amphibious operation is almost a strategic sneak attack. It isn't about sealed orders or intercepting the fleet—the plan from the first is to ignore the Entente Alliance fleet.

The Northern Sea Fleet is going beyond the parameters of its original mission and sortieing for the sole purpose of receiving a huge number of reinforcements in the High Seas Fleet and performing the landing operation. The Entente Alliance ships that will surely come to stop them will be kept at bay by the High Seas Fleet. If the Northern Sea Fleet can complete their operation during that time, the war situation will see a literal reversal.

The success of a strategic sneak attack is tantalizing. You could say a winnable battle is just dangling in front of us. It's a comparably safe opportunity to achieve things and get promoted. I'm not the only one—there's nothing strange about a soldier wanting to join a winning battle.

Actually, the ones left behind with no prospect of sortieing get depressed or look for an excuse to go. Anyone is happy to be told they're going on the attack.

If there's one problem, it's the weather. History tells us units sent into harsh winter conditions always end up getting stuck in some lousy situation. And we'll be performing an airborne operation. If we fall into the ocean, we'll freeze to death like *Titanic* victims.

Even the bright red Soviet Army met with all kinds of disaster in winter wars. The Imperial Army isn't used to such conditions, so if we fall into the winter ocean, we'll be turned into frozen meat packs.

"This means almost all our main force is going, but that's just how big the objective is…" The fleet commander leaves it as implied for just a moment, then solemnly states our target. "…the Osfjord. We're going for a direct strike on their rear communication lines."

The Osfjord… When everyone grasps the significance of what they've been told, a momentary silence descends.

Fjords are bad news for naval ships. The detestable narrow bodies of water with terrible cliffs on either side enable the enemy to shoot at them from any direction. Even without counting the threat of mines, if there are guns on both sides, any ship that makes a run for it can only lament its fate to be pummeled to death. The gunners will surely shower the marks with shells as they struggle to maneuver in the narrow waters.

And although their navy may only have a few destroyers left, if that, the cramped space forces us to worry about torpedoes.

What's more, given the geographical importance of Os, the Osfjord will be more heavily guarded than the average fjord.

"Under these circumstances, we need to go in ahead of the fleet's advance and capture the enemy guns."

From the time General von Rudersdorf gave her secret orders to prepare for an airborne operation, Tanya has pretty much been expecting this. *Neutralize coastal guns in an aerial mage sneak attack* is practically the same thing as *support the fleet as they make a run down the fjord.* For what other reason would the army pit their elites against a rear echelon coastal stronghold?

She finds herself balling up her fists inside her sleeves. Capturing enemy guns ahead of the operation to take the mouth of the bay… In other words, our drop operation is a gamble that could decide everything. And we won't be walking leisurely down a gangway in this cold weather but parachuting out of the sky with our computation orbs and rifles in hand. If we fail, it will be a huge disaster.

"Our aim is to disable enemy guns in a short amount of time to allow the fleet's entry."

It's easy to order someone to *get in there*, but it sounds pretty outrageous to the one told to go.

The purpose of the airborne operation is fine. I can grasp the military need for it. At least, I understand that it has to be done. But what's this about us securing the guns? The operation is in support of the navy, so it would make more sense to have the marine mages do it, since they train closely with the fleet. If instead we seize the guns and sweep the area, it'll be basically like rolling out a carpet for the fleet to waltz down.

"Our troops are having difficulties, so in order to support them and deliver a decisive blow, I want us to do this right."

…That's easy to say, but can we? Can we really capture enemy guns on bad, snowy footing in the fjord? If we were told to suppress enemy forces in that region, well, that just would have to be done, but the responsibility of seizing all the enemy guns is enormous.

Talk about mission impossible.

That said, there's a limit to how much mages can do as direct support for the fleet, and if guns remain, it's entirely possible that the ships won't be able to enter. So someone has to get saddled with this unlucky operation. Annoyingly enough, that someone is the 203rd Aerial Mage Battalion.

"And the vanguard will be… We're expecting great things from you, Major von Degurechaff."

"May I say something?"

"What is it, Major?"

"My unit is an augmented battalion. Setting aside the issue of firepower, I may not have enough men to take all the guns and cover the enemy reinforcements who are bound to attack."

I hate resisting superior officers. There is nothing I want to do less. But that's why I have to be bold at times like these.

Anyone can smash you if you oppose them with a subservient attitude. But if, on the contrary, you make your case so confidently that it must be logical, it sounds more persuasive. And if people think you're giving a constructive suggestion with the aim of accomplishing your mission, then even an excuse transforms into the genuine truth. So I have to be the donkey borrowing the lion's skin. I just want to probe slightly. Even if I fail, this isn't rebellious enough to cause me trouble.

"Don't worry. We were fearing that as well, so we're arranging for two regiments of marines to reinforce you thirty minutes after your drop."

"Understood. So in a worst-case scenario, do I have the right to suggest aborting the operation?"

Her attitude says she doesn't feel at all bad as she masks her request. Any sign of hesitation can be interpreted as cowardice, but if a request is stated with conviction, it will most likely have a measure of persuasive power.

It's not about who's right or wrong; it's about who makes their claims in a loud voice with confidence.

"…What do you mean?"

"Simply that if my unit fails, the fleet may be exposed to needless danger."

What if, hypothetically, we fail?

That we would have to withdraw is self-evident. Put another way, we'd be able to avoid unfeasible orders to "just do something" so the fleet could get in. Once we decide to fall back, all the mages have to do is fly away.

Even if the right to call for withdrawal isn't granted, the record of me asking for it would make it possible for me to argue that I made every effort to avoid risks.

"You mean, we should prioritize the safety of the fleet in the event you can't neutralize the guns?"

That's level one cleared. If I haven't been flat-out refused, it shows he's willing to listen.

A good officer would give serious consideration to the risks the fleet would face if we failed to take the guns and they were in working order. An officer concerned with self-preservation would be worried about being blamed for the results of a forced charge under such circumstances.

Either way, he has to carefully analyze what I've said, weigh the pros and cons, and see what he thinks.

"If we don't take preserving the fleet seriously enough, we may let the Republican or Commonwealth fleet slip in. That would render the blockade meaningless and create a very dangerous situation."

So I give him a little push. The concern of weakened patrol in our waters. I just prod his instincts as an officer of the navy by asking whether we should really conduct a landing mission at the risk of our command of the sea. It's really too reasonable. Whether he's out for self-preservation or not, he can't ignore this. Of course, I can't push too hard. Balance in this, too, is paramount. That said, if I don't mess up the pressure level, I can persuade him without upsetting him too much.

"...That's a reasonable concern, but we can't leave our course of action up to a single advance unit. Major, if you fail, fall back to join your reinforcements and try again."

"Understood, sir. But due to a quirk of the command structure, I can neither command nor be commanded by marine mages..." Having gotten this far, I just need to give him an excuse. He must know how things work. The navy's original job is only providing escorts to the mouth of the bay and maybe firing their cannons. I'm sure he doesn't want to exacerbate mage command structure issues. "In light of that, I'd like permission to advise aborting if the marine regiment commanders agree."

It's an adjusted step to save everyone's faces and avoid any bothersome disputes.

It doesn't take any time at all for him to agree.

"...All right. You have it."

A few days later, the operation is to be carried out as scheduled, and Tanya and the brave members of the 203rd Aerial Mage Battalion are in a transport plane being taken to the drop zone as the vanguard.

The plan is to jump at the crack of dawn and capitalize on the enemy's confusion in order to seize the guns. As the ones performing the operation, it seems risky, but coastal fortifications are extremely vulnerable to attacks from behind, so it has its logic.

"I guess we might be able to do this...?" Tanya murmurs, inwardly seeking comfort in reason.

Coastal fortifications are put in place to prepare for attacks by enemy ships and units. When she tells herself there is no reason for the backside to be protected because all that's there are the communication lines to the rear echelon, it feels like they have a chance of succeeding. Even if the enemy is on guard against a sneak attack, their units are likely to be only lightly outfitted.

The coastal fortifications would say that the army should protect the rear and that their purpose was to prevent attacks by sea. And a century ago, they wouldn't have been wrong.

"I've cut the engines! We're gliding!"

The announcement from the cockpit alerts them that they have entered the final prep stage.

Loath to betray even the sound of the engine, we make our careful gliding approach. Naturally, our drop will be performed with airborne gear and not rely on magic. If we can't descend undetected, Tanya's fate is sealed.

"All right. All hands, prepare to jump."

She can only hope the troops she has trained will put all their talents on display. Her only tasks now are to increase the probability of success and eliminate obstacles.

And a commander can't wear an anxious expression moments before an operation. That's why she orders them to prepare with the carefree tone of someone announcing picnic plans.

It's a bit surreal to see mages in full gear jostling around in the cramped plane, but they're getting ready, anyhow, so that's good.

"You've heard this before, but our targets are the guns and mines guarding the fjord. Capturing them is optimal, but if that proves difficult, disabling or damaging them to inhibit effective functioning is fine." She doesn't insist that she believes in them but reconfirms their objectives matter-of-factly. "I think you know this, but if we fail, the landing unit will get stuck in the fjord."

Guns are not fortresses, which means they aren't impossible to capture. Most importantly, their muzzles are pointed at the sea. They aren't set up to fight mages dropping in on them from behind, but they still have the power to trap the fleet. That's why this operation hinges on us.

"There isn't much wiggle room in the schedule. Thirty minutes after we drop, marine mages will arrive ahead of the fleet to back us up, but the plan is for them to deal with enemy reinforcements on the ground. Basically, we have to do this ourselves."

If things get bad, I can make a joint suggestion with the commanders of the troops coming later to abort the operation, but the consequences would be the sacrifice of my career and worse. I'd be ruined. I have no interest in going to ruin by myself, but to avoid ruin entirely, if possible, is surely the modest wish at the root of all human emotions.

"Destroy all the positions as best you can in thirty minutes. I expect you to all be putting the true power of aerial mages on display out there."

So Tanya is expecting a lot out of her subordinates. No, not even expecting—all she can do is hope. *Don't fuck this up. Please show me you have more than it takes.*

"Lieutenant, head up the capture of the Albert battery. I'll take the Narva battery as planned."

"Understood. What time are we lifting radio silence?" Vice Commander Weiss confirms for the third time.

"If you fail to seize the position, contact me immediately. Otherwise, the plan is to maintain radio silence until our reinforcements arrive."

"What about enemy reinforcements?"

"Come crying to me if you can't handle them. Otherwise, crush them."

"Yes, ma'am."

Reconfirming everything to make sure we don't miss anything and keeping the troops informed of relevant information—we're model communicators. Anyhow, we can't say for sure that we'll succeed, but there are blatant reasons we could fail, so there's no better way to prepare than getting rid of them.

"Okay, Lieutenant Serebryakov, you're our reserve commander. If Lieutenant Weiss and I go dark, order the retreat."

"Retreat, ma'am?"

"The operation is a failure if you lose our signals. If well-outfitted enemies show up, you have no chance of winning. We're just like canaries."

A canary in a coal mine gives its warning by dying. The point of view that resulted in this method is exemplary in its practicality. Of course, we face the vexing reality that the army values us and canaries equally.

That said, though Tanya made this troubling simile, she has absolutely no intention of nobly sacrificing herself. If need be, she'll make a scene screaming about the danger to everyone as she makes an airborne escape; that's how far her loyalty to the Reich goes.

"Then I'll try to sing my sweetest."

I kind of have to hand it to Weiss for that joke.

"I'm not interested in hearing you sing, Lieutenant. Get ready to move out!"

"Yes, ma'am!"

As each soldier briskly checks over their gear, Tanya grabs her parachute, makes the last pre-jump checks, and nods in satisfaction.

If I have no choice but to go, I should at least do a good job.

"Okay! Go!"

When it came to zeal for one's work, Colonel Anson Sue of the Entente Alliance Army was like Tanya—the kind of person who made rigorous preparations for battle.

"Enemy attack!"

"That's insane! We can detect their mana signals from this far away? What's the suppression squad doing…?"

Colonel Sue's unit had just been stationed there out of a need to protect the sea, and although they weren't in perfect fighting condition, they were already on guard—no doubt because he had learned the horror of completely losing the initiative in battle.

And especially considering their situation now… Ever since they had carelessly started the war, the pressure had been growing.

"They were attacked in their sleep? Is the army even training people properly anymore?"

Which was why Sue couldn't hide his displeasure with the chaos descending over their coastal guns and clicked his tongue in annoyance. The discipline was probably so lousy because they were calling up reserves from the rear.

"…Enemy status?"

At that time, he was regarding the attack as a mere bit of harassment. But even a harassing attack on the guns was a nasty move that could lead to a dispersal of their forces in the name of stationing additional troops in a rear echelon city like Os. One might say that he still had the where-withal to lament such things at that point.

No, more accurately, he was sighing while keeping a hopeful eye on the situation. Colonel Sue himself probably didn't understand the core of his emotions.

But up until then, at least...he didn't grasp how grave the situation was.

"Unclear. I have reports that the coastal units are engaged...and it seems the patrol boats haven't made their regular check-ins."

"What? Ask the patrol line what's going on. Could be a sneak attack by mages flying out of a sub."

Approach in secret and attack. In that sense, a commando unit and a submarine went together perfectly. That was why Sue persistently appealed to the military to adopt submarines, but sadly, the Entente Alliance Navy was really only a slightly thicker-skinned version of a coast guard. They didn't have the resources to allot submarines for use in magic operations. The few they had, frustratingly enough, had gone on their periodic deep-sea exercise before the start of the war and then wound up getting disarmed as warships in a neutral country. That disgraceful situation meant they had zero operational submarines.

Reflecting jealously, Sue wondered if they could perhaps capture one as he had his men get ready to sortie. He had the radio operator connect him with the picket line.

"I've been calling them, but none of the ships are replying..."

"Do you think there's some kind of confusion and they can't connect?"

That was when he understood the situation.

The picket line ships had gone dark. If it were only one of them, it could have just happened to be near the submarine and gotten attacked, but if the entire surface warning line went quiet, that was not a minor problem. No, it meant the root of the trouble was on the surface!

"...Crap! They're targeting the guns? We're moving out! Scramble!"

Enemy mages were sneak attacking the batteries. And they had lost contact with the ships on the sea.

"Huh?"

"The guns are all facing forward!"

It was the enemy. An enemy attack. *A major methodical attack! The fatherland, my country…the home I must protect…*

"In the air now! Scramble! Engines on!"

Sue's unit, taking off with determination in their breasts, was an unexpected newcomer for the Imperial Army. The Imperial Army General Staff thought it was a newly organized unit that had just been stationed there. They had also grasped that the enemy troops were not very content and tended to have insufficient logistical support, and the General Staff's intelligence wasn't wrong. So the staff officer who had analyzed the data came to the utterly commonsense conclusion that it was a static guard with a measure of defensive capabilities that was protecting the city of Os.

And that was why he thought the troops would be able to clean them up with the strength of their main force.

He had figured that by the time that unit had assembled to counterattack, the main imperial force would have already landed.

And he wasn't entirely wrong. Only his conclusion was.

After all, at face value, Colonel Anson's force was a puny mage battalion, a mix of wheat and chaff that was undertrained and lacking unity.

But the Empire didn't know why these troops were fighting. Because it didn't need to yet.

Still, from a totally objective standpoint, the unavoidable truth is… The Imperial Army commander, Tanya, muttering mainly curses at either God or the devil about the arrival of these unforeseen enemies, has to come up with a way to handle the situation.

"Major! New enemies!"

The rapidly approaching formation is a battalion-sized group of mages. Both their speed and altitude are quite impressive. No doubt about it, they're a first-rate interception unit—and a horrible nightmare for the 203rd Aerial Mage Battalion suppressing enemies on the ground.

"I see that! Lieutenant Serebryakov, take command of First Company and stop them!"

"Major, it's too dangerous with only one company! I'll share some troops from my group."

"Lieutenant Weiss, you just capture that battery! We'll figure out some way to handle this."

Tanya decides without a moment's hesitation to go meet them herself.

I'm at wit's end, but I can't run away. If I send my subordinates up and they get the shit kicked out of them, there'll be nowhere for me to run. If that's how it'll go, Tanya feels more at ease intercepting them herself from the start and preparing for trouble.

True, she isn't terribly keen on facing an elite-seeming enemy battalion with a force the size of a company, but it's better than the fear of having them on top of her. If she doesn't want be made into a target, she has to get above them.

"R-roger!"

"First Company, follow me! We're intercepting!"

The moment their short exchange is finished, Tanya accelerates to climb hard. As she swiftly ascends, aiming to occupy a combat altitude that is even with or superior to their opponent's, she catches sight of the tiny dots drawing nearer every second.

And as one side got visual confirmation, so too did the other.

"We can't get through to the surface!"

"I've got visuals! They're on their way up to meet us!"

As Colonel Sue's battalion raced across the sky in a messy formation and reached the Osfjord, the situation was as he had feared. The batteries had descended into chaos due to a sneak attack.

Not only that, but enemy mages were smoothly gaining altitude while maneuvering into combat formation, as if they had been skillfully lying in wait.

He could instantly gather from their impressive aptitude and clean formation that they were formidable opponents—in other words, the kind he hated.

"They're fast!"

"A company? They must think we're wimps!"

"These guys parachuted in. Don't underestimate their training! Put our numerical advantage to good use! Let's go!"

That said, they couldn't cower. *How much do you think numerical superiority will really matter?* the realistic part of his head sneered, but he suppressed it and encouraged his unit to drive the attackers away from the batteries.

"Beat them back!"

What else could he say?

"Go! Get 'em!"

All he could do was scream and lead his troops in the charge.

He chose to do it, but it was also his only choice. *But* it should probably be said…

Sue looked up at the sky. *I guess God isn't smiling on me.*

"Ngh?! That's—"

"Colonel Sue?"

Dear God, why…? Why is she here?

"This one's pesky as rust. Take some distance and fire to suppress. Do *not* let her get in close!"

She's got that obnoxious alias White Silver or whatever. When it came to an enemy who fought bitterly against his own unit and got an award out of it, he remembered news from an enemy country. *With all the blood she has on her hands, her alias is White Silver? Ha, the Empire has no talent for coming up with names.*

Might as well call her Rusted Silver, looking like that.

A devil spattered and rusted in the blood of his fellow soldiers. There was no way for him to mistake that detestable girl—his sworn enemy.

Dear God, I pray. Give me the strength to destroy that devil.

Sue even prayed as he shot the formula, and just as an attack filled with fervent hopes should, it plowed into the enemy formation.

Or rather, things happened as he expected.

They scattered, taking barely any damage, and sped toward him with no hesitation. Still, that didn't mean he could back down. There was no way he could withdraw.

He was carrying a submachine gun. If that mage would just get in range, he would turn her into honeycomb. With that thought in mind, Sue eagerly charged.

In terms of inability to withdraw, Major von Degurechaff's unit is in the same boat. Tanya inwardly feels that she is being seriously overworked for her salary, but even if she wants to declare, *This isn't in my contract* and fly away, that's not how the army works.

Rules have to be followed.

If a regiment of mages had moved in to attack, perhaps she could have used numbers as an excuse to run away. But when both the enemy mages and your own are battalion-sized groups, you can't get away with excuses—though she wants to flee, she can't. In a case like this, the army says to put up a fight.

"Tch! These guys are tough. Attack in platoon formations!"

As she thinks how badly she wants to run, she realizes that if she did, the career she had spent all this time building up would disappear, and she would be helpless to stop it. Reluctantly, even grudgingly, she has to take on some degree of risk and fight.

The only way to thwart gaps in firepower and numbers is to dart in for melee. At close quarters, there is a greater danger of misfire; as a result, the imbalance in firepower stemming from the disparity in numbers decreases somewhat. More importantly, if they bring the fight to an individual level instead of organizational, the imperial mages will definitely have the advantage.

"Get above them!"

"Don't let them get above you!"

Crisscrossing gunfire and formulas. The scene displays the very essence of mana science technology, a fantasy where the practical modern advances of civilization are having their day. Sadly, it's a picture painted only in blood and iron.

In the end, though, the impact of numerical superiority will be felt. If it becomes a battle of attrition, the side with more matériel and men will be declared the winners.

"Oh, the reinforcements are here?"

"Shit! Again? More reinforcements?"

A regiment is approaching. Openly jubilant as she notices indications of their arrival, Tanya is sure of her victory, while Colonel Sue is devastated. As such, their voices reflect their situations—the former's is very cheerful and the latter's sounds helpless and bitter.

"Major von Degurechaff, what's the status of the seizure operation?"

"Below they're sweeping up, but I'm currently fighting an enemy unit. Requesting backup."

"Understood! You two battalions, support the major! The rest of you, head for the interior."

And in her straightforward exchange with the commander of the reinforcements, her remarks are businesslike to ensure the operation proceeds smoothly. The two of them are so in control of the situation, they're no longer worried about whether they will succeed or not; instead, they're thinking of what comes next.

The coastal guns are being seized, the enemy unit can be eliminated, and the imperial transport ships are coming into view across the bay. The scene below makes all the Imperial Army soldiers feel that they are moving step-by-step closer to victory.

Victory… It will be an established fact in the Imperial Army's near future.

Colonel Sue's beloved fatherland no longer had the power to object.

>>>>　　　THE SAME DAY, THE REPUBLIC, CHANNEL COMMAND　　　<<<<

"Alert from the early warning line!"

The observation units along the warning line had an alert. What that meant was clear: The imperial fleet was on the move.

This was the chance for a naval battle they had been hoping for. The tension at Command peaked all at once.

"Order DEFCON 1. So they're finally coming out."

We've been waiting.

That's practically what the commander was saying, and his feelings were shared by all the other members of the Republican Navy. While the army was fighting a grueling battle on the Rhine lines, the navy was ridiculed as slackers. This was an opportunity to clear its name; they had been looking forward to this chance to support their troops.

"Er, they have…transport ships with them? Why?!"

But the enemy movements they had longed for completely betrayed their expectations. The latest update on the imperial fleet indicated that, contrary to their hopes, it had no intention of engaging in a naval battle. The fleet maneuver they had predicted was happening, but the warships were leaving the port accompanied by several transport ships.

Unless the movement was a long one, it was hard to imagine a unit of battleships sailing with slow, vulnerable transport ships—which is precisely why upon hearing about those vessels, the clever ones among them immediately speculated upon what might be inside and were assailed by a type of foreboding.

...*What could be in there?* Common sense would say coal, oil, food for the troops, ammunition, spare parts, and so on—things the unit would need on a long operation. But there was no way the Imperial Navy would take a leisurely cruise around the world right now. In that case, the ships had to be taking something important to where it was needed.

The Command personnel all waited with bated breath for the next report. The atmosphere was so tense their uneasiness was burning them up inside.

"Spike 04 to HQ. The imperial fleet is setting course to the north. I say again, course to the north!"

"Ngh! An amphibious operation?"

Of course, they all felt like they'd been whacked in the back of the head when they understood.

After all, this was the worst possible development for the Republic. It had been their worst nightmare ever since one corner of the encirclement, Dacia, had crumbled—the fear that the Entente Alliance would collapse as well. And now as they could see the Imperial Northern Army Group planning an offensive, the Entente Alliance's main forces were tied up on the front.

...If the rear logistics base were seized in a landing operation, it would mean they had failed to avoid another Dacia. War could no longer be fought with superior ground forces alone, and if the rear supply lines were cut, the army's fate would be tragedy.

In the back of their minds, a few senior officers remembered the plans for the Imperial Army's amphibious operation, delivered in utmost secret from the Commonwealth. If the Entente Alliance were to fall like Dacia, how much would that increase the burden on their beloved fatherland?

"Ready the fleet and the marine mages to sortie on the double! They're planning to land in the Entente Alliance's rear area." In came another enemy status report. Increasingly agitated, Command notified them that they should hurry up and send out the fleet. But one report made them all freeze. All the hubbub faded in an instant and dissipated.

"…Are you sure?"

"There's no mistake! Subs and enemy mages are forming a restraining line!"

The primary mission of the Republican Channel Fleet was to confront and annihilate the Imperial High Seas Fleet. But while the Republic had to split their main forces between the north and south, the Empire could concentrate their naval power in the north. With the Northern Sea and High Seas Fleets combining forces, the Republican Channel Fleet would be forced into a disadvantageous position.

A fight that was once seven on seven had just been joined by three enemy reinforcements. Fighting a ten-on-seven battle wasn't impossible, but it was far from the numbers they would like to see.

Even if they got backup from the Entente Alliance, it probably wouldn't help very much. Meanwhile, the Northern Sea Fleet may have been small, but it featured a lineup of relatively new models. Its flagship, the *Helgoland*, was the first of the state-of-the-art Helgoland class. In terms of capital ships, the Channel Fleet would be overwhelmed.

If under those circumstances, the Empire had chosen them as its opponent, even if they ended up getting cut in the process, they could probably have thwarted its aims.

But that hope was only feasible if the imperial fleet chose to meet them for a knife fight. Instead it was futile because the enemy ships were paying them no mind and heading in a different direction. They were leisurely escorting the transport ships north. It was certain—completely certain—that if they landed successfully, the Entente Alliance would fall. So the only time to take a risk was now. They had been lucky to discover them so early.

If they had naively gone out to challenge them to a naval battle unawares, they probably would have been sneak attacked and forced to flee in a panic. Discovering them first was truly good fortune. The problem now was how to handle the situation.

"Request backup from army mages! Send in the patrol boats and do anything necessary to beat a path to the capital ship!"

Will we make it? It only lasted a moment, but the doubt that flitted across the minds of the Channel Fleet Command personnel was serious. Whether or not the Republic's nightmare of the Entente Alliance collapsing came true hinged on them making it in time. *We just have to.* They were determined.

"Send out any ship available! Full-power sortie!"

Sadly, they were out of luck.

As they raised fists and were about to advance toward the enemy, they received bad news from the military attaché in the Entente Alliance and understood. They had been too late. And so they swore with all their might that *Next time... Next time, we'll get them.*

>>> **DECEMBER 4, UNIFIED YEAR 1924, COMMONWEALTH, *LONDINIUM*,** <<<
UNDISCLOSED LOCATION

After the shocking report that the Imperial Navy had taken an amphibious force to the Osfjord and launched a decisive landing operation, the atmosphere in the room was unbearably bitter.

The agony of the deteriorating situation was so terrible that it even dashed all hope for the nearing Christmas leave. Contrary to the Commonwealth's futile wish that the Empire, Republic, and Entente Alliance would just destroy one another, the Empire continued to pile on victories. By virtue of their shared view on the situation, the entire group of people connected to the Commonwealth's intelligence agency had fallen to the gloom. But the office itself wasn't out of sorts. The unpleasantness of the situation was due to the foul mood of the office's chief occupant, Major General Donald Habergram, which was permeating the room to a preposterous extent. He had a difficult personality to begin with, and now he was especially irritated.

Heads would roll at the first careless remark. The radio operator who saw the next notification that arrived was truly lucky. Normally, delivering a report was as nerve-racking as being shoved into a minefield, but this time was different.

To be blunt—it wasn't bad news! How many days had it been since he had nearly run like this to inform his superior? Since Dacia had fallen? Of course, since it was his job, he couldn't be swayed by likes or dislikes, but it was true that there was nothing he hated more than reporting bad news.

"Urgent message from the auxiliary ship *Lytol.*"

"Let's hear it."

Without flinching at the disgruntled tone, he relayed the facts in a straightforward way. They had received reports from their intelligence-collecting ships disguised as civilian vessels as well as their armed merchant cruisers, but out of all the messages, this one was sent at the highest emergency-level priority, even using a onetime pad.

He'd thought it would be exceptionally horrible news, but when he deciphered it, to his surprise, it wasn't bad, at least. Well, he wasn't sure if it was something to get very happy about, but anyhow.

"The Entente Alliance is requesting transport of a VIP."

The content of the request was transporting a VIP. More specifically, the person in question was one of the ten councilors of state who, in practical terms, held the most authority in the nation. Essentially, the Entente Alliance, no longer concerned about appearances, was shedding decorum in order to establish a government in exile. That was much better than the country obediently surrendering to the Empire. And it wasn't necessarily a wholly bad development in terms of the Commonwealth's national interests, either.

"…Isn't that Foreign Office business?"

But to the one receiving the message, it seemed like the matter was out of their jurisdiction. The job of the Foreign Strategy Division was planning and analysis. They were decidedly not a contact point. In fact, they wanted to avoid any actions that could compromise their intelligence gathering, as much as possible. Honestly, they were loath to get involved.

Ordinarily, it was the Foreign Office that accepted diplomatic requests. In the case of the Entente Alliance, the official channel was through the embassy on the ground there. And would the heads of a country really try to negotiate asylum directly with a room in the strategy division of the intelligence agency? It wasn't unthinkable to assume they must have just contacted the wrong place.

The radio operator understood the higher-ranking officer's suspicion immediately. He had the same doubts. Still, he had to give a short explanation, even to General Habergram, who hated wasting time.

"Someone from the Entente Alliance Navy made contact personally."

"Did they find us out? If so, all I can think is that we have a huge security leak somewhere."

"No, it seems they've contacted all our vessels."

They hadn't called a ship from the Commonwealth's intelligence agency. No, the ship just happened to be the auxiliary ship *Lytol*. Actually, they had tried every vessel stopping at the Entente Alliance.

Though they were deeply concerned about the possibility of an intelligence leak, in this case, the request was simply the natural outcome. Surely the caller was just trying their luck. In that case, however, they were dealing with a bothersome amateur.

"No regard for appearances, hmm? What a bad move. Do you have the list?"

"Here it is. It seems the others were just regular ferries."

This had to be the worst way to go about it. If you seek help indiscriminately, word will definitely get out somehow. As more people learn a secret, the risk of it being leaked grows exponentially. And their opponent in this case is the Empire, waging war seriously as a world power. He couldn't imagine that imperial intelligence was slacking off. So if these guys were trying to pull off a secret asylum operation, they should probably proceed with a bit more caution. Well, maybe he couldn't expect so much from the Entente Alliance government, now in a state of panic and dysfunction.

Even if they weren't planning on doing it in secret, the fact that the heads of government were preparing to flee would no doubt demoralize the citizens…although they may very well shift toward nationalistic resistance, so it was also possible to imagine a hopeful outcome.

The timing was delicate, given they were expecting a large-scale imperial offensive on the northern lines at just about any moment. Honestly, if word of this spread now, it could weaken Entente Alliance resistance. But if it held out heroically and the government called for resistance…it might have a chance.

If that happened, the Empire would be forced to tie up troops in Entente Alliance territory, unlike in Dacia.

"What should we do, sir? If we're going to accept, we need to hurry."

Actually, in the case of Dacia, things had happened so quickly that the government-in-exile idea didn't work out. With that failure behind them, they knew that this issue demanded a rapid response. They were receiving the message right when they keenly felt the need to play a card. An Operations officer asked a question, taking the initiative to suggest it wouldn't be wise to pass on this turn: "Shouldn't we make a move?"

"I'm opposed. I don't think anything good will come of drawing attention to our armed merchant cruisers."

From elsewhere came a proposal for cautious handling of the situation. After all, armed merchant cruisers were already in violation of international law as well as various states' laws. If their orders to collect intelligence and disrupt trade were exposed, there would be an uproar. Disguising armed vessels as merchant ships to get them into the port was a legal problem. In a worst-case scenario, all the crew members would be declared pirates and arrested.

Even if breaking international law didn't nag their conscience, every evil organization needs calculated reluctance based on profits and loss.

You weren't supposed to break treaties; you were supposed to force the other party to break them.

At least, General Habergram intended to toe the line of what he could get away with at the bounds of international law.

"I want to avoid being boarded either way. How's the loading going?"

Although they shared the same thought, the leader's idea was somewhat different. After all, they knew a little bit more than the others—that

Chapter **III**

Intelligence was proactively working to clear their bad name after Dacia and had learned several interesting things.

"I think it's almost done…"

"…Then at this point a little extra cargo won't make much difference. Who is the VIP?"

After all, the Intelligence agents had counted their chickens before they had hatched and suggested it was because Dacia collapsed so readily that the Republic and the Entente Alliance had more time to construct third lines. They thought this would be a good time to redeem themselves. Intelligence collection and analysis was proceeding at a fantastic pace on the northern lines, and they were really getting results.

The intelligence that the auxiliary ship had so rapidly acquired and the machinery they had used was secretly on board. They had even learned that the Imperial Navy was planning a landing operation.

So it went without saying that an inspection of that ship would be bad. That said, they already had so much dangerous cargo that adding something new wouldn't do anything.

He didn't think throwing in a little more problematic cargo would change their situation much.

"A councilor."

One of the ten councilors of state establishing a government in exile in the Commonwealth was fraught with political implications. Officers couldn't work in Intelligence unless they had a nose for understanding politics, so it was evident to all of them. That probably went for any outstanding staff officer.

It was no small thing for a politician at the level of minister of state to be appointed as a government in exile by the previous government with the proper authority.

And General Habergram was far from inept—which was why he hesitated.

"…Wait a moment."

It was certainly true that if they succeeded in getting him asylum, that achievement would overshadow their previous failure. They might be able to prevent the nightmare of the Empire smoothly building government organizations, as it was doing in Dacia, from happening in the

Entente Alliance. That was how well the man in charge here understood
the issues.

But that would all only happen if the bid for asylum succeeded. If it
failed, the political and diplomatic risks were huge. Additionally, the
fallout was so far-reaching that this matter was far above what General
Habergram could decide on his own.

And he was a person who knew the extent of his authority. He understood very well what wasn't up to his discretion. That was precisely why
he was selected to hold the reins. His ability to make calm judgments
and not go off the rails was valued.

In actuality, the reason they had thrown someone so toxic in there
was to get the department under control. He swiftly had a document
prepared, took it, and stood. This was a matter that demanded extra
attention to confidentiality. And so, taking a few escorts along, he left at
once for the Office of the Admiralty.

"Habergram here. Is the First Lord of the Admiralty in?"

A military policeman stood guarding the office. Habergram had to
put up with the duty officer's suspicious look, given the man's job.

He himself had always been terribly nervous when he had to stop officers of a higher rank when he was younger. With that in mind, he made a
mental note that this officer had to be quite a serious-minded young man.

"He is. Do you have an appointment?"

"No. There's an urgent matter I'd like to ask him about."

After the duty officer confirmed a few things, the general was shown
into the office.

As soon as he ran inside, he asked everyone else to leave. After all the
attendants had been sent away, he made sure no one else was around and
then gave his report.

"General, I trust you can make this quick."

"Sir, something I'm unable to handle on my discretion alone has
occurred."

He passed the First Lord the summary he had prepared. At the same
time, he gave him the outline verbally. As he watched his superior look
over the document, he supplied more detailed explanations as necessary
to help him understand.

Anyhow, every second counted. There could be no hesitation, but at the same they couldn't act thoughtlessly. That was why the basis of the decision, the report, had to be given as quickly as possible. The Entente Alliance was collapsing with each passing moment. The life of the country, measured by an hourglass, had begun trickling away. If they wanted to save its invaluable political fruits, they had to act basically right now.

"An Entente Alliance councilor is requesting carriage via our auxiliary ship."

"What a hairy situation. There aren't any civilian vessels of Commonwealth nationality anchored in the area?"

Politically, creating the government in exile and getting in the Empire's way was a promising choice. But it was the difficulty of the task that he was considering and thus asking about.

The reason was crystal clear. Any major political achievement that came without risk-taking was a dream. While a government in exile would be an excellent way to harass the Empire, getting the core members out of the country in secret and then taking them home to a supposedly neutral country was so difficult that calling it "hairy" seemed dismissive.

Yes, the issue was how to transport them. How could they get them to Commonwealth territory? Even if the *Lytol* was in disguise, it was still unquestionably conspicuous.

After all, it was registered not as a ferry but purely as a cargo-passenger ship. It wouldn't be strange for them to call at any port, but anyone watching the mouth of the bay would definitely notice.

It was too great a risk to carry someone so important in such a vessel.

"Four or five. But they're all regular liners. I'm sure the Empire is watching them."

The problem was that most ships of Commonwealth nationality had been avoiding docking at Entente Alliance ports. More accurately, since the start of the war, anything trying to call at Entente Alliance bay facilities was being blown out of the water. It wasn't so much a matter of neutrality; the Commonwealth was simply worried about getting mixed up in a fight.

So the only boats in the ports right now were the regular ferry lines scheduled beforehand. But they were almost completely filled with ordinary citizens trying to evacuate and get asylum. Apart from a slim minority of charter ships, there were no other vessels anchored besides ferries. It would be weirder if the auxiliary ship didn't stand out.

He couldn't imagine the Empire overlooking it. Even if they weren't deliberately keeping watch, it was a ship from the Commonwealth—sailors at the port would find it a rare sight, and hopeful civilians would be literally begging to board. The Empire was bound to hear of it somehow.

The ship stood out so much, the Office of the Admiralty was considering sending a diplomat to go retrieve the intelligence.

At least the *Lytol* wasn't armed in a conspicuous way. But it was moving at 29.5 knots, which was faster than a cargo-passenger ship ever needed to go, and on top of that, it was even secretly carrying a seaplane, nominally for sightseeing flights, and a measure of firepower. They were disguised as hoses and recreational equipment, at least.

If it weren't for the confidential materials, even if the ship was boarded, there wouldn't be any issues under international law. The crew might be made up of mages, but that was a decision a business could freely make. After all, the Commonwealth was a free country.

But if they were caught assisting with asylum from a country at war, things would get tricky. It would raise the issue of whether they should give the refugee up without resistance... The Entente Alliance would probably want him to be guarded; it would be furious if they just handed him over.

So what would happen if he had the crew fight the imperial boarding unit? The answer was obvious. It would come around to bite them in the ass.

"*Lytol* can move at a fairly quick clip, but can it outrun the imperial patrol boats?"

Even if the *Lytol* was fast, it had its limits. And considering marine mages or aircraft might be present, it was impossible to say whether it could make a clean getaway. To go a step further, was a ship really even the best transportation method in this case?

"All right. We'll transfer them to a submarine on the water."

That must have been why the First Lord of the Admiralty made a daring decision. The ship could certainly sink. Or the living quarters could be attacked.

But if they used a vessel that could operate underwater, they could stay hidden.

"A submarine? We have one we can use?"

"Admiral Meyer guarantees it. In any case, we need to consult with the submarine squadron."

We weren't given torpedoes but eels. Maybe load your
tubes with development personnel instead.

————— Imperial Navy Internal Submarine Manual, *The Torpedo Crisis* —————

Upon hearing the news that the city of Os had fallen, coupled with the Imperial Army's advance on the interior, everyone of that generation understood that this was the end for the Entente Alliance leadership. Some lifted a glass to toast the Imperial Army's victory. Others downed bitter drinks in anticipation of that victory. Everyone saw it as the end of the Entente Alliance.

But they cried out to encourage the ones directly involved, who were beginning to break in the face of their fatherland's looming fate; it wasn't over yet. The Empire's victory was not certain. Only the government had given up.

The civilians, the people, were not defeated.

"…So are we ready to sow our seed?"

"The Republic agreed and…the Commonwealth also agreed to take someone as a diplomat."

Resistance could continue outside the fatherland.

Yes, the war against the Empire would carry on beyond their borders.

"Well then, shall we jointly sign over our authority?"

"In that case, I think the recipient should be Foreign Affairs Councilor Abensoll."

"No, I think we should send the youngest, Culture Councilor Korsor, as our ambassador."

"I disagree. You're the better man for the job, Councilor Abensoll."

Someone had to survive and continue the fight, to declare, *We're still here.*

And it was the soldiers who would act based on the councilors' intentions. The reality was obvious, but the army did what the government demanded. Everyone would do all they could for their country, which was how it should be in a unified nation. If there was one thing that was often forgotten in the big picture, it's that those soldiers who are asked to give their all and sacrificed by the politicians in the name of the fatherland have families and happy households. And so that day before deploying, the Entente Alliance mages had only a short time to say their farewells.

"Good luck."

"…I'm sorry," Colonel Sue quietly apologized as he embraced his tearful wife. She would evacuate to another country to avoid the fighting. The fact that they were a family who could choose that option was Sue's only consolation as head of the household. He should probably have been happy he could have his family go to the Unified States.

Still, the way things had turned out meant he had no choice but to send them away. *Probably the only thing I—no, every Entente Alliance soldier—can do is hug their family and exchange hopes of safety. Our fatherland is no longer safe.*

"Dad?"

"Mary, look after your mother. And take care of yourself."

"…You can't come with us?"

"I'm sorry. I have work again."

He forced himself to remember that he was still lucky. He had the connections to at least get his family to safety. Given the congested maritime traffic and issues with controlling the sea routes, it wasn't an option open to many people. He did feel a bit guilty, but if he could protect his family, he had no regrets.

Of course, it wasn't what Sue wanted. He would have preferred to spend peaceful days in the warmth of his family. If he had known this was going to happen, he would have gone home more often. *Why didn't I appreciate what a blessing that was to have my home so close at hand?*

I should have spoken to my daughter more. There are so many things I still want to tell my wife. So many regrets. It was stupid of me to believe our lives would go on unchanged forever.

It was a feeling even he couldn't explain, but when he loosened the arms he had unconsciously wrapped around his wife, as if sweeping away

some awkwardness, he managed to put on a smile as he crouched down to his daughter's eye level.

"Anson…"

"I may not have been a very good parent, but I hope someday you'll think of me as a father you can be proud of."

"It's okay. You're my dad! Oh, but you should shave."

She was such a sweet girl. He had hugged her in spite of himself; he wanted to grin at her ticklishness.

"You're right. I really should be good and shave."

"Get it together, Dad!"

"Yeah, you're right. I gotta get it together."

The most Sue could do as a father was laugh like that with a wry smile. The moment where his daughter scolded him for not shaving often enough—that was normal life. The essence of his precious everyday world.

"Well, this is no good… I can't have you worrying about me. I'd rather remember you with a smile."

"Please stay safe."

The fact that his wife bravely wished him well, even after she had broken into tears, pained his heart. He wanted to board the ship with them, to live out their lives together. But he was a soldier bound by duty.

Duty. Aghh, annoying, noble duty. O Fatherland, I give myself to thee. So, God, please bless my home, the country my family loves.

"Dad, it's a little early, but…Merry Christmas!"

As Sue steeped in sentiment, his daughter pointed at a large case before she boarded the ship with her mother, telling him to take good care of it.

Momentary relief filled his heart as he watched them go, as well as the sadness at their parting that could very well be final. But if there was one thing he didn't want to do, it was regret the moment. There was nothing unluckier than tears in a send-off. He forced himself to smile and then suddenly realized the case was gone. He was confused until he noticed an old acquaintance holding it out to him with an easygoing look on his face.

"Sue, a Christmas present from your daughter. Take it with you."

The bizarre remark came from Councilor Cazor, who was present to see the evacuees off. Wondering why the councilor would know about his daughter's present, Sue grabbed the case only to be puzzled by its unexpected weight.

There weren't cookies or a wool sweater inside. It was something much heavier.

"Councilor Cazor, what is this?"

"Go ahead and open it. That's an SMG from A.S. Weapons in the Waldstätte Confederacy. Durable with a body like an LMG."

At the councilor's suggestion, Sue moved to the shade and opened the case. What greeted him was a brand-new submachine gun—a fairly costly model that would work well in conjunction with his orb. Clips, magic bullets, a set of maintenance tools—it came with everything.

"How did she get ahold of something like this...?" He admired the solid yet light build as his examination continued. It accepted the same caliber as his rifle and had a shorter range, but it was easier to handle in a close-quarters fight. It was a good choice for facing anyone who snuck up on him. Additionally, the limited range meant a comparatively lower risk of accidentally shooting an ally, so that was a big plus.

That's why he had to wonder.

How in the world did my daughter get this?

"It's a personal gift from a lousy Commonwealth fellow. For a country with such horrible food, they sent us a good man, wouldn't you say?"

"Sorry?"

"Apparently, he saw your daughter crying in the park. He put your initials on it."

"Oh, the A.S. is for my name?"

He was sure the engraved letters were the factory's logo; the level of effort made him smile.

I don't know if my daughter is sinful or if heaven simply loves her, but she sure wooed that intelligence agent... Now and again, those Albion chaps actually can do something nice.

"Surely it's the initials for Arnold & Smith Weapons."

"No, apparently, that's stamped on the underside." Councilor Cazor looked somehow amused as he explained.

"That vexing Commonwealth gent was probably moved by your

daughter's tears and gave her a discount. Apparently, she paid the special price of a hundred pounts. That's surprisingly cheap, Colonel."

Thanks for giving your dad such a great present, sweetie. He wanted to give her a kiss if he could.

…So this is what the strength of a hundred men feels like.

"I'm proud to have such a happy family."

"I'm sorry, Colonel. I'm afraid we're going to have to ask too much of you."

"You arranged the ship for me. For my part, I'm prepared to protect my family's home with my own two hands."

"We're counting on you."

One man bowed, and the other smiled in receipt of the gesture. They didn't need to say anything more.

〉〉〉   DECEMBER 11, UNIFIED YEAR 1924, EMPIRE, RHEINE HOTEL   〈〈〈
DINING ROOM

For Tanya, it's a wonderful autumn lunch. The appetizer had been a delightful pâté of seasonal fish. The skillfully prepared dish used fish so fresh it seemed almost a waste to make them into a paste. No praise would be enough. It was simply sublime.

The potato soup was legendary. She was used to eating potatoes, so it felt strange to enjoy them so much. That said, it wasn't a bad thing. Battlefield rations could hardly compare when it came to the level of care devoted to their creation, and as such, the dish was an embodiment of humanity's delightful creativity.

She has heard the main course, which hasn't yet arrived, is whitefish. The waiter explained the dish so proudly she has high expectations. If the hotel's waiter says it's that good, not only should the quality of the ingredients be high, but she's certain it will demonstrate the chef's skills, too.

And the fact that her dining mates are also happily expectant makes the meal even more fun. With her are members of the reservists association and notable figures from the region. To think that she gets to network with them. She can only marvel at her luck.

As they have an understanding of soldierly habits, the gift from the troops up north, Koskenkorva,[10] is going over well. I can see why this stuff is notorious for increasing your chances of becoming an alcoholic.

Though they're old soldiers, they're mainly just men well-known around town who are getting on in years. They're probably just surprised by the curious flavor. And if they're happy to have an interesting story of receiving such a gift from a child of my age, even better. With her scheme going to plan, conversation flows naturally, and Tanya is able to enjoy herself quite a bit.

Even if she can't drink with them, it was worth the trouble of confiscating a case of the stuff for private use at parties. She's most satisfied.

As she's thinking how happy she is about the results of her labor, she's looking forward to enjoying the sautéed whitefish when the waiter brings not the highly anticipated main dish but the receiver of an ominous-looking black telephone.

"Miss von Degurechaff?" He deliberately asks her if she will accept the call. She's on her way back to Central, having lunch with these local reservists and celebrities as an excuse to pass through a resort town. Who gets a wartime phone call in that setting?

My best day off has turned into my worst in an instant.

I'm also now dubious that I'll really get to spend Christmas on leave like I was promised.

She takes the respectfully proffered receiver with reluctance. If it weren't her duty, she would want to run away. This has to be just how Churchill felt getting woken up by the news that his capital ships had been sunk.

Would someone make me a hellish cup of black coffee?

"This is Major General von Rudersdorf of the General Staff. Major Tanya von Degurechaff?"

---

[10] **Koskenkorva**　An alcoholic drink.

Chapter **IV**

"Yes, sir, this is she."

She knew before he even spoke. It was obviously a call from a military person. No statement of purpose or seasonal greeting. Not to mention, General von Rudersdorf is still at this moment on the forward-most line fighting the Entente Alliance. The implications are the opposite of this gorgeous luncheon—the telephone call will be an invitation back to the wretched front lines.

I want to go home right now. How could I have been so dense to come to this meeting where everyone would know exactly where I am?

"A notice from the General Staff Office. 'Assemble Major von Degure-chaff and her unit at once. Report in as soon as this is done.'"

"Understood, sir. We'll proceed to the nearest garrison at once, and I'll report in as soon as we're all gathered."

...It's an impressively impossible-to-misunderstand order to mobilize.

She has already responded to a pile of unreasonable General von Rudersdorf orders, but it seems he's going to work her some more. If this was going to happen, she should have blocked the radios and taken her time going back under the pretense of training.

Well, there's no use crying over whatever. She replaces the receiver and slips the waiter a generous tip.

It's not his fault the news is awful. She doesn't like it, but services must be compensated.

"Oh. Good news, Major von Degurechaff?"

But apparently, people give big tips when news is favorable. I can't help but think of that as emotional, illogical behavior, so I don't do that...but it seems the amount I gave was a signal to these local names, who hadn't heard, that the message was something fortunate.

I'm probably supposed to smile at these gentlemen and politely reply, but I'm not sure I can manage it.

In the end, her face wears an unrefined frown as she shakes her head. "No, sir. Unfortunately, it doesn't seem to be very good news."

"Oh! That's..."

The man with the expression of utter compassion on his face is truly a good person. Well, they have the goodwill of men who don't have to go to war.

To someone being sent on the assault, it's complicated, but it is what it is.

Polite manners are one of the most basic tools for keeping mistakes to a minimum. As such, it's only a matter of course that I follow the rules. At their core, human beings are political animals, but at the same time, they are social ones.

"Apologies, but I have orders. I'll have to leave early."

"...I wish you well, Major."

Can I say for sure that none of them are feeling lucky it's not them? Tanya decides it's a groundless suspicion and puts on a polite smile as she swallows her bitter thoughts and stands.

"Thank you. I hope you'll forgive my rudeness. Excuse me."

With those parting words and a bow, she takes her overcoat from the waiter and pays her bill. She's dressed formally—in uniform. Her overcoat, having been designed for practical use, is quite substantial. Somehow it bothers me, but the army can be irrational in the strangest ways.

Of course, I also have to wonder about people who wear trench coats as fashion...

While she was picking up her coat, a military vehicle had been sent over. A thoughtful waiter must have alerted the orderly in the waiting room. A car with her subordinate at the wheel is already standing by. The efficient arrangements make her feel a little better. Humans have to live with a positive outlook.

And so she finds the situation genuinely wonderful. She was right not to be stingy with the tips for the waiters.

It's also nice that they open the door so courteously. She quickly gets into the car, and it pulls out.

"Corporal, back to the barracks. Sorry, but if you can step on it..."

"Yes, ma'am."

The corporal takes off, and amid the slight jolts along the way, she decides to share her misfortune. I don't enjoy suffering alone. However, I don't mind making others suffer alone. Without even giving herself time to sink back into her seat, she boots up her computation orb. She connects to the garrison and calls the Officer of the Week. The fact that he answers on the second alert means he passes.

"What can I do for you, Major?"

Well, it's bad news. Rather than beat around the bush, I should just get to the point.

"Leave's been cut short! Issue mobilization orders immediately! All hands should assemble as of right now."

"…Yes, ma'am, mobilization orders, understood. I'll call everyone back from their half-day leave."

Well, my rest in this resort town is certainly over sooner than planned. Then Tanya has a vexing thought: the possibility that even before she applied for leave, General von Rudersdorf had been "kind" enough to hold her unit up near a naval base for a few days as nominal time off. It's totally possible. If, during a large-scale operation on the northern lines, they were transferring a unit that could keep itself safe from espionage, the General Staff certainly might have the 203rd Aerial Mage Battalion withdraw.

It's actually quite practical.

"Hurry. It's orders from the General Staff."

"Understood."

The fact that they single her out to give the orders makes her think the General Staff wants to hide something. Yes, upon closer consideration, there is something very unnatural about all this. Why now, of all times, is General von Rudersdorf from Operations personally in Norden on the pretext of an inspection?

>>> **TEMPORARY CAMP OF THE IMPERIAL ARMY'S 203RD BATTALION** <<<

"Telegram from the Imperial Navy Northern Sea Fleet Command!"

"…Read it."

From the fleet? That's the doubt in my mind. Tanya shares the question behind the puzzled looks of the 203rd Aerial Mage Battalion officers. Why did the fleet's command go to the trouble of sending us a telegram?

The fact that they aren't going through the regional army must mean this is what the General Staff wants? Or are they intervening directly?

Either way, I have a bad feeling about this. As Tanya interprets the situation, she presses the radio operator to read the telegram.

As the officers listen with question marks on their faces, he responds to her request and reads the mission orders. "These are search and destroy combat orders for the 203rd Battalion. All previous maneuvers are to be halted immediately. You are requested to proceed directly to the waters indicated, locate the enemy, and block off the area. That is all!"

Geez. They say "search and destroy" like it's nothing. Plus, nobody uses search and destroy these days! And mages don't have any way to navigate over the water, so how are we supposed to find enemies and block off an area? Talk about mission impossible.

As Lieutenant Serebryakov brings the document over, Tanya stares crankily at a navigation chart of Norden's coast spread out on her desk. She doesn't even usually look at these things. Realizing this, she can't help an inward sigh. It confronts her with the reality that she'll have to fly in airspace with no sense of place, and it makes her awfully depressed.

"Lieutenant, get me the combat control map for the Northern Sea area. Call Norden Control." This is making my brain hurt. Tanya shakes her head to clear her mind as Lieutenant Serebryakov brings her the requested map before trying to establish a line through to the local controllers.

"Yes, ma'am. Right away."

She hands over the map and receiver with crisp motions. It's Norden Control. We exchange just a word or two, and the radio operator connects me to someone from the navy. It's the worst when they don't pass you off irresponsibly but actually have good lateral cooperation.

At this rate, I won't be able to slack off and blame it on bad coordination. Maybe being *too* efficient is a bad thing. I suppose I should at least praise the integrity with which they do their work, though. I'm a good citizen, so it's only right that I commend my fellow countrymen for performing their duties.

When I think of that, I guess all I can do is stick it out for the public good.

Since I have no other choice, I make all the necessary calls without a minute wasted. Griping is a luxury and a waste of time. There is not a day in the life of a corporate warrior that they are allowed the indulgence of wasting time. In order to spend their off days as they wish, the highest level of job performance is essential.

For a soldier, not a thing changes.

"Lieutenant! Where is the Northern Sea Fleet now?"

"I'll ask right away!"

The military machine is starting to move, and I'm one of its gears, Tanya automatically thinks. And this gear needs to know the positions of the remaining Entente Alliance ships, as well as her friendly fleet. She has crammed the general memo on the Entente Alliance ships into her head at least, so she dredges it up while quickly confirming the crucial points.

Even if the Northern Sea Fleet deployed in this area isn't the Empire's strongest, the High Seas Fleet, it has some powerful vessels, including capital ships. Their training is trustworthy, and ever since the landing operation a few days ago, we've been able to coordinate to some extent. But an unplanned battle is a different story.

Tanya manages to consider all the most important facts while having Lieutenant Serebryakov make phone calls. She has no choice but to handle this efficiently, but it's in an area she has no experience with, not to mention a rapid response mission. Maybe that's why she can't calm down and has only a tenuous hold on the urge to give a thousand different instructions.

She takes deep breaths—small ones so no one around her will notice. Sometimes it's useful to be short. It makes you less conspicuous, but at times like this, it's really handy.

Still, we've never even done an exercise over water, and now we're being thrown into a real marine battle? The target is a group of fleeing Entente Alliance warships. Missions to assist in pursuit are so hard. It's like trying to negotiate an acquisition without knowing anything about the other side. If we're in such a superior position that these talks would work out, it begs the question whether negotiations are even needed in the first place.

Hence, each minute feels like a hundred years, and when the situation report that Tanya is waiting for comes in and Lieutenant Serebryakov hands her the receiver, she snatches it away. With her other hand she holds a pen, ready to make notes at any moment on the map she had Lieutenant Weiss spread on the table.

"This is Major von Degurechaff of the 203rd Aerial Mage Battalion. We received a mission to support your ships from the General Staff. What's the situation?"

"The second fleet of battle cruisers has left the Kiël naval base. Submarine Task Force 13 went out ahead of them to build a patrol net."

Luckily, someone from the navy who knows what's going on fills her in. According to him, the emergency-dispatched battle cruisers are already searching for the enemy.

"So we'll be the vanguard for the battleships? Thrilling!"

Lieutenant Weiss has a penchant for keeping things lighthearted, and Tanya makes a mental note. A vice commander who stands out by paying attention to the atmosphere of the troops is hard to come by. But what he said is actually correct. Just being the vanguard would make them look good.

"What are you getting all excited about? We're a rapid-response mage battalion—it's what we do."

Soon enough, she receives the report that the unit is ready to sortie, so she goes to meet them.

"Your commander!"

Battalion Commander Tanya von Degurechaff's expression must look normal to Weiss and everyone else as they meet her with salutes. I'm confident that I act the part of an unflappable officer that well. She returns their salutes nonchalantly, glances around, and nods in satisfaction. Well, internally she's over it all, but still.

"Thanks. At ease. Lieutenant Weiss?"

"Ma'am. I'll give the briefing."

Having one's subordinates do the annoying stuff is the privilege and duty of all officers throughout history. An organization runs on hierarchy by nature. If a superior is stealing work from their reports, that workplace is topsy-turvy.

"Yesterday before dawn, a scout plane belonging to the 224th Night Reconnaissance Team spotted a gathering of vessels."

Chapter **IV**

Photos on the board show multiple Entente Alliance battleships, including a coastal defense ship. The Entente Alliance is hardly a naval power, but it's still an armament lineup on par with what you'd expect of a player on the world stage. It's a formidable threat even the Empire can't ignore.

To Tanya, the obsession with big ships and their big guns is passé. Still, she is aware they have to be wary of heavily armed combat vessels. As one data point, take the fact that a battleship's naval gun fires way more iron than an entire division of infantry. On top of that, the porcupine-like anti–air fire and marine mage interception makes it a difficult net to slip through.

Still, they should be easier to approach than the U.S. ships in the Marianas were. It's a question of how much easier.

"Upon analysis, the General Staff has concluded these are the main remaining forces of the Entente Alliance fleet attempting to escape. It's obvious, don't you think?"

We've estimated the various paths they might take, from a beeline for the Republic to a meandering route to the Commonwealth. But it's clear that their goal is to shake off imperial pursuit and get away. Naturally, the pursuing side wants to locate and annihilate them.

We've received reports that the Commonwealth Navy is doing exercises just outside our territorial waters, which is a real headache. We've been notified to avoid firing stray shots. On the other hand, we've notified them that regardless of what happens on the open sea, anything violating imperial waters will be shot at. Overall, it's a delicate situation that puts a huge strain on the nerves.

"Fleet Command has ordered all ships to find and annihilate the Entente Alliance vessels. The General Staff's order for us is to support them."

Lieutenant Weiss narrows down the broad range of meanings *support* could have. Then he looks to me as if the rest is my job, and yeah, I don't want to look like I'm getting paid to do nothing, so I take over.

"Battalion, it's as he said. Reconnaissance Mage Task Force 2 with Northern Sea Fleet Command has gone out ahead of us. And apparently, a 'neutral country' is hard at work doing exercises in nearby waters. Take care not to hit them."

It must be really hard for the scouts to stay on top of them in this rain. Although I must say, it seems backward to send a unit to watch the Commonwealth exercise while we're trying to find the Entente Alliance. But there's no reason to lower morale by making that kind of remark.

"We're going to head north and meet up with them as soon as we get data. This goes without saying, but we'll be playing it by ear."

"Understood."

"According to Intelligence, the enemy is fast. And apparently, they have marine mages. The scope of our mission includes eliminating those, but reconnaissance is top priority."

Our mission is of the common enough "search and destroy" variety—we're just being told to prioritize the "search" part.

"Meet at the exercise ground runway in sixty minutes in full gear. Any questions?"

…Well, they're my war-obsessed underlings. They're full of fight.

Without raising any questions, as usual, the unit eventually takes off an hour later. We head west at cruising speed as we climb.

Apart from a few irritating false reports from friendly submarine units, there is no news. If there is anything to say at all, it's that the wind and rain have picked up, and our visibility has rapidly deteriorated.

I look around, but I can't even see my battalion.

I'm confident in our ability to fly in formation, so I'll be pretty upset if we get separated and can't bring our full power to the fight. Our saving grace is that we shouldn't have anyone with a sense of direction that hopeless in this unit.

"Control to Pixie. No reports of contact."

"Pixie 01, roger. How about the weather? Can we expect it to improve?"

Still, I'm fed up with these tiresome reports from the rear. No reports of contact means that even though we've been flying all this time, we have to keep searching.

If we wanted to get above the rain clouds, we would have to climb awfully high. Instead, we just get wet. Even though our defensive shells repel water, getting rained on doesn't do much for the mood.

"Sending war zone data from Urban Control... Looks like it won't for a while. I feel for the ground troops. They must be in hell with this cold."

"The whole combat zone is hard rain and storm winds. A level-two flood warning and flight restrictions are being issued? Got it. How are the other units in the operation doing?" Tanya checks the data as it suddenly comes in and gets confirmation that the weather is only getting worse, which boggles her mind. That said, if the flight warnings become no-fly advisories, they can return to base.

"First Squadron has left Kiël naval base on a search and destroy mission. The air force is sending up a special force recon company. Make sure you don't accidentally shoot them."

We have other forces searching? I suppose that's better than not. Guess we should keep searching till we get permission to go home. That was what she was thinking when...

"Pixie 01, roger. Can you let me know where the exercising Commonwealth ships a...?"

Far down.

Even in the downpour, an unmistakable roar and the sound of gunfire abruptly draw her focus to something below her.

"An explosion?"

It was the dull boom of something detonating underwater. It reverberates more than you would expect, especially in the quiet night sky.

When she squints, she can just barely make out several floating shapes.

The next moment, her eyes pop open. In the searchlight are enemy ships.

It was an awful sight for the men on board the submarine belonging to Imperial Northern Sea Fleet's Submarine Task Force 13. The captain, who was looking through the periscope and saw the huge splashes the moment the explosions sounded, was so shocked at first that he couldn't get his mouth closed again. When they realized they didn't hear any secondary explosions, everyone looked to the heavens.

The torpedoes had gone off early.

The six *aals*[11] they'd only just been issued really were more useless than actual eels. The furious sailors spewed strings of curses, swearing that next time they'd load the torpedo development team, who were only good for wasting the budget, into the tubes and fire *them*.

To them, the results the devs had gotten meant nothing.

The Entente Alliance vessels they'd discovered wouldn't sink; the six torpedoes they'd launched after making careful calculations in anticipation of success had gotten impatient and blown up too soon.

It was no surprise that the navigation officer who had gone to such pains to get them into a striking position was looking dazed. Even the captain's thoughts froze for a moment at the sudden scene that seemed to scoff at all their hard work.

What he saw through the periscope was the Entente Alliance fleet changing formations for counter-sub combat. Then marine mages began sweeping the water's surface for periscopes. As the crew hurriedly pulled theirs in, they found themselves furious—they didn't want to die because of such a stupid failure.

Actually, they didn't know it at the time, but…given the outcome, they had actually pulled off a fantastic assist. When the Entente Alliance fleet realized an imperial submarine was targeting it, it entered counter-sub combat. As a result, if only for a moment…everyone was looking down.

And that's why their response to what came out of the sky in the next moment was delayed. Make them look down, then have the real attack swoop in from above for the kill.

To Colonel Anson Sue, who realized they'd been caught, it was an awfully cunning one-two punch.

"They got us, those bastards!"

"Where was the leak?! No, now they're— Those fuckers!"

---

[11] **aal** Pet name for German torpedoes. In German, *aal* means "eel."

Chapter IV

It was truly the worst possible timing for the Entente Alliance fleet. Since they had transitioned into counter-sub combat, the destroyer escorting the flagship had moved away. Not only that, but the marine mages had rushed out to suppress the submarine, and the lookouts, staring into the darkness, were all scouring the sea so as not to miss any torpedo wakes. That was when it happened.

The enemy mage battalion that had been lurking in the sky made a full-speed charge at the flagship.

Only a few managed to take off, including Colonel Sue.

But the imperial mages plunging down, trading altitude for acceleration, were far faster than they were, and the fact that they had control of the air meant he couldn't think of a way this desperate situation could get any worse.

Still, all Sue could do was climb. If he didn't, that ship and the seed of his fatherland's future would be sunk.

Major von Degurechaff's feelings at that moment, the time, the place, would be the subject of many inquiries in later years. In reality, the 203rd Aerial Mage Battalion, including Tanya, is in partial chaos at finding themselves in an unexpected encounter, but they manage to charge as a training reflex.

"Battalion! Break! Break! Prepare to attack!"

Making the split-second decision to engage, Tanya enters a headlong dive; she has no experience fighting ships. The reason is that supposedly great balance of power. Thanks to diplomatic efforts, the leading nations have avoided serious armed conflicts up until this war. In other words, this is practically the first mage attack on a ship in history.

And that was why it's all they can do to act according to their exercises. She scatters the unit, and dodging anti–air fire all the while, everyone swoops in at the same time. It's a tactic championed by a doctrine that has only been verified theoretically. No one knows whether it will work or not until the 203rd Aerial Mage Battalion tests it with their own flesh and blood.

Really, the receiving end of the attack was in the same boat. The ability of aircraft to attack ships was only just starting to be discussed, so no one was focused on mages, who have less firepower. As a result, they had only just touched on anti-mage combat in training exercises.

In a sense, it was an extremely crude firefight for both sides.

"Pixie 01 to CP! Contact! Contact!"

"CP to Pixie 01. What is it?"

It's hard to do your best when you find yourself stuck in a battle where you weren't expecting to get shot at. In that sense, Tanya can't help but hate the easygoing CP radio operator. Internally, she can't stop griping, *What the hell did you mean, telling us there'd be no contact?* But a calmer part of her brain isn't very impressed with the enemy's anti–air fire, which is a relief.

Actually, the enemy's protective fire is so poor it doesn't even come close to the American empire's anti-aircraft fire Tanya is thinking of. It's sparse enough that she can evade simply by flying aimlessly, inwardly outraged and wondering what the other search units have been doing, so it's evident that it isn't much to worry about.

"I'm taking fire! That's definitely the flash of a battle cruiser gun. Two hundred off the coast of Wiengenberg."

As she makes the report, she immediately breaks formation. After all, naval guns are a much greater threat than small arms or even most field artillery. Even a single autocannon uses 20 mm ammunition, the same class as a heavy machine gun on land. The powerful high-angle cannons are 127 mm. The shells they're aiming at her won't allow anyone with a human body to just walk away from a direct hit. If we stay in tight formation, the enemy anti–air guns will have their way with us.

"Battalion, don't bunch up! Make sure you attack the mages *and* the ships. Don't get too distracted by one or the other!"

Everywhere around me is dark, but I'm sure I'm exposed. When she realizes that, she can hardly believe how unexpected this is. Her mission was to find the enemy. If the submarines, the scout planes that went out ahead, or the company of recon mages discovered the enemy, Tanya's unit might have taken over monitoring, depending on the situation; it was supposed to be an easy mission. Entering the effective firing range of enemy ships and engaging was never part of the plan.

But if she squints, she can see a light reminiscent of a muzzle flash from

Chapter IV

below. It must be one of our submarines torpedoing them. *If it wasn't for the noise from the explosion, I probably wouldn't have noticed it.* The thought that she had narrowly escaped making an error frightens her. If she hadn't noticed, she would no doubt have ended up being grilled by an investigative commission. Boy, am I glad the torpedo's wake caught her eye. But I can't be completely happy because if she had been a little farther away, she could have noticed and been fine.

"Ngh! Anti-mage counterattack detected! Anti-air disciplined fire incoming!"

"I'm picking up mages! Damn it! We've got marine mages incoming!"

Her talented subordinates have an appropriate understanding of the situation, so she isn't actually very worried. But any commander asking their subordinates to act in a situation they haven't been trained to handle has to at least acknowledge their right to scowl.

"All hands, engage at will! Follow your company commander's lead!"

As long as they are receiving an organized interception, it has to be dealt with, but she decides that rather than trying to control an entire battalion in the dark, it's better to let each company operate individually. We have to regain some degree of discipline and get out of here!

"Visibility is poor. Don't lose your depth perception! The air is dense, but don't forget we're over the sea! Take the humidity from the water into account. Our opponents are used to it! Maintain your altitude!"

The lower companies, Second and Third, seem to be in good positions. First and Fourth were on guard above, so they have some leeway in terms of their altitude. And as long as I'm personally commanding First Company, I want to push all the dangerous stuff onto Fourth. She makes some quick calculations and decides to adjust some things.

"Ngh, draw the mages away from the ships! Second and Third Companies, you're the vanguard! Keep those mages busy!"

Marine mages are a threat to aerial mages. It goes without saying that exposing myself to anti–air fire and enemy mages isn't a hobby of mine. Even the majority of my war-crazy subordinates probably aren't into it. We'd all like to avoid working in dangerous areas.

"Fourth Company, guard the rear. Help Second and Third withdraw. A shoot-out with the ships is out of the question."

Really, I want Fourth Company as my shield, but that's too much to ask for.

In that case, increasing the number of decoys will probably get me the best results. From the enemy's point of view, it must be easier to target the entire battalion.

"First Company, lament your misfortune—or sob with joy at your opportunity to earn commendations! Rejoice, for it is we who will harass the ships! Follow me!"

I'll have my underlings do the dangerous counter-mage warfare, and I'll mess with the boats.

""""Understood!"""""

"Plunging into the fleet is a bold move! Allow us to be the vanguard!"

The elated personnel of my company volunteer, but it won't do for me to follow their suggestion.

"Sorry, the commander leads the way. Get back."

This is the only time believing that commanders should lead the way is useful. Don't get me wrong, it's not like I want to expose myself to enemy fire. Nobody with common sense *wants* to be out front charging into a hail of bullets.

But that's an amateur's calculation. Of course, I don't *want* to do it, but since I know it's the safer option, I choose it without hesitation. Reason trumps fear.

To explain it simply, most of the bullets aimed at the leader of a pack will end up hitting the people behind them.

In a little more detail, with deflection shooting, if they open fire assuming I'm coming in at two hundred fifty, all I have to do is approach at three hundred. The difference will keep me safe in the lead. But what about the ones behind me? Yes, the enemy will correct their deflection to my speed, and it's the ones who follow who will rush straight into that.

Also, when moving away after the attack, it goes without saying that I'd rather have a shield behind me. Our eyes are in the front of our heads.

The more you think about it, the more dangerous the rear starts to sound.

In other words, being the bold commander out front is the safer policy. It's said that in war, whether you survive or not is determined by how cowardly you can be. I'm a coward, so I want to calmly maneuver myself into a safe position.

"Follow me. I say again, follow me."

For the moment, I look for a ship that isn't firing so heavily.

I don't even have to stop and think to know that only war junkies want to get up close and personal with the dense anti–air fire of cruisers or battle cruisers. You can see it in war videos or special reports. The anti-aircraft fire density of American ships was nine parts bullets to one part sky. I would practically despair just watching.

I don't care how strong mages' defensive shells are—I am absolutely not flying into a 127 mm high-angle gunshot.

This is a night battle, but even if we can expect some help from the cover of darkness, it's too dangerous to aim at one of the big ships known for anti–air fire.

Of course, the sensible way to do this is to attack a destroyer. In war, picking on the weak is justice. Hooray, justice.

"…Ah. Is that a destroyer? Well, whatever it is, let's get it!"

I can't really tell because it's dark, but there's a turret firing at random, so I can make out the shape of the ship.

Considering there are no ships in consort, it must be an isolated destroyer?

In that case, we don't have to worry about backup from other ships in the enemy fleet.

Based on that interpretation, we get into assault formation.

In order to dive all at once from forty-five hundred feet, we maintain the spindle shape and make minute adjustments to the angle of our assault.

"Gah! I'm hit! Heading back to base! No escort necessary."

But I guess you can't underestimate a destroyer. Just as we were about to strike, one of my men gets hit.

The main gun on a destroyer is 127 mm and can be effectively used for anti–air fire, so I reappraise the situation and decide we can't take it lightly. My mage who got shot seems able to fly, well, fine. Still, he doesn't look very good, so he has to drop out, I guess.

Since his mouth works, he'll fly back to base on his own. There's nothing else we can do for him. About the only thing we can do is hope he's good bait.

"Go on, get outta here. Okay, everyone, prepare explosion formulas. Given a typical destroyer's armor, we should be able to take it out if we aim for exposed depth charges or the torpedo tubes."

Tanya's able to instantly twist her body to evade a shot as she approaches, most certainly a result of her training. "Well, would you look at that? I can dodge them," she murmurs. She makes a mental note that her unit probably needs additional training as she returns fire.

The ones firing off interceptor formulas from below must be Entente Alliance direct support. *Since they're a destroyer's escort, there are probably only a few, but if they're brave enough to come up here, they can't be discounted.*

Just as she's thinking that, she seems to recognize one of the enemies, a mage who gave her a lot of trouble in the fjord. *He looks an awful lot like that fanatically patriotic monster.*

Maybe it's a coincidence, but you can kill a lousy enemy with less guilt than a good one. In that sense, it's a plus that this guy resembles a lousy one. It'll be refreshing to shoot him.

She changes gears and turns her attention to how best to attack. A heavy explosion type would blow up a wide area, but she'd be a sitting duck while she's using it. Out of the question. Shoot with her rifle? That probably wouldn't even count as harassment. Rejected.

That's when she realizes: *A dive at this speed must have a ton of kinetic energy.* All I have to do is literally assault him—with the sharp end of my rifle.

A fleeting intersection.

But Tanya's bayonet, propelled at the speed of her dive, cuts through the Entente Alliance mage's defensive shell and twists into him. A bayonet thrust by a mage going over four hundred knots is far more damaging than a lance charge from a medieval heavy cavalry member.

She jabs it in and, in satisfaction, watches the stunned face of the enemy soldier, who seems hardly able to believe something is piercing his abdomen, but when she tries to pull her bayonet out, she frowns slightly because it seems to have gone too far in and gotten stuck. Even the barrel is sticking into him, and Tanya struggles a bit to remove it.

"M...Mar..."

The enemy soldier, murmuring something that's not even a word, is fatally wounded. *Geez, what's that about?* she thinks, when she realizes he's groping at the air, trying as hard as he can to bring his writhing right arm around to the submachine gun on his back. So she decides to make a trade.

"Auf Wiedersehen." She murmurs the curt farewell with a smile. I admire him for his unexpected stubbornness, but I don't have time to go along with his futile resistance—I have to hurry on ahead. Shoving his right arm out of the way, she steals the submachine gun. Then she kicks the corpse away, already pushing it out of her mind, and takes a quick look at the weapon she's acquired.

It's a standard submachine gun. But oddly enough, it accepts imperial magic bullets. How nice, this trophy will prove unexpectedly useful. A Christmas present to myself. *Anyhow.* Tanya smiles at her clear path, feeling quite refreshed, and murmurs, "Now there's nothing in my way."

Yes, she's literally kicked the obstacles out of her path. All that's left is to evade the ship's wimpy anti–air fire, strike her blow, and disappear under the veil of night.

That said, war is a gentlemanly fight for survival wherein one must be the first to do what the enemy hates. And as a civilized individual with an education, Tanya will not use her pretty hands for a sophisticated game of cricket;[12] she understands the need to unhesitatingly kick the enemy's ass.

This situation demands the enemy's intentions be thwarted.

So what is the best way to bully them?

It's simple. The enemy fleet is currently being pestered by submarines, so they have to take counter-sub measures. If I use an explosion formula with short activation time and get either the ship's depth charges

---

[12] **pretty hands for a sophisticated game of cricket** A typical English thing to do. When a British pilot taken prisoner by the Germans was missing a prosthetic leg and asked to be sent one, I guess the British dropped one with a parachute in addition to some bombs or something. When the Germans said it was bad manners, the British were like, "This isn't a game of cricket!"

or their torpedoes to blow in a secondary explosion, this thing will go down easily.

Those torpedoes can be used against even a battleship. If I can get them to explode, the destroyer won't stand a chance. If I concentrate my attack on the stern, even with low expectations, there's a possibility of speed reduction and rudder damage, too. And if it dumps the torpedoes to avoid the danger of secondary explosions, the destroyer's ability to counter the submarines will definitely take a dive.

Not so much risk on my end. This is perfect.

"There's no law that says a mage can't sink a ship. I'm gonna rock this!"

"We drew off the mages! Holding them at a distance now!"

And the one thing I was worried about, the marine mages, had been pulled away right on schedule. They made it extremely easy by dropping their altitude to work on the subs. Now I should be able to dive without worrying about being attacked from above like an idiot. And I'm nominally here to harass them, so this is too perfect.

"Good. Keep them far enough away that they can't support the ships."

""""Roger!""""

It'll probably be difficult to hold them until our fleet can get here, but they'll surely be rewarded for hastening the enemy's attrition. After all, we already did a great job by locating the enemy fleet, and we're even coordinating with our submarines, though that was rather sudden. All I have to do is report to the brass that we did all we could with a split-second decision.

The best thing to do right now is give the enemy one good hit and RTB.[13] Fighting the ships is a secondary objective.

If we return fire, I figure our part of the search and destroy mission is accomplished. Destroying the Entente Alliance ships is the Northern Sea Fleet's job.

"Okay, First Company, if you don't want to be called a bunch of no-achievement knuckleheads, it's time to go to work."

---

[13] **RTB**   Return to base.

We begin accelerating again to dive. Unlike air-to-ground attacks, the humidity from the water makes this descent uncomfortable. But we're also in the rain. As expected, the intercepting shots can't catch me, and they fly past.

Unless the enemy are hopelessly incompetent, the rest of the company behind me is in danger. Using your subordinates as bait to survive and climb the ladder is a constant in a corporate setting and the military.

"...All hands, deploy your formulas!"

That said, to my happy miscalculation, no one has dropped out. Considering it's a destroyer, maybe the last guy who got hit was a fluke? That would make sense.

The company efficiently deploys their formulas. The concentrated attacks fly one after another toward the stern of the ship.

"This is Fourth Company with an impact report. The enemy ship seems unharmed."

After confirming impact, I pull up sharply to get out of there. Even if my subordinates are acting as a shield behind me, human flesh is fragile; their presence is enough to ease my mind somewhat, but I still move at full speed.

Only an idiot gets shot down while hanging out observing the results of their attack. A unit spotting from a distance reports the outcome.

And according to Fourth Company, regrettably, the ship is apparently fine. I knew already since there wasn't a secondary explosion, but it's still disappointing. All we do now is hope is that they've jettisoned their torpedoes.

"Good enough! We achieved our aim of throwing them into confusion! Let's get out of here!"

Following the swiftly withdrawing First Company, the other three also begin to move away, keeping the marine mages in check as they go.

In order to get out of there all at once, I pull us into return formation as fast as possible. Well, we didn't do so badly.

We failed to take out the marine mages, but the strategic win of locating the enemy can't be ignored. Basically, any further combat would just wear us down without gaining anything. We should let our fleet get some of the credit here.

"How did we do?"

"Six mages down and probably moderate damage to an unknown ship. For a destroyer, it's moving pretty slowly. Its engine must be hurting. If we're lucky, the submarines will confirm. What's our damage?"

"We also have six with serious injuries and a bunch with scrapes."

Anyhow, no one died. That's a blessing in this curse. If we had been up against an American ship, there would probably be heaps of corpses...

Taking a look at the actual damage, it's not as bad as I expected. Considering we were up against a destroyer, we could have come out far worse. I'm kind of glad VT fuses[14] aren't unleashing their fury yet.

"...We basically lost. How can we show our faces back at base?"

But the mood is heavy because we weren't able to deal much damage. The lack of secondary explosion could mean that they had already used up their depth charges, but still... *That's probably wishful thinking*, Tanya laments.

"But if we encountered the enemy in these waters...they're advancing too quickly!"

"Major, if you'll forgive me...considering the speed of a destroyer..."

"Yeah, you're right. It's possible. Still, I can't believe we missed our chance to take out a destroyer..."

All Tanya can do is bemoan the unexpected encounter. In other words, she wasn't prepared. It was possible for the Entente Alliance ships to be moving faster than the estimate she'd been given if they had a group of faster than average ships.

And for just a quick destroyer...it was definitely possible.

Calling it unexpected was basically a confession of incompetence.

"It's possible, but...what about the enemy coastal defense ship...? This is going to give me a headache."

Still, the fact that a superior was wrong is no small matter. Well, the fleet coming after us has a powerful attack in store. This probably won't be viewed as that much of a problem. After all, to our fleet of powerful ships, a destroyer is easy prey.

---

[14] **VT fuse**   A proximity, aka "magic," fuse. A revolutionary gadget that makes shells explode when they are near the enemy.

At this point, it's more constructive to think about the damage my unit has taken and apply for their retraining and rest periods.

Thinking it nearly makes her crack a smile. Of course, I have plenty of experience controlling myself and faking a sorrowful expression. Nah, I should be genuinely sad. The damage to the unit I spent my time training really gets me down.

"Mages were able to hold their own against an enemy battleship. That's a fine achievement."

"We'll leave the rest up to our friends. Back to base!"

We accomplished our mission, Tanya consoles herself, biting back a sigh, and orders her soldier with the long-range wireless set to radio Command. After a few coded exchanges, Tanya is told she's gotten through, so she takes the receiver and gives a straightforward summary of the situation.

"Pixie 01 to Urban Control. That's it for my report."

"Urban Control, roger. We'll take care of it. Can you stay on the enemy?"

The enemy fleet is several ships, including a battleship. They're on a course heading north. They've had contact with our submarines. When I promptly gave Command coordinate data and the details of their speed, they asked us to pursue.

"With all due respect, we've been flying patrol for hours and can't take much more fatigue. Is it possible to spare us further anti-ship combat while we're flying with wounded men?"

"Understood. I've made arrangements for you to land at the nearest base. Wishing you a safe return."

"Thanks. Over."

To Tanya, all she had done was say indirectly that she wanted to go home. The controller probably hadn't been expecting much when he asked. She had no problems getting permission to return to base.

But Tanya doesn't know that on the way to the nearby base the controller was considerate enough to get them accommodated at, she's about to have a rather lovely run-in.

Magic Major Tanya von Degurechaff is the most senior officer in the airspace at the moment. And the senior officer has to make a decision at one point or another. That's why they're given the responsibility and authority. And the decision, when it comes down to it, will be whatever they believe is the best thing to do.

There's something you learn if you read a lot of self-improvement books: Decisions that aren't made in time are pointless. Judgments that come too late mean nothing. Of course, it goes without saying that careless decisions are prohibited.

In other words, the most important thing is balance. We can call it an essential skill for any managerial profession.

And on this most inauspicious day, the sky over the freezing Northern Sea has poor visibility. Not only is this the absolute worst possible weather to fly in, but also the fact that we encountered a submarine of unknown nationality over the water on our way home is a turn of events so unlucky I feel like something is wrong with the theory of probability.

And now that we've found it, Tanya, as the most senior officer, is forced to deal with it.

She has her troops fan out, and when she glances at their faces, she sees eyes so serious it makes her sick. Just one shot can kill almost a hundred of our own species. And their expressions mean business—these soldiers will do their best not to miss. I really hate this world. May ruin befall this place where humans can't act like humans.

And fuck the war laws, too, while we're at it, Tanya grumbles in her head.

Way to blow it by having no provision about a right to innocent passage for submarines. Were you planning on appealing to the principle of legality? Or waiting for a decision from a maritime court? This isn't a joke.

Before my eyes, a submarine of unknown nationality is attempting to rapidly flee underwater from us, the Imperial Army. This has to happen when I'm in charge, of all times. It's moving awfully fast and will probably be completely submerged in less than a minute. But although a minute isn't much, we do currently have it.

Right now, we can still make it in time.

Submarine armor is as flimsy as paper. My battalion is prepared for anti-ship combat, so we can sink a sub instantaneously.

I can't help but feel the eyes of my men turn to me, hoping for permission to attack. It's practically the same look a hunting dog uses to ask permission from its master. Externally, Tanya's unfazed, but inside she's raging.

I'm the one in charge. To put it another way, I have to take responsibility.

Sink a boat of unknown nationality? That'd be idiotic! thinks Tanya, flatly rejecting that fantasy.

The law of war doesn't permit fighting except between countries in conflict. And the worst part is that there are boats from the Commonwealth sailing near here. I should break war laws right in front of a neutral country?

The various ensuing problems would wring my neck. It'd be a way bigger issue than compliance. If I don't want to become a political scapegoat, I have to maintain at least a veneer of reason.

So do I let it go? Before my eyes? Without inspecting it even though we're right above it? *That* could develop into a huge hairy mess in the Imperial Army. It already looks like I'm forcing a lot of issues in the military org (even though I'm doing it because I have no choice), so if I let a sub of unknown nationality get away, they wouldn't just let me off the hook. It's an unknown boat operating in *these* waters. It must have some awfully important cargo. I can't overlook that, either.

And with a little effort, that sub can get away in two days underwater. As long as we don't have sonar of some kind, it'll be practically impossible to find it again if I let it go now.

…Why? Why must I be driven into this kind of corner?

What started all this, the root of Tanya's suffering in this dilemma, was a radio message received after the fight with the Entente Alliance ship as we were on our way back to base.

"…Commander! Urgent report of a suspicious boat running dark in our territorial waters at two o'clock."

I didn't expect to find anything, but if we're flying we get paid for it, so we headed away from base and ended up involved in a fight with the Entente Alliance.

It happened just as Tanya had started grumbling about how if she couldn't warm up by the fireplace with a warm cup of coffee she wouldn't be able to go on.

A report of a suspicious boat arrived. Apparently, some industrious guys found it.

Who is doing more work than they get paid for? She was half-impressed and half-disgusted as she cocked her head and then sighed in irritation that she would have to work extra hours—with no overtime pay—to deal with it.

My battalion was somewhat worn out by the unforeseen battle we had just been in. I couldn't imagine wanting to *actively* enter combat. But we weren't hurting so badly that we had to avoid it altogether.

"Well, we can't ignore it. Challenge it."

It was a situation that couldn't be ignored, and even though my battalion was on its way back to base, I acquiesced since we were the nearest force. Albeit reluctantly, Tanya and her battalion arrived at the reported sector that had been reported, and they discovered the suspicious boat.

"Is it one of our transport ships? Check the nationality."

"It's a cargo-passenger ship from the Commonwealth, the *Lytol*."

When she called and got a response, it was even more troubling.

It wasn't strange for a Commonwealth cargo-passenger ship to be there, but that didn't mean she could just let it go.

"…Tell them we're boarding."

"Are you sure? If it takes too long, it will affect our return time…"

"We can't ignore it now that we challenged it. It's in waters between countries at war."

The boat's nationality was too problematic to ignore, which was also a pain.

Yes, ships from neutral countries have the right to come and go as they please, but at the same time, we have the right to board in the territorial waters of the country at war. Obnoxiously, if we didn't inspect this ship, I would need a good reason for it.

It's just one thing after another. How annoying. I want to do my job efficiently, but it's not as if I want to work, so there's no way this will end well.

"*Lytol*, this is the Imperial Army General Staff's 203rd Aerial Mage Battalion. We order you to submit to inspection. Cut your engines immediately. I say again, cut your engines immediately."

"This is *Lytol*. We are a vessel from a neutral country, the Commonwealth, so we do not believe we are under obligation to comply."

"*Lytol*, this is the Imperial Army. Are you carrying any military personnel? Or are you operating under the orders of military personnel?"

"*Lytol* to the Imperial Army. We're not required to answer those questions."

"Imperial Army, roger. *Lytol*, if that is your decision, we're unable to recognize your immunity to boarding as a neutral country's warship. This is a warning that if you refuse inspection, it will be considered a hostile action and you will be classified as a hostile nation's vessel. I say again, if you refuse inspection, it will be considered a hostile action. We will have no choice but to sink you."

"*Lytol*, we've cut our engines."

"Good. Start the inspection. Lieutenant Weiss, your company is the boarding party."

"Yes, ma'am."

"The rest of you, keep watch over the area."

Tanya wanted to pull her hair out, the legal exchange was such a pain in the ass, but just as she was pushing the boarding duty onto her subordinates and having the smallest acceptable party pull up alongside the ship, something else happened.

"Wait a minute. What's that?" Lieutenant Serebryakov asked, pointing at something on the surface. She seemed to have found something in the mist over the sea. Drawn by her question, several people followed her gaze and...bingo, I suppose you could say? There was the cargo-passenger ship flying the Commonwealth flag *plus* a submarine of unknown nationality.

...And if I wasn't seeing things, they seemed to be transferring something.

Chapter IV

It goes without saying that these were two British ladies[15] enjoying a secret meeting.

They couldn't be unrelated. I most certainly wanted to inquire about their relationship. I might have seemed like a paparazzo, and you could say it was bad manners, but I just hoped they'd find it in their hearts to forgive me.

Another extra job to do? Tanya lamented. As she was about to send out another boarding party, she was suddenly unsure what to do.

Submarines go underwater, as their name implies, but war laws cover only surface boarding rules; there's nothing pertaining to boats that can dive. After all, submarines are a relatively new type of vessel.

Since they are used in proxy wars, there is research being done into counter-sub combat and ways to stop them, but most navy personnel are extremely under-informed. Still, it's crazy that there is nothing in the naval war laws about submarines. I realized it was only a matter of time before unrestricted submarine warfare was declared.

But every second Tanya fretted, the situation was developing. The sub was trying to dive before her eyes. In a few minutes, it would be deep enough that our attacks might not reach—it would be able to make a calm getaway.

"Ngh. Lieutenant Weiss, capture the *Lytol* with your company!"

I figured we should hurry. I wanted to keep them from hiding evidence before the inspection.

But what about the critical submarine?

If it refuses to be boarded, I can shoot, but first it has to be a warning shot. That's the standard protocol demanded by the law of war. Submerging isn't denying inspection. Annoyingly, my opponent has slipped through a legal loophole.

I love slipping through legal loopholes, but I hate it when other people do it to me.

What suddenly crosses my mind is compromise… *Does it really matter how deep the mire goes?*

---

[15] **two British ladies**   Ships are female, and British women are ladies. You all need to play Paradox Interactive's game *Victoria* (aka *Vic*)! Or maybe take a look at Britannia (the goddess).

I'm in this bog already. If I'm already covered in mud, it's not a big deal if another kind of mud gets involved. I'd hesitate to get clean white sheets all dirty, but throwing a ball of mud covered in mud into the dirt won't hurt it.

"...All units on standby, prepare to attack the submarine! Ready a warning!"

"Major?!"

"Fire sniping formulas! If it doesn't comply with orders to halt and starts to dive, blow its conning tower off!"

All we can do is shoot.

"All hands, at the same time, prepare to subdue the target. Avoid direct hits. This is for intimidation purposes only."

So I'll choose the route that isn't pitch-black, even if it is dirty.

The law of war doesn't prohibit shots across the bow. As long as we don't hit them directly, we can claim they were warning shots. We can't call diving refusing inspection, but it's not exactly cooperative, either. If we're firing warning shots to urge compliance, legally speaking, that's got to be the whiter part of gray—in other words, white.

"All hands! Assault formation! Prepare to fire warning shots!"

The company commanders repeat the orders. My men have just enough self-control to wait when told to heel. If I tell them to intimidate, they should intimidate. Submarines have such wimpy armor that one depth charge is enough to crush it. If we blow multiple heavy explosion formulas in its immediate vicinity, it won't be able to keep diving. Then all we have to do is stroll aboard once it surfaces.

"You got that? No direct hits!" So I repeatedly emphasize that we're not trying to sink it. If it sinks, I'll really be in trouble. "The opponent is a sub. One depth charge is enough to cave in its armor. Stop at a few near misses! I'm not listening to any excuses if you sink it!"

What did they put on board? Depending on that cargo, this could be a major achievement. We can't go lending them a hand by sinking them and erasing all the tangible evidence.

We have to secure it.

"*Jawohl*, Frau Major!"

"Good! Gentlemen, that Commonwealth vessel is watching. Make sure you don't humiliate us!"

Everyone swiftly gets into formation. The sub doesn't have any anti-air fire to speak of. Actually, anyone who would be scared of that should be shot. So yes, everyone has calmly—leisurely, even—assumed their positions. All that's left now is to decide how much distance to keep.

Heavy explosion formulas are different from the simple kind. About ten meters away should do it.

Converted to gunpowder, they're a hundred fifty kilos at most. There won't be fragmentation; the water pressure will be enough.

"Stay ten—no, fifteen meters away from the hull!" The worry that ten meters won't be enough suddenly crosses my mind.

Submarines are fragile. I'm not about to have them too close and send it to the bottom. Considering it's half-intimidation tactic, half-warning, fifteen meters should be good. It might even be a little under-confident, since the water will dull the shock.

That said, it can't be interpreted as an attack. We may be in waters where the Empire and Entente Alliance are at war, but that doesn't mean it's okay to sink a vessel of unknown nationality. Which is precisely why commanders forced to make quick, delicate calls can never relax—I hate it.

"Warning fire at a distance of fifteen!"

"All right. Fire!"

That's why I have them keep their distance.

I shout over and over, so there will be no confusion, that this is only for intimidation.

It must be recorded in the unit logs.

And the fact that I clearly stated to keep fifteen meters away should be in the firing data table. In other words, I'm compromising myself as little as possible. We've seen it, so the best thing we can do is perform our duty.

I pour a hefty dose of mana into the computation orb in my hand and put it in firing mode. The cores regulate the energy, and I aim near the submarine my unit is trying to keep from diving.

It's a company's worth of disciplined fire from 360 degrees and fifteen meters away—the heavy explosion formulas burst in the water.

The huge splashes obscure the unidentified submarine.

"Second Company, descend! Prepare to board the sub when it comes up."

Well, they were warning shots, but at that range, the sub is probably taking on water.

That's the weakness of these vulnerable submarines. I'm sure a bunch of confidential materials will get ruined, so we have to capture it as soon as possible.

Meanwhile, the captain of the Commonwealth S-class submarine *Syrtis* was nearly panicking due to the report of an incoming mage battalion.

There's a mole[16] *in the intelligence agency.* He was aware of the rumors. He and his submarine crew were not about to lose to the subterranean, but unfortunately diving into intelligence and diving into the sea are two different things. They knew they had taken measures to preserve utmost secrecy.

Security was so tight that when they were dispatched, he could only tell his crew that they were performing an utterly normal navigation exercise. Only the captain knew the true identity of the "technical officer" from the Office of the Admiralty who was on board; only the captain knew about the sealed orders.

They had been so thorough that even the navigation officer wasn't informed until after they had launched and were setting their course.

However...

There they were at the rendezvous point only a handful of people should have known about. They managed to make the transfer just as the report came in that the Imperial Army was approaching, and the situation rapidly deteriorated.

If that hadn't happened, all they would have had to do was play dumb and get past the Imperial Army patrol line. What did it mean that an imperial mage battalion appeared out of nowhere just then?

---

[16] **mole**   A spy, or a double agent. Usually the kind who infiltrates a nation's domestic organizations.

The shock was so great that he momentarily locked eyes with the "technical officer" from the Office of the Admiralty.

"Multiple Imperial Army mages incoming! They saw our rendezvous with the *Lytol*!"

The enemy must have known about the cargo and the schedule. If not, they wouldn't have shown up here. An auxiliary ship might have been conspicuous, but it's nominally a civilian vessel. The Empire couldn't be rough with a civilian vessel from the neutral Commonwealth.

But if the vessel was of unknown nationality, handling it as a belligerent to some extent would be permissible.

If they had known that much planned a raid, there had to be a mole.

"They're ordering us to halt!"

The radio operator's shout jerked everyone back to reality.

The captain had to set aside his doubts for the time being and make it through this moment. An S-class submarine could dive to a depth of over a hundred meters. Even mages would have trouble following them if they submerged.

It would be a different story if they took a shot to the hull, but the law of war wasn't clear on the definition of halting their ship.

No, submerging was not officially recognized as fugitive behavior. After all, the rules were written before boats went underwater.

"Cut off all radio communications! Emergency dive!"

All they had to do was dive before the mages were on them. Maintain radio silence, refuse transmissions, and dive, just like that. He thought they would be able to escape that way.

But his forecast was naive. Just as they opened the vents…

The observer shrieked a warning, and the captain learned, whether he wanted to or not, their opponent's lack of scruples.

"M-multiple mana signals detected! All hands, brace for…"

They were going to shoot. When he realized that, his head told him to grab hold of something, but the warning was so unexpected that his body wasn't moving the way he wanted it to.

Not many on the crew could get their bodies to cooperate. *I have to move.* Everyone thought so, and when they reached their hands out, they heard a roar. Then came a series of huge shocks to the hull, the captain noticed that he felt weightless as the attacks landed, and he lost consciousness.

"Captain?! Shit! Medic! The captain's wounded! Get to the conning station!"

He awoke to the sound of someone's raised voice but not for long. Noting the captain's condition, the first officer prepared himself to take command. The scenario was about as "worst-case" as it could get. Multiple hull breaches. Rapidly spreading flooding.

On top of that, the water pressure around the bridge had destroyed the periscope. The engines were just barely running, but there was a problem in the battery compartments—they were emitting chlorine gas. They needed masks for poisonous gas, but it was all he could do to just get the battered crew moving.

Between the flooding and the gas, the environment in the sub would deteriorate quickly. It was only a matter of time until disaster.

To make matters worse, the rudder wouldn't budge. It had probably been damaged by the water pressure. So they wouldn't be able to move properly.

There was a limit to the emergency repairs they could do. Only one of the drain pumps was working, so they would eventually lose balance. With their reserve power situation looking dire, the only choice they had was to surface.

"...Sir, we can't take any more." He addressed the technical officer.

"There's nothing you can do?"

He had to make a hard decision—and fast. The first officer didn't really think the mysterious technical officer was a mere officer. So he hinted at him that all they could do was surrender.

As long as the captain couldn't command the ship, the first officer was responsible for the lives of the crew. Since they were forced to surface, he had no choice but to say it. "We're not going to last long. If you need to take care of the cargo, let's do so quickly."

"...Understood."

A murmured exchange, and then the technical officer and the first officer went to quickly "deal with" the cargo. It was an awful decision to make...but it was the only way.

Chapter IV

"What were you doing?!"

An unassuming building stood tucked away in a quiet residential area. Isolated from the outside in an inconspicuous way, the building's interior was in the midst of a storm that struck a perfect contrast with its quiet environs. Not so much as a molecule of the genial Christmas spirit of the world at large could survive there.

Particularly violent was Major General Habergram of the Foreign Strategy Division, who was abusing the line of intelligence officers. He pounded the desk with his clenched fist almost hard enough to break it. A half-assed explanation wasn't going to cut it. The intelligence officers standing there were as pale as prisoners about to be executed by firing squad.

Well, it was only natural. Of course the general's fury would be violent when he'd been woken from a nap because the plan he'd forgone sleep or rest to realize was ruined in the span of a single night.

He'd figured out the Imperial Army aerial units' patrol lines and analyzed their Northern Sea Fleet's patrol routes. He'd checked the speed of that fleet and adjusted the Commonwealth Navy's exercise schedule accordingly as a distraction. In a single moment, all his efforts went up in smoke.

General Habergram was by no means the only person in the Commonwealth grinding his teeth in disappointment; the need for a sweeping investigation into the causes of the problem had been acknowledged. At this point in time, the ones getting the murderous looks were the security officers; their stomachs probably couldn't take much more.

"Why were there imperial mages over there?"

The failures of the intelligence agency had been in question for some time, but now there were getting to be too many to brush off as coincidences. One or two incidents could be unfortunate mistakes, but by the time the third one happens, it's inevitable.

When the voluntary army that had been sent out to gather intel and observe was pinpointed and bombarded by mages, it was still possible to suspect coincidence.

They were working on improving the apparatuses after they concluded that reverse detection of the surveillance waves could have been the cause. It wasn't out of the question to call it an unfortunate accident or coincidence.

But this time, it was too hard to fathom as a coincidence; he couldn't accept it. They were targeted so precisely.

"We're performing a thorough investigation, but we can only imagine it was a coincidence!"

"The Empire might have a good intelligence team, but I really don't think they could have known about this…"

"Then explain this video."

The footage of the battle he projected shut up the officers who were trying to object. Even though the details were hazy with static thanks to the dense concentration of combat mana, what it showed was clear.

The imperial mages moved in perfect formation toward a single target. Other ships tried to draw their fire by attacking, but the enemy unit ignored them. Not only were they not afraid of getting hit, they maneuvered as if they weren't even taking the possibility of damage into account.

Then they held back the marine mages who went up to intercept them and dived in assault formation.

The log blacked out when an Entente Alliance mage who went to intercept fell as a corpse into the sea after being mercilessly bayoneted and kicked away. The last image was the enemy mages darting straight for the battle cruiser.

Yes, one glance made it obvious. They were clearly aiming for a specific ship and paying no attention to the others.

"I ask you—why?" It was the question of a man about to explode at any moment. "Why is the Named who was supposedly deployed in the northern zone lying in wait for us here?"

Then his thunder crashed. All the intelligence officers could do was pray for the storm to pass. According to their careful analysis, the imperial Named had seemed to be providing support to the northern lines.

Central had taken the trouble to dispatch this Named unit. And the intelligence officers had given a partially incorrect warning that they were going to be supporting an offensive.

Against their expectations, the Named unit appeared far from the sector they had been stationed in. At first, they wondered if it was an unknown elite unit, but the recorded mana signatures answered that question immediately.

They matched the signals of the Named unit who had just previously been spotted in the Entente Alliance.

Looking at the combat logs, it was obviously the same unit who had been so kind as to demolish the voluntary army there just the other day. Really, it was hard to imagine them being here. Considering the Imperial Army's rotation of combat and rest, it was too soon.

"The fighting in the north is intensifying. And they're planning an offensive to mop up the Entente Alliance. Why would they dispatch a powerful mage unit out here?"

Yes. Their analysis said the Imperial Army, which had carried out a landing operation that ignored communication lines and the power of the Commonwealth's Navy, was preparing an operation to finish off the Entente Alliance. Why would they just happen to send an elite unit to this area at a time when the Northern Army Group probably needed all the help they could get?

These were the guys who were massing all available arms, ammunition, and personnel for the northern lines, so this maneuver clearly had to be the result of a plan, not a coincidence.

This was the same Named unit who was spotted during the landing operation. If it had been pulled and then appeared on the Rhine lines, you could call it proof that the Empire was prioritizing the Rhine front. But just when they noticed they had stopped seeing it on the northern lines, it was instead lying in wait for departing Entente Alliance ships and their submarine in the Northern Sea.

"Most importantly, look at this. They make a beeline for the middle of the fleet without even looking at the vanguard."

The attack was too efficient to be explained as a chance encounter. For starters, look at how the mages suddenly attacked just as a sub distracted the fleet with a torpedo, causing everyone to look down. How elite mages dropped out of the sky just when everyone's minds were blank, and physically, the fleet had broken formation to perform evasive maneuvers with too-perfect timing.

But then they didn't even touch the vanguard destroyers.

As a result, they were able to go undetected for some time. They ignored the intercepting attack that had just barely occurred at all and headed straight for their objective. If that was a coincidence, it had to mean about a dozen ladies of luck were smiling on the Empire. But that seemed impossible.

"We also have record of some kind of transmission above the fleet."

Were the mages filing a report right before going into assault formation? There was not *no* chance it was a report of enemy contact, but in that case, you'd think they would have done it sooner. If they were there to restrain them, they wouldn't have had to approach so closely.

But if they were an attacking unit, there should have been a combat control team.

Unexpectedly encountering an unguided battalion of mages? Don't be ridiculous. Plus, it happened right after the submarine attack. If it wasn't planned and it wasn't the kind of coincidence only God can conceive of, it wasn't possible.

"They started drawing off the escorts straightaway, and on top of that, one company went right for the battle cruiser. All you can do is laugh."

Anti–air fire doesn't score that many direct hits. The navy and even the army know that. But the difference between knowing something and experiencing it is night and day. Would you charge a battle cruiser lined with autocannons simply because the shots don't usually connect?

Normally there would be some hesitation. Even if they didn't hesitate, there would have been various ways to go about it. If attacking was their aim, deploying barrage formulas at range would have been one option. A mage's extra-long range barrage formula would be able to get past most anti–air fire.

Of course, the marine mages were there to keep them from doing that. But they had been pretty much caught by surprise, so although the handful of direct support mages put up the best resistance they could, it was futile, and they were scattered. The enemy mages were emitting such tranquil signals we didn't discover them until they were right on top of us, so they must have been working really hard to conceal them.

"Look. From the mana signatures, it seems like the Named is leading the formation."

Did the Entente Alliance miss the signature of the Named because they're incompetent? Observing the mana isotope of the flight leader[17] is the most basic step to take. It's easy to detect it as long as the mage isn't limiting output to conceal themselves.

A unit putting a check on enemies might be able to limit output. It was a standard way to extend one's time in the air and liked for the way it lowered one's chances of being detected. But could a battalion flying at high speeds do it?

It did temporarily increase your endurance, but in the end, your fatigue would spike. It would be out of the question to enter combat. So perhaps they were limiting output for some other reason, not a sneak attack…

But then right after that, the same unit raided the waters where their auxiliary ship and submarine were meeting. No matter how optimistically someone wanted to interpret the situation, it was only natural to suspect a giant leak. Rather, if the enemy was acting this boldly on their intelligence, they probably weren't even trying to hide that they were getting it.

They considered saying it was so obvious it was unnatural…but they thought they had looked deep into all the circumstances…and yet they still couldn't get the possibility out of their heads—and that was the demands of their job. In an information war, truth was never guaranteed. Even if something seemed correct, the mere appearance of accuracy wouldn't help them. And that was why they had to suspect every possibility—including the hypothesis of a leak.

"…What did you find out in the hunt?"

---

[17] **flight leader**   The one in front who guides the others. They mark bombing objectives, guide aviation units, and so on, so it's a job for veterans. Leaders are important.

Acknowledging that hypothesis had serious implications. If there wasn't a leak, they had no explanation for the enemy's actions.

Naturally, the intelligence agency had launched a major operation in great haste to whack all the moles and clean out the organization, the assumption being that if they could just find the culprit…

Everyone was about ready to cry because they hadn't found the slightest sign of the enemy. The people in charge of the investigation had come up with no evidence and no support, but if there wasn't a huge leak, then they were saddled with the bigger problem of having no explanation for the situation. They really were at wits' end, about to break down sobbing.

"We considered code issues, a double agent, or betrayal, but so far we're clear."

"We're still waiting for the actual results of the investigation, but I can't imagine the code is broken. We're not using anything except one-time pads."

"A double agent or traitor isn't terribly likely, either. The number of people with access to this information isn't even double digits."

"It's possible they were a lookout on the flank of the main imperial fleet headed north. Perhaps it really was just an unfortunate coincidence…"

It wasn't as if the intelligence agency and its officers were doing nothing.

They had arrived at this word *coincidence* after suffering through investigations that exhausted every other avenue. Now all they could do was tell their irate boss their troubling conclusion…that perhaps it was simply chance. Over the course of the hunt, a few moles had been discovered and purged. Still, they were clear.

At this point, wasn't it just an unfortunate accident? It was only a matter of time until a number of people began to think that. Actually, some were even saying it, given the report that the Entente Alliance fleet had been able to escape the Empire's Northern Sea Fleet to meet up with the Republic fleet in the end.

But that idea was rejected due to one piece of unmistakably clear evidence: the reports from the intelligence and naval officers dispatched to the Entente Alliance ship as military observers.

Chapter IV

The details written there were enough to silence anyone claiming it was a coincidence or an accident. No, it blew them out of the water.

"...A big augmented battalion of mages just happens to encounter the battle cruiser with the councilor who would form the government in exile, and they just happen to attack and concentrate their fire on where that vital politician is?"

And immediately before, the submarine torpedo attack with perfect timing. Right as the ships abruptly shifted to counter-sub combat and the direct support marine mages were flying low on patrol, the imperial mages used their altitude to their advantage and swooped out of the sky.

It was awfully well coordinated if they weren't waiting for us.

Then, as if they had done what they came to do, the enemy mages left after only one strike.

For General Habergram, the bad news they had woken him up for was enough to make him nearly crush the pipe in his hand. The attached photo made it clear that they had focused their attack on a single area—an area that was almost never considered a strategic target. In anti-ship warfare, there aren't many methods of effective attack; maybe a heavy explosion formula or a gravity formula aimed beneath the target's waterline.

But they took the trouble to aim for the living quarters with anti-personnel explosion formulas. Maybe against the bridge it would be understandable, but they aimed at the living quarters. That is, the entire company concentrated their fire on them.

And this had been noted already, but according to the reports, after recklessly charging in and bombing their target area, they all left without any further combat actions.

They left as if they had no time to lose. They must have been on their way back to base. Theoretically, it was possible to insist that coincidences had just stacked up.

But what are the astronomical odds of the coincidence where an enemy who waited so persistently, only to strike once and rush away, subsequently runs into the Commonwealth's auxiliary ship and sub "on their way back"?

You don't even have to think about it.

"And is there anyone who believes that it was a coincidence that they ran into our boat on their way back just because it was bobbing out there looking suspicious?" It was a rhetorical question containing his fury.

He was all but saying that if anyone did, that fist pounding into the table would smash into them instead. He squared his shoulders imposingly while inside him the hurricane was raging.

"What a priceless fluke! Of all the coincidences that could possibly happen, this one's a real riot!" Shouting, he slammed his fist into the table again, paid no mind to the fact that he'd started bleeding, and fell silent as though he'd lost the power of speech.

He had always been praised as an unflappable paragon of composure, and yet...

>>>>   **SAME DAY, IMPERIAL ARMY GENERAL STAFF OFFICE, JOINT**   <<<<
CONFERENCE ROOM

The situation was bad if the Service Corps staff, the Intelligence staff, and the Operations staff were all at wits' end. Maybe there was some kind of political strategy problem or some kind of military issue. It was natural that the staff officers would be worried about how to get things under control.

Well, they had probably also started thinking about who to blame.

"What? We lost the Entente Alliance ships?" That accurately summed up the sentiment of all the army officers present. No, all the participants' thoughts could be expressed that way.

Not that they'd had them trapped like rats, but everyone had believed it was certain, given the power balance, that they would deal the enemy ships a serious blow in this naval battle. It had been finally a chance for the idle navy to shine and show some results, but the staff's expectations had been magnificently betrayed.

"...The Northern Sea Fleet failed to relocate them."

"Even though we succeeded in building up superior fighting capabilities?"

"Yes, it seems they got away."

They let them get away? Not that the fleet was perfect, but they had managed to gather a fair number of capital ships. They were also able to choose the battleground. It was only natural to have high expectations under those circumstances.

Were all those fleet maneuvers just a waste of heavy oil?

The stern gazes from the army seemed to contain a rebuke. *What is the meaning of this?* The confused naval officers bearing the brunt of it were forced to present materials and attempt to explain.

"No, the weather was so horrible. The fact that we even made contact twice was a fluke. It's incredibly difficult to relocate a fleet."

There was nothing easy about finding something in the sea. Even a fleet of warships is nothing but a speck in the wide-open water.

Unless you controlled all sides of an area, it was impossible to patrol it perfectly. How well you could do was practically up to probability. For that reason, the navy prioritized inferences based on past experience. To put it another way, the Imperial Navy's lack of experience was enough to break them down into tears. Though the expansion of their "hardware" was on schedule, the personnel operating them still required improvements.

"But that's your job."

Still, it was true that griping wouldn't get them anywhere. They didn't need to be told that doing their best with what they were given was demanded of military men. In that case, the navy had to supplement their perfectly adequate hardware with "software" that could operate it in the form of quality manpower.

"Still, I guess saying any more at this point won't change anything." Major General von Zettour figured that was enough useless finger-pointing and chimed in to end the venting.

As far as he could tell, the army had already expressed most of their complaints and discontent. The navy was getting near the end of their rope. Any more of this was just a waste of time. Yes, he made up his mind to end the witch hunt and proposed that they work toward a realistic solution.

"All we can do is consider our next step. Does the navy have anything to suggest?" After finishing his question, he gave a stern look to any army officers who seemed to have more to say and slowly took his seat. An officer from the navy stood, apparently waiting for the chance. *What a young kid*, Zettour thought as he changed gears.

"We would like to prevent their meeting with the Republic by getting some assistance on the diplomatic front."

In the documents they'd been given, there was a plan that included an opinion from the Foreign Office. There was not a problem with the proposal per se. He actually thought it was fairly well put together. At least, it was reasonable.

"Making use of the duties of neutral states, hmm? But do you think the Commonwealth will actually fulfill them?"

But reason is not all that matters in a fight for the survival of a state. If that were the case, the world would already be Utopia, and the absence of a heaven on earth made their position clear.

"The Foreign Office thinks it's tricky. But honestly, they won't, right?"

The Commonwealth would probably just demand they leave within forty-eight hours. He didn't think it would actually take measures to disarm them like it was supposed to. The military attaché's confirmation would be resisted with procedural delays.

By the time permission was granted, the boat would have left the bay.

"In which case, those ships will waltz over to meet up with the Republic fleet."

"Ugh. That means Entente Alliance resistance will drag on."

Inconveniently for the Empire, the Commonwealth and the Republic had more than a little adjacent territorial water. Since it was out of the question to battle in the Commonwealth's territory, there was no real way to prevent the ships from getting to the Republic once they'd lost them.

And if the Entente Alliance ships were fighting with the Empire, it could create issues with convincing them to surrender. *Look! Our navy's fit as a fiddle!* the enemy could say. They were trying to discourage further resistance at this juncture, so the issue had the capacity to develop into a headache.

"…There's not really anything else we can do but sink them ASAP."

Chapter IV

There was no other way to rapidly gain control of the situation and minimize damage. They had to sink all those Entente Alliance ships.

Missing a ship or two was one thing, but they had let them get away. Sinking a few enemy vessels was no longer enough to resolve the problem.

The only option their current situation permitted was to swiftly sink as many ships as they could. That was the only way to stop the issue from evolving any further.

"So the orders for the Northern Sea Fleet are still to promptly sink the ships?"

"That works."

The navy had no objections, either.

"We'll continue to provide support. I just want to get this resolved as soon as possible."

 GARRISON OF THE 203RD BATTALION, BATTALION HQ ◀◀◀

It had crystallized into something pure and tranquil...a madness that had precipitated as a faintly black sediment, then festered and condensed.

Those nightmarish eyes seemed to invite insanity into everything they fell upon. It was all you could do to resist the bewitching gaze if it landed on you.

"Your orders, please, Colonel."

Lieutenant Colonel von Lergen exhaled lightly and finally drew air into his lungs again. Sunlight streamed in through the window.

It seemed a warm day for winter, but his body felt like it was enveloped in cold.

The reason was simple—the incarnation of madness before his eyes.

"Major von Degurechaff, you're being transferred."

Preparations were under way for a large operation on the Rhine front—planned and drafted with an unprecedented amount of leverage from Major General von Rudersdorf, deputy director of Operations, and the support of Major General von Zettour.

So they needed reinforcements.

And they would need support for those reinforcements.

Of course, as a bit of an obnoxious errand, there was a court-martial waiting for her at Central—a formality. After all, though she hadn't realized it was a neutral country's boat, she had sunk a Commonwealth submarine as a suspicious vessel in an unfortunate accident. That said, it would be a court-martial in form only.

"Of course, I can't say it won't be a bother...but it's really mostly a formality. I'm expecting your best."

"...So this'll be a chance to redeem my reputation?"

But the little major before him didn't make an effort to understand any of that. Apparently, she was taking the unofficial transfer orders he'd shown her as bad news. Maybe she was also a bit nervous about the trial.

She had a warped sense of responsibility, but the thought of being called to account made her shiver. A mere major had to take responsibility for everything. He had a strange feeling that something more horrifying than chilly air was blowing through the room. Or maybe like he had been hurled into the fissure separating normal and abnormal.

"You succeeded in locating the enemy unit. It's not your fault. Nobody was asking any more than that of you."

"I had our sworn enemy right in front of me, and I let them get away. Next time, next time, I'll get them for sure."

His intercession didn't accomplish anything. But the words weren't just for show.

That her unit had located the enemy at all in those horrible weather conditions was impressive. They had also dealt some damage to the enemy marine mages.

Even if the results were not perfect, there was probably only one person who didn't acknowledge them as acceptable.

"Major?"

"Don't worry. I won't repeat this mistake. I swear to you that it won't happen again."

But that person wouldn't acknowledge anything less than perfect. Horrifyingly, her frame of mind seemed to be a combination of bloodlust and patriotism molded into the form of a soldier's psyche. Rather than a soldier, she was more a doll shaped like one.

Chapter **IV**

The words she repeated over and over, practically delirious, exuded a strange urgency.

One time—just one time—she had gotten merely satisfactory results, and this was her state. *How much of a perfectionist can you be?*

She has no interest in anything except for following her orders to the letter. *What kind of education do you have to give a child to warp them like this?*

"...Don't fret, Major. We're pleased with what you've achieved. All you need to do is accomplish your missions."

"Don't worry. I won't leave a single ship behind."

I'm not getting through to her at all. It looks like we're having a conversation, but something is making us talk past each other. All I did was encourage her to accomplish her missions; why does that make this ball of insanity overflow with a will to fight and declare her intent to annihilate? How war crazy can you get?

Though she's the best the Empire has ever produced, she's the worst war nut we've seen. Can a mere person be so joyful about killing their fellow men? Can a mere person carry out any and every military duty so faithfully with no hesitation?

Unless your foundation as a human being was off-kilter, this level of incongruity was impossible.

"No one at the General Staff Office has any issues with your actions, Major."

It was a fact he had to express to her as a messenger. Customarily, typical notices to unit commanders conveyed expectations that they eliminate enemy units. They were practically season's greetings. But what he had to express this time was not superficial consolation but unmistakable forgiveness.

But, but... In some corner of his mind, reason was warning him. *This monster in front of you might actually do it.*

"But, Major..."

Thus...

"...if you do want to contribute to the fleet's efforts..."

He gave her as much consideration as his discretion would allow.

"…it is planning a war game in the Northern Sea. I don't think anyone would mind if you participated before going to the Rhine."

"I volunteer."

"Great. I'll make the arrangements."

As she gave the reply he expected, Lergen caught himself feeling relieved that this would bring closure to the matter.

"I wish you and your unit much success. Good luck."

Feeling a slight chill, he dutifully answered with the required encouragement, speaking quickly. She and her men were on his side, at least. *As long as the tip of her spear isn't pointed at my beloved fatherland, what is there to fear?* He suffocated his mind with that question to deceive himself.

"Thank you."

Whether she knew it or not as she bowed, Major von Degurechaff was an outstanding model soldier.

>>> BATTALION GARRISON, LARGE AUDITORIUM <<<

To express the feelings of Magic Major Tanya von Degurechaff in a nutshell: *I've escaped by a hair.*

I was trembling in fear of a rebuke. But when I opened the envelope my friend Colonel von Lergen brought from the General Staff, it was just an administrative note. I really expected a reprimand over my failure in that mission, but I guess the brass is more lenient than I thought.

Relieved, Tanya drains her cold coffee with an involuntary sigh and smiles wryly, thinking of how uncharacteristically nervous she's been feeling.

There's the court-martial coming up. But it's supposed be nothing more than a discussion held as a formality, which means Tanya's been unofficially given a mostly unexpected pardon. She was only informed verbally, but given that it was the word of a staff officer, it has to be true.

In other words, the fact that Lergen, someone she knows, delivered the note had to be a token of consideration from the higher-ups. Lergen's report must be a roundabout way of saying that the brass hasn't forsaken me yet. It's a kindness that says, *We'll keep you around, so show us you can still get results.*

If I'm receiving this sort of understanding, the General Staff must still have high expectations for my unit and me. I mean, they were nice enough to spare me mental stress by giving me a heads-up, albeit only verbally, that I would be found not guilty.

If it were me and *my* subordinate was being incompetent, I wouldn't give a damn about their mental health—I'd advise them to resign. Wouldn't anyone? Even in the army, where you can't lay someone off, they'd have to be ready for some sort of disciplinary action.

But apparently the higher-ups are letting me off the hook this time and giving me a second chance. To put it another way, I can't expect them to be so lenient again.

They're even giving me an opportunity to show off my abilities in this war game. I definitely have to live up to the expectations of the General Staff and the brass this time.

"Still, I wonder... Who's the one making allowances for me?"

If I'm getting off so easily, someone in the totem pole is pulling the strings. There are only a few people it could possibly be. Someone who has influence higher up but would also deign to do me a favor—it has to be someone in General von Zettour's camp.

"Hmm, I'll have to thank him sometime soon," Tanya murmurs, her mood improving slightly after considering her good fortune to have such a great superior in the army, where soldiers don't have the luxury of choosing their bosses. I really can't thank him enough.

Then, with a single deep breath, I amble leisurely to the room next door. In the worst-case scenario, I thought the battalion might even be broken up, so I had summoned them all in case I needed to explain; they're already waiting.

Everyone's exhibiting proper concern, and they seem ready to listen, which is endearing. I'll tell them the good news. Tanya slowly begins to speak.

"Battalion, I don't believe in God. Not even a little bit."

If you do exist, grant me the power to feed Being X to pigs after cramming him through a shredder.

Tanya doesn't say that part aloud, but I think it.

Nothing happens.

I sigh inwardly. The troops lined up here are way more useful and a hell of a lot more loyal than some nonexistent god. A great commander of ancient times said that the hundred men you have are better than the ten thousand you don't, and he was quite right.

Of course, if I loosen the reins, they'll go racing off to the battlefield, so that gives me a splitting headache, but… Anyhow, I have a chance to make up for the mistake. She takes the dais and decides to give her troops a few inspiring words so that she can restore her reputation.

"Gentlemen, I believe in the General Staff. It's a bastion of logic and wisdom. Dear God, if you're so great, try being ethical. Then I'll show you that the General Staff's wisdom is greater than yours."

The Imperial Army General Staff exists for real; God or whoever only exists as an idea. In other words, he's a fantasy.

That's ethics. If you want to oppose the rule of law, the generally accepted universal principles, then you have to show us something greater.

To neglect them, unilaterally claim you exist, and declare your own laws is to ask us to fulfill a one-sided contract.

On that point, the kindhearted General Staff shows mercy even when we err and gives us chances to redeem ourselves. But Tanya won't forget her failure. Colonel von Lergen and the General Staff are considerate enough to be indirect about it, but it's torturous. It's our—in other words, my—failure.

I want to impress these things on my disheartened troops, so I issue a declaration. These are the kinds of subtleties middle management has to instill in their subordinates.

"People don't expect anything from an entity with minimal presence. My brothers-in-arms, the General Staff—maybe even the Empire itself—has expectations of us. Our duty and dedication are our honor."

Of course, Tanya was convinced the higher-ups were disappointed in them. She could have done nothing if they had been deemed useless.

Chapter IV

If a person in manufacturing somehow made an inventory management error by going out on a business call? It wouldn't matter how well he did in the meeting.

He would have to endure castigation for his incompetence.

"It is the will of the army to give us a chance. We've been granted an opportunity to atone for our mistake."

The General Staff Office even sent someone in person. It means we haven't been forsaken. There's still the danger of being sent to serve in some penal battalion, but we'll just have to overcome it by amassing achievements.

"I don't care if it's purgatory—we'll go there, and we'll conquer it, because that's what soldiers do."

We go anywhere we're ordered. That fundamental principle goes without saying, but it's important to constantly review the basics. Heinrich's Law is a warning against letting minor errors pile up.

Taking a heavier hand to prevent accidents is elementary.

"So let's do a mission right now. Let's do it ourselves."

"Commander?"

Vice Commander Weiss is interrupting me? Am I repeating myself too much? I feel rather hesitant, but something from my education at the military academy crosses my mind: *Never waver in front of subordinates.* But I'd rather regret doing something than aimlessly doing nothing.

Having made up her mind, she just barely maintains her unconcerned expression and glances around. Well, the battalion personnel don't seem to be so sick of my insistent confirmations. People who value the basics are the kind of talent I wish I could just put in my pocket.

"Let's show the Empire how great their watchdog is."

I make sure it registers. Basically, the army is an instrument of violence that serves as a watchdog. We need to show that we have no intention of bucking the state's control. You never know whose eyes might be out there glinting as they watch.

It's good to appeal to their loyalty to a slightly underhanded degree. It's a million times better to have them laughing at me than putting them on their guard and trapping myself. Besides, I can just give anyone who laughs a beating.

"Let's teach those rats that no matter where they run we'll be on their tails."

Let's think a step further. I'm acting like Tsuji right now. Would anyone with common sense like him? Fat chance. I have the feeling they probably hated him. Why? Because he would act without consulting anyone?

...Of course. If a sensible person like me had a subordinate like Tsuji, they would stand him up before a firing squad. After all, he was the kind of guy who'd go making his own arbitrary decisions. How useless can you get?

And does my vice commander have common sense? In other words, has he concluded that I'm a Tsuji who might go on a rampage?

Well, that's no good. I'm actually a sensible person who feels shame. I don't want to make decisions on my own and then shove the responsibility onto others. Plus, following rules is the meaning of my existence. I don't break them; I find loopholes!

"Lieutenant, we're being transferred to the Rhine. Some of you have fond memories there. Yes, gentlemen, the Rhine!"

Sweating bullets at this misunderstanding, Tanya racks her brain. Honestly, I want to avoid being seen like Tsuji, General Brute-Guchi, and those guys. If Lieutenant Weiss thinks of me like that, I'll need to have a talk with him.

Though brooding inside, she concentrates on getting through the current moment.

"The Rhine?"

"Well, we'll be in a rush, but they're expecting a lot out of us. We're going to do a counterclockwise sweep of the battlefield."

We just bop the guys who have the gall to show up. That's it.

We don't get paid to do more. There's also the idea of working hard to get promotions, but in the army, getting promoted doesn't always mean you'll be happy. As long as that's the case, I'd like to cut off my efforts where my pay grade ends. *Why in the world is this happening? No, I know Being X is at the root of this*, Tanya laments. I think twice about acting too much like Tsuji.

Next time maybe I should speak frankly with my troops. Should I ask

Chapter IV

Serebryakov what they think of me? Or should I ask Weiss how they're doing?

"So?"

"Yes, but before that, we're going to play a little game of marine mages. Rejoice. The navy has better food, right?"

But that's a job for later. For now, I have one piece of good news that is worth telling them. Navy meals are much higher quality than the army's. The navy lambastes the army for spending too much on "hardware," and frankly, the army can't deny it—because on the "software" side, the navy surpasses the army with their quality food. From a welfare standpoint, the navy is certainly a much more desirable workplace.

"Huh?"

"Courtesy of Colonel von Lergen. We're going to go help out the fleet."

》》》 JANUARY 18, UNIFIED YEAR 1925, IMPERIAL NAVY, NORTHERN SEA 《《《
FLEET COMMAND'S EXERCISE AREA 2

At one hundred feet.

Scowling at the spray, Major von Degurechaff gives the order for boarding assault formation. The idea is to practically skim the water without dropping their speed and charge their target. Responding to her directions, the companies all get into formations that support one another.

Beneath her serious expression, however, Tanya is shocked… They were told they'd be flying into anti–air fire, so despite it being an exercise, she expected an appropriate interception. Instead, she is compelled to worry. *Are they actually shooting?* She's puzzled by the weak intercepting fire. *Surely, they're going to fire on us, even though it's an exercise.*

We're performing an attack on a ship using visual combat maneuvers with a clear view. According to the scenario, we've already deployed a smoke screen to foil the intercepting fire. Tanya hides in the smoke and gets down to business, finding it disappointingly easy to reach boarding distance.

"Enemy mage incoming on the starboard side! Prepare for a close-quarters fight! Anyone not occupied, come starboard!"

A few petty officers on deck begin moving to handle the situation, but they're hopelessly slow. It's already too late. Once you let a mage get this close, you can't avoid a fight on deck. Maybe they weren't expecting it, but this is still pathetic.

Inside, she wonders: *Is this a trap?* Like the wily ones people used to plan back in the age of sailing ships? I'm pretty sure I've read nautical novels where confusion on the deck turns out to be a trick.

But no matter how I look at it, the opponents running hither and thither everywhere I can see seem a bit too inexperienced. The deck may be narrow, but I even see some sailors tripping. If that's acting, they would have had to spend an awful lot of time training to fall so naturally.

"Magic blades up! Company, on me!"

Anyhow, leading the charge again, Tanya has no choice but to maintain her speed perfectly and swoop in. She even deploys an interference formula right into the panicking cluster of sailors.

As some of them go flying, the sailors grow even more confused, and the marine unit that came running gets caught up in the mess. The rest of my company coming after me hinders the marines' efforts to restore discipline. They miss their chance to stop us, too busy with the exchange of checking fire.

"Don't let up! Keep shooting!"

"Fix bayonets! All hands, fix bayonets!"

A handful of officers and sailors just barely manage to fight back, but they're not enough to keep the force of the attack at bay.

Tanya and her company easily break through their defense. Then they stab the second bridge's soft shrapnel shielding and cling to it with their magic blades. We didn't slow down at all; one of the internal frames probably got dented.

Watching us come in is probably freaky as hell.

"Land and capture! Go, go, go!"

Even though they smashed into them pretty much head-on, the members of the 203rd Battalion are enthusiasm incarnate.

With brisk movements, they promptly establish a bridgehead. From there, they set about taking the main areas of the boat. Though outnumbered, their coordination keeps everyone well-covered.

"Destroy the anti–air gun mounts! Take the next set of points!"

"Gunners, don't let them get any closer!"

"We're taking the second bridge back. Form an assault team around the marine unit."

It takes a little while, but they manage to finish setting up their counter-attack team consisting chiefly of marines.

We may be a battalion, but our strength is our mobility, and that can't be used to its fullest in the closed space of a ship's interior. That's why the marines and marine mages are able to put up a fierce fight inside.

"Here's the counterattack! Marines!"

"Dump 'em overboard! Get rid of 'em."

But the members of the 203rd Battalion capture point after point with surprising efficiency.

Normally, mages focus on mobile battles and aerial maneuvers and tend not to be so great at close-quarters fighting. The vanguard might be different, but the members in the rear usually have a hard time with it. But training is about eliminating weak areas.

"Show them what the marines are made of! Don't let those landlub-bers think they're so tough!"

"The next group has arrived! I'm sending them in now!"

And so the 203rd Battalion and the marines, each with their own take on close-quarters combat, clash and refuse to give any ground. The marines have a slightly better position, but the situation is fluid.

As both sides struggle to make their next move, the follow-up company lands.

We shall be victorious. Major von Degurechaff and the company commanders grin. Meanwhile, the marines who had allowed reinforcements to arrive display their disgrace in their expressions. They're running out of fighting resources to tap into. Sailors would be some help, but they can't be pulled off the cannons. They hesitate slightly, and their actions get delayed.

"All unoccupied personnel, prepare for hand-to-hand combat! We're going to drive them off this ship!"

Still, if the bridges, engine block, and magazine get captured, your ship is done no matter how much you have left to throw at the enemy.

It's that crisis that makes them hesitate a bit before they scrape together what muscle they can for a counterattack.

The captain issues the order to gather up any spare fighting power. And when it comes down to it, a ship has quite a lot of personnel on board. Though it isn't their primary task, sailors can shoot guns. The mobilized officers and petty officers form provisional naval brigades and start to reinforce the marines.

It was hopeless to begin with. Their idea is to push and push till they push us off the boat. It's quite simple, but it's still a valid attack plan for the narrow space inside the ship. If this is all, though, the 203rd Aerial Mage Battalion can push right back. Humming, I cheerfully lay down a smoke screen, and just as the cunning fire from the attacking side has distracted the defenders—

"All hands, I don't care if they're marines! Teach them what a bad idea it is to mount a frontal attack on my battalion! Remember that the useless ones who die in war get sent to hell!"

With that shout, she attacks in a flash to bring the fight into close quarters.

The pressure of two companies is hitting the resistance hard.

Just as the sailors begin to retreat from the mages and their ogre-like game faces, Tanya takes a small unit on a detour.

While everyone is focused on the fierce fighting inside the ship, she seizes the opening and launches a sneak attack on the port side.

"We're pincered?! Shit! Move some of the crew to the port side!"

"They're all confused?! Success! Major von Degurechaff got around behind them! Now we destroy them!"

Our opponents look ready to run once they've been pincered, but we don't let them. Each company commander works to improve their results. The iron law of war is the harmony of impact and confusion.

Break their composure, disrupt their discipline, and then crush them.

Chaos is spreading on the defensive side between the rear attack, pulled off efficiently in loyal accordance with the principles of war, and the intensifying frontal attack. Just like we wanted.

An intense impact crushes the marines faster than they can close gaps and rebuild the interception line.

Chapter IV

"We're clear."

"Us too."

Directly after that, Tanya gives each company their own target as she mops up the defenders, who are no longer able to operate in an organized way. "Good. First Company, to the bridge. Follow me. Second and Third Companies, go to the engines. Fourth Company, to the magazine. Capture your objectives quickly." After eliminating the main enemy resistance force, we need to gain control of the key parts of the ship.

The plan is to approach each area in order by sweeping outward from captured locations. We manage to maintain speed by going around any pockets of enemy resistance, and the decision to share the burden across the battalion is implemented with high standards.

Once the ship side realizes that we've stormed the critical areas, they give up resisting. Discipline has collapsed inside, and the sailors look like they're about to flee. At the same time, their pretend enemy joins up with reinforcements and seems ready for more. The defense's fighting force is already practically nonexistent, and their methods of resistance are limited. They're forced to gracefully admit their defeat to the referees.

"Okay, rush them in your two-man cells. Vanguard troops, brace yourselves!"

"Major von Degurechaff, that's enough, that's enough."

The message comes just as she's about to step onto the bridge.

For the referees, who were forced to follow all those insane maneuvers, the end couldn't have come soon enough. Honestly, so many things had gone through their minds when she told them to come with her because she was going to seize the second bridge.

"The exercise is over! I say again, the exercise is over!"

The call ending the game echoes throughout the ship over the loudspeakers.

Hearing this, though they're concerned about all the things on the ship that were damaged, everyone is finally able to relax. It had been a rare joint combat simulation. Many things were broken, but there hadn't been any accidents.

"All right, stupid corpses, you can move now."

All the sailors and marines who were judged dead and ordered to lie still, facedown, sluggishly get to their feet.

We may have been using exercise-grade rubber bullets and low-power explosion formulas, but that doesn't mean they feel good.

Some of the injured even have to go to the infirmary to get treated by a surgeon.

For example, take the sailors who were unlucky enough to get caught up in the firefight between the 203rd Battalion and the marines. They said that, despite ducking down, they came out of it worse for wear because stray bullets kept hitting them.

Although such bad luck was rare, no small number of people were hurt in the melee on the interior of the ship. A team of medics and surgeons was on call and prepared for efficient intake, but I imagine the infirmary will still be crowded for a while.

And in the midst of all that hustle and bustle, Magic Major Tanya von Degurechaff is in the wardroom, which has already been picked up. Although it's small, some thought was put into the design, so the atmosphere is relaxing. It's now packed full of officers. In her hand is a cup of coffee she was given; it's supposedly better than the stuff the army serves. Something smells faintly like baked goods. Surely only in the navy, where they're allowed to bring their own rations and cookies, can you enjoy that.

Naturally, we're not just having a tea party for no reason. After the exercise, it's time for the main event.

"Very well, let's review the full fleet close-quarters exercise."

The seamen have been permitted port and starboard liberty and raced off to the PX still in a holiday mood now boosted by post-exercise cheer, but unlike them, the officers' real work begins now. We have to go through the referees' commentary and the reports from each unit commander to find areas of improvement and reflect on what happened so we can put the lessons to use in actual combat.

This time was different from the usual exercise in that it included a boarding scenario that aimed to be extremely realistic. But to *only* do that would be a waste.

"First of all, it's still early in the year, but I think we can say that this exercise was meaningful."

The all-important ratings showed that the participants thought the exercise was worth doing.

The navy, who provided the base and ship as the venue, are desperate for anti-mage combat experience; they can never get enough. Although their main job is counter-ship warfare, they've learned through battle that marine mages can't be ignored.

But they never have enough marine mages for an exercise, and how few mages they do have allotted internally is a matter of constant contention. Yes, the borderline-overworked marine mages are in such great demand that they don't have the wherewithal to participate in war games. And so, the navy was thrilled to have this joint exercise to gain some of that missing experience.

At the same time, Tanya herself and the 203rd Battalion had little experience with anti-ship combat or battles to capture ships, so the exercise was in their interest as well. More than anything, it was what the General Staff wanted. They had no choice but to participate. That notwithstanding, it was still a useful experience.

And when the referees said it was meaningful, they meant it. When it comes to results, although they were up against particularly elite mages, building some experience handling that situation was clearly valuable for the navy.

"All right. First some complaints from Captain Grän of the warship used in the exercise, *Basel*."

Captain Grän stands and bows to Major von Degurechaff. "…To be blunt, you creamed us. And on top of that, the year has only just started, and we've taken all kinds of damage." His expression is somewhat resigned as he acknowledges his ship's defeat. No one died during the exercise, but that didn't mean the ship wasn't laid to waste.

It was more than a few broken windows. The formulas and grenades may have been exercise-grade, but they were still hurled all over the place. Naturally, the crew did cleanup as an exercise in damage control, but still.

"Damage control went fairly well. The crew was able to make prompt repairs."

The results were all right. They could at least be satisfied with them. There were no issues during the operation inspection after interior maintenance was performed, mainly on the engines.

…That said, although the damage isn't bad enough that the ships need to be docked, there are a number of repairs that need to be made—broken glass exchanged, dents fixed, and so on—that will take some time.

Luckily, it'll be patched up by the time the Entente Alliance ships have to leave the neutral port, but the captain still isn't happy about it.

As such, Major von Degurechaff bows as well. Honestly, it might be a bit weird that the child among all these adults is the one being so considerate. It might be weird, but I guess I just have to go with it, since it's better than being seen as uncaring.

"Our most urgent task is to reevaluate our anti–air fire. I can't believe we didn't even graze the incoming mages." He looks like he wants to rough up the men of his who boasted that they wouldn't let the mages anywhere near the ship.

The gunners who upset him are sure to be trained extra hard for some time. Still, everyone is relieved that they learned their lesson in an exercise rather than in actual combat.

The observing captains are also sure to tighten up their training regimens in the same way. If things go downhill when the enemy reaches a ship, then they have to drive the enemy off before that happens. Learning that is a great outcome for the exercise.

"Major von Degurechaff, do you have any suggestions for improvement from the attacking side?"

"I believe the fundamental problem is a lack of firepower. I can't imagine anything but a dense barrage of anti–air fire will prevent an approach." Tanya, who was actually one of the mages to so easily break through their defense, has an even simpler opinion—the utterly straightforward one that they don't have enough guns.

Tanya would tell you that if intercepting is a matter of probability, the only way to raise the probability is to increase the density of anti–air fire. The idea for this comes from the simple knowledge that at the end of their trials and errors, the navies of countries outside this world all went running for the solution of adding more anti–air fire. If you don't outfit ships like porcupines, they'll be vulnerable to an attack from the sky.

Plus, Tanya adds in her head, *even the aircraft carriers the Americans used near the end of World War II that supposedly had great anti-aircraft fire couldn't completely stop a certain all-in approach taken on the assumption of not returning.*

"*Basel* has some of the most powerful anti–air cannons out of all our existing capital ships."

To someone who *doesn't know yet,* charging a ship with a mountain of autocannons seems like suicide.

The navy officer who brought it up, looking confused, seems to have done so because he thought the ship had enough firepower.

And it's not such an outlandish thing to believe.

It's a practical truth that human beings, while intending to take in things objectively, only accept what they themselves can understand subjectively. In a surprise twist, Lippmann's "stereotype" paradoxically describes how far the human intellect can expand.

A warship with a pile of autocannons is a floating fortress. Among them, *Basel* boasts outstanding defensive firepower, so the question arises: *Isn't that enough?* To the officers in attendance, it's a natural question. Or at least to them, it's not a strange one.

"From the point of view of the attacker, it's not much of a threat." But Tanya puts an end to it easily. "To be honest, it really wasn't even an obstacle." That matter-of-fact murmur is significant. She has hinted that anti–air fire is not actually an efficient defense against attacks from the sky. All the Northern Sea Fleet Command, previously lacking in anti-mage combat and exercise experience, can do is register anew what a threat mages are.

Still, that's just the opinion of one major, and they would like to hear from a third party who participated in the assault. The head referee gathers that and discreetly eyes the referee in charge of the attacking side.

The referee takes the hint and begins giving his general opinion. "I agree with Major von Degurechaff. I accompanied her on the charge and was surprised to find the firing line not so imposing." But contrary to most of the officers' hopes, he essentially repeats what Tanya said. "Overall, I'm forced to say that our current anti–air fire is about as useful as a bunch of firecrackers."

"...Our defensive firepower is that weak?" The claim is that they have been overestimating their defense, and in response the officers ask a question that shows their consternation: *Is it really, honestly that weak?*

"Yes, we're lacking even more than I expected. In order to halt approaches, we need to increase the number of guns until the ships are like porcupines."

The reply from the second referee is simple and leaves no room for misunderstanding.

"I agree. And we should be adding not just 20 mm autocannons but 40 mm as well."

Tanya concurs more strongly than anyone. She believes the American military provided the best example of ideal anti–air fire.

In this world, it's completely unheard of, but it's already been proven in combat. She indirectly proposes the innovation as her own contribution, albeit dispassionately.

"What do you mean?"

"This is just my opinion, but 20 mm are for short-range defense; in order to create a multilayered interception shield, I strongly recommend adding midrange guns," Tanya answers. From what she can tell, the 20 mm guns have the advantage when it comes to handling and speed, but in terms of range and power, they're weaker. It's logical to add 40 mm autocannons for intercepting at midrange.

Most importantly, mage defensive shells and aircraft have no chance of withstanding a 40 mm shell.

From the attacking point of view, capturing a warship with multibarrel gun emplacements all over like a porcupine would be a difficult task.

"If possible, I'd like to focus on numbers. We probably need ten times the current amount."

"Captain Grän, what do you think?"

"...It's an interesting suggestion, but we can't change the number of cannons without doing major overhauls, such as removing the secondary guns on the flanks."

"To go a step further, I would say that secondary guns are worse than useless. We need to increase the priority of air defense." Tanya knows it's disrespectful, but she sees a chance for the navy to take a decisive step forward and chimes in. After all, she knows the era of aerial warfare better than anyone here. She's sure the time will come when warships will be assigned to aircraft carriers as direct support.

Really, she would like to urge them to change the doctrine from obsessing about big ships with big guns to focusing on their air forces as their main power. Incidentally, she's also a believer in fire action and values warship cannons for their supporting fire.

That said, even one-shot lighters were able to send the then state-of-the-art *Prince of Wales* and the *Repulse*, which had been reconstructed for the modern era, to join the seaweed. Of course, we should concentrate on removing the secondary guns already and increasing the amount of high-angle guns and other autocannon emplacements.

She also knows that until a comparable incident occurs, it will be difficult to convince the ship warfare–oriented navy to accept an air force–centric doctrine.

At the time, the fleet's original mission was set as counter-ship combat, and the use of mages was not yet so widespread. I've heard that requests for vessels to be upgraded for anti-mage and anti–air combat began pouring in this year as a countermeasure. Honestly, everyone still thinks mages fight on land.

Computation orb functionality and aircraft specs are both improving. As a result, the idea that maybe orbs and planes might be threats is only just starting to spread.

Only someone who understands the history of how aviation advanced by leaps and bounds during the Second World War can understand. Until then, no one had dreamed war would drive scientific and technological advances like it does.

"Hmm. It's not that we're taking air defense lightly, but…"

"We'll have to think about it if issues arise fighting off other ships."

In truth, even officers who are far from inept have deeply rooted views. Ships are equipped to counter ships because the navy can't escape the instinct to keep their original counter-ship combat mission in mind.

And thinking in terms of counter-ship doctrine, they'd like to keep their secondary guns. Though the importance of being equipped for close-quarters fighting has lessened, the need to fight off torpedo boats and destroyers, which do press in to attack, is a factor that can't be ignored to them.

"We'll have to discuss it with Technology. Please let navy command and the Technology Department handle this issue."

In the end, the conclusion is not to reject the idea but take it under advisement, which essentially means to shelve it. Well, in a way, by saying her piece Tanya has done her duty. After all, it's no skin off her back if the anti–air fire isn't strengthened.

As long as it's not a ship I'm on, where it sinks has nothing to do with me. Besides, the Empire is a continental state, not a maritime state.

Without breathing a word of any of that, she camouflages herself with a sober attitude, but she is in utter earnest. The best thing for ensuring my own survival is training my troops.

Of course, she is passionate about identifying issues in this postmortem. Well, she has to be. She believes that preventing mistakes is best.

"All right. Are there any other remarks from the attacking side?"

"I would say there are cooperation problems."

"Of what sort?"

"The marines and sailors don't seem to be very well coordinated. I felt like the disorder of the sailors was tripping up the marines."

She had noticed it on her approach—the deck was a real mess. Her impression was that the two different corps had trouble working together.

If they had been units stationed there today, below-par coordination would be understandable, but for units that are shipmates, it's a bit problematic. From what I could tell, it seemed like the marines felt their job consisted of ground and landing battles.

Of course, I can't deny that those are their primary duties, but we don't want them to suck at fighting on board a ship. And the confusion and failure to cooperate with sailors is completely unacceptable. In an organization where sales and systems engineering become estranged, they have to compensate with a death march. In the military, the *death* in *death march* is literal.

Considering that I could end up a casualty of poor cooperation between our own troops, it's absolutely critical to suggest an improvement. Having reached this quite reasonable conclusion, albeit via a selfish argument, Tanya speaks eloquently on the necessity of increased coordination. Her idea at its root is self-preservation, but at the same time, she's altruistic; it can't be said that she isn't acting with the aim to benefit the majority.

And that attitude, for the good of the majority, leads to a proposal that is acceptable by the whole.

Probably everyone was vaguely aware of the poor cooperation. The head referee questions the concerned party. Naturally, he does it in a way that is sensitive to their sense of honor. "I see. What do the marines think about this?"

"I'm embarrassed to admit that we haven't trained much with fighting on ships in mind. I acknowledge the need for retraining."

In response to the comment from the marines, Tanya declares her unit's need for more training as well. "After having actually fought inside a ship, I think my unit is lacking experience, too."

She's half using inadequate training as an excuse; though the 203rd Aerial Mage Battalion is elite, the group is made up entirely of mages, and their lack of knowledge of other fields is a real problem.

That's why Tanya hopes to do joint training with the marines, who have the most experience on this front.

You can't hesitate to borrow wisdom from experts if you want to stay alive. The plan for what happens next can come *after* you survive.

If this meeting runs long enough, the navy will feed us dinner—that is, the good food that navy officers get. It's no problem at all if the exercise schedule takes more time than planned.

In this way, Tanya continues her hard work, cultivating a heartening friendship with the navy while keeping an eye on her next battlefield—though it runs against her own thinking—and thus she takes one step after another toward victory.

A shovel is an implement born of civilization.
Hooray for civilization.

Tanya von Degurechaff, *Analects of a Rhine Front Commander*

It's a familiar dream for the old man who lived through the Rhine.

He would have the same dream again tonight. As one of the soldiers who served in the Great War, it's all burned into his mind.

Back then, back there—in a way, it was where the rest of their lives were forged.

Even now, unceasing gunfire echoes in his head like a broken record.

Before he knows it, his thoughts return to that battlefield full of memories. Even after the war, the sights and sounds are too raw in their minds to fade. It's the past, but they can remember that world so clearly. The fucking battlefield. The most horrible thing the human race ever created. That battlefield where mud and flies reigned.

Ahh. He groans at the recollection. *The Rhine was the very gates of hell.*

The old man has that dream over and over and is reminded again and again. *I'll probably never forget it.*

I remember the events of that day in detail. As shells crisscrossed just over our heads, me and the rest of Company G were steadily advancing under orders to move to a new attack position. Of the five regiments composing the front line, Company E was seeing the most intense fighting, and our mission was to support their flank.

I was in a machine-gun squad. Our job was simply to set up the guns at the trench dug by the vanguard unit and create a firing position. The Imperial Army was supposed to have the Republican Army pretty well suppressed in that area, but the lines themselves were complicated as always. They were almost fluid. In other words, the battlefield was a bloody, chaotic jumble of us and them.

The bombardment had blown away all but one tree in this mire—the sort of place where resources were wasted, blood ran in rivers, and when you would peek out of the trench to see what you could see, it would be all artillery smoke.

Still, the blasted enemy artillerymen made nothing of the awful visibility and shelled us constantly at a varying pace. Our company's trench mortar squad returned fire, but they barely made a dent. Despite the smoke obscuring the battlefield, we could see a number of muzzle flashes from the Republican Army positions.

I remember how much we struggled with the mortars. They didn't have a stable place to shoot from because the duckboards were sinking into the mud. Conditions were so bad that for the machine guns, too, even the highly trained gunners couldn't control their lines of fire.

I remember that as far as the eye could see, it was soldiers covered in mud, doing everything within human power to secure their attack positions.

I remember that day very well.

The field guns set up in the trench were trying out some observed fire, and the designated riflemen were digging foxholes with all their might. Looking back on it now, these were superhuman actions from the few who stepped up in one corner of the harsh battlefield. Not allowing themselves to be discouraged by the maggots, the muck, or the shells raining down, enveloped in the stenches of rot and death, with no decent cover, those men advanced through the mud. They had trench foot. Their display of bravery is burned into my eyelids, and it even appeared divine; I respect those men to this day from the bottom of my heart.

It was a shocking picture from a world you can't understand unless you've experienced it; you can only understand by being there.

"I can't believe this. Those toads. They must really like the mud!"

"Yeah. The gunners want to turn this land into a swamp and jump right in."

"But the ones getting shot at are Company H. I feel for them."

The team's banter eased our nerves somewhat, but the chatter from the guys in a nearby foxhole reminded us of reality. The ones under fire were Company H, who had gone ahead of us. Frustratingly, the brass at the time seemed convinced we could break through the enemy's defense with human bullets.

How many lives do they think this muddy tract of land is worth?!

"Air support still isn't here?! Shut up the enemy guns already!"

Someone let out a groan that echoed the sentiments of the whole company. We were supposed to push the lines up in places under local air superiority. That's how the operation was supposed to work.

Those despicable bigwigs said we would have *complete* air support, but we wanted to scream that they must have meant a *complete lack of* air support.

"I told ya, didn't I? You can bet your Easter turkey that was an empty promise."

High explosives crisscrossed over the battlefield. A near hit from one of those was enough to blow a human body to bits. In a situation like that, close, full support was a pipe dream. So I don't think we were expecting much in the first place. Regardless of how the new recruits rushed through training felt, the old hands knew that there was no promise less reliable than one made by the brass.

Everyone ended up like that. The soldiers exposed to the squall of heavy shelling, faced with the inescapable pain and mental strain of long hours under fire, couldn't help their eternal skepticism.

If they didn't, gruesome reality would slay the beautiful propaganda in a single blow, and the soldiers would go insane. In order to survive the horrific war, you couldn't rely too much on hope.

"Ngh! I'm hit! Damn it!"

"Medic! Medic!"

I remember being able to hear, for some reason, the sounds of someone in a neighboring dugout crumpling to the ground and their friends panicking, even over the roar of the battlefield. I suddenly realized that one unlucky bastard had been done in by a stray shot or a sniper. Since the entire trench wasn't blown away and there were no follow-up shots, it had to be a sniper.

We quickly ducked lower and sprayed harassing fire anywhere it seemed like he could have been lurking. *We don't wanna die.*

"Send out a stretcher! Cover them!"

Chapter V

Then...

I'll never forget those four stretcher-bearers racing out under diligent cover to try to get their injured brother to the rear. Emblems of courage and integrity. The medics are the only ones those of us headed away from the battlefield can rely on. Because the medics, called *Sanis*, were with us, we were guaranteed some humanity in that hellish world.

Unlike people working easier jobs in the rear, if there was a fellow soldier who needed them, they would always charge into hails of bullets even we would balk at. Even when they were blown away with a painful impact, more of them were ready to go out after their fallen teammates. It was proof of their courage.

They were the only ones I really, deeply respected. They were the only ones we could trust no matter what. I still feel that way.

"Lay down a smoke screen!"

"Hand grenades! Throw everything you got!"

The mortar squad shot smoke shells, the designated riflemen threw grenades, and we just put up a curtain of fire. The stretcher was a sight for sore eyes when it safely appeared. Our trustworthy friends with their magnificent bravery. *Sanis* had to be protected if no one else; they were the only ones who would save us.

And at the same time, I guess you could say, due to our covering fire, the Republicans spread out across from us seemed to remember the target they were supposed to prioritize. They were determined to crush not the swiftly receding stretcher but the smart-aleck machine-gun nets. Thanks to that, we were showered in concentrated fire, and I lowered my head without thinking, unable to take all the blasts of dust filling the air from near hits. Facedown in our trench with our ears alert, we smiled weakly at the thought of how many Republican artillerymen must be treating us to shells.

But that strange calm only lasted so long. After the *whiz* of something cutting through the air came a big, heavy *boom* we weren't used to. It sent chills up our spines.

Those weren't 128 mm shells; they'd brought out their precious 180 mm field guns.

"Listen up, troops! Friendly reinforcements are on their way! Let's stick this out!"

At that moment, we were happy for instructions over the radio from our battalion commander, but our sense of futility was greater. Our battalion had no shortage of replacement troops. We'd nearly lost our will to fight, so I guess they were throwing us a line to cling to.

Maybe that line would work on guys who didn't know how unreliable it was, but we understood all too well how that illusion would hold up.

"So when the hell is that support unit getting here?"

Someone on the machine-gun crew expressed what all of us who knew that battlefield were thinking. We really needed reinforcements. The way it was going, we figured we would all have to die defending that quagmire and covered in its muck.

So we really wanted backup as soon as possible.

"I want reinforcements…preferably before we die." Was it me who murmured it? Or the fellow next to me? I still don't know, but I'm sure someone did.

That was when the nearby radio operator started shouting at the top of his lungs. The operators were the guys monitoring enemy transmissions, making sure they didn't pinpoint us. Usually they were full of bad news, but later I would think over and over how sometimes they did have something good for us.

"Reinforcements! Reinforcements are here!"

I remember very well how people thought the operator was shell-shocked and sent him pitying looks. But then we saw something we could hardly believe, so there was no time to think about that.

Or rather, we heard it.

"O Fatherland, my love, be at peace."

On every channel over a wide area, the words were broadcast so powerfully even a regular soldier with no magic ability could hear them.

Clouds of dust were blackening the sky, and the mud seemed to be swallowing up everything on the battlefield, but the voice that rang out over the chaos was surprisingly calm.

It was no wonder we questioned for a moment whether we had gone crazy as well. The phenomenon seemed that unreal.

It was the code for a unit of reinforcements. We cocked our heads thinking the backup couldn't be real, that it had to be an auditory hallucination.

"O Fatherland, my love, be at peace."

But we weren't hearing things and we weren't crazy; someone was really repeating those words in the official language of the Empire. And it was the single-use password to show they were friend and not foe at that!

"*Guardians of the Rhine! Ye are loyal! Ye are rocks! Ye are loyal! Ye are rocks!*"

The operator boosts the signal to the highest output possible, and the answer from the radio dugout was the happiest sounding I'd ever heard. The stream of words coming out of the machine-gun squad's radio will be forever carved into my eardrums.

We always laughed at what silly codes they'd come up with. The radio operators, especially, would make fun of them, but this time, just this once, I think all of us were truly consoled by them. The widespread interference only mages could employ. It could only be mages. It could only have been the elite mages of the Imperial Army.

So it's lucky they didn't know—that their saviors, their reinforcements, were hazardous, could bring utter destruction to their allies.

She was supposedly on their side, but even the Imperial Army brass treated her as a god of death. It was a battalion for war nuts by war nuts, and they had arrived on the battlefield.

Slicing through the haze of clouds and gunsmoke, she bristles with nerves. Major Tanya von Degurechaff, internally sick of this, externally expressionless, is leading her response unit to the Rhine Air Defense Identification Zone Sector D-5.

"Code confirmed. This is the 203rd Aerial Mage Battalion, call sign Pixie. We're en route. Arriving in 160 seconds."

Tanya isn't particularly keen on trench warfare. The only job I hate more is turning on the charm for propaganda.

After all, now that I've been turned into a girl, I'm faced with this annoying military framework where men are superior. Just the thought of my promotions being blocked by an invisible glass ceiling is enough to dampen any desire I might have to act all girlish for propaganda. Trench warfare, on the other hand, is just too dangerous.

Apart from that, the Empire's personnel system has adapted extremely meritocratic principles for the war, in a way, so I'm more or less satisfied with it.

So even though hugging every contour of the land to maintain the lowest-possible altitude as she speeds toward the battlefield is dangerous, she is satisfied because at least she'll be valued.

That said, she's in command of a mission to cross an area littered with spent shells and assault the enemy artillery position with gunsmoke curling high into the air. Even if it came with hazard and war zone pay, it didn't feel great.

"Troops, you'll be performing supporting combat. Ready anti-surface ordnance, diffusion explosion formulas, optical deception formulas, and counter-bullet outer shells. Take on counter-air and -mage fights as you like." Gripping her rifle and computation orb tightly, Tanya gives the necessary instructions in a matter-of-fact tone.

Supporting combat is actually a pain for commanders. Bombing the wrong side is unforgivable. If we blow away our own troops, next will be a shower of bullets from the firing positions on the ground, no question.

The trenches and positions are built in such a way as to limit damage, but even so, nobody is happy to be blown up by accident. Only the USA is allowed to accidentally bomb whatever the hell. That they somehow get enough leeway to—*oops*—bomb the Chinese embassy in Belgrade makes me jealous, in a way.

Setting those thoughts aside, the only viable option for this support mission is to swoop in close to the enemy position and go to town. In that case, the best plan is to maintain as high a speed and low an altitude as possible and invade all at once in a sneak attack.

But that's theory. The ones actually maintaining that speed and altitude are already fed up. No one will tell you that flying fast near the ground is comfortable.

Although this allowed me to escape the trouble surrounding the sinking of the Commonwealth submarine, getting sent to the Rhine front was bad luck.

"CP, this is Pixie. Send the target."

"Roger, Pixie. Take out the enemy artillery emplacement pummeling G and H Companies."

"Understood. I'd like to request five minutes of supporting suppressive fire starting now. We'll get them during that time."

Still, I'm glad that on this type of arena Tanya's managed to retain the measure of autonomy that naturally comes with being a Silver Wings Assault Badge recipient. For starters, I can choose my targets freely.

And the rear base may not have been perfectly tidy, but it was way better than getting all muddy, being ordered to defend a position, and ending up the target of a barrage in the confusion.

The place just barely counts as a rear base, though. The meals aren't the standard portable trench rations but proper hot food. On top of that, if I may broach an indelicate topic, the waste management situation is also better. It's only our first spring. If the air when I'm flying low reeks this badly, I can only imagine they're doing the exact opposite of what hygiene dictates.

As the cultured man with a commonsense grasp of hygiene I was before trenches, becoming a little girl, and what have you, I can only say it's a difficult environment to withstand. It's about as bad as being aboard a submarine sinking into an out-of-order toilet.

Instead of that, I have work commensurate with my pay striking field guns, with their feeble anti–air fire, from the sky.

And as long as there are no intercepting mages, we'll just be duck hunting. They'll be great targets. I want to rack up as many accomplishments as I can and fulfill the requirements for leave. I may be here as punishment, but if nothing's on paper, I must be allowed to exercise my rights.

I want to hurry up and get transferred to the rear to find a safe post.

"Five minutes? That won't even suppress the anti–air fire, much less the artillery."

After all, even a strike mission, which is comparatively safe for the front line, forces you to run some pretty lousy risks.

For example, the observation squad is going out of their way—

volunteering—to support us. If the frontline observers are acting as guides for us, that has to mean the situation is less than ideal. Usually, the observers would be out there spotting impacts. If they have time to kill, it must mean our side doesn't have much artillery.

If we deploy our mage's outer shells at full power and fly in anti-surface assault formation, there's no way we'll get shot by our own, at least.

If by some miraculous chance we suffer direct hits, we should be able to escape fatal injury thanks to the new orb model. More importantly, defense from artillery is drilled into everyone in boot camp.

"That's no problem. And don't worry about us—keep firing after we go in."

After all, keeping an eye out overhead is the commander's job in an anti-surface assault. Having one unit strike while another unit provides air cover is a basic necessity in an air battle.

I'm sure I don't need to explain that if I fly with direct support, the danger of getting caught in a barrage lessens to an incredible degree. Plus, I can finally increase my altitude. Escaping that sticky, thick air even feels a little nice.

Anyhow, leaving the smell and the danger zone is enough to improve Major von Degurechaff's mood.

"Lieutenant Serebryakov, we're getting five minutes of supporting fire. After all the artillery shelling drills we did, I don't believe there's any numbskulls in my battalion who would take a friendly shell to the head."

"Understood."

Frankly, it still feels weird to call my being "she," but anyhow, this little girl is wearing a rare smile. She pays no mind to the rather strained quality of the reply and, noting that it's time for work, cheerfully starts on an upward trajectory. Since we'll be attacking the ground, we don't have to climb to freezing cold temperatures—another plus.

As a result, Major Tanya von Degurechaff is decidedly chipper. Her expression even relaxes into a grin.

And that scene is carved into the mind of the former soldier who was there watching it. How many years has it been since the war? Yet his memories of the time are still clear as day.

Chapter V

*　　*　　*

Pleasantly surprised by the news of reinforcements, we figured things would work out somehow. That said, the threat level we were facing might have dropped a bit, but lowering our guard as well would see us turned into silent corpses.

So our company used the little extra time we'd been given wisely. The dead were moved aside, and stretchers were prepared for the wounded. And the machine guns had just worn out, so we arranged to swap in replacement barrels. To our dismay, however, although they had plenty of the all-important barrels, apparently Logistics was too understaffed to deliver them to the firing line in the middle of a large-scale battle.

When they told my team to send someone, I was called upon to settle my tab from that ritual both traditional and sacred known as cards. In other words, "You owe us!" Come to think of it, I think the cards hated me back then. Or I just couldn't see through the clever cheating of my company mates. It pains me that now I have no way of knowing.

But at the time, those things weren't even a dream in my mind as I set off, grumbling and crawling to the base dugout. There I negotiated with the formidable Logistics NCO and ended up stuck carrying the parts.

People tend to have this misunderstanding that it was safe in the rear, but on the Rhine front at the time, safety was a fantasy.

The closest distance between firing lines was only a few dozen meters. I wish I had been staring down the enemy in one of those. Since the trenches were so close together, the risk of accidentally hitting friendlies was high, so they couldn't usually conduct bombardments.

Even if that wasn't their situation, artillerymen apparently hated firing into dangerous areas where they might lay waste to their own along with the enemy. Whether Empire or Republic, we all had the common desire to avoid blowing up our fellow troops.

Rather than drop high explosives on our own positions, shoot for the enemy, even if you miss. It was common sense for both armies, so if you watched out for snipers, land mines, and rifles on the forward-most line, you weren't likely to be an instant fatality.

But I should probably add that it wasn't rare for artillery to mistake the position of the front line or to have trouble telling friend from foe in the confusion. I was once in a position nearly overrun by the Republican Army, and I saw all the invading soldiers get wiped out in an instant by Republican Army shells. Our respectful nomination of the enemy artillery for the Field Artillery Badge made it into the official gazette as a bit of a gag. *We applaud the Republican artillery's great demonstration of their training and contribution to the imperial war cause.*

That's the kind of battlefield we were dealing with, but there was only one reason the rear was considered the most dangerous place to be.

It's the radios. Any strong waves that aren't your own are obviously enemy command or a base dugout. It doesn't take even two days to crush a newbie's delusions of safety because of our sturdy underground fortifications.

If you can't achieve much firing on the front line, then aim a storm of steel at the communications apparatus you can find, or so the thinking goes. If heavy armor-piercing rounds hit, dugouts are practically meaningless.

You're holed up in a cellar one minute, and then next, you're being plowed by artillery shells—the end. A suffocating death under a collapsed trench would be dreadful. Nobody was eager to set foot in a radio dugout.

At the time, they were so dangerous it was taboo to keep the communications base in the same dugout for more than forty-eight hours. Nobody talked about it, but everyone avoided doing it.

The reason radios were brought to the front despite those conditions was that we needed them. You can't keep something as big as an army together with semaphores and trumpets alone. Wireless technology has proved effective amid the fog of war, so it's no wonder armies continue to depend on it even now.

And listening in on the flood of messages was second nature to not only the radio operators but also the rumor-starved soldiers in the trenches.

That's why I was keeping my ears open by habit and heard it. Something so unbelievable I wondered if the fray had ruined my ears.

"There aren't any numbskulls in my unit who would get hit by a friendly shell. We need to prioritize keeping the enemy under control and holding them back above all else."

A commander asking for a bombardment to be shot over them? I was about to shake my head, thinking there must have been some mistake, when—

"CP to Pixie 01. These are high-explosive shells with fuses timed for air bursts, you know!"

"Pixie 01, roger. That's fine."

Despite the static, I could tell she sounded cheerful. I'm still confident in my hearing ability even at this age, but that time was the one occasion I didn't trust it.

She sounded so excited. Her tone was lighthearted, but her message was disturbing. What I heard over the radio was definitely the voice of someone having fun. She thought nothing of a direct hit from an air burst. She wasn't worried about shrapnel coming down like rain?

Without thinking, the NCO I didn't even know and I looked at each other. We had to make our artillerymen bombard our own mages? I couldn't believe it. If they hit them, there would be hell to pay. Even if they were forgiven, they would have killed their own.

"...Is she serious?"

"She can't be. Why do the mages listen to her?"

But either God is a piece of shit, or he has some farsighted design us lambs can't even begin to imagine. She was serious.

In the case of friendly fire, it was impossible to tell which emplacement had hit the wrong target, so incidents were handled with silence. They were unfortunate accidents, and no one said a word.

But it's a different story if the artillery is executing an observed fire mission on an area with our troops in it. Their reputation would be ruined. No one would forgive firing on our own troops, even if it was an order.

"...Major, do you...?"

"Don't worry about us. Continue the bombardment."

Even more invigorated. It scared me that such good cheer was coming over the radio. No, even now I'm not sure exactly what I was scared of.

The fear of being shelled for hours on end, holed up in a trench praying to make it through. The terror and the urge to scream at the top of your lungs, *Just put me out of my misery!* Only someone who has experienced that horror can understand it. There was something strange about some-one who could laugh off the fear of a bombardment.

I wasn't this scared even when the sniper was aiming at us. I was cold. It felt like my body was frozen to the core. *What the hell is this chill?*

"Pixie 03 to Pixie 01! Detecting multiple mana signals! Two company-sized groups of enemy mages are on their way up! Time to contact is 600!"

I remember that the warning someone issued brought me back to myself. And the radio operator frantically relayed the enemy info to other stations.

It was either just a new enemy unit or an intercepting unit. Even so, that was daily life on the Rhine lines, so I felt a strange happiness at returning to the normal from such an anomaly.

I remembered that I had to take the replacement parts and ammuni-tion and return to the firing line. I had to get back while the communica-tion trench was relatively tranquil. So it must have been about the time I thanked the NCO, grabbed the stuff, and was about to set off running?

I definitely heard the click of a tongue and a sigh over the radio—the same radio that cheerful voice had been coming from until a moment ago.

"First Company, prepare for counter-mage combat. Follow me. These idiots don't have an appointment, so we're going to beat them back. The rest of you, on the artillery. Finish that quick and join up with us."

The spirit in her words was like a blizzard. You don't know that spirits can dwell in words? It's a pretty well-known topic on the battlefield, but, well, it's probably better not to know. Maybe it'll be easier to understand if I say it was like the devil reading prophetic writings at random.

In other words, chaos.

"Pixie 01 to CP. We'll meet the incoming enemy mages, but no changes to the original plan. You don't have to watch out for air combat."

Normally, that would be condescending and overconfident. The ones under that commander must have been unlucky. But when I replay the memories in my mind, I can't help but shout, *You monster!*

A hero, a star, an outstanding magic officer. You, ma'am, were a great officer. To all of us imperial soldiers serving on the Rhine lines, you were a god.

Chapter V

"A new commander with a lot of mana and not much else? She must have a death wish." Unfortunately, whoever uttered that comment is no longer alive.

"Pixies…? I'm pretty sure I heard of them from some Great Army guys. They said she was a god of death."

The rumors from those guys who thought they knew a bit about Major von Degurechaff were true. Yeah, she's a god—an immensely powerful one who presides over life and death.

"Things are getting fun now, troops. You're having fun, right?"

Her words, brimming with a spine-chilling anger, swept over the area as if she was planning to attract all the enemy hostility like moths to a flame.

Major von Degurechaff had bared her fangs. It invited a violent reaction.

The Republic wanted to hunt the devil. In other words, they devoted all humanity's wisdom to killing the god of death. Gods don't die, but those of us next to them?

…They were right to call her a god of death.

She killed the enemy, and the enemy killed our men. Then the noble major, with a glance at all the dead in the mud, took her leave.

Fucking hell.

>>> FEBRUARY 24, UNIFIED YEAR 1925, THE SUBURBS OF BERUN, IMPERIAL <<< ARMY MILITARY COURT

Tanya would tell you that an army, at the end of the day, is a state's instrument of violence. No matter what rhetorical flourishes are employed, its fundamental nature doesn't change. Those who get indignant and ask, *What do you mean, "instrument of violence"?* either don't understand the military or do understand voters, one or the other.

Either way, regardless of the definition, the army must be controlled. Thus, regardless of how trustworthy those making up the organization are, they must be put on a leash.

The emperor's army, protectors of the Empire, vanguard of the people, shield of the nation... Even the Imperial Army, showered with such praise, is no exception.

Imperial subjects are proud of their soldiers. That's why deviating from that ideal inspires such reproach.

The imperial military, as one of its standards, desires all officers and men to be model citizens. These expectations apply across the board, even to lowly privates.

A natural consequence of this is that proper conduct is demanded of honorable officers with special emphasis. In a way, during peacetime it's even more important than your caliber as a soldier. As a result, the military authorities have a maniacal love for rules, meaning they have a court-martial waiting for you if you break one.

As a class in society, military officers are ashamed of being court-martialed. But that's during peacetime. The peaceful era of prioritizing honor and worshipping causes is over.

Now we're at war. The matters dealt with in military courts, too, become issues of whether you unflinchingly carried out your duty or not.

So according to military logic, it's difficult to overlook that this was an officer just doing their duty who got mixed up in an international political deal brought about by improperly maintained legislation.

On the other hand, in a foreign affairs sense...a few of the high-ranking officers and most of the diplomats are pulling their hair out. *"Please consider the politics!"* they demand. *"You intend to make an officer who did her duty a scapegoat?"* comes the retort. The combination of these viewpoints makes for a volatile courtroom atmosphere.

There we find the governance of a trial according to law.

"Major von Degurechaff, this court is dismissing your case." The legal specialist acting as the judge stands and reads the decision, amid a forest of thorns formed from the gazes of uniforms and suits alike.

They're *throwing out* my case. Which is to say, this compromise lets them avoid having to reject the claim by saying there's no reason to make one; they're getting around making a judicial call by saying that the case doesn't technically meet the criteria to be considered.

The acting judge can do nothing but read the paper in his hands with an expression like a Françoisman who has been served the best Albion cuisine in the world three nights in a row. They need to save face on both sides, but if the positions are in marked contradiction, sublation is the answer. In other words, shelving the case is the only choice.

"The attack on and sinking of the neutral country's vessel was an unfortunate accident."

But by adding that extra bit at the end, he is able to express his regret about the affair. It's clear to all seated in the courtroom that the presiding legal officer inserted the line to absorb some of the shock.

To Tanya, this is the reconciliation she was expecting. She knows that someone who is faithful to the logic of the organization is in no danger of being disciplined unless they do something to harm the whole.

And the group from the Foreign Office had been prepared for that decision as well. They went in with the gloomy thought that the army would probably not give them the decision they wanted, but they understood. Not that understanding does anything to soften the looks they're sending Tanya's way from their seats in the gallery, fists clenched.

Meanwhile, as Tanya, I feel that receiving these murderous stares as if she's killed their parents was rather unfair. Of course, I understand what the Foreign Office guys think. They very badly want a scapegoat to appease public opinion in the Commonwealth.

For better or worse because the Foreign Office types value the entire state, they apparently don't consider an individual's interests with the same framework as the national concerns.

Well, that's annoying. Tanya wants to sigh, but seeing as they are already seething internally, she figures keeping her mouth shut is the smarter plan and remains silent.

"It is a grave truth that international relations have been harmed by this accident, but in light of both precedent and laws and regulations, although it is our moral obligation to debate Major von Degurechaff's negligence, we find that in terms of legal authority, the matter lies outside our jurisdiction."

The statement he reads is, in a way, declaring an ambiguous position. While speaking of moral obligation and whatnot, they indicate, in a roundabout way, that they intend to evade responsibility via the bureaucratic reply that the matter doesn't fall under their legal authority. That said, Tanya's not the only one who can understand that to not judge her means the same thing as to not blame her.

"In addition, having taken into account the lawful nature of the mandate Major von Degurechaff was given, we acknowledge that at the time she had very little room for discretion and that she acted in faithful accordance with her orders. In any event, however, we dismiss the case."

But it seems like the General Staff or someone at the top put pressure on them. Even to Tanya, that last bit on the conclusion was a strangely favorable addition.

She grins. Without realizing it, her glossy lips have twisted into a faint smile. With this, she is as good as innocent.

But in the courtroom, the only one looking so cheerful is the girl at the center of it all. Among a majority of people who are willfully suppressing their expressions, the smiling defendant can't help but draw attention—all the more so because the happy face belongs to Major von Degurechaff, who is rumored to have rather emotionless features.

"For the aforementioned reasons, we lift Major von Degurechaff's detention order."

All those involved think it best not to mention that she wasn't ever under one.

That said, confronted with her smile, many of the attendees fret and wonder if this was really the right thing to do. But the decision has already been made. And the superior mage the front lines want so badly will be released from custody...exactly as the General Staff expected.

The Rhine lines call for urgency. Having a usable mage detained due to a political issue would be intolerable.

They can prioritize the allotment of shells and other supplies to the Great Army but not mages?

If they could fight the war like that, then no one would have to worry. *Give us more mages! Even just one more!* When wailing entreaties like that are coming in from the front lines, the General Staff don't have the resources—anywhere—to let a decorated Named just loaf around. And how would they? If they had such resources, the war would surely have been decided a long time ago.

We need her on the Rhine. It can't be helped. For those sorts of reasons

alone, the matter was decided from the start. Well, no, if she had actually been negligent, things might have been different.

Those are the only reasons. She's proud and visibly relieved that her previous judgment has proven correct.

According to the rules of military and international law, I threatened
a submarine of unknown nationality that was either violating or deviating from established standards. Though unfortunate, the accident was
caused by warning shots fired according to procedures that were not created with submarines in mind.

If there had been even one mistake in execution, the diplomats probably could have gotten the heavy punishment they wanted so much. But
when there wasn't a single error? That's right—if there are no grounds
for a sacrifice, what do you think will happen?

If they were going to force through disciplinary action on me under
these circumstances, this would turn into a scandal involving everyone
from the Ministry of the Interior and the people from the army and navy
who drafted the rules to members of the Foreign Office. My most significant military achievement has been to complicate things.

*I'm a promising mage and a recipient of the Silver Wings Assault Badge.
In other words, they can't afford to cut me off.* And Tanya's analysis is
correct.

The army's Railroad Department, the Service Corps, Operations in
the General Staff, and even the Technology Division had been putting
pressure, albeit informally, on the legal officers. The person in charge
of practical matters in each department had gone directly and hinted
that they were deeply concerned that an outstanding officer's reputation
might be ruined. It was probably so much pressure it gave the legal officers stomachaches.

I'm so important that multiple departments came together to protect
me. Not that anyone made direct threats, but the expectations multiple
military organizations have for me put an awful lot of pressure on the
legal officers not to disappoint them.

So the legal specialists' hard-won achievement was showing that they
were ready to court-martial me and deliberate. I can say that's a job well
done.

But that's only an internal matter. Someone within the organization may have resisted, but to an outsider, the end result wouldn't look any different.

Of course, in terms of international law, the matter between the Empire and the Commonwealth is officially settled. It was an unfortunate accident. The deal is that the Empire expresses their regret, the Commonwealth makes an announcement to the effect that they hope this will be prevented going forward, and there ensues some finger-pointing where each lays most of the blame on the other.

But that's between diplomats. I highly doubt the people will accept that just because the government does. The Commonwealth's public is furious that one of their warships was sunk and people died as a result; they have no reason to bury the hatchet so easily.

...On top of that, and I'll say it without mincing words, Commonwealth authorities are happily inciting such opinions.

The atrocious Imperial Army.

For someone who knows their geopolitics, their actions are actually natural. It's obvious what would happen if the Empire defeated all its opposition on the continent. Having to face one giant country would have to be a nightmare. So if the people aren't on board with fighting the war, there's nothing strange about the authorities starting to stir them up.

Into that situation comes an event, an *unfortunate accident*, perfect for propaganda. No matter how dirty it is, they'll shout their anti-Empire views endlessly. And reading the complicated legal details of the discussion in the paper is too much trouble.

Officially, of course, both countries declare it an accident and speak of it as an unfortunate misunderstanding.

The official line from both sides is that the Commonwealth submarine's communications and navigation equipment were malfunctioning from the start and had broken down, so the sub lost its way in imperial waters, was unable to pick up the radio contact from the imperial mage unit on guard in the area, and began a training dive as part of its scheduled exercise. Then, as a result of warning shots fired according to the law of war, a high level of water pressure was applied to the hull of the submarine. About to be crushed, it performed an emergency blow.

Then both sides, implying that the other is to blame, deliver the ambiguous conclusion that as a result of lifesaving operations performed by the imperial mages, many injured crew members were treated at an imperial hospital, but for those with serious injuries, the rescue was in vain, and they perished. It is also confirmed that the emergency mechanisms didn't function in time and the submarine sank due to flooding. Additionally, both countries agree that the loss of life is regrettable and that there will need to be discussions about how to prevent similar accidents going forward.

So according to that story, it was more of a shipwreck than a sinking by attack. What that means politically is that both sides admit to mistakes, but they agree to look together for a way to prevent future accidents.

But if the Commonwealth wanted to, it could paint a very simple picture.

Empire Sinks Commonwealth Vessel

That would prime their public more than enough. It'd be like pouring gasoline on an already smoking fire. That's precisely why the Empire's Foreign Office is so anxious to avoid any further deterioration of the situation.

No, to be more precise, everyone knows. Everyone knows that at this stage, the world is asking whether the other powers will allow the Empire to be the sole winner and invite the birth of a hegemonic state or intervene to stop that from happening in the interest of balancing the powers.

So this is an excuse. Nothing more, nothing less. In reality, everyone has braced themselves. If you have commonsense powers of judgment, it's plain to see.

The policy makers in both the Empire and the Commonwealth are aware that the clash between the two countries is only a matter of time.

As such, the handling of Major von Degurechaff, one little magic officer, is not top priority.

Basically, it's politics. But it's also true that as a result of all this, her presence is a bit complicated. So being sent to the Rhine is understandable. In one respect, this is where Major Generals von Zettour and von Rudersdorf were pushing to put her anyhow, so it can be done now without any awkwardness.

The General Staff is sending me and expecting results. The diplomats expect me not to cause any more issues. If possible, they'd like me to die out there. Then the legal specialists can escape this pain in the neck.

Anyhow, now that everyone and his brother wanted to send her and her troops west, the Devil of the Rhine sneered.

And the situation on those lines became even more hellish.

》》》　　　　APRIL 5, UNIFIED YEAR 1925, THE RHINE LINES　　　《《《

Life with shells from breakfast through brunch. Waking up to find your friend who was sleeping right next to you dead is a rarity that happens all the time in service on the forward-most line. If you relax in the trenches, you get burned. That's why you have to smile, keep your mind sound, and watch out for your health. They say you can't fight a war with a smile, but wars without smiles are dangerous.

If the troops lose the ability to smile, that's a bad sign. Times like those, you need to make sure they aren't drinking too much. If you don't want to get sniped at, you have to give up cigarettes.

As that thought occurs to her, Tanya realizes with a start that she'd like to give herself a pat on the back for not wanting to drink even though they've confiscated so much alcohol. The only ones in the battalion who are getting enough drink and tobacco despite no rations are me and Lieutenant Serebryakov. Someone must care about us; we even get playing cards and candy.

Cocking her head, wondering whether girls are unexpectedly more suited to this type of warfare, Tanya is once again forcibly reminded how harsh life is in the trenches. Even the soldiers most loyal to their nations might turn traitorous if cards, one of their sole leisure activities, were taken away. There are tens of thousands stationed on the front lines in this delicate mental state.

Even on the most peaceful day in those trenches, the weather is rainy with a chance of shells. Apart from when we deal with snipers and harassing fire, we can just lie around in the damp and the mud, but we're probably only able to get away with that because mages are so scarce.

Mages have leeway to take a quick break in the rear and get cleaned up. We're worked that much harder when we get back, though, of course. On sunny days, vision is good, and we fight huge, fierce battles where blood demands blood. In this world, the number of shells flying around has reached the point where a single division consumes one thousand tons in a day. How could they say, *Artillery plows and the infantry advances?* Sure, it's half-true, but we can't advance.

Anyhow, both matériel and men are being used as if they are worthless, and when Tanya steps back and thinks about it, it's unusual; the more she thinks about it, the more she wants to frown. It's such a huge waste that she can't imagine a bigger one. Even I think human assets should be better taken care of.

Once the troops receive their red slips and get called up, it costs money to train, outfit, and feed them, but here's this war where we're going through them like they're sold at bulk discount. Our meetings may not be with stockholders, but it's a wonder we don't get criticized.

We're firing with such wild abandon I want to grill them for about an hour to see how much kickback they're getting from Grupper for these shells.

Tanya doesn't doubt the importance of a curtain of fire. Of course, she understands that without the views of her esteemed superiors.

But she has told them they should at least cut costs. The rear is such a mess that she has to sincerely wonder why there need to be seven or eight different standards for railway guns alone.

Never mind the 20 cm guns and whatnot. Why does there have to be so much variety among 80 cm railway guns used by thousands of men? As someone with rotten experiences with an engineer, I suspect the imperial engineers just made them because they wanted to. I wouldn't put it past them.

Still, shouldn't they be at least a tiny bit interested in mass production?

Anyhow, faced with this scene, I can see why the military-industrial complex prefers war.

So that's why Japan was booming during World War I. Ditto regarding "special procurement" during the Korean War.

There's no way sales don't climb when you have consumers plowing through supplies at this tremendous rate. It's a perfect example of supply and demand. The market is so attractive it almost makes me want to start up a private military company.

Ah, the heartlessness. If they're going to waste us like this, they should at least raise our wages. They have the money to shoot these shells at the Republic like so much water, and those cost who knows how much a pop. They should give some thought to employee welfare. I'd like to receive more than just candy and snacks.

Tanya is lost in these utterly normal thoughts for an employee to have when Lieutenant Serebryakov interrupts her with an administrative notice.

"Major, we've received word that the fresh mages have arrived at group command. They say they'd like you to stop by to see about them…"

"Fresh mages? …Even if I wanted to replenish the battalion, we haven't lost anyone." Zero casualties. Tanya intends to be performing the most cost-effective management on the insane Rhine front, so she doesn't understand the relationship between her battalion and new recruits. "Are you sure they weren't stationed here by accident? Or did the message go to the wrong person?"

"Though it's presumptuous, I did, er, check myself…and there's no mistake, ma'am."

I'm confused. I didn't even request any replacements. But Lieutenant Serebryakov says she didn't mishear, that she confirmed there is no misunderstanding. So Tanya has to think. Her adjutant understands that a battalion with no casualties doesn't require replacements. Command understands this logic even better than Serebryakov, so it couldn't be them.

On top of that, the battalion is already an augmented battalion. For a unit under a major's command, that's about as big as they get. And it's difficult to imagine being promoted and receiving new personnel so suddenly under these circumstances.

The only logical inference to make is that we're in for some trouble.

Why? I'm such good person, cost conscious, and a stickler for compliance. If Fate exists, I can guarantee she's a jerk. Well, she's probably in league with Being X.

"Uh, this isn't for sure…it's only a rumor…but I heard Command might want us to act as an instructor unit."

"What? And where did you hear that?"

"Well, a classmate from the Cadet Corps is attached to Command as an observer on the Rhine. She's in a different sector, but…in a personal letter, she said, 'I heard you're going to be a teacher. Nice work.'"

Hearing this plausible rumor through a random personal connection, Tanya finds herself asking for clarification.

"Lieutenant, your friend's ears are a little too sharp. Not that it's anything to be upset about."

The duty to instruct recruits who aren't used to the battlefield yet… It's a bit late, but someone must have noticed the rate at which new troops fall. That's all well and good, but how did they conclude that we should be the instructors?

"But an instructor unit? If that's true… No, with the war going as it is, I doubt they'll have us fall back to the rear. So they're telling us to train rookies at the front?"

One of my men snorts as if he can't believe it. Exactly. Fresh recruits on a battlefield are deadweight that can't even be used to deflect incoming rounds. Honestly, they should be hauled off somewhere else.

I don't want anyone in my way, and yet they assign me recruits to train? Frankly, I want to scream at them to come over to the front and see for themselves whether that is even possible.

But just as I'm thinking that, First Lieutenant Weiss yells it himself. "Unbelievable. I guess they think we can babysit while fighting a war!"

They all start shouting with no way to vent their indignation. Well, they're honest guys. And as one who's spent time shivering in a trench, I can sympathize.

"So we're supposed to keep the shells off them? Have you ever heard something so stupid?"

"Well, umm, everyone was a new recruit once…"

Still, Lieutenant Serebryakov's cautiously stated comment is correct. Watching after panicking newbies is a bona fide pain in the ass, but we were all new once. Going a step further, Tanya's already fought on the Rhine while babysitting once before.

Maybe it's because she has that experience that the brass is pushing it on her again.

"Yeah, it's true. I taught you on the Rhine, Lieutenant."

"Yes, Major, I've come this far thanks to you."

Considering that, contrary to my expectations, I managed to find a useful subordinate, maybe we just have to do our best and see if we can dig up someone good.

"This might be rude, but the major's training seemed pretty harsh. I can't believe you..."

"What's that, Lieutenant Weiss? If you have something to say, go ahead and say it."

"Never mind—excuse me!"

From the looks on my bickering subordinates' faces, it seems like they'll take care of the recruits. And it's an order, after all. Tanya unwillingly braces herself. Resigned, she has to force herself to accept the task.

The reason she still can't think positive is that she knows reality.

They're throwing new recruits into a world where you'll go crazy if you can't endure the misery of suppressive shellfire. She'll want to pull her hair out the day an untrained newbie makes a scene in the trenches or the lodgings at base. At least if it's at the base, she can shove them on the medical staff in the rear, but if they panic on the front lines, we won't have time for that. I won't know what to do.

More importantly, panic is contagious. If one handsome newbie's face crumples into a teary mess, and then the brave ones who've been enduring everything start making a fuss, I won't be able to control it. If someone pukes everywhere, it'll start an unacceptable chain of nausea for everyone. In a worst-case scenario, I'll have no choice but to produce silence with a shovel.[18]

Shovels are fantastic for rookie education—we can bury their waste products, shut them up, and, if necessary, bury them as well. They're useful no matter where you are—trench, base, or graveyard.

"Well, that's fine. Gentlemen, if that's our duty, we have no choice

---

[18] **produce silence with a shovel**   To shut someone up by hitting them. Doesn't really distinguish between knocking someone down, knocking them out, and killing them.

but to do it." That said, orders are orders, and it's not as if this one has been issued yet. It's important to confirm these things. "Anyhow, first let's inquire with Command. If it's the truth, it'll be tough, but we'll just have to do it. We'll give it our all!"

If I ask for confirmation on the rumor, I'll learn whether I want to do this or not. If it's true that we'll be rearing greenhorns, then we'll have to do it in a way that doesn't break our backs. Tanya braces herself. We can't be expected to hold their hands every step of the way.

Of course, I know that wasting precious human resources is a folly to be avoided. Which is also why I think I'd like to do this only as long as it doesn't put too much of a burden on me.

"This is Major von Degurechaff. About the new mages…"

So Tanya hazards a simple guess and receives confirmation right away.

In a nutshell, the mission we've been given is to break the newbies in. From the phone conversation, Tanya makes a fairly certain guess that her unit will be training them.

Then the first thing to do is have them observe the firing line as soon as possible. I'll just be glad that the battalion shouldn't get thrown into anywhere actually dangerous.

The front lines will teach them reality far better than a million words of explanation. Apparently, my troops agree.

All right, I need to plan a training schedule is what I should have been thinking.

Yes, what I should have been thinking.

"Gentlemen, welcome to the Rhine front!"

The fresh recruits were sent over more efficiently than I expected. Tanya was thoroughly at a loss as she gave them a word of welcome. When Command does something promptly, things are not normal. It's an anomaly, and you need to prepare yourself for the worst.

In the army, not having to worry about Command's mess of administrative procedures is the kind of aberration that should put you on guard. Supplies get held up, reinforcements are delayed, but they'll send trouble over right away. In other words, Command being efficient is bad news.

Which is why even Tanya wants to rip her hair out over the group of newbies they've pushed on her. Even though she knows it isn't becoming, she gets cranky and frowns.

She braced herself, but…why are these replacement personnel so utterly green? Lieutenant Weiss and the others all groan as they look over the careers of the recruits they've been assigned.

They aren't here for retraining or changing arms—they're literally a slab of fresh newbie meat. We're being given raw recruits, whose only use is fodder for the meat grinder, and being told, *Don't mince them! Evolve them into fighting chunks of steak!*

"I'm your instructor, Magic Major von Degurechaff."

If this was what was going to happen I should have never gotten assigned to the instructor unit at Central. Tech Research wasn't a proper workplace, either, and the Elinium Type 95 is one more reason my head hurts. I guess I haven't been able to take proper advantage of my promotion opportunities. I just end up with more and more unfortunate connections. Tanya can't help but lament her circumstances.

"As you know, the Rhine is hell. It's a graveyard, so to speak."

She smiles weakly, thinking how it won't do for all the fresh meat to drop like flies, and describes the battlefield to them in frank terms as a warning. It would be better if they had received a little more training that's actually useful for their situation; soldiers who don't understand are deadweight. Then again, on second thought, that's exactly why someone thought of making them a proper fighting force with this training mission.

"To break it down further, this is the wonderful Rhine front, where the Republican Army will throw periodic welcome parties for any useless bodies who deserve to be disposed of, and you can get promoted two ranks in no time at all."

Still, the high rate of attrition on the Rhine lines can only be lamented. It's a fundamental problem. I'm only a major, but all the superior officers here when I arrived were busy getting their posthumous double promotions or, if they were lucky, getting transferred or sent to the rear.

Before I knew it, as a major, I was closer to the top of the command structure than the bottom.

Oh, competition is so fierce in the Rhine lines labor market it'll make you pale. What would Darwin say if he saw this? Is this the ultimate progression of the theory of evolution? Or is it a desolate place where the theory of evolution breaks down? It's definitely a fascinating question.

"So anyone who wants to be a hero should go play with some snipers."

Any time you spend talking to idiots who don't listen is for nothing, and having them hang around using supplies is a waste.

The best thing they can do is go make an enemy sniper use up a bullet. If I can get rid of idiots and tire out enemy snipers at the same time, it's not a bad deal.

"The rest of you. Do your best not to get in the way."

Well, if they follow instructions they should at least be able to act as bullet repellant.

"Okay, gentlemen, we'll probably only be together a short while, but let's all get along."

Guess that's about it. Now then, time to work as much as I get paid to.

Shovels are great. Shovels are the quintessence of civilization.

With a shovel, you can dig a hole just deep enough to hide yourself. Or if you gather a bunch of people with them, you can dig a fine trench.

If you change your viewpoint just a little, you can even dig a tunnel. You can smash a sturdy enemy trench with mining tactics (not that they get used often).

A shovel is a good friend to any and every type of soldier. And a shovel is the best gear for a close-quarters fight in a trench.

Longer than a bayonet, simpler to handle than a rifle, sturdier than any other tool. Not only that, but they are extremely cheap to make, so they're perfect for mass-producing. Plus, I don't have to worry much about damaging my mind.

This is it, the ideal piece of equipment. This is the point humanity was meant to reach. Civilization has developed the shovel as its implement.

Above all, it doesn't rely on magic, so it's optimal for stealth kills. With a shovel, it's possible to educate numbskulls who are dependent on magic scanning— *Klang!* We can say it's an indispensable item for nighttime raids. Of course, it's an excellent general-purpose tool at any time of day.

"The shovel is truly an implement born of civilization," Tanya murmurs, leading a unit to wish good evening to the enemy with their shovels. On this nighttime outing, they get all muddy as they crawl over the ground on their bellies. Her objective is clear—it's part of the new recruit education she has undertaken.

Tanya has no problem forcing them to wriggle through this morass if she can beat into them that the only ones who can dress nicely on the Rhine are dumbasses or corpses of heroes being sent to the rear. She doesn't want to, but when it's an order, she has no choice. And so, she's reluctantly crawling at the head of the group, biting her lip.

If it were possible, she would want to go back this instant, but she's advancing across no-man's-land. Since the snipers have given up their day off and are going for the perfect attendance award, she and her troop, clad in the gray camouflage of the trench dress code, drag themselves inch by inch toward the enemy camp.

Sneaking forward, jumpy as a mouse, with a heavy steel helmet on your head is the height of humiliation. What torture that we can do nothing but sneak like this covered in mud! This place is utterly insanitary; the putrid reek of the unrecovered corpses of both sides has completely numbed my nose. *Agh, how extraordinarily disgusting!* Though conditions are severe enough that I lament as such, work is work. I curse the fruitlessness of this 3D (dirty, dangerous, and demeaning) labor from the bottom of my heart.

…Why are the higher-ups always asking for the impossible?

To find out how all this started, we have to go back several hours to the beginning.

Whether you see it as a comedy or a tragedy will depend on your point of view. The incident does, however, become the momentum for marked improvements in the Imperial Army's chain of command and communications channels.

"I'd like to hear your opinion on improving field battle capabilities." The Operations staffer attached to Command who had come to visit Tanya that day handed her a circulating notice. On it were the loss rates of new soldiers stationed on the Rhine lines as replacements, separated by arm of service. What jumped out at her when she scanned the page was how high the numbers were. You could say the Empire's new soldiers were literally dropping like flies.

As a frontline officer, she put the notice on her desk and sat down with a sigh. *These are what the rates will be if you have to deploy new recruits with not enough training or experience.*

"If I may be blunt, this is surely due to insufficient training and accelerated education. I should think that instead of learning how to march in formation, they need to be trained how to lie in a trench. Aside from that, perhaps they should also be baptized in the most difficult parts of trench warfare under conditions that minimize casualties."

"They certainly have a ways to go to be useful, but…we can't very well stand them up in front of the machine guns, either."

Seeing the important colonel sigh, bring his coffee to his lips, and grimace, Tanya's face stiffened. On the forward-most line, there's no way to provide adequate hospitality. She had given Lieutenant Serebryakov strict orders to make it the best cup of coffee she could, but there probably hadn't been enough fuel to boil the chalk out. The colonel had drunk some, so she did, too, but it tasted awfully tainted.

"…You don't like it, sir?"

That said, she showed him what it was like on the front lines by implying that that's just how it tastes there.

"I don't mean to nag you about conditions on the front, but…this is horrible. It reminds me of the dining room at the central General Staff Office."

"They must have better luck with water there, though. This is the firing line," Tanya murmured, staring sadly into her butchered coffee, oozing a bit of helplessness. Even the taste of these luxury items wasn't the same on the front. They were in another world, removed from daily civilian life. It would be no easy task to throw in new recruits with only accelerated training and get them acclimated.

"You're saying we should give them a taste of this experience in the rear?"

"If possible, they should be informed of the realities of the trenches so as to shatter their illusions about war. The numbskulls who want to be heroes end up killing not only themselves but their fellow soldiers."

The newbies who try to pull off heroics in the trenches really are numbskulls. If one of them succumbs to the rush of adrenaline and does something reckless or makes a futile charge, at least the damage can be minimized to affect just him, but oftentimes they have the nerve to involve others.

On top of that, though you can't really blame them for a physiological phenomenon, I'm also really sick of them polluting the trenches with all varieties of incontinence and creating hotbeds for every type of infectious disease.

"That's why, with these young ones, I just..." Tanya groaned, burying her head in her hands. "...Hmm? What was that, sir?"

"Oh, I just thought it was strange, given how young you are, Major."

"The one with infant military careers are useless. Of course, I'm sure it's a different story if they can manage to survive two months on the Rhine."

"Ahh, no...uh, forget I said anything. Let's get back to the topic at hand."

I wasn't really sure why the colonel was mincing words. The whims of superior officers don't always make sense. Tanya politely did as she was told and switched to their main topic without asking anything further.

Tanya's age might be strange from an objective perspective, but subjectively, she could only think of years of service, similar to the way someone would say how long they'd been working at a company.

"Yes, sir. At present, we can't hope for large-scale mobile battles. All we can have them do is hole up in the trenches and maybe shoot their guns."

Anyhow, Tanya's idea about the loss rates, that they would improve a bit once the soldiers acclimated, was a violently realistic one—i.e., that's just how it goes in total war, where you're in a competition to literally grind up human resources. Even if it made sense to be concerned about high losses, she thinks they're overly worried about the effect such losses might have on the lines. To Tanya, you can afford to overlook losses that aren't big enough to affect the ability of the organization to continue fighting.

To put it another way, if they were dropping as fast as they were in *All Quiet on the Western Front*, things would be pretty much like the title of the movie—all quiet.

Even if divisions attacked by night, like in the Russo-Japanese War, it would be a cinch to repel them with machine guns and mage support. Well, we would have to be practical and expect casualties within some permissible range, since the newbies would still be learning the ropes.

After all, I wasn't the one who'd be dying. Not that I wanted them to die if we could help it.

"Indeed. It is difficult to imagine a large-scale mobile battle breaking out. You're probably correct that we should focus our instruction on other areas, but..."

Ultimately, the colonel didn't say anything that negated what Tanya had said.

What came through in his anguished reply were the emotions he couldn't shake, the feeling of wrongness and hatred for this way of fighting that involved sending so many young to die.

"...neither can we ignore the damage being done in these smaller engagements. The problem is that even if the losses are small, they pile up. Worst of all, morale will start to flag."

"But if an engagement is small, it shouldn't be resulting in too many losses."

Wait a minute. Tanya seemed to be the only one present who thought those losses were within the permissible range. Compared to the rate of casualties in World War I, these little scuffles were adorable. But a normal person wouldn't usually use deaths in World War I as the yardstick even if they were aware of it, and if they weren't, they would undoubtedly shiver at the inconceivable numbers.

"At most, a harassing raid would only kill the ones who would die anyhow, so that doesn't seem like such a big deal."

A serious raid would be too high risk, so the most the enemy can do is take a company of infantry for a sneak attack. The limit for mages would be a battalion-sized harassing attack. If that's all, the casualties the imperial side could expect wouldn't be unsuitably high.

Speaking in extremes, of course. With that thought, Tanya drained her awful coffee and reached for a mint candy as a palate cleanser.

The large gap in experience between veterans and newbies can only be explained by how much actual combat they've been through. My unit's rate of loss was far and away the lowest, but the replacements from other units were starting to get injured, albeit gradually. The soldiers who got their first taste of combat in the easy Dacian War were lucky. If your first time is this rough, it must take a long time to get used to it.

"Major von Degurechaff, don't you think with your instruction and direction the loss rate could be lowered?"

"If you order me to do it, I'll do my utmost, but ultimately our only option for these first-time combatants is to teach them step-by-step."

On a battlefield with snipers, pointing at a moron who got shot is far more persuasive than telling them, *Don't stick your head out!* While trenches diminish the effectiveness of field guns, concentrated fire from large-caliber heavy artillery reduces even reinforced concrete to rubble, *so don't all hide in the same place!* They'll understand well enough if you make them recover the bodies of the poor radio operators who suffocated when they were buried alive in a pillbox.

Take writing the alphabet, for example. If you don't go A-B-C step-by-step and actually teach how to write it, there's no point. When that occurred to her, Tanya realized her battalion still hadn't experienced some things on the Rhine, either.

The obstacle of trenches certainly changed the way night battles were fought. They changed the way guard duty was performed as well, and the replacement troops were definitely not used to it. Newbies and veterans alike had to deal with warnings being given at the drop of a hat. And maybe this was compounded by the mages not having much opportunity to be in the trenches during the day.

"That said, it seems to be as you say. From what I've seen, I agree that we should be able to improve a bit more," said Tanya upon reflection.

In other words, she needed to educate the fresh recruits under the assumption they were unfamiliar with the trenches. The change in environment and premises requires retraining.

"Yes, that's right. Their combat in environments where they can't rely on magic is particularly unbearable to watch."

Tanya nodded in response to the colonel's observation. The mages were trained under the assumption they'd be deploying both protective films and defensive shells, so they really did suck at stealth combat. The shameful sight of newbies unconsciously protecting themselves and then getting targeted by the enemy annoyed her.

"It's true that even though they're under strict orders not to use magic in the trenches, there are too many examples of people leaking signals without realizing and getting picked up by the enemy."

Having said that, it really started to hit home. *Oh, right, there was also an incident where a whole unit got blown away because some numbskull gave away their position while they were getting ready...*

There had been an inquiry, but did anyone attempt to reevaluate replacement training as a result? *Aha, it really is an issue when one person's mistake multiplies the damage.* Having jumped to that conclusion through logic incomprehensible to others, she was touched, thinking it was good that the higher-ups cared about improving the situation.

"You're worried about even the small-scale battles with recruits this under-trained?"

Right, Heinrich's Law. There is always the risk that letting small errors go will lead to getting majorly burned. And Murphy's Law teaches us about the dangers of ignoring the possibility of failure. Humans are numbskulls. If there is a way to fail, someone will figure out how to do it at some point.

In that case... Tanya, shocked at her own pride, felt her heart stop. *The higher-ups must be apprehensive about the shaky new recruits not for some baseless reason but because they've discovered some risk that officers across the front have been carelessly overlooking.*

How perceptive. I need to hand it to them, from an HR perspective. There's no guarantee that these issues won't worsen if things develop into a massive battle, so if there are even small ways to improve, we have to work at them.

"That's exactly the issue. Large-scale engagements notwithstanding, these smaller skirmishes..."

Even if the current assumption is that a large-scale battle won't break out... The Operations staffer emphasized that even the present human losses couldn't be ignored and felt (as a decent person would) that this level of harm, this mass production of corpses, was wrong somehow.

Meanwhile, Tanya nodded—*quite right*—at everything the colonel said but nevertheless took no particular issue with the losses as such. Rather, she thought the biggest problem was that many of their units were inferior due to being formed mainly with replacements.

Certainly, even if the chance of a large-scale fight was negligible, they were currently leaving open the possibility of failure and piling up small errors.

Actually, after having this pointed out to her, her most serious concern was the very real (if sporadic) instances where one person's error had caused catastrophic damage—too much. She worried that newbies who couldn't function without relying on magic could be a major component of failure on a high-risk mission.

"You were on an operation in Norden where you couldn't rely on magic, right? I imagine you have a handle on the gist of it."

"As you say, sir. I'm ashamed to say I hadn't been thinking about it, but I'll keep it in mind when I'm teaching."

The idea of requesting error-prevention measures indicates, in a way, healthy operation of the organization. In civilian life, trouble can usually be dealt with by firing the person who made the mistake. In the army, however, one person's mistake can mean everyone dies. One for all. All for one. It's a truly wise saying. If one person fails, everyone dies, and if everyone else messes up, one person's fierce fight won't be enough to win in the end.

"About that..."

I appreciate that instruction is happening, but it's far from enough. The issue really is lack of actual combat experience. The colonel was enthusiastic, thinking that he'd gotten her to understand his opinion. Thus, he and Tanya entered a strange misunderstanding without realizing the incongruity of their views because they saw only their agreement that something needed to be done.

"Yes, what is it, sir?"

Chapter V

"Can you give them some experience?"

What they needed more than protected experience in a large operation was thorough repetition and review in small-scale battles. That is what Tanya believed, so although she didn't want to, she resolved to go on a non-magic raid.

Yes, combat experience should be gained alongside a well-trained unit with extraordinarily low loss rates. Experience trumps schooling.

"Sir! Experience, yes."

There was no point in training corpses. There was no telling on the ground when the chance would arise to do a large-scale mobile battle or breakthrough or difficult operation like an infiltration attack. As long as that was the case, troops should be kept trained up so they could respond to orders at any time; Tanya kicked herself for her careless neglect.

I didn't want losses in my unit, and I figured if I put the newbies out to pasture, the battlefield would turn them into master soldiers, but that was the wrong way to go about it.

"Yeah, if there's a chance to train them in the trenches for a while, I'd like to have them fight with your troops."

It was true that having her battalion go to the trenches with the new recruits as an instructor unit would reinforce the front. *The Empire sure gets all they can out of their people.* The shocking truth had just started dawning on Tanya that in the abnormality of war she had lapsed into irrationality and laziness. *This is why war is bad,* she thought. *War numbs humanity and reason and drives you crazy with rotten fantasies.*

When that thought crossed her mind, she had been on the verge of resisting, saying, *You're telling me to leave the rear and throw myself into the trenches? And not only that but take a bunch of deadweight with me and train them?* She was terrified to see how tainted her own thoughts were. Even though I know that being hasty and shortsighted is most likely to cause a failure, once I experienced it, I got a good taste of how easy it is to fall into that trap.

"Understood! I'll do my best to instruct the unit."

"Great. I'll prepare the written orders immediately. Sorry for the pressure, but we're counting on you."

"Yes, sir. Leave it to me! I'll have results to show in no time."

And so, neither of them realized there was a definite contradiction in their views, and Tanya moved ahead with carrying out her orders.

Taking her time to enjoy her dinner, she has the company commanders under her prepare for a night battle and confer with the leader of the recruits. She also points out to her batman that the potatoes are inexcusably old. When he replies that the supply unit is bringing canned goods as a top priority, she is forced to reluctantly back down...because she senses her superiors are focused on logistics network maintenance and efficiency.

The light railway is handling about as much traffic as it can take, so they're probably prioritizing canned goods since those keep for a long time and can be transported according to a preset plan. In other words, I shouldn't expect raw vegetables or fresh meat or fish anytime soon. The calories, at least, should be up to regulations. *Still...* When she hits upon that prospect, she has to accept the reality that her already simple table will become even drearier.

Well, I guess the only ones who get to expect decent meals at war are the navy. Or maybe just the submarine squads—I've heard they get treated well. Of course, everything else about their situation is the worst...

Basically, they're beginning to prioritize ease of transport, and that makes sense to her. She certainly can't argue against it, so with nothing else to do, she lays down her sword on the food issue and continues her meeting.

That's how essential close cooperation and maintaining leadership will be in the upcoming operation. After all, discipline in a normal mage battalion night battle would be managed via magic. But if they were to cast interference formulas in the middle of no-man's-land, they'd be detected; no individual radios will be distributed, either. Fighting a night battle under these conditions with fresh recruits is incredibly reckless.

Operation Eagle Claw heading for Iran probably had a higher chance of succeeding.

So should we split into autonomous platoons for the raid? Just one imperial mage platoon is said to have firepower equal to a company of regular infantry. Well, practically speaking, an infantry company and a mage platoon really can probably deliver the same amount of damage. Plus, it's a night battle. If we hit them with that much firepower under the veil of darkness, we can probably expect widespread confusion. But then to continue fighting, we'll have to rely on magic. That means the second we cast interference formulas, it's possible that the enemy retreats and the whole area gets bombarded indiscriminately.

Well, or we could just take checking machine-gun fire.

So should we infiltrate as companies? It's realistic but on a whole new scale of difficulty. It's not a bad idea to have each group perform a feint and then attack from four totally different locations. But sending in all four companies would mean that even as an augmented battalion, we wouldn't have any muscle in reserve. I want to stay in the rear under the pretext of commanding the reserves, so I can't accept that plan.

I will take the most highly trained First Company. Having all the other companies perform the raid would be best for me, but my subordinates are advocating for a plan where First Company is the main attacking force. They want to go without reserves and have the others feint.

The objective of our night battle is the abduction of enemy soldiers, which is relatively less difficult. Basically, we'll invite enemy sentries from a warning trench to be friends for Intelligence to chat with.

"In other words, you all want to avoid engaging as much as possible."

"Yes, Commander. Honestly, it'll be impossible to fight with those recruits along."

…I suppose it is important to avoid combat. My orders are simple. "Give them night battle experience." Period.

If you know the enemy and know yourself, you need not fear the result of a hundred battles. Or endeavor to understand one another in an advanced, civilized manner. To that end, a bit of nocturnal hiking to invite enemy soldiers over isn't so bad.

No, it's not bad. Well, it's not good, either. I guess things can't be declared simply good or bad.

"I'm concerned about speed. More than anything, this'll demand a swift withdrawal." Without thinking, I've already voiced a worry. Well, as the one in charge, I have to consider and prepare for all eventualities.

I can't get away with saying, *Oops, I didn't think about that.*

If I say it's possible and fail, I'll be laughed at. If I say it's impossible, I'll be reprimanded as inept.

I'm compelled to raise concerns; we need to think seriously about this. Any resisting enemy soldiers won't be killed but knocked out. Well, that's easy for a mage to do. We get a lot of practical experience on how to leave people neither dead nor alive in the military academy and basic training. The venerable Daigongen and Zusho come in surprisingly handy.

We're up against soldiers instead of farmers, but in terms of governing theory, the result is the same. Well, no, I'm actually much more comfortable doing it to civilians.

We could also tap them lightly with the flat side of a shovel. If you swing a shovel sideways, it slices, but if you hit with the flat, that's one down. They really are convenient—so much so that I'd almost like to have all the recruits participate armed only with shovels.

But what do we do once we capture our guests? If the warning trench sends out an alert, our only options will be to fight or run. As long as our objective is to take prisoners, fighting is pointless. When all you've got is the muscle of a group on force recon, dealing with the counterattacking unit in a trench fight is a completely futile battle of attrition. And if we were to miss our chance to pull out, we would literally die in vain. That's why after we achieve our appointed objective, there's no reason to stick around.

When your work is done, there's nothing better than going straight home.

Which is why we can prioritize speed without fretting over the mana signals we'll have been concealing up to then and go literally flying out of there with flight formulas. There is no better way to let your mana signal loose and hightail it away from the battle lines than a flight formula. Hooray for flight formulas.

We'll have to run for our lives for a couple minutes, but if we can't get away, we'll get blown up in a hail of SOS fire.

Well, another way to look at it is that as long as whatever gets us makes a clean hit, we won't have to suffer.

That said, everyone wants to enjoy life.

Even suicidal people aren't born in such a passionate state of despair over their existence that they want to kill themselves. If they are able to believe in the future, humans all have the wonderful potential to build a bright, peaceful tomorrow. Humans are irreplaceable; we're all unique. At least, I don't know about other people, but I have no substitute. That's why I want to survive, no matter what it takes. No, I *will* survive. To that end, I'll even praise the devil as God for those couple minutes to go full throttle.

I'm saying that we'll keep an eye out for each other as we withdraw, but I'm definitely not stopping. Falling behind means being taken prisoner if you're lucky or death in battle if you're not.

"...Well, seems like you're appropriately nervous."

Apparently, all my subordinates have screws loose. I mentioned a concern, so why are they talking about "appropriately nervous"? Was it a mistake to gather a bunch of war addicts when I formed my unit?

I want to take a little space. I hunt for someone with some other—some normal—opinion. When I scan my troops, I see Lieutenant Serebryakov raising her hand.

"Major, the last few minutes are the dangerous part, although we do have to give the new recruits support on our way over as well."

This is a much more sensible viewpoint. We'll be fine on the approach unless someone makes a sound or some numbskull gives off a mana signal.

"Lieutenant, you and I have seen enough newbies screwing up on the Rhine to make you sick. You can handle them, right?"

"...If need be. But, Major, I'm going to do my best to cover for them so that won't be necessary."

"Hmm. Well, let's go over the opinions we've presented."

Let's round up the most sensible conclusions we have.

1. Do all we can to avoid combat.

Peace is best, of course. No reason to oppose that.

2. Send the strongest unit.

This is irritating, but in terms of military sense, I can't argue with it. Accepted for its prudence.

3. If we don't get discovered, the approach is possible. Withdrawing will be dangerous.

These are the points we collected. It's probably the safest plan. That is, if we arrange for a steady advance and a swift withdrawal, I guess we shouldn't have any problems. And if the troops make a mess of it, they'll have officers and NCOs with plenty of Rhine experience to back them up. Lieutenant Serebryakov and the others who have come up through the ranks will probably do a proper job of that.

"Good. I'll notify them of the plan."

Now, which of the fresh mages will I take on our first picnic?

Dinner was potatoes. And a little bit of fresh meat. Everything else was canned. *Mages are usually treated well, and I'm even an officer, but this is what I get. This is still the rear base, so I'm told it's on the good side; I wonder what the situation is on the front line. I hear the Great Army is putting pressure on the enemy lines, but Logistics is probably still struggling.*

With those things on his mind, Magic Second Lieutenant Warren Grantz, who had finally just been commissioned, ate his food quickly like soldiers do. The meal was better than the rations at the field exercise grounds.

At least it satisfied his appetite, and his tongue didn't reject it. But even if the food was better, he'd actually been feeling depressed for a few days. After all, he was being sent to the district with the fiercest fighting.

No, when he left the academy, he even trembled with excitement at being sent to the Rhine sometimes. He even thought he'd rack up brilliant exploits and become a hero.

But that enthusiasm withered the closer the military train got to the Rhine district on the way to the front.

What he saw were shell craters and burned, blistered things. Everything in his field of vision was gray. All of it, scorched fields. By the time the pungent odor began invading his nose, his spirit was deflated. And the thunder of a large gun, maybe an imperial railway gun, intensified his worries.

Before he knew it, he and the others were restlessly glancing around, noticing that many of their fellows wore the same anxious faces.

During that journey, one of the few ways to pass the time was sharing rumors. As he'd heard, the old stagers either slept, played cards, or spread rumors. Grantz dozed now and then, otherwise chatting as the train rocked along. He heard some rumors he knew of, too.

For example, one legend at the academy said a second-class student had once murmured that Cadet Degurechaff was more terrifying than the battlefield. *She certainly is scary.* Such were the thoughts running through his mind as he presented himself at Rhine Command.

When he arrived, he heard he would be attached to an instructor unit, which was a relief.

According to Command, he'd be retrained as a replacement before getting his assignment, so the first thing to do was get used to the front lines.

Maybe I can do this! It was several days ago that he had thought that.

"Gentlemen, welcome to the Rhine front!"

If the devil exists, it has to be our instructor, the commander of the 203rd Aerial Mage Assault Battalion, the legendary Major von Degurechaff.

The way she smiled. The way she looked at us like we were maggots. The way she seemed thirsty for blood.

I'd believe she had tried to kill a rebellious underclassman or crack his skull open. *If I screw up on the battlefield, she'll definitely kill me.* That's how threatened I felt by the instructor who just had to also be my advisor.

…I wanna cry.

Out of all the replacements, I was the only one who had been through the academy. In other words, everyone either didn't know the rumor that she was a demon in the guise of a little girl or laughed it off. The ones who figured they could handle war if that little kid could were on the safer side.

Just the thought of what the ones who underestimated her might do made my stomach hurt. I've never hated the words *collective responsibility* so much.

Tonight, I'm off duty. I should go to bed early. It happened just as I thought that.

We were summoned. The 203rd Aerial Mage Battalion was ordered to appear in the briefing room, grouped by platoon, within three minutes.

"Hurry up! Run!"

I urged my platoon, who had been finishing dinner; raced over to the briefing room; and just barely made it at two minutes and fifty-one seconds. No other platoons had arrived yet. Well, no, in ran Seventh Platoon; they'd been competing with those of us in Fourth Platoon. That second, the three minutes were up.

And the next second, the superior officers broke into broad grins and went to go get the tardy platoons. Did the others even feel bad for being late?

In any case, we all assembled quickly. And our smiling battalion commander announced a night picnic plan. Not that it involved anything like a picnic.

"Unfortunately, gentlemen, I think that aside from Fourth and Seventh Platoons, you deserve penalties."

This was the major who had once said during a speech at the academy that deadweight should be killed. I pitied the groups who hadn't been able to make it in three minutes because I figured they would be thrown into hell, but that wasn't right.

"In order to teach you the importance of haste, I'm sending you to the trenches. Since you don't seem to understand when I tell you, you'll experience firsthand what happens to slowpokes."

They'd actually be *buried* in the *depths* of hell. The shocked mages were immediately assigned to the warning trench. The warning trench on the front lines of the district with the worst fighting... They would be what are commonly called "canaries," the first to get attacked on the forward-most line. The mortality rate was naturally the highest; it was a position where you couldn't rest for even a moment.

By the way, they're called canaries after the caged birds that are taken into mines. The comparison is made because of the criticism that the raison d'être of anyone in this post is to stop responding.

But I shouldn't have been relieved.

"Now then, you fine, punctual fellows, I have a reward."

She looked at us one by one as if she was going to tell us something wonderful. My platoon mates next to me seemed to be expecting a reward, but I wasn't.

I had a really bad feeling.

"You get a little amity-building recreation. We'll go on a picnic, make a toast, and invite some new friends to come back with us. I guess you can call it a party."

As soon as she said that, someone handed us a pamphlet that said *Field Trip Guide*. Picnic procedure?

"First, equip hand grenades and your shovel; then ready your rifle and computation orb. Dress in night camo for CQB. By the way, if you use your computation orb or rifle without permission, you'll be shot or beaten to death. Republican soldiers are people, too. That means you can make friends with them"?

Then why did we have to knock them out with shovels?

"...In ancient times, people made friends by talking with their fists"?

"Civilized people of the present use the implement born of civilization, the shovel..."?

This is crazy. No one said it aloud, but it was the look on everyone's faces. This was a nighttime mission to abduct enemy soldiers—a so-called intelligence-gathering mission but extremely dangerous nonetheless. If we were going to drag enemies back with us, it went without saying that we would have to approach the enemy trenches.

Basically, we had to sneak up to the enemy position—where machine guns, all types of heavy artillery, infantry guns, snipers, and tons of soldiers were waiting—and abduct enemies out of the warning trench, which was the place that was on highest alert.

"...We're gonna die."

It was from there that things would get really intense. *"After using your shovels to mingle with lots of friends, let's invite some to our house. But I think all our friends will try to keep us from leaving in various ways. The field trip lasts until you shake them off and make it home"?*

"Incidentally, I'm not too worried about you punctual fellows, but one thing..." She beamed. *Oh God, please save us.* "If you're too slow, we're leaving you behind. Yes, anyone who wants a quick double promotion can stay out there. We wouldn't want to hinder your success in life."

She said the same sort of thing when I first met her. I didn't realize it was word for word the truth!

Magic Second Lieutenant Warren Grantz realized he was shaking.

My survival instinct was screaming. I wanted to avoid the war, the combat, the killing. I was hesitating.

But one glance from Major von Degurechaff was enough to subjugate that instinct. She was far more terrifying. We sallied forth like lambs being herded by a sheepdog. No one raised so much as a groan. We advanced under the cover of night, crawling in silence.

The commander was the first to strike. We heard the thudding of her shovel followed by the grunts of several people. We whacked the enemy soldiers caught with their guard down, too, as if our lives depended on it.

How much time passed after that?

It felt like the experience lasted a lifetime, but in reality, it was only a few dozen seconds.

It was a short moment. During that tiny amount of time, all the enemy soldiers in the specified area of the warning trench were either incapacitated or deep in a sleep they would never wake up from.

I could still feel the shock of the shovel impact in my hand; it was different from the recoil of shooting like we were taught at the academy. That particular feeling, the sensation of crushing something, was still impressed upon my body.

If I had been left like that, I wonder what would have happened to me.

"It's time. Company, carry the prisoners. Newbies, you're support. In thirty seconds, the magic ban is lifted. We're flying outta here. Sync your watches—three, two, one, start."

But the orders delivered in a calm, unruffled whisper brought me back to reality. Combined with my training, they slowly got my body moving. That's what I had been drilled for. My training saved me.

As instructed, thirty seconds later I started up my computation orb at full throttle and took off.

We really hightailed it back to our own defensive lines. It only took a few minutes. All we had to do was fly—simple. But it was horrible. My heart raced with every artillery shot. It hurt to breathe.

I was so terrified I hardly felt like myself anymore.

When we climbed up high to avoid being shot accidentally and set a safe course for the rear base, all the stress left my body at once, and weariness washed over me.

…How could the major just calmly sing a hymn?

Today, after completing her morning exercises and eating breakfast, Major von Degurechaff reaches for her pen as if she's made up her mind.

In the rear base, the mail can get through. Naturally, it's possible to send a letter if necessary.

It's military mail, so sometimes there are delays, but in general, things can be sent and received like any normal letter.

Of course, someone like her with no relatives doesn't have any personal letters to write.

She only ever writes on official business or unofficial business.

What she's writing this time is official. That said, in a rare case, she takes out her stationery hesitantly, and her pen moves over the paper awkwardly.

She's already written a pile of these documents. She just accepts that they're work and gets them done. But today the tip of her pen feels heavy.

Well, it would be stranger if a person could write it without trouble.

To the dear family of Warrant Officer Anluk E. Kahteijanen,

I am Magic Major Tanya von Degurechaff, his superior officer.

I regret to inform you that your one and only young Anluk E. Kahteijanen is being discharged with a disability.

He became abruptly ill during an operation, and the surgeon has judged that it would be difficult for him to endure lengthy military service.

His recovery will most likely require a long recuperation period at home or in a military hospital.

The Personnel Division has agreed to go ahead with this treatment plan.

Please speak with him and ensure he has a restful convalescence.

And please forgive us for returning your child in such a condition.

He is an outstanding mage, our irreplaceable brother-in-arms, brave and trusted by all.

We are deeply saddened to no longer have Anluk E. Kahteijanen in our ranks.

Small consolation though it must be, I recommended him for the Field Service Badge First Class and the Disability Medal, both of which were approved.

I hope he makes a full recovery.

Sincerely,

[xxx] Unit Commander, Imperial Army Magic Major Tanya von Degurechaff

…To think the day would come when I'd lose a man to some bad potatoes. Apparently, the legendary remark from an American Thunderbolt pilot that even a veteran can't beat food poisoning wasn't a joke.

So those potatoes really were rotten after all. Tanya puts away her pen, irritated by the worsening logistics situation.

Sending a letter to the family when something happens to a subordinate is the superior officer's responsibility, and I'm not against writing…but food poisoning from potatoes? Tanya has finished the letter, but she has complicated feelings about the incident and can't get over it.

He had eaten, participated in a night raid, and shocked me upon our return by throwing up and complaining of an awful stomachache. I was dumbfounded. A veteran writhing about like that, I was sure he had to have been hit by an NBC weapon. Those work even on mages. I hurriedly cast a medical formula, but it only eased the pain. Protective films provide comprehensive NBC coverage, and I remember we were on the verge of panicking that some new weapon not on that list had been developed.

When the surgeon rushed over and examined him, we were finally able to sigh in relief. In other words, it was just sudden, acute food poisoning. And it only hit unlucky Anluk E. Kahteijanen.

He was a good mage, damn it. I never thought I would send someone away from the front like this.

But it's really great that Personnel treated his condition as a disability. This way, he gets his pension, and his honor as a soldier remains intact. And I, as an officer, won't have the blemish on my record of a dishonorable subordinate.

I mean, you can only really laugh at an officer who loses a man to bad potatoes. Who would have thought I had a guy in my unit who would be taken out by his own stomach...? Nah, it's not even funny.

The Republican bombardments come as always, shaking our position like clockwork, but I must feel oddly reflective on this auspicious day because I sent a man to the rear for a difficult-to-verbalize reason.

That said, what we learned from this lesson was promptly applied. As such, this morning's breakfast was bacon, hard biscuits, and ersatz coffee. The vegetable soup featuring the guilty potatoes was hastily disposed of. Personally, I worry about my diet being unbalanced without vegetables, but there's nothing I can do about it.

I had someone go to get supplies first thing this morning, so I figure maybe we'll get a chance to eat canned vegetables with lunch. And well, even if we are on a battlefield, we can't escape falling into routines, and I'm a bit sick of it. It'd be great if we could get a meal that's not part of the rotation.

Aside from these things, our daily battles in the trenches take place in the world of *All Quiet on the Western Front*. We basically repeat the same pattern day after day. The only novelty to keep my attention is whether the recruits training on the front lines are doing well or not.

Well, I only put them in yesterday. Tanya expects that after a week's baptism of war in the trenches she'll find out whether they're usable or not.

If not, all she has to do is send them back and apply for their retraining.

So although she regrets war's brand of tunnel vision, she devotes herself to instructing her troops. First, just as her boss said, she gave them the most difficult test first; despite the risks, she reluctantly took them on a night battle, but to her surprise and delight, they only lost two.

Though she'd told everyone they were leaving in thirty seconds, that pair couldn't keep up and were blown away in an artillery barrage, a fact confirmed by one of her subordinates. That was all. Apart from that, the newbies all followed instructions, and no one went insane. As Tanya mulls over the recruits' misfortune to be blown up together in their two-man cell, she finds herself in a somewhat philosophical mood and begins to wonder about the role of luck in food poisoning.

In any case, she's doing what she needs to do.

But actually, even though she's doing what she needs to do, she sometimes gets doubtful looks.

For instance, she reported in, *"I'M INSTRUCTING THEM ACCORD-ING TO YOUR ORDERS."*

And the response she received was *"ROGER. GOOD LUCK."*

But then when they went on the night raid and lost only two men, the higher-ups told her to be more careful next time. She began wondering if maybe they wanted her to do it with zero losses.

But this is a battlefield, she argued, *and we went on a high-risk operation. Losing two newbies under those circumstances is not bad.*

But when it comes to luck, it seems Tanya has to admit that she needs to take certain things into account.

Still, she finds it lamentable that just because they don't want any losses and her unit got unlucky, the blame is laid on her as the commander who was present.

I know history repeats in little ways, from private companies to the Yankee military. For example, when that guy MacArthur ordered his subordinate Eisenhower to plan a parade and then insisted he had no memory of it—there are a number of rotten incidents like that throughout time.

Still, Tanya is feeling really sad. *Ahh, I might start to cry. I mean, I'm a girl, you know!*

…??

When her thoughts stray, she suddenly realizes she feels off.

Her mind floods with the horror of psychological contamination.

She runs off in search of some kind of help as if her life depends on it.

A doctor! I need to see a doctor!

Chapter V

"Well, it's the appointed hour, so I would like to begin the joint meeting between the Service Corps and Operations surrounding the pros and cons of the Rhine offensive plan."

The officer presiding over the meeting spoke, but no one followed him, and silence reigned.

In contrast with the splendid exterior of the building, the expressions of the high-ranking men in the meeting room were dour.

Some of the officers were practically tearing their hair out with incessant worries, unsure what to do, and among them was Major General von Zettour. The situation changed from moment to moment, and just getting a handle on what was going on was incredibly difficult. Moreover, the Empire was learning from the rising pile of corpses, courtesy of the Republicans, how fundamentally impossible a frontal breakthrough was in trench warfare.

That is, the price of a front assault on the trenches was too high. On the other hand, a large-scale firepower offensive would put too much strain on the supply lines.

They had just improved the supply-line light-rail to the front, but there were already requests from every post for reinforcements coming in day after day.

The burden on supply had blown through prewar estimates long ago.

The Entente Alliance was essentially collapsing, and it was necessary to allot some military strength to the area for a short time to ensure it, which also weighed heavy on Logistics.

Even the local army group alone was enough to secure overwhelming superiority for the Imperial Army in the north, but the harsh winter weather had held them back. They weren't in a situation where they could spare troops to reinforce the main fighting lines on the Rhine. These lines would probably be frozen stiff until next spring. In other words, it would be a while before they could expect any easing up on the supply line burden from the north.

Meanwhile, the navy was in the process of gaining superiority in the channel against the Republic, but the navy and army disagreed on whether that was a good thing or not. The air and magic forces were prepared to support either side if asked, but the army's and navy's worries were just so different.

The navy apparently couldn't wait to break through the channel. After all, their ambition was to wipe out the Republican fleet in a battle of warships. They even proposed doing an amphibious operation afterward, like with the Entente Alliance, to completely annihilate the country.

As far as Zettour could see, taking command of the sea for a landing operation seemed likely to keep casualties down far more effectively than advancing by breaking through the trenches. The issue was the safety of the route if they went by sea. If they broke into the channel between the Republic and the Commonwealth, they had to be worried about how the (superficially) neutral Commonwealth would react. Would it just stand quietly by?

He'd already been over these questions with Major General von Rudersdorf. They were both forced to conclude that if they entered the channel, the Commonwealth would probably interfere to maintain the balance of power. If that happened, the fears that made the rounds at the office in "Predictions on the Shape and Direction of the Current War" and "Theory of Total War," would come true.

Yes, *world war*. The war's expansion would be like a never-ending chain reaction, and they wouldn't be able to avoid it. If that happened, they could end up with a Rhine-like scenario on every front.

The Republican Army on the Rhine lines was quite a handful. If it was only the Republic, though, they still had a chance of winning.

But what would happen if some units from the Commonwealth showed up? They could find themselves in the opposite of their current superior position.

As long as it was doubtful the Imperial Navy could stop the Commonwealth Navy, if the remnants of the Republican Navy joined in, it would be all the imperial fleet could do to protect itself.

Of course, they couldn't twiddle their thumbs for too long, either. If they waited to act, even the Empire would run out of steam. Then they would lose the strategic effects of having brought down Dacia and the Entente Alliance.

Chapter V

And they couldn't bear the idea of being beaten from the side by the Commonwealth or some other interloping power. *What can we do about this dilemma?*

Yet, it was becoming clear that if they tolerated the current situation, anything that happened to affect the supply lines could spell disaster. That was their irritating predicament.

Since the founding of the nation, the Great Reich had obtained its historical lands but was also hounded by territorial conflicts, so there was never any lack of sparks for the next war.

Hence their distress. No one with a simple solution to a problem suffers. For better or worse, there were people present who knew the plan.

Zettour knew. He knew that all they had to do was not lose. Zettour believed, to a rather surprising degree for a member of the military, that there was no need for them to go on the attack. Simply put, the status quo was fine.

And Rudersdorf was also aware of it. He knew there was no need for them to make serious attacks on the trenches. Unlike Zettour, however, he couldn't accept the notion that this attrition war was fine. He had the lucid determination of a soldier: If they could control losses and win, then why not do that?

They finally both made up their minds and received permission to speak.

"I feel we should change the way we're looking at this problem."

Zettour didn't consider himself timid, but given the significance of what he was about to say, even he was nervous. There was just a hint of stiffness in his voice, too small for almost anyone to pick up, but he spoke as calmly as possible.

His secret plan to disentangle these snarled-up threads in one blow would be gory. The Gordian knot is just a story. A sharp sword is sharp no matter who it's cutting.

"With our existing doctrine and values, we probably won't make it. We need a paradigm shift."

Achieving victory by attacking the enemy castle and forcing them to sign a capitulation was now impossible. It would be difficult to demand a full surrender outside of instances like the Empire and Dacia or the Entente

Alliance, where there was an overwhelming gap in national strength. Looking at the current terrible war, it seemed the bloodletting would have to continue until one or the other of the powers couldn't take any more.

"Don't aim for victory, avoid defeat. If we don't do that, it will be too hard to be the last one standing."

"…General von Zettour, you mean you oppose the offensive?" a member of Operations asked him, perplexed. That was as far as their thinking went.

No, that was probably common sense. To them, the offensive was how they would overcome and trample the enemy and end the war. But they were wrong.

"No, I support the offensive as such, but I do think we should modify its operational aims."

"Change its aims?"

Go on—no, stop. The question could mean both of those things, and Zettour answered by dropping a bomb in plain terms.

"The goal of the operation shouldn't be to break through. It should be to bleed the enemy. To put it another way, our offensive plan should be to wear out as many enemy soldiers as possible."

Conclusion: Exhaust the enemy.

"We carry out a thorough bloodletting and crush the enemy's ability to continue fighting."

Degurechaff's remark.

He could still remember each and every word the young soldier said to him in the war college library. The shock of hearing her speak so dispassionately about such a horrible world was hard to forget. And now that everything was progressing just as she had said, he was even more surprised. *How much did that girl Degurechaff predict?*

Predicting the future of a war is extremely difficult.

The only constant rule is that common sense can change in an instant and a new principle of war can conquer the battlefield. *There aren't many soldiers who can adapt to those changes, so to think there's one who can* predict *them is…!*

"In other words, we bleed the enemy until they collapse. This is the only way to resolve this."

Someone unconsciously shifted, and the creak of the chair sounded extra loud in the quiet room. It was completely silent.

Zettour was actually feeling calm in the face of it. No, strictly speaking, he was sympathizing with Degurechaff. He sensed now that she had been able to speak so calmly back in the library because she understood.

She understood the cost of breaking through would be too high. Even if they could pull it off, their losses would be heavy. And if the Commonwealth, anxious about the deteriorating war situation, decided to intervene, they would be pushed right back. That would be the worst possible outcome for the Empire.

If they shed all that blood not for nothing but a push in the wrong direction, the soldiers' will to fight would crumble.

I couldn't send men in that condition back to break through again, at least. Giving the order would only lead to more waste. So why not let the enemy make that mistake?

We'll just wait for the Republic to drown in their own blood.

Zettour believed this was the only viable option for the Imperial Army. In other words, war is ultimately about not heroes or the expression of chivalry but how efficiently you can kill your enemies.

To put it another way, it was inevitable that this conflict would become total war.

"So we'll thoroughly pummel enemy soldiers and supplies. I ask that we draw up an offensive plan with those aims, and that is all I wish to say at this time."

Surely, almost definitely, our future has been decided. The frozen expressions on the faces of his colleagues and subordinates spoke to that.

You're crazy, they said.

The operation he proposed was the opposite of almost anyone's idea of common sense. *Leave parts of their territory undefended and prioritize wiping out the enemy field army. And finish them off with a revolving door? You would have the army that exists to defend the fatherland carry out this operation?* No one could help but think these things.

But sooner or later, the staffers sitting there would understand—there was no other path. He didn't know when, but he knew they would come around to the plan for its military merit, in every way except emotionally.

"I agree. Clearly, we should focus on annihilating the enemy's field army." Despite the others' hesitation, Rudersdorf made a clear declaration of his strong support for Zettour's idea. He was aware that posterity would judge them harshly, but he made up his mind and stated his position with confidence.

It's a mad world where promising youths are pit against one another in battles to the death to see who can draw the most blood… And we're likely to carve our names into history as the ringleaders. If that's the case, then let's at least improve the situation a little bit by putting an end to the war with our own hands.

"I have an idea… We advance. In other words, I believe the best plan is to escape forward!"

And therefore, he made a proposal that was devoid of rationality: Fight the war aiming not at the territory but at the army.

…Oh God, why do you let these things happen?

After vomiting up the contents of his stomach, including everything he'd eaten the night before, Magic Second Lieutenant Warren Grantz was lamenting to the heavens in a corner of his lodgings. Even the recollection of what he'd just experienced horrified him.

I hit a Republican soldier whose name I don't know over the head with my shovel and kept swinging like a madman. Then orders brought me back to reality, and soon after that, we were ordered to leave.

I poured mana into my computation orb like my life depended on it so I could race across the sky for all I was worth.

As soon as I took off, several machine guns began firing at me.

I frantically formed my defensive shell and protective film. No matter what, I had to get away. With that on my mind, I forgot about support completely and made a run for it.

That's when it happened. Whether by some trick of fate or the work of the devil, I saw the battalion commander climbing at a furious pace.

Chapter V

Despite the dark veil of night, she was singing a hymn in an invigorating voice—the battalion commander. I couldn't believe what I was seeing, but I was scared she was escaping alone and would leave me behind, so I tried to follow her.

I don't want to get left behind was what I was thinking when I started to ascend, but right at that moment, First Lieutenant Weiss seemed to come out of nowhere to grab my arm and pull me down. When we got back to base, he chewed me out—*Why would you approach the commander while she's acting as our decoy? Are you insane?*—but if he hadn't saved me, I would have been turned into mincemeat like those other two guys who came to the front the same time as me.

At the time, all I was thinking about was getting back, so my memories before I made it onto a safe flight path are really hazy.

Looking at the scenes recorded on my computation orb, I want to thank God I was somehow able to make it back from such a dense rain of fire.

It was only a few seconds. The reactions of the pair from Seventh Platoon were delayed by mere moments, but they paid for it with their lives.

One careless moment. But it meant so much.

The second I arrived at the rear base, the sensation of bashing someone's head returned to my hands, and I felt sick. No, it wasn't just me. All the recruits felt the same way.

The guilt—it was like I'd suddenly become an unpardonable criminal.

And right next to us and the worries tormenting us, the senior officers coolly began to interrogate the prisoners.

"Tell the truth. If you don't, my hand might slip."

"Relax. We follow the law of war. If you fellows take the prisoner's oath, you'll have your rights."

"Don't worry. We're not torturers. We're proper, sensible humans."

…I couldn't believe it.

I couldn't believe humans were capable of this.

This battlefield.

I had thought I understood that all manner of brutal, inhuman things would be done. I'm a soldier, myself. I thought as long as I was in the military, I wouldn't hesitate to do my duty.

…Keyword: *thought.*

But what was this?

Was this a soldier's duty, what must be done to protect the fatherland? *My* duty?

I couldn't stand the feeling. It was a strange sensation, like I was losing myself forever.

I didn't want to remember my first…my first time killing someone with my own hands.

People die too easily on the battlefield. People you eat dinner with one night disappear by breakfast.

In just a short time, I kill people, and my friends get killed.

The Rhine front is really, truly hell.

The urge to run flitted across my mind.

But then—

The batmen came to tell us breakfast was ready. Since we were at a rear base, as an officer, I had the right to use the provisional officers' mess.

Put another way, I *have to* eat at the officers' mess.

As I rinsed out my mouth and straightened out my uniform, the mirror reflected my haggard face. In just one day, I'd transformed into a monster. I couldn't believe it was me.

"…Now I've seen war."

Quietly.

My inner thoughts slipped from my mouth on their own.

Leaning on the sink, I just managed to hold back the rising nausea, and then I looked to the heavens.

Really, how can everyone act normal in this crazy world of war?

The moment I entered the officers' mess, the feeling intensified.

It was crowded with the officers from my battalion. I heard the commander had eaten and was already at work. And the officers were taking their time and chatting.

Despite what had just taken place, I even heard laughter. Everyone was smiling and talking, relaxed. Something about the gap between the insanity suffusing the battleground and this scene disgusted me.

My batman waited on me, and my food came out, but how could I

possibly have an appetite? Even so, I still had the habit I'd learned in my military career to force food down my throat if I had to.

I used coffee to break up the hard biscuits and made myself eat them along with some bacon. There was no way the flavors would register, but I figured my body needed them to stay alive, so I swallowed them down.

Humans have to eat, even at times like this. It's the same as forcing food down my throat when I was exhausted at the academy. That's what I told myself, but it took an awfully long time for me to finish my meal.

Then I found myself heading to the small auditorium for the usual morning classroom session.

My mentality was to follow orders due to force of habit from the drilled repetitions, again and again. Even times like this when I had no willpower, I was still a soldier.

Then I realized I wanted to burst out laughing.

"...Wait a minute, what happened?"

I can laugh. It was a startling, refreshing discovery.

I guess I didn't expect it because of my situation. Apparently, the human spirit is ridiculously resilient.

"Oh, I can't be late."

I took so long to eat breakfast even though soldiers, praised for their unceasing vigilance, are supposed to get that over with quickly.

As a result, I had no time to lose that morning. If I stood around lost in thought, I wouldn't make it to the lecture on time. When I realized what time it was, I dashed off to the hall.

"Magic Second Lieutenant Grantz coming in."

"Grantz? Sure, come in."

But when I got there, the desks were empty aside from a few company commanders and key officers giving me puzzled looks.

Am I too late? The worry flitted across my mind, but when I looked at the clock on the wall, I had just made it five minutes early.

Everyone was supposed to be there by that time.

Normally, I would never be the only one rushing over here.

"What is it? You guys are supposed to have off today."

Lieutenant Weiss must have understood why I was confused, and I finally realized after he said something.

"Sir, embarrassingly enough, I thought we had class today."

I guess the shock from last night was so great that nothing they told us registered. Wincing, Lieutenant Weiss explained that after we got back we'd been granted leave. With my head full of other things, I had gotten up unsteadily this morning, but apparently they thought I was taking my time with breakfast to enjoy it. In other words, the superior officers figured I was having a relaxing breakfast on my day off, so they didn't check on me.

I should have realized sooner.

"I'm sorry."

"What? You're fine. But while you're here, tell me what you thought of the raid," said Lieutenant Weiss, pointing to a seat. The other officers didn't seem to mind, so I decided to join them... Well, it was a good opportunity. You reap what you sow, after all.

"Honestly, I was in a trance. Before I knew it, I was back at base."

I didn't want to die, so I had been completely absorbed in taking action. If you ask me what I actually did, though, my memories are hazy.

It was embarrassing, but I was honest with them.

"Yeah, that's how it goes, I suppose."

"Well, nice job making it through. With that as your first combat experience, your next one should be a lot easier."

But the officers didn't really seem to blame me. At the academy, I would have gotten chewed out—*Keep your head screwed on out there!* On the front lines, they're more realistic; they recognized that I had survived.

They were actually nice to me, as if being considerate were the norm.

"Everyone has to run that gauntlet. Well, if you survive the commander's training, consider yourself more or less fine."

"Lieutenant Serebryakov toughened up just by flying after her."

"Well, yes, that's true... Would anyone like to trade with me?"

"Ha-ha-ha-ha. I'm second-in-command, so I can't fly with her."

"It wouldn't do for company commanders to bunch up, so unfortunately the reality of my duties prevents me from trading with you, Lieutenant."

"It really is too bad." Lieutenant Serebryakov puffed out her cheeks and pouted as if she were really fuming.

The collection of individuals here creating this peaceful atmosphere were the old stagers who had been working so furiously the other day.

I suddenly felt like I might sigh out of relief. Up until just a moment ago, I was so shaken, but I was starting to calm down a little bit.

Nobody said so, but I'm sure they had all been upset the first time they shot and killed someone.

But now they have those memories, and they aren't upset by them.

"Don't think too hard, Lieutenant. Just focus on staying alive."

Someone patted me on the shoulder, and they let me go. It was proof that the more experienced officers accepted me as a little bit tougher than a chick newly hatched.

The next day...

To Tanya, everything is going too well. For starters, when she wakes up, breakfast and coffee are already neatly prepared for her.

There are no harassing bombardments and no enemies wandering into their airspace, so after eating in peace, her first administrative tasks of the day go smoothly. Awfully smoothly. A request that would normally take weeks to fulfill gets accepted in one try, and the supplies are delivered right away.

How horrifying can it get? Parsimony is the supply officer's job, but he hands over the special bullets for loading with interference formulas and the casting detonators with a smile. Meeting a grinning debt collector or auditor would feel more real— No, actually, they're all unthinkable.

This is the first time everything has gone according to procedure; I never would have imagined that supply delivery and paperwork inspection could be done so amiably. Thoroughly astonished, Tanya has no choice but to be on guard at this unexpected efficiency.

After all, supply and paperwork inspections operate on the iron rules of precedent and not rocking the boat. In other words, you can practically describe them as a naturally occurring phenomena.

If they are acting unusual, it has to be a sign of abnormal conditions.

Chapter V

I guess I should avoid going out for a while, if I don't have to, Tanya thinks; she's not averse to preparing for any eventuality.

Today is definitely going to be trouble. Convinced of this, Tanya steels herself. She'll give strict orders to the troops in the trenches to be on guard. She'll have her unit at combat readiness level two. She'll keep an eye on the enemy and make preparations to ensure a rapid response is possible.

Then, for some reason, nothing has happened and it's lunchtime. Food is served. It's a real steak with sauerkraut. There's even rhubarb juice for dessert.

It all just arrived via the unusually smooth-running supply lines.

The members of her unit all dig in enthusiastically, but she still can't believe it and inspects the food a bit before eating.

I'm jealous of the guy who struck gold with that potato condition and got to fall back to a safe area.

I'm wondering if they want to send me to the rear already due to the nudge I may have given foreign policy regarding the Commonwealth. If I got food poisoning, they'd happily sacrifice me, so I can't be carelessly getting sick.

Of course, watching my subordinates wolf down the meat is torture.

Being the only one who has to wait is sad, indescribably so if it turns out nothing's wrong. I can't stand it anymore. Reluctantly balancing reason with desire, I am about to start on my meat, and that's when it happens.

Lieutenant Weiss comes running over with a telegram, and Tanya ends up missing her chance to eat.

"Major, it's from Command."

With no choice but to lay down her knife and fork to exchange salutes, Tanya is the very definition of *displeased.*

If he weren't so sensible I'd throw him out right now.

At least read the situation. It had better be awfully important if you're obstructing my opportunity to have a fine meal on the front lines where we have almost nothing to look forward to. Unbelievably outraged, she can't help but reply grouchily, though she knows it's an emotional reaction.

"…I'm eating, Lieutenant Weiss."

Her tone doesn't veer into criticism, but her discontent is faintly audible. Most subordinates would hesitate if their superior spoke to them in such a voice. No one wants to incur their boss's wrath. But in unusual circumstances, they don't yield. And this is one of those rare situations.

"My apologies, but it's quite urgent."

And from the fact that he presents not a message tube but simply a short cipher, she smells trouble.

"Hmm? It's not orders?"

Usually orders come by telegraph.

As long as it's addressed to the commander, no one can read it before them except for the radio operator.

So short ciphers are used when it doesn't need to be telegrammed or can't be.

Basically, it's going to be either stupid or utterly annoying *and* stupid.

"No, you've been summoned to appear immediately."

"Summoned to appear immediately? Understood."

Agh, what a day.

It's going to be horrible.

Even an ordinary human, if given a reason,
can commit any level of wickedness. The evil
done in Arene was that commonplace.

——————————— The final report from Arene ———————————

I always get depressed this time of year.

Good evening, everyone.

This is *WTN* Special Correspondent Andrew.

…Today, we won't be bringing you the usual documentary.

We'll still be looking back on what happened during the war, but today we'll be doing it with a prayer. This will be a memorial broadcast.

First, let's talk about the disturbance in the Arene-Roygen region. The video you're all seeing right now is invaluable archival footage of residents of the occupied area revolting against the Imperial Army… This program contains numerous violent scenes. What happened during that time? Because our aim is to confront the truth, we've been granted permission under the ethics code to broadcast this material, but viewer discretion is advised.

Now then, are you still with us? What you see in the upper right-hand corner of your screen is Karelian Cathedral. It was also the scene of a tragedy we'll discuss later on.

All right, we'll keep the prefatory remarks to a minimum, as we're connected to the venue of the memorial ceremony now. Here is video of the commemoration of the victims of the suppression. This year, we can finally see ambassadors from each country in attendance.

The controversy goes on, but we should be glad the reconciliation process has reached the point where the two nations are having a joint memorial.

After all, this is a day to remember: They're unveiling the new Karelian Cathedral, raised out of the wreckage by the citizens' own hands.

The city of Arene burned. This is the story of how its people overcame their suffering and rebuilt.

Tonight, we discuss this wartime tragedy with an eye on those who are thinking of the future.

Here is Arene in the immediate aftermath, ruined.

This was recorded in secret by a newscaster from the Waldstätte Confederacy, which was one of the few neutral countries.

Can you tell that the partially collapsed building in the foreground is the famous white cathedral Karelian?

This all started when a hunt for partisans turned into a military clash. Arene had always been staunchly anti-Empire. It didn't even take a day for skirmishes to develop into a full-on uprising. We're told that the Imperial Army was shocked upon receiving the report that anti-Empire riots were spreading and that they no longer had control over the city.

"This could cause the collapse of supply lines servicing the Great Army on the front."

Having made this judgment, the army feared the collapse of the front, where it had dedicated its bodies and souls, and it responded without mercy.

Upon receiving word that anti-Empire riots had broken out in Arene, Major General (at the time) von Zettour proposed a swift, ruthless way to "cope." Major General von Rudersdorf of the Operations Division immediately called an emergency meeting of the Imperial Army General Staff and got the operation approved as a joint proposal from the Service Corps and Operations. With that, the army had permission to send military forces into the city.

One of the main points of controversy, even today, is that the Imperial Army unhesitatingly chose to gain control of the city with *not police power but the army*.

From that decision, it is generally believed that the Empire regarded the uprising as irregular warfare, and people speculate that the mission given to the Imperial Army units envisioned not suppression of the partisans but elimination.

On that point, the Empire argued at the time that partisan activities or the support of them was to forfeit the protection of the law of war.

And so the flames engulfed Arene terribly quickly.

We have here testimony from citizens of Arene who just barely escaped. They've told us that they weren't revolting but that their protests had simply intensified.

…Of course, history tells us that no matter how things started, the Empire's reaction was fierce.

Due to some documents being lost and others remaining classified, we don't know the details, but a battalion-size, possibly larger group of mages was the first to attack.

After receiving what barely counted as a warning, the citizens were beset by a storm of mages.

"They gunned people down like they were so many targets in a firing exercise."

"They got 'points' for shooting people."

"People had blocked themselves in, so they used heavy-explosion formulas to bombard whole districts."

These are all painful memories of the tragedy being shared today.

Even counting only the confirmed deaths, the city of Arene lost half its population that day. The worst incident occurred at the Karelian Cathedral I mentioned earlier.

The swift, disproportionate mage assault they witnessed was only the vanguard. Once a train brought in a multitude of reserve units to sweep through and gain complete control of the city, the residents were left with few places to hide.

To protect themselves and their families, the only options remaining to the men and women who took up arms were to put up a hopeless resistance within the city or risk a desperate escape through enemy forces.

But with no other way to do battle, the sad reality is that the citizens were forced to barricade themselves in. The great majority of them took refuge in and around Karelian Cathedral.

The actions the Empire took in response to this are still debated today, and they have many critics. At the same time, you can't help but notice a strange discrepancy between the complicated laws and common sense.

After all, legal scholars agree that the massacre wasn't in violation of any laws of war. To you viewers at home, that fact must come as a shock.

It's not as though citizens participating in the armed uprising were wearing military uniforms. They were irregular combatants. In other words, international law didn't even guarantee them the rights of prisoners.

Perhaps that's why the Imperial Army surrounded them and gave a word of warning.

"Release unaffiliated members of the general population immediately. We can't allow your slaughter to continue. We demand the release of imperial citizens according to article 26, paragraph 3, of the Rules of War on Land."

Records of what the citizens did are sparse, due to the chaos. But we do know that a small number of pro-Empire people attempted to escape and were shot in full view of the Imperial Army.

Now, why did this tragedy occur?

It recent years, scholars have pointed to the possibility that it was an unforeseen result of Republican propaganda. They had been expressing their intent to dispatch a rescue to take the city back.

Some Republican soldiers were even prepared to fight the Empire.

A number of historians say that atmosphere spread to the populace of Arene. More than a few suggest that the arrival of Republican Army mages led the citizens to make the wrong decision.

And in fact, many of the survivors report a prevailing attitude that they could hold out until the Republic saved them.

Then the Empire issued its last warning.

"This is a warning for the irregular combatants of the armed revolt. In accordance with article 8, paragraph 5, of the Rules of War on Land, I demand someone meet with our representative to discuss the subjects of the Empire you so unjustly imprison."

In response, the city of Arene said, *"We are the citizens of Arene. There are no prisoners. We are just people asking to be free."*

And so, according to the Rules of War on Land, since there were no prisoners and no imperial citizens among the irregular combatants occupying the city, the Empire carried out an operation to capture it.

In order to avoid the heavy responsibility for each soldier that would result if they went into the city and had to visually confirm their targets, they aimed to cause widespread fires via artillery bombardment from positions surrounding the city.

A portion of the documents shows that they had chosen targets that were likely to spread the flames as proof-of-concept for a firestorm.

This notorious atrocity perpetrated by the Imperial Army is commonly known as the Arene Massacre.

We have with us Professor Walter Halbom of Londinium University. Professor Halbom, we'll jump right into it. Why did the Imperial Army take such drastic military action with no hesitation?

"Well, you have to understand how the imperial soldiers were thinking. Their paradigm tended to have military leanings. To put it another way, they wanted to apply that logic to everything.

"In other words, they were thinking in terms of strategy and whatnot.

"You can probably understand the significance of riots behind the Western District Army's front for guys with that mind-set.

"Let's take this step-by-step. First, the Empire's Arene-Roygen region has always contained sparks of partisan resistance. The Imperial Army hypothesizes that someone is inciting the area's anti-Empire faction.

"I think the real problem was that that possibility couldn't be completely denied.

"And if you consider that the uprising cut off the western Imperial Army rear areas from the front, the rest is simple.

"What the Imperial Army General Staff feared first and foremost at the time was the western army getting pinned down before they could scrape together the troops for a unit to suppress the revolt. Most of the Empire's forces were committed on the Rhine lines, so an attack from the militia while the troops were pinned down by the Republican Army might have been enough to cost the Empire the western industrial district.

"The second possibility was that the revolt would stay contained within the Arene-Roygen region. In that case, they would be able to protect the industrial region, but…Arene was a major city on the supply rail line. I think that played a major role.

"Because, you know, if there is pressure on the supply lines, the troops won't be able to fight for very long no matter how tough they are.

"The potential was there for the Empire's worst-case scenario to come to

pass—at least, it wouldn't have been an unexpected line of reasoning for the imperial side.

"*We can see that the anti-Empire movement uprising gave the Empire a tremendous shock in terms of strategy.*

"*I myself can declare, from my experience serving, that the mere notion of the communication lines to the rear becoming paralyzed is terrifying for anyone.*

"*So I think the Imperial Army was imagining the Republican Army Command would throw their weight around. If that happened, the imperial forces would be requested to urgently eliminate the resistance, but they would have to worry about Republican mages joining and strengthening it.*

"*At that point, the army was already short on troops for the front, so stabilizing the rear at the same time was a practically impossible demand.*

"*With these two difficult problems, the Empire now faced a major dilemma. The only good thing—or perhaps, the disastrous thing—was that they had an intercepting mage unit as reinforcements.*

"*The mage units Command kept on hand as reserves for the army had a measure of firepower. That gave them the option to suppress the separatist independent movement.*

"*Of course, if they mobilized them here, they wouldn't be able to use them to resist an invasion.*

"*Naturally, that led to worries that the main battlefront could collapse. Additionally, in a battle to capture a city, the mage units would really only be good for intimidation and diversions.*

"*But on the front lines, they could wipe out or repel enemy units.*

"*Should they prioritize fending off attacking Republicans? If they did that, with the rear devoid of soldiers, the revolt was liable to spread. If that happened, it could have a markedly negative effect on the supply lines, causing enormous losses in a battle of attrition. On the front lines, where they were already fighting close-pitched battles, it was hard to imagine they would be able to take such losses.*

"*So should they put down the revolt first? But spending the time of their only reserves to suppress the revolt could prove fatal. If the reserves got tied up and lost time and the Republican Army broke through, the invasion could result in an immeasurable increase in casualties. All the lives lost countering the sneak attack and pushing the enemy back would have been lost for nothing, and that would not be acceptable.*

"For the Republican Army, on the other hand, success was guaranteed. No matter which objective the Imperial Army chose, the Republicans would achieve something in the end.

"It is here that the Imperial Army commits an obviously atrocious deed, leaving a mark on history no country should make.

"Who ordered it is unclear. We don't even really have a record of who carried it out. These were truly soldiers who had to be left out of the records.

"While they were soldiers of the finest caliber who pulled off a miraculous defensive battle, they were also the lowest of the low who deeply stained the Empire's honor.

"Now in the postwar period, many soldiers criticize them. Personally, though, I defend the people who were put in that difficult position. Under the circumstances, they had no alternative options, and additionally, it came down as an order.

"What is certain is that someone saved the Empire's battle lines, although I have to say, the method is not one I personally agree with."

Thank you, Professor Walter Halbom.

Now, take a look at this next video… Professor Halbom offers this internal document from the Imperial Army General Staff.

She might call it "an extreme form of 'practicality.'"

Command has removed her restraints. Wisely, to achieve victory, they took away her limits. These are the orders of the army, of the Empire, and as a soldier, I am forced to obey. The impulses that were successfully suppressed with logic will be unchained for this great cause. Or perhaps it's that the cause she had to hesitate will disappear.

Whose responsibility is it when a beast bites into a meal thrown in front of it? I believe those responsible are none other than the ones who threw the sacrifice to the starving animal.

Chapter VI

*A scribbled note discovered in a wastebasket at the Imperial Army General Staff Headquarters

》》》   MAY 4, UNIFIED YEAR 1925, THE RHINE FRONT   《《《

"As chief of staff, did you know this might happen?" the army corps commander generously pretended to ask, trying to hide the tremble in his voice at the seriousness of the situation.

Actually, though he was controlling his expression, he was seething internally. The Republican Army had moved far more quickly than the Empire had anticipated.

News had come in that, completely contrary to their expectations, mage reinforcements, albeit a small number of them, had entered Arene.

Arene's defenses would probably grow stronger as more time passed. *Meanwhile, our plan has utterly failed.* The initial confusion had finally been brought under control, and they were getting a grasp on the situation, but he wanted to shield his eyes from the pathetic spectacle of panicking troops. *Is this really our Imperial Army?*

Even the suppression unit the central General Staff promised them had gotten held up, and this was the result. He wanted to chew out the Railroad Department, who was responsible for managing the schedules, and ask what the hell they had been doing.

But the necessity of such complaints showed how bad the situation was in Arene. If the trains that ran through there were paralyzed for even a day, the supply line delivering tens of thousands of tons of ammunition and food to the front would be physically disrupted. Unless each division was sent at least five hundred—but a thousand, if possible—tons of supplies, the frontline troops would find their ranks thinning out. That statistic was now basically the General Staff's nightmare.

To make matters worse, there was no alternative line. Arene was a main relay point that even had a switchyard. There were branch lines, yes, but as for whether or not they could serve the front, the hopeless, pale faces of the Railroad Department members said it all. The Imperial

Army was realizing again what an Achilles' heel logistics trouble was when invading—especially after cutting off its enemies up north.

So for a moment, what crossed the commanders' minds was the furious scolding they would unleash on the Feldgendarmerie, since they had failed to quash the sparks of rebellion.

The army corps commander wasn't the only one softly sneering, "You good-for-nothing freeloaders."

He didn't know where the military police's precious Feldgendarmerie had been napping, but talk about lazy. *If you have a siesta custom, get your asses back to the countryside.* Though no one said it out loud, they all groaned and spat on the ground.

Circumstances were so lamentable that someone murmured, "We could have avoided this if we had one of our brave, loyal mage companies."

The situation was rapidly deteriorating. They couldn't help but fear the worst.

Riots in the rear. Thanks to that, the units were stuck.

If we move the front, won't the Republic react? As long as that worry remained, they had to keep movement of troops to a minimum. But if supplies were interrupted for even a few days, they would soon lose the ability to fight.

So the threat in Arene had to be eliminated. Well, that was easy to say. It would be very difficult to get rid of the rebels quickly now that Republican mages had joined them.

"Yes, sir, there was some idea. Operations, please explain."

But as expected, you could say, it took the staff corps very little time to collect their analyses of a scenario like this. Plans made in advance may not be everything, but they can help you tackle your problems.

"Sir. We have a plan drawn up from a purely military view to achieve a very limited aim that was created as part of strategy research."

"What? Is it actually usable?"

The only issue was whether what they came up with was usable or not.

After all, the situation was bad. A half-baked scheme wasn't going to cut it. He would accept anything as long as it solved their problem in one shot.

...But from the sound of it, he couldn't expect too much.

"Well, it will definitely achieve certain results. But it will require a, uh, very important decision to be made..."

Just spit it out, he stopped himself from shouting.

"We don't have time for this. Tell me what it is."

"Yes, sir. It's a plan by the war college's strategy research committee submitted with the idea of eliminating enemy units building defensive lines in an urban setting, including mages, in an extremely short amount of time."

As far as the dubious army corps commander could tell, it sounded like an effective plan. If the strategy research committee at the war college had submitted it, that meant they acknowledged its practicality. If they could really use it to quickly take out mages and other defenses in an urban setting, the plan would be invaluable in their current predicament.

"...This is quite groundbreaking, isn't it? Why didn't it get passed around to all the armies?"

If it's so useful, then why not share it?

"Does it violate the Worms Convention?" Perhaps wondering the same thing, the chief of staff voiced a possible worry—an international treaty.

They imagined that the rapid capture of a city and elimination of resistance would be difficult without using gas or heavy artillery. Of course, gas wouldn't be allowed in a city. And even the General Staff probably didn't have a plan to defend against gas.

"No, the legal specialists say it doesn't conflict with any existing treaties."

"Even better. So what's the problem?"

There shouldn't be any reason to hesitate if it's legal. Honestly, we don't have a second to lose.

They didn't have time to debate with the legal specialists. The army corps commander banged the table in irritation and urged the hesitating staffer on with his eyes.

"The plan was written on the assumption, from a purely military point of view, that there are no noncombatants in the city, only enemy forces."

"What is that supposed to mean? How can we use something based on such an improbable assumption?"

He nearly shouted that it was stupid. There aren't any cities where only enemy soldiers live.

Cities are mostly civilians. At most, civilians with militia among them. And they had confirmed when they occupied Arene that many civilians lived there.

"Well, we'd create those conditions by following a legal procedure."

Both the one answering and the one asking spoke in a monotone to conceal their emotions.

"In short, it's a sort of deceit. According to the legal specialists, the plan is only valid upon ruling out the existence of noncombatants, so we'll just make sure there are none."

"…So we'd just be killing everyone regardless of gender or age?"

It was unmistakably clear. In everyone's heads appeared an urban battle. Yes, a bloody slaughter in the guise of an urban battle. Everyone understood that if they were being told to take this rotten fight seriously, they couldn't bother with legal practicality.

"We would employ the simple, straightforward method of burning the city down."

I just want to be done with this is what the tone of the Operations officer seemed to say as he continued the requested explanation. He wasn't the only one who wished there was nothing to continue.

"A fire attack? Well, that's classic. But against mages?"

"Have you ever heard of a firestorm?"

A terrifying report or a proposal from hell. The one who thought of this was either a lawyer so cunning the devil would invite them to join forces or a criminal. This way of thinking is practically inhuman. Only a devil who forgot their reason and conscience in their mother's womb could come up with such a tactic.

That someone would equate having the technical capabilities for an operation with actually doing it… Are they deranged?

"No, it's the first time I've heard of it."

"It was proposed after the idea was verified by looking at large-scale conflagrations of the past."

Urban warfare has many different legal constraints. The topic of the research was how the army should deal with them, but nobody would have thought to look for a plan that removed them.

No, for better or worse, outside of the specialists, no soldiers felt like confronting the laws at all. To put it nicely, you could call them simple; to cast it negatively, you could say the army had an anti-intellectual streak. So they weren't used to explanations of legal principles.

But from a soldier's point of view, the rules of engagement were to some extent self-evident, and indiscriminately shooting civilians was like police groping for a solution to a hostage crisis and deciding to shoot all the hostages along with the criminal. Certainly, apprehending the culprit would be the highest priority, but would you arrive at a plan to eliminate the hostages instead of save them? Ideas that are purely unthinkable for a normal person are a soldier's common sense.

Of course, there is the delicate issue with military wisdom that the ethics and morality tend to be old-fashioned, due to the inevitable reference to wars of the previous era for its standards.

Still, a soldier's way of thinking was generally rational. This way of thinking was such a single-minded pursuit of purposive rationality that it was anomalous.

"It seems they've arrived at one conclusion, which is that, ideally, the operation should be carried out by mages with fire attacks."

"Never mind the theory. Has it been put into practice?"

"When it was attempted on army exercise grounds, a phenomenon approaching the projected results was achieved. If fire attacks are coordinated from multiple locations, it's plenty possible to create."

And when he understood, the army corps commander was frightened of the plan his army had received.

...Ohhh, oh God.

Why, why must I do such a thing?

Why must I be ordered to carry out a plan conceived by the devil?

When I respond to the immediate summons, an Intelligence officer wearing the rank of captain meets me. In other words, *I'm sure he is the bearer of bad news.* Having made that conclusion, Tanya takes a deep breath to brace herself.

Always be calm and collected.

But that thought promptly crumbles. That's how shocking the news is. The news that...

"The rear has been cut off."

One of my forerunners gave me a piece of advice: *"What's important when being brought bad news is whether or not you can find the silver lining."*

Ever since then, I've remained faithful to it.

For instance, right now, I have a cup of real coffee in my hands, a treat from the rear headquarters, and I'm glad I'm not drinking it because doing a spit take or choking on it would have been a terrible waste of such a valuable item.

...Of all things, the rear is cut off? The supply lines?

"Yes, Major von Degurechaff. It's a partisan uprising."

"Now?!"

What occurs to me is Republican leadership. The rear cut off. The collapse of logistics. If that happens, our entire army could be sent fleeing in a disorderly panic.

Even a child could imagine that much. The partisan movement intensifies at a strategic point in the rear while the Imperial Army's main forces are pinned down? There's no way the Republicans won't pour oil on that little fire. And after such libation, there's no way the partisans won't go a little pyromaniac. The logic is self-evident.

No doubt, a huge fire is about to start raging. Detrimental situations tend to go downhill fast. There is only a handful of exceptions.

"Yes, now, ma'am."

I want to tell this situation to eat shit.

Tanya's natural reaction to the news is for her facial muscles to tense. The command personnel are all wearing expressions of pensive distress. *I probably have the same look on my face, too,* Tanya observes in a somehow calm way, with a tinge of self-derision. Maybe I shouldn't look this way in front of my subordinates, but all I can do is wish. All the officers who heard the news got the same look on their faces, and they're probably just as self-conscious.

"What's the situation?"

"The military police and some of the troops garrisoned there are doing their best to bring the area under control, but it seems things are getting worse fast."

"That's no good. Can they put it down?"

In a way, it's as bad as I expected. The inept Feldgendarmerie screwed up, so they got caught when the fat hit the fire. If we leave them alone, the rear will get burned. But if we put out the fire, our front lines will get trampled. One wrong move, and it'll be trench warfare without ammunition or food.

No matter how optimistically you look at this, it's bound to be an utter disaster with piles of corpses. We should even be prepared for the lines to break.

"I don't know, but I think we need to be ready to respond."

"Right. Give standby orders. Make sure we can move as soon as we get the word."

What I'm hoping, what I'd like, is for this situation to settle down on its own. It could happen. But my optimistic speculation that the fire might just fizzle out misses the mark.

In reality, my wish means nothing, and the situation rapidly deteriorates. Signs of a Republican offensive are confirmed, and Command is forced to make a decision.

As a result, we end up in the pursuit of pure military logic and nothing else.

The deciding factor is a report that Republican Army reinforcements have joined the partisans. At this point, the army reaches a conclusion that is quite straightforward. As long as there is a line that can't be crossed, holding it has to be made priority.

"An airdrop?! Crud! They're mages. The Republican Army is conducting an airborne operation! Looks like they're meeting up with the rebels!"

Shrieks from Control.

If they were just armed insurrectionists with no mages, it would be hard to put them down, but there was the possibility that police power would be enough. Or maybe it could be resolved with a division of infantry.

But in urban combat up against mages, even heavy infantry will have to prepare for insane losses. After all, a city is a three-dimensional battlefield full of cover and obstacles. It doesn't get shouted from the rooftops, but it is said that mages actually do their best work in urban battles. So this will have to be a serious fight.

"Is someone intercepting them?"

And that's why mages helping to defend the city is so hugely significant. Just one infantry division plucked from the mustered reserves would probably be enough to suppress an armed mob, even if it took a little time. With the manpower of the police and Ministry of the Interior, they might have been able to suppress them, even if they had to shed some blood to do it.

But once mages are the defenders of the city, it's different from intercepting on flat ground or from defensive positions, and military intervention is required. But even then, just throwing a ton of matériel at them won't be very effective. You need to literally disregard any damage and capture the city district by district.

For that reason, mages should be stopped with their weak point, air-to-air combat, and there should have been an air defense network covering 360 degrees. That was how it was supposed to be.

"They didn't make it in time and got diverted."

But there is a glaring chasm between the plan and our present situation. There should have been some leeway in the rotation of the aerial forces, but it has been broken down for a while now. The Imperial Air Fleet was basically out in full force every day and having trouble making up for losses in the Rhine Air Battle.

The air units have more types of missions than expected—not just securing supremacy in the sky. As a result, the plan created before the war started meant absolutely nothing when it met the reality of borderline overworked air units being mobilized for missions they weren't expecting. It was only once the air units had been sent in that the military began to understand the necessity of the types of missions they could perform; the army is much more aware of how important controlling the sky is than they were before the start of the war.

Dacia, where the ones who soared through the sky ruled everything, has been taken as a model case. *For that reason alone*, perhaps you can say? Or *precisely because of that?*—the Imperial Air Fleet put all their forces into securing command of the air near the front lines.

As a result, they've succeeded in stabilizing the battlefront and managed to establish a degree of supremacy in the sky. It's somewhat ironic that they should be lacking the forces to prevent a sneak attack in the rear... This is practically like Norden with offense and defense reversed.

"This is bad. We can't let them secure a bridgehead."

"So it'll be a counter-mage battle? Against mages who are ready and waiting for us?"

Yes, that. The longer it takes to suppress them, the worse things will get.

We don't know how many mages they sent in, but if we consider how many it would take to organize a resistance, we can get an idea. After all, the Imperial Army pioneered this tactic. We understand it even if we don't want to.

"...Major von Degurechaff. Report to the commander's office immediately."

And so.

Things happen without anyone making a definite decision.

History, to a surprising extent, is a series of miscalculations.

》》》 APRIL 13, UNIFIED YEAR 1924, RESEARCH ROOM 17 (JOINT STRATEGY 《《《
RESEARCH MEETING HELD AT THE IMPERIAL WAR COLLEGE)

"As you can see, as the war situation changes, the chances of combat in a city will become extremely high."

The instructor finishes his explanation in front of a war map spread on the desk. It was a review of the war situation touching on how the Imperial Army has been making a comeback bit by bit on the Rhine front.

The two armies are still competing for a scrap of barren land, but the

Imperial Army has been gradually advancing. Progress is progress, even in baby steps. It's huge that we've gone from being invaded to being able to plan a counterattack.

And that's why at this new stage, all variety of combat in Republican territory is starting to sound more realistic, thinks Tanya.

It'll come down to urban warfare.

It's difficult to imagine the Republic simply neglecting key strategic cities that function as transport terminals. And unfortunately, a lot of civilians must live in urban areas. Some of them will certainly have taken shelter or been evacuated, but we have to assume that enough people will stay behind to keep the city functioning.

"So the General Staff has tasked us with coming up with ways to handle urban warfare."

As Tanya expected, the task the instructor has for them is planning countermeasures for just such a battle.

The law of war is extremely critical of involving noncombatants in urban battles. I don't know if it's true or not, but supposedly there is a trigger clause that allows unlimited economic sanctions against countries that purposely attack in a way that involves noncombatants.

Actually invoking the clause would be up to each individual country, but…it's still a troublesome provision from the Empire's point of view. That's why this request was made—it's necessary to capture a city without giving the major powers a rallying cause.

Of course, even if we did that, it would only buy us time. After all, geopolitically the other powers have plenty of reason to intervene.

Well, that's why we should try to keep them from intervening for a bit longer.

"To be frank, the only option we'll have if we don't involve noncombatants is to surround and starve them into submission."

Everyone present knows how unrealistic the request is.

But despite knowing the extent of the problem, they understand well enough to curse to hell how critical it is strategically. That's why she uses an indirect expression shrouded in rhetoric to say, *Don't order us to do the impossible!* Crying like that is all that is ever possible under political pressure.

She said to surround and starve them into submission, but it would be incredibly difficult to keep them surrounded until the city finally fell. Even sending in three times the force of the enemy would put an unimaginable burden on Logistics.

"I think we can free ourselves from this type of issue by leaving the front lines where they are and devoting ourselves to defense until the enemy can't take it anymore."

Purely in terms of the principle of concentration of force, it's better to defend than invade. Even though that is only one of the assumptions made internally, more than a few officers think that way. *Even they want to win*, thinks Tanya. *Still*, she thinks again. The officers of the Imperial Army aren't excitable enough to think they can fight a war with their arms and legs tied up.

"But we were able to do it in the Entente Alliance."

"Consider how much stronger we were, please. Besides, doing it that way is why we now have so many troops stuck up there."

Though she is listening to the debate going on before her, Tanya has already accepted the fact that it's impossible to be considerate of civilians in urban warfare. Even the American Army tried to conduct urban warfare with kindness to civilians and is now stuck writhing around in agony.

In this age of total war, Tanya has no choice but to give up on kindness to civilians.

What's worse, most of the surplus forces are tied up in the north and west. The burden on the supply lines has far surpassed prewar estimates. We're up against small powers that we beat in terms of both muscle and population, and *this* is where we're at. A huge war between the major players will require full power not to get eaten alive. At this rate, it'll be impossible. Tanya regrets it, but they are no longer in a position to observe international laws and fight with concern for civilians.

Even with an industrial base that can manufacture a vast amount of matériel, the supply lines are shrieking, and the people in charge of logistics in the rear are flailing around, trying to prevent a shortage of food and other consumables.

"…I don't mean to be rude, but is this discussion really necessary?"

That's why she interrupts. Aware that she's not being very cute, she speaks calmly in a deliberately flat tone.

Normally you would be rebuked for such a comment. But Tanya didn't think she would have any problems.

"That's a bold remark from a student, Degurechaff. Tell us what you mean."

"Yes, sir. Encircling and starving the enemy is a leisurely tactic from medieval times or, at best, a previous era."

Specifically, the Ottoman's siege of Vienna or Napoleon's campaign in Italy. An army fighting a modern war can't use tactics from an earlier period when there weren't even railroads.

If you're going to end up using that strategy, you're better off not fighting.

"So…"

True, there aren't many realistic options besides starving them into submission. She understands that. But that's a problem that *everyone* is aware of.

We aren't gathered here to debate something so well understood.

If you can't brainstorm, it's better to look for a legal loophole.

Setting aside feasibility, failing to consider every possibility would be a big mistake.

As an individual with what passes for an intellectual education, it would be an inexcusable error.

Therefore, Tanya is simply convinced that even if it's just debate for the sake of debate, they should try approaching the issue in a different way.

As someone who, in a way, is familiar with urban warfare as historical truth, the question is *how* to fight an urban battle.

"…shouldn't we try to think of a way to make fighting in a city legal?"

Urban warfare is restricted by international laws? Groping for a way to defeat them besides urban warfare is like playing by their rules. It's like negotiating an important deal at the other party's office.

You'll never win that way. What you need to do is flip the situation so they're coming to negotiate with you.

In other words, isn't it possible to shift our point of view and ask how to make urban warfare legal? Of course, having seen Iraq and Afghanistan, I seriously refuse to actually do it. Having thought that, Tanya realizes, *But if we could lay waste to whole blocks like they did in Warsaw, this urban warfare thing would be a cinch.* She even begins to calculate. *It would be a pain to go into all-out war, but it's definitely a possibility.*

"...Degurechaff. Haven't you learned about the war of law in your classes?"

"Yes, I completed the subject. It's terribly interesting."

I hadn't studied laws since I was a student taking Jurisprudence (including constitutional theory) and Civil Law A and B. I did learn a little about international relations theory, international administration, and international law. In that sense, getting the chance to study law, the ruler of civilization, was genuinely fun.

And that's why she can make her declaration with confidence even in terms of the legal basis. There's nothing wrong with her idea, and it doesn't come into conflict with any legal principles.

"...So you're saying this with that experience in mind?"

"Yes, Instructor."

After all, any law has room for interpretation as a matter of course. That's why there are so many opportunities for jerks to twist them to fit their aims and annoy the rational marketplace. Legal opportunists can even profit from something as time consuming as patent litigation... That's why in litigation societies like the United States, there are a ton of lawyers waging great legal battles. Basically, what you can and can't do under a law changes any number of times depending on how it's interpreted and enforced—to the point where some peaceful island nation can be a weird country that says it doesn't have an army while equipping it with all kinds of fantastic weapons. Well, that's a better idea than abandoning the notion of an army completely, but it just goes to show how broadly laws can be interpreted.

What's wrong with the ever-serious Empire doing a serious reinterpretation of the law? To Tanya, it's nothing but an utterly natural course of events.

Of course, domestic laws are ultimately interpreted by the one with the sovereign rights, His Imperial Majesty the Emperor, and impinging on his authority is prohibited…but the military studies international laws; they're totally safe. Tanya believes, without question, that gray is white.

"It's a problem of interpretation. Anything the international laws do not expressly forbid is only restricted depending on one's interpretation."

"Specifically?"

"This is only one example, but there is a clause that says, 'Armies are prohibited from indiscriminately attacking areas where there are noncombatants.'"

If you just look at that, it seems like you couldn't possibly fight in a city. Tons of noncombatants live there. But think of it flipped around. The enemy is limited in the same way. After all, armies have the duty to protect.

"At a glance, it appears to be a clause that restricts the attacking side, but naturally, it also limits the defending side. It's possible to demand that they protect those in the shelters according to law. In other words, if they don't take the evacuees and withdraw…it's possible to interpret that as meaning there are no civilians."

"…I see. And then?"

If I have permission to continue, then I'll do so.

Well, legal debate is half-sophistry, half-finger-pointing. A court might make the final decision, but the way each country interprets the law has a major influence on international legal cases.

"According to the law of war, we both have the duty to protect non-combatants. So we'll be expected to do everything in our power to fulfill it. It depends on how you work it, but I think we can use it."

For example, what would happen if we had a small unit infiltrate an area where civilians lived, and we got attacked? If there was even one stray shot fired our way, we could turn it into a justification. Well, that's an extreme method. There's a more legitimate way to go about it.

"Or if we make them tell us there are no noncombatants, the restriction will be instantly lifted."

"What?"

"If they say that every person down to the last civilian will resist us. If we interpret that as meaning that every last civilian is militia, then we don't have to recognize any prisoners' rights."

Chapter VI

...The former Yugoslavia said all their citizens were soldiers. *Then if*
everyone's a soldier, we can blow them up and it won't be a war crime would
be the logical end to that interpretation. That said, if you pursue this
sort of interpretation to extremes, it's possible to twist reason itself.
So of course, justice and fairness are warped as well.

Yep. And? What about it? Concepts are concepts, and bad laws are still
laws. In the first place, this is a world where a god or a devil—this Being
X guy—is getting his way. If you want to think seriously about the question of what justice is, maybe the guy who stipulates the world should be
at war is the evil one.

In other words, I'm just one good person doing my duty.

QED.[19]

>>> X-DAY <<<

Luckily, an army corps commander summoning a mere major is exceedingly rare. But the army corps commander probably had a hard time
being happy about the infrequency. Exceptional though it was, it
meant there was a chance he might have to summon this monster again
someday.

Telling him it was only a possibility wouldn't make him feel any better.

"Rejoice, Major von Degurechaff."

"Sir."

Doing his best not to look directly at the monster straightening her
posture in front of him, the army corps commander accepted that it was
for work and met her. As far as he could tell from a normal person's perspective, mages were more than a little foreign.

They were humans who could fly by their own power and use magic to
interfere with the world. Even if he understood them logically, when he
met one face-to-face, his emotions couldn't catch up.

But this he could state confidently: The principles behind the actions

---

[19] **QED** "It has been proven."

of this major in front of him were impossible to understand using *anyone's* logic *or* emotions. Her inorganic eyes compelled you to conclude that her thoughts, her frameworks, her way of being were all warped. She may have had blue eyes and a pretty face, which probably gave a gentle impression, but the emotions in those eyes said everything and made her look different.

"You've got a special mission from the regional command."

She was commissioned before her age hit double digits.

When he had heard that, he had laughed and said, *"A fabled child soldier, then?"* But when he met her, his first impression was *combat machine.* He immediately corrected his perception of her, but he didn't begin to think he had understood her. The reputation that had preceded her—*for a recipient of the Silver Wings Assault Badge, she looks like a fairy, albeit one who was born to fight*—must have been true to the letter. Maybe it was her symmetrical features, but she seemed like the type who might get called a vampire behind her back.

"The orders will be issued at 1422."

When she had been ordered to do some simple field training, she had, unbelievably, taken her recruits on a night raid against an enemy outpost trench. And yet the unit's loss ratio was surprisingly low. Though they fought hard with dauntless bravery and got results, their loss ratios were lower than that of all the other units. *Honestly, if that was all, she would be a great soldier.*

She's too perfect. There's nothing about her to criticize; she's so logical and has achieved so much. So no one can stop her. It makes sense that Lieutenant Colonel von Lergen failed when he tried to eliminate her. Well, the legal specialists letting her go and the Foreign Office giving up are probably bigger factors...

"Promptly eliminate the enemy mage unit that has penetrated the rear city of Arene. After that, join up with reinforcements and suppress the city. That is all."

Republican mages had dropped into the city of Arene in the rear, in a sense, completely outwitting the imperial lookouts. On top of that, the partisan riots were growing. If they couldn't suppress Arene, they couldn't use the railway. If they couldn't use the railway, logistics would get cut off.

And then, the army corps commander concluded, somewhat self-mockingly, if the logistics got cut off, they would starve. At that rate, even a child would be able to understand where the war was headed.

For exactly that reason, the brass was not fooling around. No, they had probably already braced themselves. Their determination could be felt in the orders.

Apparently, if there was *no other way*, they wouldn't stop at turning Arene to ashes.

Evacuation orders had already been issued at this point, as well as a curfew to prevent people going out at night, accompanied by a stern warning. If things proceeded according to the plan he'd been given, if the rebels didn't obediently surrender, the entire city would be "dealt with appropriately."

And she was so trusted to get things done that she would be assisting. Well, she was frightfully capable.

"Any questions?"

"If you could tell me what size of enemy force to expect…"

"At least a battalion."

The vanguard would be the 203rd Aerial Mage Battalion. They would be sent in to eliminate the mages obstructing imperial suppression of the city.

Really, the top seemed reluctant to burn Arene. They must have been thinking that resolving things without burning it *would be best*. The artillery and air units had only just been ordered to prepare to attack, so they weren't ready to do it at a moment's notice.

So is it as an alibi, then, that they're to issue a warning to surrender after the 203rd Aerial Mage Battalion eliminates the mages? The problem was that if the people of Arene didn't lose their will to fight with that, there would be no options left for the Imperial Army.

"What kind of troops?"

"Apart from a small number of Republican mages, they're militia. Many citizens of Arene have already become casualties."

But there was another horrible truth right next to him. The magic major before his eyes had presented striking views on international law at the war college. And these were not your average "striking views."

To speak in extremes, she had a brain diabolical enough to foresee today's situation and come up with a solution.

After all, I know she's the one who came up with the justification to sacrifice the people of Arene in this operation.

General von Zettour in the Service Corps gave me all the details, but I never thought I would regret taking her on this much.

That bastard, he should be more considerate of his superior's stomach.

"How sad. By the way, I overheard a little bird twittering about partisans…"

"It's a problem for me if you can hear too well. You must have mistaken some other sound."

"So our enemy is the Republican Army, then?"

Just in case. Yes, she was *only* checking to make sure their enemy was the Republican Army. *Who does that? A normal officer wouldn't even wonder.* On the Rhine lines, "the enemy" meant "the Republican Army."

"Isn't that a given? They don't follow the Land War Convention. We need to get in there and protect the noncombatants."

But he could see why she reconfirmed her definitions. This wasn't a mission you could perform if you didn't know what *enemy* meant.

"So we'll get to flex our muscles. You mean that we should buy time cheerfully despite being fatally outnumbered?"

"Ha, Major. You can choose victory or Valhalla, either one you like."

"Is that an order to annihilate them and win, sir?"

Well, I can see how it could be interpreted that way.

Cause widespread destruction, theoretically with no legal restrictions. *Is there any other way to win?*

It's like we're ordering a bloodbath. There won't even be combat.

Even if you believed the war college's interpretation of the laws was correct, this plan was clearly designed with a massacre in mind.

And I heard rumors she was involved in the plan. This expression, this calm… Maybe the rumors are true. That was how inhuman she was.

"Yes, and yesterday at 1100 hours Arene was given an evacuation warning. So you can assume the entire city has already been captured."

"Which means?"

Chapter **VI**

"The higher-ups are saying to eliminate everything. Legally, only the Republican Army units are there."

I'll just be frank. There's not really any reason to hide it. After all, the only thing this war machine soldier needs is permission and orders.

She adheres to the rules. That is, she doesn't do anything beyond them. Apparently, she limits herself in a strange way.

"How awful. It'll be hell no matter what we do," Major von Degurechaff said coolly.

But then why is she smiling so happily?

What is that delighted smile glowing on your cheeks?! What are those fangs peeking out of your mouth?! Why are you happy enough to grin? ...You vampire.

"...A battle to capture a city is a fight against time."

I hope no one noticed that I just flinched, thought the army corps commander, sensing that he was distinctly afraid of her.

"The city is already under enemy control, right? So can't we lay waste to entire blocks?"

"Major?"

"If civilians were there, they would limit us, but if the city has been overrun, then no worries."

No worries about what? He deeply wanted to ask what she was planning to do, but he held back. He told himself it was surely better not to know.

"But this is really too bad."

With this, the die is cast.

For the one responsible, there was probably no die more nauseating.

"Yes, it's *really, truly* awful. But we're soldiers. If it's an order, we have to burn even the beautiful city of Arene."

You devil. Zettour and Rudersdorf, you wicked men.

Apparently, they'll do anything to win the war. They would literally do any and everything.

They mean to win this war by any means necessary, even if they go insane. Soldiers they may be, but they're cracked.

"...No one should ever be a soldier."

"You're right about that. But not everyone gets to live the life they want."

That's right, Magic Major von Degurechaff.

But there is probably no one more suited to being a soldier than you. Perhaps you feel at home in hell on the Rhine front.

I was wondering why I was summoned from my standby dugout on the forward-most line to the safe command dugout farther back under the highest-priority orders, and now I have a mission to eliminate enemy mages invading a key location in the rear. Fighting enemy mages is a totally ordinary mission.

The difference this time is that the "field" will be a city. Not just any city, but Arene, a critical node in the Empire's rail transport network. According to the orders, we have to be prompt and speedy... *Use any means necessary to eliminate the enemy* is the missive from my superior's superior's superior.

Having wrapped her head around the situation in her own way, it doesn't seem so difficult. Her position, in a nutshell, is like being told to crush the Prague Spring.

The enemy mages are apparently joined by a battalion-sized militia, so it's a simple order to take care of the uprising along with their tanks—the mages—with our artillery.

If the order is to crush this mob, Tanya is almost bored, knowing history and how common such orders were. Of course, considering the supply lines are in danger, it's not a trivial mission. Tanya is well aware of that.

But that's all. If a riot starts, just give the order to put it down. She double-checked so many times because she was startled that the local army corps commander had to call her, a frontline officer, over to discuss it.

Once she realized the orders were simply to deal with a mob, she could barely keep herself from grinning. *This isn't going to be so hard. And it's a great chance to get away from the front lines.*

Chapter **VI**

Having made that conclusion, she dashed over to her battalion's headquarters to start getting ready just a little while ago.

…Then I finally realize that there's something bothering me about the written orders I was given. We're legally in the white, but then why do they hint at the possibility of indiscriminate strategic bombardment?

If the remaining troops don't surrender after we eliminate the enemy mages, the next steps are terrifying. When Tanya realizes that, she kicks her brain into high gear. Yes, the WTO,[20] who crushed the Prague Spring, were the WTO. It's not as if they were acting under a banner of democracy or anything. In other words, history can denounce it.

After all, this plan calls for doing as much damage as possible to stone buildings using high explosives and explosion formulas. Militarily, it's a great idea and will expose the buildings' flammable innards.

After that, I guess we just drop mainly incendiary bombs? No, we can probably burn things fine with artillery time bombs. If all the Imperial Army units assembled here concentrate their fire, Arene will end up having something in common with Dresden.

…It'll be a massacre even if we don't screw up. Ehh, but we'll basically be substituting artillery for carpet-bombing, so it's like in the Warsaw Uprising; it *is* within the realm of the typical.

One regrettable thing is the gray zone where those bombings will be evil for the country that loses, but the ones the winning country conducted don't even get questioned, much less written off as a result of said nonexistent questioning. One wrong move and I could end up nominated as a war criminal. I refuse to put myself in such danger.

But wait, that'll only happen if the Empire loses. Which means that supposing we don't lose, if I refuse to follow orders at this point, I'll be shot for insubordination, fleeing before the enemy, et cetera.

After all, orders are orders. And at this point, there is nothing wrong with the ones I've received. I have no grounds for refusing them and no reason to worry. I don't even know if my superiors would listen to me if I tried to talk to them. Well, there may not be time for that, anyhow.

---

[20] **WTO**   Warsaw Treaty Organization

On the other hand, I could devote myself to actions with no legal issues now, but given that laws were retroactively enforced in the Military Tribunal for the Far East, I'll definitely need to be humane. And on top of that, I have to act in such a way that a bunch of people won't accuse me of things later? You mean I have to pretend to be nice?

In that case, obeying the laws to the best of my ability won't cut it. What the heck? But I guess my life is in danger unless I act humanely? I'd like to take it easy on the people, but doing that for no reason and ending up low on achievements will be problematic...

No, wait. I have a reason. I have a bunch of burdensome new recruits with me, don't I? With them slowing me down, the other units will probably arrive by the time we finish eliminating the enemy mages. At that point, we can say we have casualties and withdraw.

Then I don't have to get my hands dirty. At least, if the battle takes some time to unfold, maybe I can pull my punches without anyone thinking poorly of my abilities. Ah, if this was going to happen, maybe I should have been more understanding of the recruits.

Hmm? Ugh, but the commander is the one held liable. What would happen if one of the new recruits accidentally shot a civilian? It goes without saying that I, their leader, would either face a tribunal or a kangaroo court. But I guess if the Empire wins, the tribunal wouldn't be so bad.

If I'm lucky I can expect to be acquitted. Of course I can. It's a question of how much responsibility I can really be expected to take for these newbies. But if we lose, I'll probably end up the victim of revenge. That would suck. I thought this was a good idea, but now it seems like it's not going to work.

For a moment, she considers a way to keep it a secret. Should I just eliminate all the witnesses? But she immediately puts a lid on her indiscretion, as even massacres have survivor testimonies.

Almost zero is not zero. And with a look at history, you can see that any number of witnesses can be created. How many countries would hesitate to create a witness where none existed?

"...I'm so not keen on this," murmurs Tanya, because that's all she can do in this situation. There's not even much time left until the sortie. And her talented unit is such a bunch of war nuts that when they heard there was a sortie they assembled right away.

We can probably already transition into sortie readiness. If this was going to happen, I shouldn't have had them get prepped ahead of time.

With eyes like a dead fish's, her pleasant features distorted, Tanya has mixed feelings watching her subordinates as they ready themselves with an irritating briskness. She wonders what she should do.

People might think I'm hard-line imperialist just because I received that superficial decoration. No, they must. If that's the case, the life waiting for me will be pretty unpleasant. Just take a look at Germany. No one who was a zealous Nazi during the war met a good end. People still give the SS a rough time. About the only ones who got decent treatment were the ace pilots. Even so, after the war, albeit for a brief time, many of them were interned by the communists. Is there no loophole? I can't get interned like Hartmann.

...No, wait a minute. There was one guy. There was a soldier named Rudel[21] or something. He was hard-core—we're talking reinforced concrete—anticommunist and pro-Nazi. But after the war, he even managed to enjoy his life pretty well. Him. I'll emulate him!

To Second Lieutenant Grantz, it sounded the same as usual.

"Okay, battalion, we're going on a picnic!"

From readiness level two, they were assembled, and he'd run so as not to be late. When he arrived, he was met with the commander, a displeased frown painted across her entire face. She wasn't just irritated, she was furious, apparently, with nowhere to vent her anger.

This can't be good.

The other day they'd been made to follow a unit of enemy mages fifty kilometers past the enemy lines in what was called parallel pursuit.

He had to at least be ready to venture out to the enemy trenches by night.

---

[21] **Rudel**   A great pioneer of enlightenment who turned a certain lying encyclopedia honest. Or the king of destroying tanks.

"Those idiots in the air let enemy mages slip past, and they've invaded Arene."

But the words that came out of her mouth would have hit him hard even if he had been expecting them. He'd heard whispered rumors, but having it confirmed by a superior officer was demoralizing.

The disheartening truth was that a major supply relay point had fallen. Anyone who learns the trains that bring them their food won't be functioning after the next day can understand how huge an impact on logistics that will have. Even a private can comprehend that war without supplies is a strategic nightmare.

The situation was so tense that even ever-indifferent Major von Degurechaff couldn't conceal her bad mood. After all, Grantz himself had been shocked to hear the rumor that enemy mages had invaded the rear by airdrop. *How could we miss the transport planes gliding into our airspace?*

"And apparently they joined up with the militia. Arene has fallen into the Republican Army's clutches."

That was bad news. But honestly, what did it actually mean? For a moment, Grantz and some of the other mages couldn't quite grasp the gravity of the situation. The battlefield paradigm required no thinking past *Eliminate the enemy.*

In other words, as far as Grantz and the others knew, the situation would be resolved if they eliminated the militia and the mages. Defending an entire city probably wasn't possible with just mages and militia. With no infantry arm, occupation was a dream within a dream. The militia could compensate to some extent with numbers, but he didn't think they could hold up in real organized combat.

In contrast, the 203rd Aerial Mage Battalion was, for better or worse, a child of war that had learned to fight on the front lines and made achieving results their standard.

"Naturally, we're taking it back."

As she says it, Tanya herself is convinced that as a legitimate-enough conclusion, recapture is the only option. It's a kill-or-be-killed battlefield. All they're going to do is change positions on it. Compared to the horror of supplies being cut off, sortie orders are somewhat familiar.

Both Grantz and Tanya tended toward agitated thought patterns, so they felt attacking was just what you did on the battlefield.

"Now here's the tricky part."

Even though she always conveyed their simple operation objectives without wasting any time, she took a deliberate breath.

When he looked around, the other officers' faces were tense, too.

What the heck could it be? Grantz braced himself slightly.

"Arene…"

Grantz waited in uncertainty for her next words but then realized something with a shock. *She said "Arene" and isn't sure how to continue.*

An officer who would indifferently order a charge on hell was hesitating.

She was shaking something off and doing something she found difficult to endure.

Whatever it was was grim and oppressive. The unit had fallen completely silent, and nothing made a sound. Something was wrong. The soldiers who had been distracted by the impending sortie began wondering what was going on.

Then, as if to interrupt their thoughts, she managed to continue.

"Arene is now occupied by the Republican Army. Troops, to take back the city, we need to eliminate *all* the Republican soldiers."

Huh? That sounds totally straightforward. If Republican mages have joined up with the militia to occupy the city, it'll be too dangerous if we don't eliminate all the mages. Doesn't that go without saying?

Would it even be hard? Grantz didn't really understand.

No, actually most of the replacements didn't see anything different from normal orders. They would be told to go as always, and then they would. That's what they thought.

Hoping to see if anyone knew what was going on, Grantz glanced at Weiss. The first lieutenant's face was just slightly stiff. That seemed strange. He looked clearly nervous and shaken. Then he took a deep breath as if he was trying to steel himself.

Steel himself against what? What was so horrible that it could rattle a Rhine front old stager so experienced he could be called a veteran?

"It goes without saying, but firing on *noncombatants* is strictly prohibited; however, as we've been given *permission* to cause *property damage*, that won't count."

She emphasized the rules of engagement. Their ROE was utterly ordinary. If there was anything of note, it was the exemption from responsibility for property damage. But even obtaining that exemption was part of normal procedures.

"Furthermore, before engaging the enemy mages and after eliminating them, we will issue warnings to surrender."

Am I…am I missing something? A vague, confusing anxiety enveloped him.

"Be sure to temporarily cease combat while the warnings are being issued."

She was giving them the same instructions as any sortie. The only difference was that it would be a city battle.

Of course, a few of the constraints would be different. But even with those alterations, the primary objective of eliminating the enemy mages wouldn't change.

…At least, it shouldn't.

If he thought harder about it, maybe the warnings? But it's obvious that an urban battle will have fewer casualties if you have the enemy surrender instead of finishing them off. And if they refuse, then you just conduct the moderately obnoxious battle to mop them up.

"If they accept the warning, that's great. *If they don't, we transition to wiping them out.* That is all."

And actually, the tone of his superior's voice was utterly flat, concealing her emotions as always. *If they surrender, that's great.*

If it didn't work out, they would transition to taking them out as usual—totally normal.

If pressed, he had to admit something felt strange. He sensed some kind of dissonance, something that didn't sit right. *That said, should I really be getting distracted right before we sortie?* Having made that conclusion, he began performing the final pre-sortie checks on his computation orb and rifle. Rather than being unable to use his weapons on the battlefield due to insufficient maintenance, it was better to forget his other thoughts.

The recruits had had it beaten into them that learning was the first step toward survival, and with each passing day, they were growing more familiar with war.

The next thing they knew, they were on the battlefield that Major von Degurechaff had led them to as planned.

"Bravo Leader to Combat Control. It's a Named! Sending data now. Please confirm."

As expected, the Empire's response was prompt in the strictest sense of the word. *They sent over a battalion of mages in a matter of hours!*

Apparently, they're taking this quite seriously. I guess the pain of air-dropping in was worth it?

The commander of Mage Second Company of the Republic's special ops forces, Lieutenant Colonel Vianto, was somewhat relieved to find some meaning in the operation he hadn't been terribly keen on. Though he'd been nervous, he'd done it. He finally had the wherewithal to glance at his annoyingly stiff hands.

The Republic was in a fairly tough spot. It had been looking forward to Dacia's participation in the war, only to have that backfire. Republicans had to grit their teeth and watch the Entente Alliance collapse after the fleet tried to prevent the landing operation but didn't make it in time. This nightmare was slowly wearing them out.

The Republic's below-the-surface contact with the Commonwealth was an open secret, but the Commonwealth was acting for its own national welfare. As a condition for its assistance, the Republic was liable to lose all its overseas interests.

Considering the gravity of endangering its voice as a major power, the Republic felt a need to resolve things on its own to the extent possible.

We need to push them back as far as we can before the Commonwealth joins the fight. It was for that political reason that Vianto was carrying out this crazy (to him) rear invasion.

I can't believe they pulled the so-called raison d'état card.

"Data confirmed… The Devil of the Rhine? They brought out the big guns."

But apparently when it came to raison d'état, counting your chickens before they hatch worked. They had succeeded in drawing the unidentified Named known to every soldier on the Rhine front off the main lines.

It was the Named who excelled in high-maneuver warfare and long-range firing, as did the elite unit she commanded. They were an annoying bunch who, as a mobile unit in the Imperial Army, defended a sizable territory; taking them out was high priority.

This unit was even capable of mobile defense. Drawing them away from the front lines was more significant than drawing away any other mage battalion.

Diverting this unit with a veteran Named, who could strike at their weak points, had an important effect on the battlefield that couldn't be measured with numbers.

"That said…they won't be easy. I'm not looking forward to this fight."

Capturing a city the size of Arene would require several divisions of ground forces. It was up to the Imperial General Staff whether to scrape them away from the front lines or mobilize reserves, but apparently, they had gone all in. *If only they would have underestimated us and sent troops in piecemeal.*

In any case, if they could hold this transport terminal, the Empire's supply lines would dry up in less than a week, which meant they would definitely get results if they could hinder enemy reinforcements for just a few days. They could only hope that the troops on the front could pull off a major counterattack during that time.

"Charlie Leader to Combat Control. You're telling us to fight that battalion at range?"

Even for an elite special ops force, fighting the Devil of the Rhine at a distance would be tough.

They had anticipated doing little more than chipping away at the enemy.

"No changes to the operation. The long-range fighting was only to distract them anyhow. Work to delay them."

If it didn't work out, that was fine. There hadn't been terribly high expectations for the ranged fighting, so it was no problem.

Maybe a line of distracting fire? The point is to force them to evade, tire

them out, and break up their formations. Anyhow, slowing them down is
crucial. Time is on our side.

""Roger.""

They promptly began their maneuvers according to the plan.

Some mages lurking in buildings opened up with harassing fire.

Those shots weren't very likely to connect in a major way, but on the other hand, they couldn't simply forgo it given that their enemy was Named.

And after all, disciplined fire was the Republican Army's specialty. If the enemy flew slowly, they could score direct hits.

"The enemy mages are breaking. They're evading our sniping."

But apparently, they were dodging the attacks. Well, that would be the natural thing to do, but Vianto had hoped to deal at least a little damage. *As it is…we'll only do a tiny bit or barely any.*

"But huh, they sent in a whole battalion right away. They're making snap decisions that ignore the effect on the front sooner than I expected."

And they responded even quicker than we heard they did, which is a pain. With his plans upset, Vianto wanted to pull his hair out—even if it was good that they had managed to weaken the enemy's frontal attack. If the Empire was committing a battalion of elite mages with no hesitation, he and his men had to be ready for the arrival of far more ground troops than anticipated and much sooner than expected.

They must want to take Arene back as soon as possible. In the worst case, where they're prepared to withdraw from the lines, things could get hairy.

"We're containing the Devil of the Rhine with two companies. What else can we do?"

These were mages trained for special missions. Two companies of them had been sent in. Containing the Devil of the Rhine was really only one of their objectives, but his adjutant wasn't talking nonsense.

"So urban warfare is the key? But we won't even last two weeks!"

If the enemy was really focusing on them more than they had anticipated, this would be awful.

At first, they thought it would be a simple charge or that maybe there would be a company of mages at most. If they were up against an augmented battalion all of a sudden, their enemy was determined.

And Vianto's biggest headache was their readiness to send in a Named. "Once the counterattack starts on the front, pressure from the enemy will decrease. Most importantly, the troops should be able to break through their defensive positions once the supplies are cut off, don't you think?"

"That's just wishful thinking. I hope we succeed, but it's going to be rough."

We have friendly backup and met up with the partisan militia, but what will happen when real ground troops show up? They would have mage support, and the Empire had more firepower than the Republic on a fundamental level. As far as ammunition, all the Republicans had apart from a small amount of air-dropped supplies were local stockpiles and what each mage had on them.

They wouldn't be able to last long, and they would probably take heavy casualties. *Even worse, we'll probably end up fighting with the civilians as our shields—something we should be ashamed of as soldiers.*

...Some of the believers in raison d'état even thought that in a worst-case scenario they could run the partisans into the ground to buy time. It was logical, but it was an ugly side of their nation.

"So in the worst case, we continue delaying and try to cause as much damage as possible?"

"That's our only choice. Either way, a soldier is a rotten thing to be."

Humiliatingly, their duty was, basically, to faithfully carry out this operation to make civilians their shields. When they were told it would make winning the war possible, they had no choice.

But there was no operation that put his raison d'être as a soldier more into question than this one. As Republican soldiers, for the Republic—to have Republican citizens die was a rotten business.

"The enemy vanguard has entered the Air Defense Identification Zone! They're rapidly approaching the city!"

But even he was a soldier. He knew that while thinking could be meaningful, there was a time and a place for it. If he didn't, he would have been dead long ago.

"Commander, then we should—"

"I know. Here they come. Prepare to ambush!"

Once the enemy was closing in, his conflicted thoughts toward his mission had to be put off until later. He would do everything in his power to survive—because regret was a privilege reserved for the living.

Have you ever been ordered to eliminate a fearless enemy assaulting an area in the rear? I haven't until now, either. Thus, while I'm happy to have enjoyed such good fortune previously, I want to lament my current situation. But I want to do a proper job without letting anything stand in my way. I realized recently that I'm the kind of person who lives to work. I want to be proud of myself for being a levelheaded person who can think with common sense.

…is the sort of thing Tanya is thinking, pretending to be upset about what a sad era it is when one gets intercepted just for flying through the sky as she deftly evades the long-range disciplined fire the Republican Army is so proud of.

Even if the beams are no stronger than the lasers shot by some organic resource recovery unit that's hostile to the human race, the hit rate is far lower simply by virtue of the fact that humans are spotting.

Well, I do dodge them fairly seriously, since if one hit me it would be powerful enough to potentially pierce my protective film and outer shell and cause me to fall. Maybe if I poured mana into Type 95 with all my might I could withstand them, but that would be psychological suicide, so I hesitate to do that. In which case, the best thing to do is evade.

"Engage! They're fast! They know what they're doing!"

That said, just as it's difficult to win a hundred of a hundred battles, it seems like breaking through unscathed will be impossible. The artillery fire is so dense Tanya is amazed in spite of herself; their history of beating up on nothing but second-rate forces in Dacia and Norden has come back to bite them.

It's good that everyone could evade a counterattack on a scale they didn't anticipate. In the process, though, their strike formation has gotten pretty disorderly—even though the formation was designed to counter the Republic's disciplined fire. She is forced to acknowledge the painful realization that they won't be able to get past the enemy firing positions with speed and spread-out maneuvering alone. The idea that speed is armor definitely has a few flaws.

We're still fine for now, but up against big believers in firepower like the reds, we might be in trouble.

"Lieutenant Serebryakov, sorry, but I'm weirdly tired... Can I get a tonic?"

As she thinks, the fatigued voice of Lieutenant Weiss comes over the radio, and Tanya frowns unconsciously. Tired? My vice commander who was put through the mill on the Rhine and in Norden is tired after just this?

Tanya promptly throws her adjutant some alcohol—soldier fuel—as she has her go take a look, and her question is cleared up when Serebryakov's panicked shriek comes over the radio.

"Lieutenant Weiss, you've been shot! Hurry, stop the bleeding!"

"What?"

"You didn't notice?! Let's get this tourniquet on! Hurry!"

From the first aid discussion and Serebryakov urging Weiss on, Tanya realizes the former was correct and sighs. Instead of subordinates who don't have enough fighting spirit, I have berserkers that get hyped up on too much adrenaline to register that they're injured; there's something vaguely depressing about that.

I didn't even give him meth and this is what he's like. It's hard to know whether I should rejoice that I have the best soldiers or lament that I've gathered a bunch of war addicts.

"...How's the numbskull who didn't even realize he got hit?"

"It's not life-threatening, but I think it will be difficult for him to continue fighting."

"What? Well, there's no helping it. Weiss, fall back."

Still, what suddenly filled my mind was apprehension about losing my capable assistant. Despite being a war nut, he's one of the ones with common sense, and more than anything, it's particularly painful to have the chain of command affected so greatly in the heat of battle. But Tanya is already switching gears because she knows she needs to consider not only current interests but solutions to future issues.

As the most sensible among her men, the good First Lieutenant Weiss seems to have a few thoughts about this operation. If he's dropping off the battlefield, that means that one of her above-average mages nearly got shot down. Normally, Weiss would be the kind of mage to attain Ace of Aces level.

...If it wasn't a fluke, the Republicans are awfully capable interceptors.

"But, Major—"

"It's fine; fall back. You're just one person; we'll be all right. Instead of slowing us down, round up the others who've been hit and RTB."

It's great to be serious, but if those serious personnel leave, that's a problem. With no other reliable people around, I'm the only one left. I'm the one sensible person among all these war crazies. Talk about a nightmare.

It goes without saying that I'll be exhausted both physically and mentally. People who can remain sensible during such an abnormality as war are exceedingly valuable. It's hard to keep a unit who has lost someone like that under control.

Sensible people—they generally keep their heads in a crisis. These modern individuals who can value reason and the market are the ones who will sustain the capitalist society to come. To squander them on this waste called war is truly horrible.

What will the Empire's economy be like after the war if it throws away its best and brightest like this? I don't even want to think about it.

Should I convert all my wages into gold and goods while I still can? I have a feeling that win or lose, the Empire's future won't be terribly bright.

"Understood... I wish you luck."

"You think too much. You hesitated, right? You big idiot. When I get back, you're gonna get it."

But first I have to survive this. It's annoying and I'm not motivated, but I have to crush the pro-Republic fellows holed up in Arene.

As a person, it's not a very nice thing to do. Logically, it's easier to eliminate them, but no one will compliment you for violating human rights. Yes, I'm philanthropic, and as such, I don't want to get innocent people mixed up in this.

Even though legally there are no problems, something surely gave good, conscientious Weiss pause. In other words, reluctance and hesitation hindered his maneuvers, and as a result, he got hit. Well, it's not as if I don't understand.

But to say one thing, if I were in the same position as him, I would have wanted to shirk responsibility in the same way. So about that part, I'm jealous. *Geez, you're that averse to taking part in a massacre?*

Well, I don't like it, she mocked herself, *but circumstances call for the death of the partisans of Arene.*

I'm only taking part in a broad sense. I'm just doing nothing, like those three wise monkeys—see no evil, hear no evil, speak no evil.

In contemporary law, it's omission. But I'm not the direct subject of the act. In other words, the issue is whether I have the duty to report it or not.

Even Rudel bombed tons of Soviet tanks, ships, fighter planes, and armored trains, and he didn't have to go to prison. Basically, all he did was sortie, and that in itself wasn't a problem.

Good. If I'm just doing my duty as a single soldier, there shouldn't be any real issues.

Ohh, laws are wonderful.

"Ma'am. My apologies."

That said, as long as there are issues at all, I won't be enthusiastic about it.

Of course, I'm pretty sure there aren't any military operations you can really shout *yee-haw* and serve in with gusto. I end up wondering why we have wars.

Even today—why am I conducting this irrational operation?

Tanya is really at wits' end, but she doesn't long for death enough to lose herself in thought in the middle of a battlefield. She switches gears to focus on dealing with the task at hand.

"It's fine. You can't help being you. Okay, Lieutenant König, take over Lieutenant Weiss's command."

"Roger."

I have no choice, so I reorganize command at my discretion. Either way, our mission is counter-mage combat with, at most, some containment.

If there are healthy enemy mages out there, we have to beat on them to some extent.

"All hands, prepare to swoop in for a close-quarters fight. Watch out for ambushes. These guys are capable. If you take them lightly, you're liable to get burned."

"Commander. The enemy mages are withdrawing! They're going to shut themselves up in the city!"

But that plan was designed with the idea in mind that the enemies would sortie to intercept us.

"Ngh. Never mind. Abort the charge. Just keep the pressure on."

Put another way, it's our job to take on the mage ambushes on the periphery of the city, nothing beyond that.

In other words, if they remove any mages from the attackable areas around the edges of the city, Tanya's mission will be mostly accomplished.

In short, if they drive the enemies to positions where they couldn't reach the bombers or artillery, their part will be over.

"Commander?"

"All we have to do is drive them off. Once we've pushed them away, we'll issue the warning to surrender."

"...Are you sure?"

It's precisely because they understand what that means that several members of the company express hesitation. Of course, these aren't the types to hesitate to attack once we've transitioned to mopping up, but it isn't as if they can't foresee what's about to happen.

"It's not our job. At least, our job is to counter the mages. It doesn't include urban warfare."

But Tanya has already taken a practical attitude. Since she is focused on how to keep the dirt on her hands to a minimum, nothing is higher priority than getting out of there after issuing the call for surrender.

This is an easy job. Even if someone ends up dying as a result, it won't be by my hand.

In that case...

"…Understood."

Despite their hesitation, no one continues to object—for better or worse. In other words, no matter what they might have wanted to say, they're all mature enough to swallow it.

Business is basically stoicism. Entertaining, layoffs, or a boss you just can't stand—there are so many things that must simply be endured. So if you can avoid them, there aren't many reasons to waver. And if you're a soldier, orders are a great excuse.

"Contact the artillery and the bomber unit. Tell them we're issuing the surrender warning."

All that's left is to get them to take over. If the enemy surrenders, that's great. If not, the bombardment will put an end to it. That's all.

Well, I know this isn't the type of enemy to meekly surrender, so it's practically a foregone conclusion, but still.

In other words, we'll have them become our justification.

"Do you want protection?"

"Second Company, you're on direct support."

Still, the best is to issue a warning. If they're logical, there's a nonzero chance that they choose to surrender. If we issue a warning first, it's also much easier emotionally, and most importantly, if there is a trial, it can be used as evidence in my defense.

"Okay, let's give them a call."

We don't lose anything by warning them. In which case, it'd practically be a betrayal of capitalism not to do it.

We pretty much know they're going to reject our offer, but I might as well give it sincerely for my own reasons. It's definitely worth it. Actually, I'd really appreciate it if they would surrender at this point. Time and ammunition are precious.

Well, in reality, a ton of them surrendering would be the bigger burden on Logistics. And the brass doesn't expect them to give themselves up, so they're already assuming there will be a fight to wipe them out. I think we should hedge, but since cutting costs is also important, I can't fault them for their conclusion.

Sheesh. Well, there's no reason for us in the thick of it to think that far. Guess I should get things rolling.

"Release unaffiliated members of the general population immediately. We can't allow your slaughter to continue. We demand the release of imperial citizens according to article 26, paragraph 3 of the Rules of War on Land."

A nominal request to release civilians. That said, the only imperial citizens who would be in Arene, what used to be a Republican city, are soldiers or civilian army personnel.

They were probably killed or lynched back when the revolt began. Even if there are survivors, I don't imagine they'll obediently let them go. There's a greater chance they'll off any survivors out of spite.

I can't believe they actually wanted this scenario. It's like the monumental difference between talking about a nuclear apocalypse in a sci-fi novel and actually waging nuclear war.

"You're watching, right? See anything?"

"...Yeah, they shot someone. Here's the video."

And as expected, the militia shoots someone dead and shouts something obscene. Well, it's the type of thing an undisciplined militia is likely to do in any era. That's why a proper army and a militia are two different things. Freedom fighters are all well and good, but freedom without order ends up with major internal strife, a kind of environmental hazard. These guys are hopeless. They could have done this themselves, but instead they had to involve citizens engaged in wholesome economic activity.

Yeah, so in that context, they're probably shouting, "Go to hell, imperial bastards!" Something like that.

Well, that's how people who aren't used to war tend to behave. They may believe in some noble principle, but as long as they aren't trained, they're slaves to emotion. So I suppose this is just what's bound to happen when an undisciplined organization of civilians has guns.

Just like a functioning member of society, a soldier, even in uniform, is useless without training, and you obviously can't expect that much of a militia. In other words, this underscores the claim of economic theory that human capital is so important.

"HQ, I'm sending video. Requesting permission to begin immediate rescue."

At the same time, this is a big chance. Nominally, we've fulfilled our duty of issuing a warning.

All that's left is to join the extermination, but if possible, I'd like to avoid that out of consideration for my future political position. It's a simple reason, and anyone would exempt me from responsibility.

This is the perfect chance. The marvelously just cause of protecting my fellow countrymen is right here in front of me.

What army could reproach a soldier for saving its own civilians? At least, rescuing captured imperial subjects is a politically clean act. Perhaps it doesn't have much meaning from a military point of view, but all that's left now is the annihilation phase.

So this is the phase during which your political conduct matters. The fact that I didn't participate directly during the battle but was engaged in rescuing fellow countrymen should work as a get-out-of-jail-free card.

At least, it should be a justification.

"HQ, roger. Get it done."

"Pixie 01, roger. I'll proceed immediately."

Okay, saving people. Let's do a good deed. For myself. Whoever said, *The good you do to others will always come back to you,* had a way with words.

To Grantz and Visha, it was a massacre painted as mopping up. No, Visha took it a little better, since she knew the ropes. She at least understood the danger of hesitating on the battlefield.

For Grantz, it was purgatory or perhaps simply hell.

"HQ to all participating units. Transition to cleanup. Get rid of the Republican Army."

Red flames added color to the black-and-gray world. Then a faint flashing was all he could see. His distracted consciousness registered a noise coming from somewhere, orders to the entire theater from HQ. The voice on the radio was so level he was shocked by how unreal it sounded.

But the significance of it was orders. Yes, orders. The individual Grantz was in this place on orders.

I came here, I pulled the trigger, I killed the enemy. No, what I killed was a person.

And he could recognize the strange tingle in his nose that had begun some time ago. Even though he was used to the smell of the battlefield, a stench was irritating it. It was the smell of burning human flesh. A freshly charred corpse whose odor wasn't masked by the reek of decay. The air, sticky with protein, stunk horribly.

He was sure he was out of things to throw up, and yet he did everything in his power to keep any acid from spewing out his mouth. He was getting used to actual combat, perhaps. The fact that Second Lieutenant Grantz had the ability to try to understand the situation meant he actually had some presence of mind.

The surrender warning and the attempt to separate the civilians from the militia had been only a short while ago. *Technically, it was probably a procedure to allow them to consider the civilians militia.* Anyhow, as soon as the civilians didn't have to be defined as noncombatants, the Empire had begun a merciless attack on the city.

Luckily, he was engaged in the Imperial Army's prisoner rescue mission. It seemed strange to him that Major von Degurechaff cared for allies over the enemy, but that feeling was gone in an instant. She was probably just deciding according to priority.

That is, soldiers are the shields of the nation's people, so if the question is whether eliminating the enemy or performing a rescue is higher priority, it has to be the rescue.

Apparently, it's a question of value standards. To put it another way, she honestly doesn't mind trading the life of an enemy for the life of a fellow countryman. Thanks to that, even if it was only during the short time before the bombardment started, they were able to rescue some of the people held captive in the city.

"We've already crushed all hostile organized resistance. Now just take out the remaining holdouts!"

The Republican civilians were full of fight, and in a conceptual sense, they certainly meant to do battle with the Empire. They had consciously stood up to protect the Republic, and the bodies and corpses of recovered army employees made their intent to do harm very clear.

But that didn't mean Grantz could enjoy the scene playing out before his eyes.

Meanwhile, the unit's superior officer, Tanya, is content to look on as the cleanup progresses fairly smoothly.

They used high explosives to smash the roofs of stone buildings. Once the flammable items inside were visible, they dropped incendiary bombs inside. To prevent the fires from going out, they used more high explosives to shatter the buildings, creating gusts of wind to help the conflagration spread.

Then more incendiary bombs. That repetition set all of Arene ablaze in a few short hours.

The barricade the civilians erected meant nothing.

Not only that, but the Republican mages probably even ended up getting roasted in the flames. Surely the city already looks more like hell than those Buddhist paintings that supposedly depict it.

On that point, Tanya's feelings are simple. God must be so upset about this—if he exists.

Anyhow, Being X apparently isn't nice enough to lend a hand in this sort of disaster. Well, what can you do? Humans are the only ones who can save humans. Forgetting that and clinging to religion must be our weakness.

That said, Tanya believes that such a weakness has produced massive changes in the history of mankind. Which is why she's keeping her hands clean and going to save the imprisoned military employees.

She takes the action that the collective consciousness of those weak people would want her to and praises herself for being a realist who doesn't neglect to create excuses for the future.

Meanwhile, for Grantz, who didn't have the wherewithal to guess at his superior's inner thoughts, the only thing keeping him sane were his pristine, pure white hands. He could defend himself by saying that he had made it through without shooting any noncombatants. He was rescuing people, not massacring them.

On this battlefield, that was only a type of fiction...but as long as he could maintain it, it provided consolation.

Unfortunately, Battalion Commander Major von Degurechaff's

surrender warning and the militia who rejected it sent his fiction crumbling to bits in no time.

Their battalion was the vanguard in this fight, and if it hadn't been for their good cause, the rescue of imperial subjects, they would have been in there participating in the killing. Now, he and his unit, the 203rd Aerial Mage Battalion, had to perform their original mission.

"Pixie 01, roger. Requesting target."

Having swiftly and soundly recovered the imperial prisoners, the battalion had regrouped and was waiting for its next orders. What everyone knew without hearing it was that it would be the mission they were meant to do, an attack. Everyone mentioned it in ambiguous terms, but unbelievably, Major von Degurechaff apparently intended to participate in the horrible thing happening in Arene…firsthand.

Whether the people of Arene even had the means to stay alive, much less fight, was doubtful. But neither the Imperial Army Command, Battalion Command, nor the individual commanders could be satisfied yet. As long as those people existed in front of them, they would devote their all to the task and accept no alternatives.

They knew no other way to resolve the situation. Everyone was reluctant to say it, but if asked officially, they had to acknowledge that there were orders for a pursuit battle. And their commander was trading messages with HQ in her usual tone of voice, telling them they had regrouped, and pressing them for the unit's next orders.

"HQ to Pixie Battalion, the remaining enemy mages are acting as a rear guard as they retreat. Can you eliminate them?"

"I see them… No problem. We can do it."

As part of his training, he was assigned to the headquarters company. The notion that the commander thought he had potential made him happy, but that naïveté had been an awful mistake… It meant he had to hear the worst news. To think he was meant to learn her style of command!

Following Major von Degurechaff's gaze, he could indeed see a somewhat orderly group of people. They were at a visible distance—there was no mistaking them. And it was true that bringing up the rear were a bunch of fellows who looked like the Republican Army mages, albeit covered in wounds.

But the view, unique to mages with a boosted observation formula, told him the people beyond the beat-up mages were *only people*. Yes, people whom he couldn't imagine were capable of fighting. On their faces were anger and fear, plus despair and the faintest hope that they might escape. By the time he realized it, Grantz himself was unexpectedly awash in a feeling that was difficult to understand. *Are we really going to rip away those people's last protection?*

"After you eliminate the rear guard, the plan is for the artillery to finish off the remaining enemies. We request that you take no more than ten minutes."

...But Command didn't seem to want to let the group of "enemies" go. Of course, they were an army. Grantz knew in his head that they were an army. But his emotions screamed, *Are you really—? Are you really going to let that happen?*

But his superior didn't voice any objections whatsoever. The orders to mop up the remaining adversaries who were trying to deploy protective formulas to defend the people from Major von Degurechaff, from the artillery—they were orders to get rid of the mages trying to help the people escape.

But Grantz had learned that his commander would give such orders matter-of-factly, with no trace of emotion... That was the right way for a soldier to be. *She isn't wrong. She isn't...wrong...*

"HQ to Pixie Battalion. That is all. Over."

The wishes of the superior who closed out the transmission were no more and no less than that.

Kill them, they said.

Once they were gone, the protective formulas would disappear instantaneously. After that, Grantz had no doubt the artillery would pulverize the people. The artillery wouldn't know the true identity of the "enemies," so they would naturally do a great job. *At least we're only fighting the mages; we won't be shooting the people behind them.* But he could still guess what would happen next.

No, he knew quite well what would happen. *We're destroying their last shield.*

"Pixie Battalion, roger that. We'll do our best."

The moment the mages were eliminated, those people would also be blown away. Concentrated artillery fire. On desolate flat country that hardly had any rubble, much less trenches. It was stranger to think they would survive.

Above all...why would artillery open fire on civilians who had no idea how to live through a bombardment? *This is insane.*

"...Commander, please reconsider this! If...if we eliminate them—"

Before he realized it—he could hardly believe it himself—he was giving his opinion to a superior.

He could sense that his face was deathly pale.

He had practically committed insubordination. He had argued against an order that came down from Command. That wasn't the type of thing a mere second lieutenant could say to a battalion commander. Plus, he was essentially rebelling against the orders.

"*Enemies of the Empire* will be laid to waste. That's great."

"But, that's—"

Maybe that was why he hesitated, but he had still objected.

Grantz was so confused he hardly understood what was happening himself, but he spoke up to try to stop Major von Degurechaff.

But she remained unfazed. "Lieutenant Grantz. The enemy you let escape can take up guns again—to shoot us."

Yeah, probably. Their expressions were filled with loathing. Undoubtedly—undoubtedly—the Republic would gain zealous new soldiers from their ranks. Since they hated the Empire, the army would have no issues with their will to fight.

So you tell us to kill them? You're telling us to kill someone who could *be an enemy?*

Perhaps she recognized his conflict, or perhaps she said it for no reason, but Major von Degurechaff added an important point at the end.

"If you don't shoot the enemy, they'll shoot you. We have to at least open fire until someone tells us not to. It's an order, after all."

Then before he knew it, he'd been knocked to the ground. He could feel dirt in his mouth. Well, more like mud.

His face complained of the pain where he'd been struck, but he was hazily conscious. Maybe her decision to sweep his feet out from under him instead of kick him down was born of kindness?

"I'll pretend I didn't hear that. This is an order. Pick up your gun. It's time for work."

Yes, it's an order. I know I have to do anything I'm ordered to. Because it's an order. Fuck. An order...

Hello. Long-distance trains aren't very comfortable, are they? First class is a lot better, but sure enough, in wartime it's really only "better." On top of that, since the army's railway guns and supply trains are prioritized, the schedules are seriously off.

About all I should be doing in this situation is reviewing documents or sipping coffee (although it's cold). For confidentiality purposes, not only are radios jammed, but I can't even leave the first-class cars. What is that about?

Yeah, the food is relatively decent, since it's provided by the train. That said, you can't really relax and enjoy a meal with this mood.

On top of that, the menu's tone-deaf main dish is beef stew.

Yes, normally I'm quite happy to eat stew, but at the moment, I'd rather not. I mean, it's good and all. It's tasty, but I just saw an awful lot of things on the battlefield I just came from, so it's a bit heavy. I acknowledge that it's delicious, though. Yeah, I don't think a meat doria would have made it down my throat.

Tanya is grumbling facetiously.

A super-fun legal debate and actually implementing those ideas are two different things! For instance, what's the point of ludicrous proposals that maybe there aren't any civilians because all your nation's citizens are soldiers due to universal conscription, or total war, or whatever?

Normally something like that would never be realized. The problem is that the plans that logically would never be used and the pressures of necessity both exist in reality. What an outrageous age we live in.

People use up their kin and throw them away as if they're not human. If they were at least using them in a clever way, they'd have room to debate, but this is completely random. Unforgivable waste, and on top of that, the idea of recycling to use resources efficiently hasn't been developed. No, they're practically ignoring it.

Honestly, I want to ask them how much human capital they're planning to invest in this. Considering the cost and the time it takes to cultivate a mage, they really can't be dropping dead all over the battlefield.

Even worse, a college graduate who continued on to get his PhD—a scientist—was stationed on the front lines until just the other day. But if we neglect science, we'll fall behind the enemy's new weapons and technology. Agh, I have no interest in dealing with what would happen if, say, the enemy had radar and VT fuses and we didn't.

If they're implementing the Manhattan Project and our scientists are dying on the front lines, isn't that playing for the wrong team? I mean, that mad scientist should die, but apart from that...

Dr. Einstein may have been no good as a military man, but he contributed to the nation, which makes him better than a rank-and-file soldier! Don't they know that rather than giving guys like Einstein and Nobel guns, they need to give them pencils and make them do calculations?! Of course, anybody with a touch of crazy like the mad scientist is a different story, but still.

Having mad scientists contribute is about as meaningless as standing Nobel up on the forward-most line. Having Nobel study nitroglycerin would be much better for society. He was also a wonderful guardian of human capital who advocated for peace in order to prevent wasting resources.

In other words, everything is for the future of humanity.

Alfred Nobel had a great reputation as a guy who "became rich by finding ways to kill more people faster than ever before" (as per Wiki), but there was no one who valued efficiency as much as he did!

If it were me, I would want to add, "He worked to protect human capital."

Ahh, why this extravagant waste of human capital? If there are plenty of posts and not enough talent, we can just pull them off the front lines. Don't you think this is why we're lacking talent?

Supposedly they are finally correcting this...

Well, all I can do is rewrite these notes as a formal opinion to turn in.

I'm on a train, but since we're at war, there isn't even any good scenery to look at, so I'm bored.

I've been summoned, though, so I guess I have to endure it.

Perhaps we'll have some breathing room after thoroughly crushing Arene. The unit was given leave, and the higher-ups will consider where to station all the troops that were assembled. Well, I expected that much.

But why am I the only one who has to appear at the General Staff Office in the capital?

I sincerely reviewed my conduct to try to find anything that would warrant me being called in, but I don't think I made any mistakes.

Yes, we saved lives *and* eradicated the enemy mages.

And before that, on the Rhine lines, I even received a decoration for my daring exploits, albeit in a simple battlefield presentation.

I don't think any of my behavior has been problematic.

And I don't recall any slipups in terms of controlling my subordinates, either. I adhere strictly to regulation in the battalion because there is no way I'm getting stuck in a military tribunal for mismanaging my reports like Mr. Yamashita.[22]

I have zero tolerance for abuse of prisoners. Due to the temperament of my unit, we rarely have prisoners, but I can say with confidence that we never torture or abuse our captured information sources. Unlike the amateurs who take more prisoners than necessary and then tear their hair out over how to feed everyone, we don't take on more than forty-eight people can handle; it does make things somewhat easier.

I have an ideal unit that both adheres extremely close to international laws and devotes themselves to their missions, which is nice and easy; they don't give me much trouble. So why am I being called in?

"Excuse me. Long time no see, Major von Degurechaff."

---

[22] **Mr. Yamashita**   Thought to be the precedent for International Criminal Court Statute, Article 8, also known as the "Yamashita Standard." In a nutshell, that's what we call General Tomoyuki Yamashita, who was tried in the pickiest way in an American military tribunal for bad things his subordinates did—command responsibility.

I'm nearly lost in my meandering thoughts when they're interrupted by a familiar voice. A man wearing a mid-ranking officer's coat stands in the entrance to my compartment. Before I wonder who it is, I look at his face and more or less understand the situation.

"It certainly has been a while, Major Uger. Good to see you're doing well." I stand up, hastily remove my cap, and bow. Well, etiquette might also require that I let down my tied-back hair. Luckily, there are no rules enforced so inflexibly near the front lines.

Hmm, but I heard that Major Uger got a post in the rear. I think it was either with the army's Railroad Department or Logistics.

Of all the officers in my class at war college, he'll probably go the furthest. He had already been promoted to the middle ranks when I got my captain's commission. He'll probably make it to lieutenant colonel rather quickly for someone not serving on a battlefield.

Ahh, I'm jealous. After you serve in Logistics, you usually end up either in the General Staff or an instructor position at the war college. It won't hurt me to stay on good terms with him.

"Yes, I'm glad to see you in one piece, too. I heard about Arene. Sounds like it was rough."

"I'm afraid military secrets are involved, so I can't give you details..."

And since we were in college together, we're a bit closer than acquaintances. Or really, although class reunions and the hierarchy of commissions operate in the background, they still influence officers to have ties to one another—connections.

"That's fine. Today I'm basically on an errand for General von Zettour. Are you, too?"

Aha, I guess I should say. He must be here as a messenger. The poor guy is really getting run around.

"Do you know something?"

"...Well, I suppose I can tell you..."

Can he keep a secret or not? Well, Major Uger is fairly sensible, so I'll be happy he trusts me.

There's nothing more handy and essential than connections, influence, and a network.

"The army's Railroad Department is being asked to plan urgent transportation into a war zone. I'm going to report that."

"...I don't mean to be rude, but I don't see what that has to do with me. At most, won't I be one of the field officers being transported?"

The Railroad Department performs a critical role in the Empire, where we use interior lines strategy. If the rails can't move troops smoothly, our force can't get where it needs to be in an efficient way, and we can't concentrate our fighting power. Then the Great Army is like an elephant with a body, so big it can't move.

A department that important probably gets asked to plan urgent transportation into a war zone fairly often.

That's fine.

But why does that overlap with the reason I've been summoned?

I don't mean to sound smart-alecky, but I'm a mage. And I'm a battalion commander—nothing more than a tactical component. At most, I'd be asked to get on such and such a train to go to such and such a place. Or, since I can fly, they might tell me to zoom off somewhere under my own steam.

There shouldn't be any reason to call me all the way to the capital.

"It's where they're going that's the problem. The higher-ups are apparently planning to pull the Rhine lines back."

"The Rhine lines... You mean, we'll retreat?"

The shock keeps Tanya from understanding what Uger has said for a moment.

We pushed so hard only to pull back?

"That's right. I guess they mean to fall back and make them bleed."

Fall back and make them bleed... So that's what they're doing? Hannibal's Cannae, on this scale?!

"...That's unexpected. It's drastic, but an interesting idea."

Agh, I guess I'm losing my edge. The Concorde's failure isn't funny anymore. We should adhere to the rule that says not to lament the money you've invested in an unprofitable enterprise but rather lament any further loss. My time on the front lines has really rusted my economic, rational sensibilities. It's horrifying.

Or does Being X mean to destroy this faithful believer in the modern, practical spirit? I have to stay conscious of the context—that I'm in this war-torn world he was blabbing about. Terrifyingly, my senses of the market and what's rational were on the verge of numbing.

Ahh, war is such a crime. I want to escape this human madness and wastefulness as fast as I can. We should quit this war with actual bombs whizzing around and have economic wars instead.

"Still...pulling back?"

But, hmm, General von Zettour has come up with a surprising idea, thinks Tanya with unstinting admiration.

It would take time and effort to push the lines forward, that's for sure. A retreat isn't so hard. And actually, even if the enemy pursues us, we can expect fewer casualties than if we charged at heavily defended trenches. It's not a bad idea. If we organize the uneven lines, we should be able to face them head-on.

And well, striking into Republican territory gives their supply lines the advantage, but if we retreat, it'll be easier on ours.

Of course, the plan will only work if they go along with it.

"That's why the information is so tightly controlled... It seems like we're going to be putting on a bit of an act."

"An act?"

"Listen, Major. That mess in Arene destroyed our supply lines. We can't maintain the front anymore."

...Hold on a minute.

That's the story we're telling about our retreat?

No matter how inept we think the Republicans are, surely they'll at least send out scouts.

"Isn't that a bit of a stretch? Whether through a third power or a unit participating in the battle, I'm sure the truth will leak out."

"No, just the opposite. We'll spread propaganda through the other country. 'The heroic citizens of Arene resisted and practically destroyed the Imperial Army's railroad.'"

Wow. I'm genuinely impressed. I'm no propaganda expert, but I can imagine how effective this could be. I honestly never expected someone in this world, and at such an age, would come up with this brand of information warfare.

I'm struck once again by how wonderful the human race is, so truly adaptable.

Of course, it's absurd that they can be this wise and still fight wars...

Well, behavioral economics attempts to explain the human ball of contradictions from an emotional angle.

I'm sure it makes many interesting points.

The citizens of Arene gave their all and fought so bravely, so fiercely, that the Imperial Army lines were shaken. The moment someone shouts, *You would waste these gains?* levelheaded debate will be overwhelmed by a torrent of emotion.

"You mean we'll take away all their choices?"

Bravo. It's a reproduction of the dance Bismarck made Napoleon III do. The Ems Dispatch incident is a truly classic feat of diplomacy. Even a mere sensible person like me can appreciate it.

This is essentially a provocation.

Well, if Bismarck's move was a provocation, maybe this is more like coaxing. Well, I'll leave the detailed categorizing to the academics, but I still want to praise this move with a *bravo* from the bottom of my heart.

"That's right. Even if they don't come to help them, all it will take is someone to whisper, 'They abandoned them.' It can't hurt to send around that kind of disinformation."

"It's a marvelous idea. I'm surprised he thought of it."

Well.

The Republican administration will probably hate getting a reputation as the type that watches resisting civilians die in the middle of total war when they need the unity of their people.

A nation can't expect its people to accept its logic that a small sacrifice will benefit the majority.

Really, the only ones who declare something like that are the Soviets or their ilk, although in Pol Pot's case his "small sacrifice" was about a third of the population.

Chapter **VI**

Well, some nations go to war under the pretext of protecting their citizens, so I guess it balances out.

Deploying troops because of murdered missionaries is a cliché by now. The Empire has a few past conflicts along the same lines.

Of course, purely as a diplomatic issue, a country shouldn't be lazy when it comes to protecting its citizens. Or rather, the people pay taxes to be protected. Even in a night-watchman state, the people want protection from their government, so that should be provided.

In that sense, security is the nation's duty. Well, it probably only goes so far, but still.

Oh, I've gotten quite off track. This is no time to let my thoughts wander.

"But what does that have to do with me?"

How does a mere field major like me fit into a grand strategy like that? I honestly have no idea. Really—how?

In principle, it's better for confidentiality—there'll be fewer leaks—if fewer people know, so I'm sure it's on a need-to-know basis only, but I have to ask.

"It's simple. Apparently, your 203rd Aerial Mage Battalion will be the rear guard for the retreat."

"…They think far too much of us."

Actually, considering what happens to people who know too much… The civilian method is to give people a large retirement allowance or pension to keep their mouths shut. Yeah, that gets expensive. Hence, all the criticism of how much golden parachutes cost.

Conversely, if you want to keep costs down and resolve things in a practical manner, you can render people incapable of talking. And if you can accomplish it legally on a battlefield, it's a no-brainer.

…Is this to threaten us into staying quiet about Arene? The thought sends a chill up my spine.

Maybe I'm thinking too hard, but it sure seems like my loyalty is being questioned. It's true that in a pinch I prioritize my own safety, but…I've still been getting results for them. And I'm pretty sure I've been displaying my allegiance to the organization at every opportunity.

No, maybe they found out I hesitated in Arene? But I don't recall that resulting in any failures. Plus, I have the great excuse of protecting our own people.

Yeah, I want to believe there are no issues. Then why are we getting stuck as the rear guard?

"Your mission will only be a delaying defense, but it'll be rough, I'm sure. You're probably being summoned to discuss it."

"A delaying defense when we're half-enveloped? Losing half of my troops won't buy us time."

We got asked this question all the time in the academy, but I never thought I would actually be put in this situation.

It's possible, but I'm not doing it and *Let's try it* are very different things.

It's easy to say pretty words like, *I'll use my subordinates as a shield,* but to actually do it takes a tremendous amount of discipline.

At least, it's too much to ask of a young officer like me.

"Half...? You'd be basically wiped out..."

"Yes, I'm sure we would be. I never thought I'd end up having to actually implement a scenario from the academy's oral exam."

I want to shout, *Surely, you must be joking!* but nothing would be more pointless. I feel like I have at least a little understanding of Major Uger's personality.

Basically, I don't think he's the type of guy to joke around.

Besides, as long as I have no idea why he would lie to me, it's safer to assume it's the truth. In other words, I'm going to be the tail end of the army performing delaying action as we retreat? What an elegant way to indirectly tell me to drop dead.

Am I allowed to say that this is something they should have a family of warriors like the Shimahdzus[23] do and not mere mages? I just barely manage to control my urge to flee out the window of the car. Running away now won't improve my situation one bit. I have to think how I can resolve this—no, how to survive. I need to find a way out.

Fortunately, my subordinates are all capable shields. I may need to use

---

[23] **Shimahdzus**   The Shimazu clan.

the Shimahdzus special, the *sutegamari* fighting retreat. Maybe I should apply to license it. Gotta follow the rules at all times.

"You're overthinking it. It won't take that long. Won't you basically be on lookout?"

"On the perpetual battlefield, you have to be prepared for the worst, though, you know? Not that I enjoy having that temperament..."

My hope is that they just get the lines moved back in a hurry so we don't have to suffer. In other words, it's only a hope. I can't risk my life on this sad, little chance. We have to be an ultra-vigilant rear guard. What the heck?

If I was going to feel this sick, I shouldn't have eaten that beef stew. I wanna throw up. Was the reason Rudel drank milk because his stomach couldn't handle anything more than that?

No, I think he was serious about nutrition and just a total battlefield addict.

But maybe I should take a page from his book and drink some milk; it'd be good for my health. I'll take some time to seriously consider this later.

"...We'll do our best and try not to take too much time."

"I appreciate it, Major Uger."

Anyhow, what the heck.

It'll be fine if I can go to General von Zettour directly and get him to take back the orders later, but...

If they're trying to shut us up, he definitely won't.

No, even if he doesn't turn down my request, the danger of being disposed of will never quite leave us.

In that case, I might have to consider surrendering to the Republic in order to survive. Well, no, I guess that would be dangerous, too... It's so unlucky that we accidentally sunk that Commonwealth vessel. At worst, I would be sacrificed for long-term friendly relations between the Commonwealth and the Republic or whatever. Actually, that's definitely what would happen.

If that's true, then the first thing I need to do is get out of this jam.

"Either way, as long as we're soldiers, we do what we must. That's how it is, right?"

Damn it. I have to pretend I don't know anything and survive. Of course, the ideal would be if this is all a misunderstanding.

It's better to be pessimistically prepared than think optimistically and fail. If you're assuming you're fine at the cost calculation stage and you put too much trust in a 5.7-meter standard for sea walls, what happens?

Of course, a corporation has to be conscious of costs. Rather, I think a nation that wages a war with no sense of cost is far madder. I choose to firmly support peace. That said, I'm all for intervening in a region in order to secure limited interests.

The costs of a war waged by a practical economic agent should be capped within a permissible limit. And how about the escargots' standards? Power plants? More like fortresses. Well, the actual fortresses they build have pretty well-known reputations, in various senses of the word, e.g., the Maginot Line.

Ahh, this is no good. It appears my intellectual curiosity and purity are making my mind wander.

"Either way, Major von Degurechaff, for now, we've reunited. How about a toast to mark the occasion?"

"All I have is ersatz coffee, but if that works, I'm happy to."

Anyhow, next time I'll make sure to have some milk on hand. Incidentally, for some reason, the Empire is famous for its milk.

Friends, lead the Empire to victory!

— Major Generals von Zettour and von Rudersdorf, *Remembering the Rhine Lines* —

Magic Major Tanya von Degurechaff is advancing with a dismal look on her face. No, she's forced to advance. As an imperial soldier, she should be relishing an attack deep in enemy territory with a plethora of emotions, but all that is on Tanya's mind is the natural human desire to not die.

That is probably the inevitable thought of someone compelled to charge by circumstances. Tanya, skillfully casting formulas and causing enemies to burst into gory bloom, is doing her best so that on the surface, at least, she is an utterly fearless field major leading the charge.

"Break! Break!"

"04, Fox Three, Fox Three!"

"Fucking hell, 13 is hit!"

"01 to 10, 11. Cover him! Then hurry up and get him to the rear!"

It's her unit's radio chatter. The troops are less calm than usual. For them to sound upset during an operation isn't so rare, but exchanges of struggling, frantic curses are uncommon for the veteran 203rd Aerial Mage Battalion.

That said, it's not exactly surprising. She looks up at the sky and finds herself fantasizing about punching Being X's head off with her clenched fist.

If God exists, he must be some inflexible being like an evil computer. With that thought, she forces herself to freeze any mental effort that doesn't help her survive on the battlefield, and she focuses on combat maneuvers.

The sky is full of shells, and "crowded" doesn't begin to cover it. Like pelting rain or hail, iron is being shot up from the ground instead of falling down. Just a ton of iron. A truly brutal amount of iron is flying toward a single target. If this unending blaze of gunfire in the darkness represents human activity, then I can declare that civilization has, in a way, evolved in the exact opposite of the ideal direction.

Hell exists on the Rhine. The trials of purgatory are taking place here today.

This is where a human's life is worth the least. No, the lowest price is updated each day after hitting limit-down at this nearest station to hell. This is where the god of the dead and evil spirits make bank. A world where human lives plunge into dreadful deflation relative to lead bullets. This is a purgatory where the boundary between life and death is the haziest it ever gets.

Distinguished mages are no exception to this rule. Mages are feared on the surface, but the Rhine is also their graveyard.

"Fairy 01 to CP, we're completely enveloped. We won't last long. What's the situation like?"

Only mages have trouble dealing damage at eight thousand feet. For fighter planes, that altitude even allows for some comfort.

On top of that, the high explosives fired at these aircraft and the dense curtain of anti–air shot could slaughter a mage with ease.

Mages deploy magic walls about a meter from their bodies as protective films.

If that defends them, it's the same as the mages receiving no damage at all. But though they're magic, these walls aren't so strong.

The biggest ordinary single shot a protective film can defend against in a direct hit is 12.7 mm.

Of course, every mage is a little different, but in a saturation attack, even infantry small arms can weaken and penetrate a protective film. If they concentrate on defense and funnel more resources into it, a film can withstand up to about 40 mm.

Even assuming that level of protection, taking direct hits from large-caliber shells is impossible. Plus, if they do get hit, they may be dazed and unable to rely on their speed to evade.

As a mage's last line of defense, the defensive shell, armor they build with their own power right up against their flesh, is as strong as you might think. But since they can't bend the laws of physics, they have to be ready for shocks from impact.

Even dispersed, the shock to the internal organs from a direct hit with a 120 mm would render a mage helpless. Even if they were lucky and only blacked out, they would still crash. And probably most of them would get minced where they lie.

For better or worse, my orb, the Elinium Type 95, can repel up to 88 mm shots with its protective film. Theoretically, it can also create a defensive shell that can stand up to 120 mm grade shots. I'm not anxious to test that.

Only researchers want to test bulletproof vests in actual combat. The people who have to use them would never do that.

Plus, when my orb blocks a shot, high-density-interference factors get scattered around and obstruct magic use over a wide area. It's possible to take advantage of that effect to make yourself nearly undetectable. A simple way to think of it is that it's like putting an ECM[24] on full blast.

It's probably exceedingly difficult to spot flying objects with optical apparatuses at night.

Of course, since it's so similar to an ECM, the interference in itself is a frank indicator.

If your radar whites out, it's self-evident that something is there.

As such, the situation is not suitable for stealth maneuvers.

If we're detected but they can't lock on, however, guided missiles or disciplined fire won't be a threat, so breaking through at high speed and harassing them a bit makes a great invisibility cloak.

The huge, critical side effect of that is my psychological suffering, but there's nothing I can do about it.

"Phase two will be finished momentarily. Until phase three orders are given, each unit should continue designated operational maneuvers."

A noise-filled radio message.

Not only is it encoded, it's a transmission between mages that uses a special format with directional waves via orbs. You can just barely have

---

[24] **ECM**   Electronic countermeasure. Can jam transmissions, among other things.

a conversation using this system, so it only really works for practical communications.

The high density of magic remaining in the air creates ear-piercing noise.

I hate that we're supposed to throw off the Republican Army observers when we don't even know the positions of our fellow soldiers. After all, we're a rear guard that is jutting—or rather, charging—into enemy territory.

Once the entire theater gets involved and large-scale maneuvers begin, concealing ourselves will become important. Although we're withdrawing under cover of night, regardless of how it would go with a division, doing it with an army group is a different story.

As highly mobile and responsive as my group of excellent mages is, we're not a big enough force to cover the entire Rhine area.

And with one somewhat undermanned augmented battalion, the normal methods would be impossible.

Which is why we have this deceptive plan to convince the enemy that we're planning an offensive using a reconnaissance-in-force mission. The General Staff concluded that it wouldn't be possible to hide the activation of the rail network that would accompany the large-scale maneuver in the theater, so instead they deliberately spread false information about it: *The Empire is moving supplies and troops in preparation for a major offensive.*

If I hadn't heard about it when I met with General von Zettour in the capital, I would have believed it myself, they put so much effort into the story.

In the capital, a public relations officer made reference to a "large-scale operation," albeit in unofficial settings.

There were rumors of "a major operation on the Rhine lines."

And there were the supplies bustling back and forth by rail. It's a huge, tricky retreat designed to draw the enemy out and destroy them. We'll need a ton of matériel. And reports on Arene are being thoroughly censored.

Thanks to that, we've convinced even most of the informed people that the movement on the imperial side is reinforcements for the suppression of the revolt in Arene. The Empire admits, blushing, that it has failed to quell the situation. The parts of the story that couldn't be blocked with a strict gag order have been turned into rumors that control had been achieved to keep up appearances. The tight plan tricks people into believing the opposite of what's true.

We don't have enough data to guess how the Republic is taking it, but people have a tendency to believe what they want to believe, so I think we can expect some results.

Even so, they're probably suspicious that the Empire, which supposedly has supply line issues, is launching a desperate all-out offensive. But I can't believe we actually fooled them, even if they are suspicious.

The trick worked brilliantly, and it seems the Republic was even on guard against our desperate offensive. The Imperial Army's most elite mages have performed a recon-in-force on an unprecedentedly deep level and met with formidable Republican Army interception, just like the Empire wanted.

Thus, Tanya and her battalion, reflecting the desperate Imperial Army's impatience, must pull off this deceptive recon-in-force mission with no regard for casualties.

And the report that the Republican Army is on guard against deep penetration by a recon-in-force unit was music to the Imperial Army General Staffers' ears. *They bought it*, they all think, relieved by the good news. *Now the retreating units don't have to worry about getting their butts kicked.*

But though she may be a staff officer, Tanya is in a fight for her life on the battlefield and thinking about awful things like a smile on Being X's face.

In order to keep the enemy from finding out it's a ruse, the battalion is forced to carry out this recon-in-force mission without regard for sacrifices.

The 203rd Aerial Mage Battalion is spread out along the front acting as a decoy and rear guard so the enemy doesn't realize the army is retreating.

Behind us, they're probably doing their best to move the clunky field guns to the rear. Once that phase is over, the infantry will withdraw.

The field engineers have already laid traps. We can expect the move to be finished within the next few hours. Hence, my unit is stuck getting shot up like this while we buy that time.

The object of the recon-in-force fishing so frequently performed on this front is to find out about the enemy's defensive preparations and positions of their forces. Since both sides see recon as a sign of a major impending offensive, the receiving end would prioritize concealing their troops and not move their reserve forces around in an aggressive way.

If that would buy the retreating Imperial Army the time they needed, then Tanya and her battalion had to go in. That's what the orders told them to do.

Of course, in order to prevent us from gathering intelligence, the Republican Army gives us an enthusiastic welcome with dense anti–air fire. Plus, since we're facing an interception from a base so far back, our rate of safe returns isn't going to be very high. In fact, the yardstick for whether it's actually recon-in-force or not is how many casualties the attacking team suffers.

"Fairy 08 to 01. I'm hit. Going to fall back."

It isn't uncommon for the guy flying next to me to be put out of commission. As for the efficiency of their interception alone, though, as long we have their radar whited out, there's no way they can use disciplined fire.

Conversely, with skilled radar observers guiding the fire, they probably would have been able to intercept more effectively.

But the Republican Army, which tends to rely on radar observer fire and mages' disciplined fire, is horrible at visual combat.

The main reason we're still taking damage is the sheer amount of iron they're throwing at us.

You can connect even with lousily aimed shots if you fire enough of them. It's just terrible.

…Seeing this extravagance, I realize I should have bought stocks in ammunition companies. I can't regret this oversight enough.

While they are consumables that cost little individually and therefore aren't very profitable, if they're getting squandered like this, the manufacturers must be doing gangbusters. I had been putting my salary into natural resources, thinking the profits on munitions would tend to be kept low, but maybe that was a mistake.

"01, roger. 06, 09, cover him. I'm gonna take two shots, so fall back during that time."

What is done cannot be undone. As I reconsider the conclusion I reached back then, I need to apply what I learn to the future.

Here it is, my constructive orientation toward the future. It's important to always have a positive attitude.

Anyhow, right now I need to fill in the hole left by my injured man. That's only a matter of course, but it's better if I can avoid danger. Then is not covering him because I fear danger the right thing to do? The answer, unfortunately, is no.

Amateurs tend to be scared of any danger they can see. They worry that if they do anything, something terrifying will happen, so they freeze up.

So an amateur frets that they'll give their position away if they shoot. Certainly, they may be right to perceive some danger there. But it's still only an amateur's thinking.

Doing nothing means losing an opportunity to do something.

What humans should fear the most is forfeiting profit. If I offer the retreating man an escort in this situation, I attach two of my subordinates to him as support. So we have a cluster of three people. If I fire two supporting shots, the sky is still full of smoke from bursting shells and searchlights. I doubt anyone will notice a couple of shots in the middle of all that.

If anything, I can expect that the two supporters will get a great reaction as decoys. In other words, while they're withdrawing, they'll monopolize the enemy's attention. If by taking a slight risk I can steer clear of danger, then naturally, that is the rational choice. And they do have the chance of falling back to a safe area, so in game theory terms, it's not too bad. It's not zero-sum, after all.

Best of all, if I send out decoys under the pretext of providing support for a retreating soldier, I can pursue my personal profit while caring about my subordinates. The chances that the idiot who got hit will be saved increase. This is it: a win-win scenario.

"Commander, it's too dangerous."

Of course, my men are pros, so they recognize the danger. They don't want to be decoys. That's dangerous. I understand very well why they want to protest.

"We have no choice. There's no time. Do it."

But oh, how sad. No, for me, I should probably say it's happy. This is the army, and I'm the superior officer leading my troops.

Of course, when she remembers that the whole reason she's stuck here suffering in the first place is because this is the army, she's sorry. In the capital, her superior officer, General von Zettour, gave her strict orders in writing to operate under the direct command of General von Rudersdorf.

The orders had come down the official route in the proper format. In other words, since I have orders from General von Rudersdorf, I have no choice but to accept them and be the rear guard here. This world is quite easy to understand.

"It's an intense mission, but I know you can handle it"?

"The higher-ups have extremely high expectations of you"?

I'm sure no one can euphemize forcibly sealing lips so well as him. Since I couldn't get him to listen to my objections, it must be that. It could be a misunderstanding, but it's best to be a pessimist and prepare for the worst.

So once I'm prepared like a pessimist, I'll be an optimist. Ideally, I'd like to build a win-win relationship with the General Staff. I don't think I have a bad reputation as a staff officer in the first place.

Then there's a fairly good chance that I've been sent here out of military necessity. Thinking that, a slight grin appears on Tanya's face. *Yeah, maybe I've been worrying too much.*

Surely it must just be that my superiors want to break out of this war situation. I want to work with both major generals again as soon as the opportunity presents itself. If possible, I'd like a chance to chat with them. Of course, first I have to get out of this. The future is important, but right now, surviving is even more crucial.

I quickly load an interference formula from my computation orb into a rifle bullet. I deploy a defensive shell in front of my troops to shield them from the disproportionate shots flying up at us.

By interrupting the line of fire, I give them temporary safety. Put another way, even the Republican numbskulls can tell I've used an interference formula to manifest some sort of wall that is blocking their shots. Naturally, they'll realize there is something behind it.

At that point, most of the hail of bullets will be aimed that way.

"01 to 06 and 09. Get a move on. That won't hold for long."

Anyhow, if the decoys move too slowly, they won't last very long, either, but I need to keep the enemy's eyes on something besides me.

Hurry, hurry, hurry!

"Roger, good luck."

"Yeah…may the Lord protect you."

Irritatingly, instead of "may your luck be everlasting" or something like that, I say some incomprehensible nonsense about the Lord's protection. I want to cry, but without the Elinium Type 95, my protective film would be blown away in an instant, and I'd be destroyed, defensive shell and all.

In a way, Being X is like consumer finance. I don't want to borrow, and I shouldn't, but I have to. *Ahh, eat shit.*

The only weapons that can intercept us at eight thousand feet are anti–air cannons, but if I get hit with one of those, it won't end well.

"CP to Fairy. Report on casualties and status."

"Fairy 01 to CP. Half of us have already dropped out. So far, we've achieved half of our scheduled numbers. Been looking for that Republican Army ammo dump but can't find it."

Thanks to that, even my battalion of tough mages is losing lots of men. No one has died, but there are probably more than a few who will never return to the lines. I'm glad I was honest about the "constant danger" when I was recruiting.

If I was accused of false advertising, I would have betrayed the first principle of sales born of the modern era: honesty. I'm not such a halfwit that I think I can fool the market by shouting about "mislabeling." A lack of faith in a trust economy is terrifying, just terrifying.

Chapter **VII**

Sheesh, I guess I should be breathing a sigh of relief. Or should I lament that just because we blew up the factory in Dacia everyone's gone off and convinced themselves that if anyone can blow up an enemy ammo dump, the 203rd Aerial Mage Battalion can?

"CP, roger. 01, got some bad news for you."

It's not as if I believe in luck, but I recall that my forerunners emphasized it as a factor. Apparently, when the great Matsusheeta[25] hired people, he asked whether they were lucky or not. Before I was inhumanely sent to this insane world, I didn't understand it.

But now I do. It may only be a question of probability theory, but luck is worth researching.

"What is it?"

"A battalion-sized group of mages is rapidly approaching the Rhine lines from the edge of our radar range. Hold them off until the end of phase three."

"...Fairy 01, roger. Transitioning to interdiction combat. Anything else?" Suppressing the rage welling up inside me, I just barely maintain a businesslike tone. They say it so simply.

I may say interdiction combat, but we're essentially the strength of two companies performing recon-in-force. We're not in close formation. On top of that, just passing through defended positions takes a lot out of us.

In contrast, the intercepting side is full of energy. The air we're flying above the firing positions is their home turf, so as long as they don't get hit accidentally, they don't have to worry about that.

It has to be much easier on their nerves.

We may be a band of elites, but I doubt our opponents are the type to unthinkingly say "yes, sir" when ordered to intercept us.

After all, they're a battalion scrambled from the surface to obstruct our recon mission.

It goes without saying that they're a select team. I don't want to kill myself by wishfully hoping the enemies are numbskulls. The only way to survive is to prepare like a pessimist.

---

[25] **Matsusheeta**   Kōnosuke Matsushita.

"You have permission to immediately abort your recon-in-force mission."
And then, hmm, that's an interesting thing to have permission to do.

It's a fact that permission to abort a mission like this isn't given very
often. Certainly, now that we have interdiction combat orders, if the
retreat is going according to schedule, aborting this mission would be
one way to limit further losses.

So it seems rational for the brass to allow it. But think about it. I definitely won't fall back. Or rather, a little thinking tells me military practicality is a trap.

If someone offers you a paved road straight to hell, even with good
intentions, it's much safer to veer off and drive across the wasteland.

"...I hope that won't be necessary."

I'm not an amateur. As an economically minded person who values
rational thought, I didn't go through training for no reason. I wasn't
built to the specifications of some impractical entity like Being X. I can
swear it on the honor of the intelligent winners of evolution who survived as the fittest, *Homo sapiens.*

"What? What do you mean?"

"The point of recon-in-force is a survey of the enemy's interception
capabilities. If we abort now, we risk revealing the deceptive purpose of
the mission."

If the recon-in-force ruse to mask the withdrawal fails, the rear guard
will have to hold out and buy time till the very end. If we fail to buy
time, that's it. What is now an orderly retreat of ground troops will
descend into chaos, and they could be trampled.

For that reason, we should hesitate to even transmit this sort of conversation, even if it is encoded.

Tanya's only choice is to have them move the retreat along as quickly
as possible. The side giving the orders will probably order the rear guard
to buy time even if they have to get literally wiped out doing it. If I were
on the side giving the orders, I wouldn't hesitate to do it that way, either.
It's logical. If there's a problem with this plan, it's that I'm on the receiving side. Fucking hell.

Either way, evading this battalion only to be pursued by every Republican unit on the Rhine front would be way stupider.

In other words, considering the risk, staying here is all we can do. I'm not the kind of person who doesn't know the folly of not investing because you're scared of a tiny risk. What matters most is the returns.

"Since we can't have them finding out until phase three is over, the only choice we have is to take out this intercepting unit and continue our mission."

"...Understood. I'll have them move as fast as they can."

"Thanks. May the Lord protect you."

In the end, I'm relieved that CP is cooperating. Honestly, this is so rough. Now then, in order to survive, I've got to be brave and do my best not to lose to this abnormal world.

I have no intention of sacrificing myself to an order to keep flying after I can no longer focus and my will is nearly broken. I'm fighting for my life, and that's it.

"Okay, attention, all hands. We're headed into a counter-mage fight. Let's teach the fools challenging us a lesson."

Geez. You could have been enjoying a nice break in the rear, but you came to challenge us? Personally, it's hard for me to praise that attitude because I know that unpaid overtime doesn't contribute much to labor productivity. Why would you proactively enter such a pain-in-the-ass battle?

I'm a peace-loving person, so this pains me. Surely there is no one who loves human beings more than I do. And yet. It's rare to be ordered to kill them so often as I am. As a rational, thinking person, it would be embarrassing to curse my fate. Still, I sense some absurdity.

It's almost as if the conceited face of Being X is about to appear in the back of my mind with all the narcissism of a transcendent existence. Oh God, if you exist, you are surely a rotten bastard.

Things really don't go how you'd like. I just want to live a quiet life.

Nothing seemed particularly different about that day. Anyone would say so: *It was a normal day.* No, *it was a normal battlefield.*

If anything was out of the ordinary, it was that there were a few military observers visiting from the Commonwealth to foster friendly relations. But that wasn't enough to register as a blip when everyone's emotions were so exhausted.

After chatting with the bigwigs over dinner, the visitors were guided by one of our officers to begin their inspection. For better or worse, it wasn't of interest to the troops. They were so tired they didn't care, so they banished it from their consciousness and went to sleep.

At that point, the Third Mage Battalion belonging to the Republican Army's Twenty-Second Division was already on its ascent. Whether sleeping on the ground or heading into the sky, the soldiers were faithful to their duties... To the mages who took off upon receiving the scramble order, protecting the sound sleep of our fellow soldiers was part of our job.

The mission was to eliminate the battalion daring to try recon-in-force, and we anticipated a secondary objective of assisting ground troops. Our biggest problem was troops not being able to sleep due to harassing sneak attacks, so the importance of the mission to restore tranquility might be difficult for someone who hasn't been on the front lines to understand.

"Control to all hands. Our guests today are pretty serious. You're going to have your hands full."

And the words from the combat controller, though somewhat grave, were overflowing with the confidence that things would work out somehow. If a division or regiment of mages had forced their way through or infiltrated to attack, it might have been different, but repelling a battalion doing reconnaissance-in-force wouldn't be so hard.

After all, despite the "in-force" tacked on, it's essentially "reconnaissance." They would probably withdraw upon making contact. Well, I genuinely had to hand it to the guys charging in that day, though—they were really going for it. It takes a lot of determination to get as far as they did. And judging from the size of the unit, they'd make quite a racket with harassing attacks, so we had to stay vigilant... Numbers is a problem in any era.

"Control, who are the invaders?"

"An augmented battalion. They're already past the third defensive line. It's only a matter of time till they break through the fourth."

Usually a recon-in-force mission would sniff around the first or second defensive line positions and fall back. At an attack position, they could expect support, and from the second defensive line, it was still fairly easy to get back to their base. If that was how it went, it would have a limited effect on the front lines, since they were prepared. More than anything, it wasn't something that warranted waking up the officers sleeping in the rear.

If we woke up the whole army for every little scuffle with these frequent recon missions done expressly as a feint or to distract us, that would be playing right into their hands.

Everyone just hoped we could get enemy engagements done quietly. The little fights between recon-in-force units and our interceptors happened so often they were facetiously treated as part of the nighttime scenery.

"They're too fast. What are the guys on the defensive lines doing?"

Maybe that's why we hesitated at this enemy coming in so rapidly. It went without saying that they had to be a pretty enthusiastic unit if they were already past the third defensive line. There was a good chance they had located our shelters and frontline command.

There were rumors of a desperate imperial offensive.

I was suspicious, but...unless the enemy was awfully determined, they wouldn't usually be able to get past the third defensive lines. What's more, usually once the second line is passed, the standby unit is scrambled. We only received sortie orders after the third line was breached, and it was fair to call that an unbelievably slow response.

"Widespread magic jamming has paralyzed our scouting network, so our response is pretty delayed."

And of course, the controller's voice reflected the frustrating state of affairs—how could it not? The situation was unclear; we were a bit miffed at the urgent order to intercept after being told repeatedly to stand by.

I can't believe we're stuck having to stop them before they pass the last defensive line. We risk damage from harassing attacks as well as them taking home intelligence. Inevitably, this state of affairs had everyone feeling ashamed.

A battalion of mages may have breached the lines, but the Rhine general headquarters should have been able to crush them easily.

Considering the intelligence they had, though, this was liable to end in disaster.

I was sure a few high-ranking officers' heads would roll because the response to the widespread magic jamming was delayed. The radio operators would surely be crawling around unrolling cable to strengthen our communications. And I bet it would be our job to cover them.

"And apparently the anti–air fire is stuck relying on optical instruments, so watch out—the enemy force might be doing just fine."

"Roger. Don't want to underestimate an injured beast. Do you have more information about them? Whatever you know is fine. Got anything?"

Anyhow, the future is the future. Today is today's mission. And it was going to be more intense than the usual missions. Everyone realized for the first time how worrisome the situation was.

And we were shocked. Unlike when we repel exhausted enemy mages, this time it was possible we'd be up against a force that had been able to conserve their energy to a relative degree. The irritating veil of night made the situation we were facing even more difficult.

Since our anti–air gunners were relying on optical instruments, we would have to worry about friendly fire, too. Considering how confusing it could be to tell friend from foe, it wasn't unthinkable.

"Due to the awful jamming, we haven't managed to identify them, but our superior says they seem like elites. There's also the rumors of a large-scale imperial offensive. Stay on your guard!"

"I appreciate the advice. Troops, game faces on and let's go!"

Our commander's encouraging voice tells us to prepare for the challenge. The determination and spirit we could hear indicated the appropriate amount of nervousness for a vigilant warrior.

But that's only in hindsight.

They were wrong. We didn't need game faces. What we needed was to be crazy enough about death to find a way to live through it.

"All hands, this is your battalion commander. We've located the enemy. Prepare to engage."

Both sides' fields of vision were narrower due to the dark, which gave us trouble.

We discovered each other nearly simultaneously. The battalion commanders engaged at about the same time, too. It was simple. Republican mage doctrine is to work as a group and overwhelm the individual strength of imperial mages using organized combat and disciplined fire. It was basically an unexpected encounter battle in an area approached by the enemy. Plus, the powerful jamming caused by high mana density.

Even a conservative estimate would say this battle would be something we're not used to. And our opponents were a unit composed of veteran mages with a wealth of experience and a talent for close-quarters fighting.

There was no way a normal unit could take the brunt of this assault honed in Dacia and Norden.

If the vanguard had held out just a little longer, maybe the rear guard could have gotten away. Or if there had been just a few more mages in the rear guard, the unexpected shots could have stopped the enemy's approach so the vanguard could get away.

But everything fell just a bit short. The results were disastrous. The shock caused confusion. A storm of formula bullets from a submachine gun heightened it.

Things deteriorated—we'd been had, and there was no way to stop the blood or the damage.

The explosion formula, loosed by the imperial mage commander at the helm, opened a huge hole in the vanguard. At the same time the breach appeared, multiple optical shot formulas were aimed to crush commanders of each company, and just like that, the Republican command chain's head was lopped off.

But Republican troops could still, if only barely, resist in an organized way. The rear guard began using suppressive fire; they knew they had to cover the gap in the vanguard.

For a short time, the rear guard managed to cover for the vanguard to plug up that hole. They had enough energy to attempt to reorganize their force. Their vigorous resistance succeeded in keeping the attack at bay, but as a result, they couldn't give the vanguard covering fire. They used their full strength preventing the enemy approach, but then had no energy left to protect the vanguard.

When furious resistance interrupted the imperial charge, the mages suddenly switched targets to the isolated Republicans out front.

It was around two companies of imperial mages versus the two companies of the Republican vanguard. But the latter had been completely stripped of its leadership, so it didn't even have support; in that cut-off state, the Republican mages were isolated sitting ducks.

As a result, the numerical balance between the two sides flipped. The rear guard had its hands full defending itself when the vanguard's fate was decided with a swift incision. Normally, the imperial mages were prevented from approaching by the Republican Army's obnoxious disciplined fire. Meanwhile, after their supporting volley, the Republicans would be able to stop the remnants of the enemy from breaking through. This time, when the two sides met, however, the imperial mages got to release their pent-up anger and cut the Republicans down.

"Attention, Fairy Battalion. Engage in pursuit."

The rest happened too easily. By the time the rear guard suddenly tried to retreat after losing its shield, it was too late.

The Republicans didn't have enough distance or speed to shake off the imperial mages, who had accelerated for the attack.

Their race to escape the theater wasn't to be. Ultimately, the Third Mage Battalion of the Republican Army's Twenty-Second Division was pronounced annihilated.

Ironically, the only survivors were a few downed in the initial explosion formula who narrowly escaped death.

The Republican Army ended up mobilizing the Rhine general headquarters' select mage battalion, but they failed to locate the invaders. On the contrary, they let them burn several supply depots. At that point, the Republican Army Command shifted its full attention entirely onto the invading battalion.

Rumors of a major offensive. Whispers of the fate of Arene.

They fought bravely to the last man.

The stirring echoes of propaganda convinced the Republic that the people had sacrificed themselves and met a tragic end. *We can't let their deaths be in vain.*

The distress of the Imperial Army and the cornered supply lines were simple enough for the Empire to fix, but the blow still stung. So it didn't hesitate to choose military maneuvers as the way to break out of that horrible situation.

To secure the front, to secure the Empire.

But that's exactly why people of both nations thought...*We're so sick of this.* So the Empire was at wits' end over its unreliable supply lines, and the Republic saw them as hope.

Little birds were twittering about the movements of the Imperial Army, and the same thing was on everyone's minds: *The Empire is not okay with the current situation.* And it was the absolute truth. The Imperial Army General Staff had realized that if they focused on beating the bothersome partisans while relying on a limping rail system for supplies, maintaining an aimless front wasn't worth it.

That objective reality fueled the Republic's misunderstanding. Everyone firmly believed that the Empire's powerful military organization solved problems through major offensives, like it did in Dacia, like it did in Norden.

And apart from the delaying at the beginning of the war, the Empire had always defended its territory to the end. Yes, its territory.

Nobody would withdraw from their own territory. That was the one-sided belief the Republicans had. But to the officers of the Republican Army who paid for a sliver of land with blood, it was self-evident truth. They were proud of defending their home with mountains of dead, so they wondered, *Who would part with their fatherland?*

And that was why they ended up misreading the Imperial Army General Staff war machine's intentions so completely it was ridiculous. Perhaps you could say the Republican soldiers got trapped in their own emotions.

That day, as a result, the Imperial Army succeeded in abandoning the front without the Republican Army noticing.

Now then, it's about time to talk about the seed of the Empire's victory.

It all started with the reality of conducting recon-in-force of heavily guarded positions. The dilemma was serious: high casualties versus tactical necessity.

The fact that estimates said even the Devil of the Rhine and her elite troops would lose at least half their numbers should speak to the danger of it.

Command and staff officers all understood and struggled with the dilemma that despite that premise, there was an urgent military need for recon-in-force.

An augmented battalion performing recon-in-force created too many casualties, but any fewer soldiers and they wouldn't be able to achieve their objective.

Facing this dilemma, the Imperial Army requested its Technical Arsenal to research a new weapon that would enable penetration into heavily guarded enemy positions and for some degree of reconnaissance. The engineers tentatively suggested a few technical solutions to the problem, and the one that seemed promising was from Aerial Technical Arsenal. They proposed developing a high-altitude recon unit to fly outside the range of anti–air fire. The aerial units that had teams for special recon missions were superior to begin with.

To the other departments, however, regardless of the latent potential in aerial reconnaissance, there was one cause for concern: Was it actually possible to achieve with their current level of technology? It may have been easy enough to talk about increasing the altitude, but the technical demands of an aircraft that could fly at high altitude presented a lot of hurdles, and they weren't sure they could handle it.

That was the moment Chief Engineer Adelheid von Schugel suggested a methodology and approach from the magic point of view.

"...What about a special apparatus for additional acceleration during recon-in-force?"

What the heck is that?

The answer to the question that came into everyone's minds when they saw the outline of the problem was simple, in a way.

Reconnaissance-in-force requires penetrating the enemy's interception lines. So if one assumes an assault to perform a quick strike and pull out, sending a fast, heavily armed unit would be best.

So all they needed to do was rapidly accelerate past the enemy positions before they could intercept. According to Schugel, putting the mages in additional acceleration apparatuses would solve everything.

By doing that, they would be able to measure the enemy defenses and interception ability, so everything would work out for the recon-in-force mission as well.

The argument that they would be able to achieve their aims to some degree using mages for recon-in-force was correct. That was why foot soldiers or mages were used more often than aircraft.

But casualties had exceeded the permissible limit. That's why the army had asked the Technical Arsenal for its opinion. This was the conclusion.

"All right. Have the mages charge at high speed."

Aha, certainly if you change your point of view, all you need to do is increase the breakthrough success rate of the mages. So it was true that having them do it at high speed would get the job done. The only problem was that there weren't any mages who could operate at such speeds and altitudes.

The one who offered this solution and wondered how to make it possible was one genius, Adelheid von Schugel.

His answer? Add speed and altitude with an external apparatus.

The criticism that his idea wasn't much different from the Aerial Technical Arsenal's only went so far. After all, altitude was a by-product in his plan, which essentially focused only on speed.

Hence, "additional acceleration apparatus."

But rather than speak of his genius, it's probably easier to take a look at his plan.

The apparatus would be equipped with an abundance of extra-large hydrazine fuel boosters. Of all the ways to secure stable flight, he used multiple single-use boosters. And once empty, they would detach along with their external fuel tank, resulting in an even higher speed near the end of the journey.

On top of that, he gave up on the biggest technical obstacle, regulating the boosters. With great decisiveness, he conquered the hurdle by deciding the thing would simply continue on accelerating. Yes, they would just launch it on a straight path. To put it another way, while it was operating, the mage wouldn't be able to adjust the speed at all.

The apparatus would come with a tank of boron additive for accelerating in enemy sky, but that was different. The boron additive, estimated to be ten times as poisonous as potassium cyanide, was for emergency evasion.

To address the feared shock waves and sudden increase in wave drag, all aeroelasticity issues would be left up to the mage's protective film and defensive shell.

(The plan was judged to be possible only with unrestrained booster consumption; aircraft definitely wouldn't work.)

With an unbelievable supersonic target speed, Mach 1.5, they would be able to leave anything in the dust.

And from a purely engineering perspective, it would be easier to realize than a new reconnaissance aircraft. More importantly, it was expected to be ready for actual combat soon.

To add one final comment, however: Due to the single-use nature of its boosters, the additional acceleration apparatus could fly only in a straight line.

After breaking through the enemy position, mages were required to return to base under their own steam. No matter how you looked at it, the thing was a one-way ticket to hell. There's no point in reconnaissance if you can't get back after you go and see.

Even if it's technically practical, a thing isn't fit for practical use unless it can be used, right? In a way, you would expect people to voice that concern, but when the whispers started…

An officer from an airborne unit murmured an idea that sounded like it came from another dimension.

"Then what about sending a 'unit' to the rear of an enemy position?" he asked.

Certainly, it was incredibly dangerous to individuals. It would be nearly impossible to return. Aha, an additional acceleration apparatus that couldn't return to base was defective as a reconnaissance vehicle.

But why limit its use to reconnaissance? It would be a more reliable way of delivering mages behind enemy lines than paradropping.

And it would get them past any intercepting enemies. After all, simply launching the thing would send it way higher than a practical altitude for anti–air fire. Depending on how it was used, the army could even anticipate sending a company of mages directly to the enemy headquarters to decapitate their operation.

At that point, Major General von Zettour from General Staff Service Corps went to visit. The research itself continued under Chief Engineer Schugel, but the General Staff requested fairly detailed progress reports.

And when they understood the value of it, they were overjoyed. The guerrilla warfare proponents were especially ecstatic supporters, and they took steps to prioritize proceeding with the plan. The project received literal leverage from the General Staff.

With that assistance, a prototype was completed just before the partisans temporarily took over Arene.

And it just so happened that the Elinium Arms Type 97 Assault Computation Orb was able to make the critical defense shell and protective film.

According to the test personnel who participated in the experiments, the assault orb functioned exactly as they had hoped.

Since a measure of reliability had been guaranteed, a first run of twenty mass production models was rolled out in a hurry.

With that success, the General Staff made a slight but significant amendment to their decisive battle plan. It was great news for Major General von Rudersdorf's strategy to lure the Republican Army in and destroy them. The apparatus Zettour had spotted while it was in development in Tech Research was written into the plan. They were both thrilled. They would achieve what was, in a way, the dream of all General Staff officers.

Schrecken und Ehrfurcht.

The first phase of the operation named "Shock and Awe" was simple.

"Attack the enemy headquarters directly to cause the collapse of their line."

That was it.

It was a clear, cold night. In the Imperial Army's 203rd Aerial Mage Battalion, Second Lieutenant Warren Grantz was on guard in a wool-lined field overcoat. It was a quieter night than they'd had in quite a while. Yes, a quiet night. A peaceful time during which he could sit in a chair on standby sipping the coffee provided as part of his field rations.

The dark hour was rather tranquil. No shells exploding nearby, no warnings to be on guard against raids. He couldn't even remember the last time they had gone to sleep without hearing so much as rifle fire. It must have been so long ago.

This calm had come about because the brass carried line consolidation with extraordinary resolve.

As a result of the successful retreat and reorganization, the Republican Army had hastily launched an advance into the wide-open vacuum the Imperial Army had left; apparently, they were too busy with that to bother with the 203rd. Thanks to that, there was a brief lull on the battlefield. The battalion commander held off any sorties and told everyone to take a break before she went back to bed, giving the exhausted soldiers a much-needed rest.

And so fortunately, perhaps it could be said, the troops were able to spend a night free of the anxiety induced by the presence of the powerful Commander Degurechaff. When was the last time that had happened?

Even though these were usually prime hours for nighttime interception missions or for conducting anti-raid patrols, everything was safe and sound.

Despite knowing they were secure in a rear base, maybe they should have been a little more nervous about surprise attacks under cover of darkness. Of course, it wasn't as if the unit had grown lax.

Even if they were so worn out they could sleep anywhere, including the mud, they could still respond to urgent orders at the drop of a hat.

Still, they relaxed a mite.

The reason was clear.

The majority of the Republican Army had advanced into the void and basically forgot about the 203rd's defensive position.

The moment the Republican Army emerged from its heavily forti-
fied lines, their soldiers zealously devoted themselves to expanding the
army's gains.

At this point, they would surely rather move into an abandoned area
and advance the front rather than expend blood and iron fighting over a
well-defended trench line.

Which explained the rare peaceful night.

Naturally, there wasn't *zero* concern about pulling the front back. But
their commander had made a confident declaration. *"Tomorrow, we'll be
the tip of the spear that will end this war."* It could have only meant the
unit was gearing up for a serious attack.

Still, though, the thought that they could end the war made things
easier. *If our commander has so much faith in the plan, then even if we don't
completely destroy the Republican Army, it should still be enough to ensure
the Empire's safety.*

*And after that, we can focus on rebuilding the territories ravaged by
the war.*

…As Grantz reflected fighting so fierce that thoughts of the future
were impossible, he received some concerned looks from his comrades-in-
arms.

Once he thought about it more closely, it felt like he hadn't paid attention to his surroundings in quite some time. Not that it had actually
been that long, but still. He couldn't believe he had so much quiet time;
it was more than enough to reflect on the harsher fighting he'd been
through.

To calm his nerves, he picked up his cup of now slightly tepid coffee. Up until that moment, he'd just been drinking it without paying
attention, but the beans were actually pretty good. He'd been told it was
ration, but the presence of beans at all was rare. Considering the scarcity
of boiled water on the battlefield, coffee was quite a luxury.

Since he was on duty, alcohol was obviously prohibited. He was thankful that they had a good supply of the coffee their commander liked.

It seemed they had requisitioned a ton of it. It was great that when he
wanted to have a good think over a cup, he could do it without resorting

to ersatz coffee. Yes, now that he considered them, Grantz noticed even the smallest details.

I must really be calm, he mused behind a wry smile... The battalion had been reorganized due to the wear and tear from repeated battles. Though their losses were low, it was impossible to get away without a few at least, so even the 203rd Aerial Mage Battalion had taken on replacements and absorbed part of another unit. And in fact, Grantz and others like him were originally incorporated as provisional replacements.

They'd basically been added upon completion of their training. Surely that was better than being transferred from the familiar unit they'd trained with to struggle in a new one. Anyhow, the unit based on the 203rd was now known as the Imperial Army's 203rd Provisional Composite Battalion on paper.

Their call sign was Fairy. Pixies, fairies, not much difference really. Basically, this was just a formality. Eventually, the personnel would be transferred on paper to the 203rd Aerial Mage Battalion and the "provisional" part of the name would go away.

Thinking along those lines, Grantz could work out the implications of a temporary reorganization for himself. The higher-ups would do the real transformation after the upcoming operation.

Mulling over all this, he quietly sipped his coffee. It was an unbelievably calm night for a battlefield. The view from the trench showed him the same sky he gazed at every night, but for some reason during these quiet moments, it looked surprisingly starry.

For someone used to the battlefield, the distinct lack of machine guns and nighttime harassing fire was actually so out of place that it was nerve-racking.

"...Relax, Lieutenant. You're acting strange."

But he if he got too worked up, others were bound to notice. *Agh. I was just thinking how I can finally get some sleep even on the Rhine lines with its storms of steel. I still have a ways to go. Do I seem like a chick with eggshell on its head to everyone else?*

"Sorry, Lieutenant Weiss."

It was First Lieutenant Weiss, who had been hit and injured in Arene.

The whole battalion was glad to hear news of his smooth recovery and finally welcomed him back the other day. Lieutenant Weiss was the sort of guy who looked out for the whole unit in one way or another—everyone felt more shored up when he was around.

And even though Grantz was the only officer who really needed to be on duty, Weiss was helping out in an effort to regain his combat instincts after some time away. It helped relieve a lot of the tension.

The main enemies of a sentry are boredom and nerves. Grantz couldn't have been more grateful that a senior officer kept them at bay.

"Well, it's not like I don't understand how you feel. I can't calm down, either."

The first lieutenant shrugged. From the casual gesture, Grantz gathered that his wound was no longer causing him any problems.

The other day, to celebrate his release from the hospital and hone his rusty skills, Lieutenant Weiss had a mock battle with the commander. *Even if that's all he can do right now...I'm relieved he recovered.*

Then Grantz suddenly seized upon one thing Weiss had said. *He can't relax, either?*

"...So you feel like something is off, too?"

"Of course. This battalion has been on the front lines ever since we mustered." Weiss smiled bitterly and drained his coffee.

He had been through hard fighting, but the smile on his face was one of amusement.

Why, though?

That question came into his mind for the first time in a while. Compared with everyone else, Grantz's time on the battlefield had been so short, but it already felt like he'd been living like this for half his life. Honestly, when he thought about it, the days had been jam-packed.

"Oh, you don't know, huh?"

Upon seeing Grantz's questioning look, Weiss suddenly seemed to remember. He'd been thinking that the youngster knew what he was talking about, but it hit him that he and the other new recruits had only recently reported for duty. He wasn't one of the grognards from the early days of the battalion.

New arrivals learned the stories of the unit from the senior members. These guys had been incorporated so hastily that no one had been able to take the time for these basics. After their baptism in combat and surviving calamitous artillery fire, the members of the battalion finally had some time to talk to one another.

Actually, this is more or less what we were told during the recruitment process, Weiss realized and cracked a smile in spite of himself.

"This is a good opportunity. Let's talk about the old days."

We have the time. It's a perfect chance for us to get to know how the other thinks.

Weiss had an orderly bring them more coffee and sat on the desk, looking up as if he were reminiscing. *I didn't realize the first lieutenant could make expressions like that*, Grantz thought suddenly, looking at his senior from the side.

...The Weiss I know is always wearing his first lieutenant mask.

It hit him again that although he had grown used to life in the battalion, his time there hadn't been very long at all.

"Did you know I was originally in the eastern army?"

"No, I never heard that before."

Grantz and the other recruits had come straight out of their accelerated schooling. In fact, they graduated early and were hurled onto the front lines that very minute. He remembered again how little time there had been.

Under normal circumstances, he would have heard stories about the service of his seniors as part of getting to know the unit, but this was his first time. Up until this moment, they'd been gripping their guns so tightly that neither Grantz nor any of the old guard had noticed.

"Oh right." Weiss nodded and began to recite something with a smile. "We guide him always, abandon him never, go where there is no path, never yielding, forever on the battlefield. Everything we do, we do for victory. We seek mages for the worst battlefields, the smallest rewards; days darkened by a forest of swords and hails of bullets, and constant danger with no guarantee of survival. To those who return go the glory and the honor."

Sound familiar? Weiss asked with his eyes. But he could tell without an answer that Grantz didn't understand.

I don't even need to ask, Weiss thought and continued his story. "That's what we were told when we volunteered for the 203rd. 'Don't expect to come back alive!'" His wry smile contained a multitude of emotions. There was regret, a little self-mockery. A flood of nostalgia. Sentiments that probably all the senior members of the battalion shared.

"I was younger. I overestimated my ability and stupidly thought I could be a hero. Mages always overestimate themselves."

"No, Lieutenant. I don't think you—"

"Nah, it's fine. I'm just telling the truth. That's when the major knocked me flat. Our training was really like being born again."

Kicked around on a snowy mountain where complaints were futile, targeted by artillery, and as if to finish them off, forced to fly so high they could barely breathe.

"I really can't believe I made it through that," he murmured, shuddering at the horrors of his past.

If the commander called something that nearly gave him two heart attacks "training," then training it was. If she called a drill with the artillery that included some live rounds "practice," all they could do was resign themselves to the truth. Their schooling was so rigorous that it may very well have been more terrifying than actual combat.

In his position as second-in-command, Weiss was more painfully aware than he wanted to be that training cost money. Their battalion had already gone through a scraggly regiment's worth of annual exercise budget. The amount generously spent on exercises—a rare exception under Major von Degurechaff's command given her hatred of waste—was considerable.

He had never once wondered what sort of battle she was anticipating. Still, after his mistake in Dacia and redeeming himself in Norden—all the different combat experiences he'd had—he finally understood to some extent. What Major von Degurechaff's vice commander had learned was a simple principle.

By thoroughly training them and then accumulating further instruction in the form of combat experience, Major von Degurechaff was hardening her battalion into a battle-worthy unit step-by-step, attempting to educate them while carrying out missions and racking up achievements.

In a way, you could say she was trying to whip her hastily formed battalion into elite shape.

That's why he'd heard her (and wondered at the time if he'd heard wrong) rail against the idea of allowing a lower standard of discipline due to the addition of new recruits.

In fact, he probably should have been surprised she even took on the assignment of rearing Grantz and the other newbies. As a result, however, it was fair to say that there was a reason the commander's philosophy changed from handpicking elites to forcing cultivation.

Or you could say she had her own form of trust in her superior officer's nose. Something had invited a change.

Some reason that she needed mages "even just for head count."

That was why Weiss had been looking out for the group newcomers. To his happy surprise, he got the impression Lieutenant Grantz would make a fine officer.

That was why, even if Major von Degurechaff wasn't grumbling, he wanted to tell the new recruits how things really were. That was his way of showing kindness.

**》》》 MAY 21, UNIFIED YEAR 1925, IMPERIAL ARMY GENERAL STAFF OFFICE, 《《《
DINING ROOM 1 (ARMY)**

Major General von Rudersdorf had heard that General Staff Office meals were prepared with the same budget and ingredients as on the front lines, for the extremely persuasive reason that it wouldn't do for soldiers back from the battlefield to be jealous of the food in the rear.

That's what he'd heard, but he wondered, as he washed down a bite of bone-dry K-Brot with some water, whether frontline food was perhaps better than what he had been served. *I doubt the food committee that came up with this even tried any for themselves* was his calm impression, dripping with the brand of cynicism particular to those with plenty of combat experience.

VII

Knowing them, they came at it purely from a nutritional point of view, debated at length, considered all the details of securing production costs and ingredients. During all that time, I'm sure not a single person paid any attention to the crucial element of flavor. That has to be it. He aired his complaint as a sigh, cleansing the lingering crumbs and awful flavor from his mouth with another drink. *Who would think to mass-produce this stuff?*

That said, across from him, Zettour had resigned himself to accepting the bread and ate it with a straight face. *Perhaps resignation is the best spice for this,* thought Rudersdorf as he decided to set aside his myriad grievances with the bread.

Their plan was proceeding almost exactly according to schedule. They were perfectly prepared for their escape forward.

Operation *Schrecken und Ehrfurcht* ("Shock and Awe") was mere seconds away from launch.

Ever onward. We have no choice but to advance.

"Are we going to eat in silence? I must be more nervous than I thought."

"Aha, hmm. I can't believe you said that. Nervous? I always thought you, at least, were a stranger to nerves, Zettour."

"I could say the same. I'm surprised *you're* nervous."

The pair bantered as they had since their college days.

But... Rudersdorf wasn't averse to admitting he was anxious.

The fate of their fatherland hung on this operation. If the revolving door didn't work as planned, if they failed to cut off the enemy's head... they would be forced back to square one.

Still, he thought.

The only way out of this for the Empire is to keep moving ahead.

We must advance.

The only thing they could do was escape forward.

Onward. Onward still.

We'll blaze a trail for the fatherland. We'll smash everything that stands in its way. Oh, we swear to forge the future of our fatherland.

""Comrades, lead the Empire to victory!""

"Major von Degurechaff to all hands. It is now 1700 hours."

At the appointed time of their sealed orders, having synced watches with her adjutant, Tanya solemnly reports the hour.

"I agree, First Lieutenant Weiss," Tanya's second-in-command attests.

After making sure all the officers present are prepared to log the contents with no room for misunderstanding, Tanya nods and draws the knife at her hip.

"All right. Let's open it."

She casually slices into the secure package with the dagger and pulls out a sheaf of documents. Judging from the texture, it's probably the extra-flammable oil paper with the General Staff's watermark. I can tell from the blurring of the letters that they were thoughtful enough to use water-based ink. It's fairly exciting.

After flipping through the documents with a practiced eye, I've gotten the gist of it.

…Ultimately, the only move we have is to pierce straight through the front. In this situation, if we can't force a path to open up, the only alternative is to gather even more strength and find a way to break through.

Which must have been why the Imperial Army General Staff Service Corps and Operations Division arrived at such a rather unusual solution.

Even I think escaping forward is our only way out of this.

So…

If there is nothing to do but advance, we have to press forward like crazy with no thought to stopping.

"Lieutenant Serebryakov, gather the troops. Lieutenant Weiss, give this a look."

Routine exchanges. Tanya sends her adjutant to assemble the battalion, fills her vice commander in, and prepares for the attack.

Afterward, the brief comment she has for her officers is the same as always.

"Attention, officers. There is only the unflinching advance. Go forward, then press on."

No, stopping won't be allowed.

"This will be an indomitable advance. Anyone who falters won't be permitted to live."

It's our first and last chance. That's why we must get through.

Only onward.

Onward still.

(The Saga of Tanya the Evil, Volume 2: Plus Ultra, Fin)

A Borrowed Cat

It was a cold, cloudy day.

Magic Second Lieutenant Tanya Degurechaff felt more alone than ever. She'd been putting up a hopeless solo resistance for seventy-two hours with no end in sight.

In a corner of the imperial capital, Berun, where the core of the Imperial Army gathered, she was alone and friendless.

The wave attack was conducted by terrifyingly unyielding opponents who had never learned how to hold back. Her mental processing was saturated almost immediately, and the situation rapidly deteriorated into one she couldn't manage.

She was supposed to be the outstanding field officer who returned from Norden, received the Silver Wings Assault Badge despite being alive, and was so graceful she was given the alias "White Silver." But in this extreme circumstance, Lieutenant Degurechaff could only defend herself in a daze like she was newly commissioned and didn't know how to fight.

This is indeed the shame of being trampled after a lone battle, your resistance proving futile. The helplessness assailing her brain gave way to an empty feeling, like her mind was being ground down to nothing.

But even then, she couldn't run away.

Running away would be a major breach of trust as an imperial soldier; as a soldier, period; and, when it came down to it, as a modern civilized person with contractual obligations. As much as she might like to take emergency evacuation measures, fleeing before the enemy meant death by firing squad.

Continuing was hell, but fleeing meant ruin.

In that case… Tanya roused her timid heart, reviving her determination to resist until the very end.

In Norden when I faced an entire company, wasn't I prepared to die?

Didn't that mad scientist force me to go along with all sorts of dangerous experiments?

But here I am, still alive. Yes, alive. I didn't break.

Unyielding spirit. Free will and an even obstinate devotion to her dignity.

Using all those things, she—Magic Second Lieutenant Tanya Degurechaff—took a firm stance with indomitable resolve, bracing herself.

"Tanya, sweetie, are you here?"

Sadly.

"Hey, today we're finally gonna get your makeup done!"

Her indomitable resolve.

"It's a special occasion, so why not, right? We got a cute outfit for you! C'mon, let's try it on!"

Her oath to resist.

"Change into this, okay?"

Her sense of dignity.

"And this is a new corset. You said the other one was too hard to move in, so I brought the most flexible one. C'mon, c'mon."

Today, under these circumstances, they would all be crushed underfoot.

…It all started with orders she received three days previously.

It was supposed to be a mission to help out with some minor business in the rear as part of her receiving the Silver Wings Assault Badge and being transferred back there. Of course, this was the "minor" of not only the military's but any organization's upper echelons. It had to be taken with a grain of salt.

But she wasn't going to become the guinea pig of a mad scientist and get blown up by his invention; she wasn't going to have to perform delaying action in isolation on the front lines; this time it was supposed to be simply supplying a word or two on some topics for a little propaganda piece.

Nothing had seemed problematic when she received the orders, but the moment she knocked on the door of the Culture and Promotion Division in her type I dress uniform, things started to go haywire.

Her hair was tucked under her well-starched cap, and her Silver Wings Assault Badge gleamed on her chest according to regulation. She could move briskly after her injuries in Norden thanks to advanced magic treatment for mages, and she thought she had made a model salute. Her boots were polished to such mirror perfection that even her sergeant at the academy wouldn't have been able to pick on her.

"Be mindful that as a magic officer, you are a model member of the Reich." She thought she had followed her orders to the letter. Like past heroes who had left behind any number of propaganda photos, she would say beautiful things and look sharp like an officer should.

First impressions stick in people's minds, so she had given her appearance extra attention.

And yet. She was forced to realize she had made a huge mistake.

The moment she walked into the room and everyone's eyes gathered on her, there were sighs.

She was then dragged before similarly disappointed military women, who grumbled at her so furiously she didn't know what they were talking about.

Before she knew it, she was stripped of her new riding breeches, the boots she'd spent half a day polishing were thrown away, and although she just managed to keep her underwear, she lost her cap.

Her resistance futile, she was forced into an outfit so mortifying she could hardly take it.

A floor-length frilly skirt, incomprehensibly designed, and a pair of strappy women's shoes that would be impossible to march in.

But all that was still tolerable compared with the smiling murmurs. Before that, she still had room to debate.

"It's great that your skin is so clear! We heard you were hurt, so we were worried…but I guess the surgeon did a great job! And your legs are so slim. Try this one for just a second."

It was another frilly skirt, but for some reason, this one left her legs exposed when she sat down. And to top it off, the corset's restraints were pulled impossibly tight until she could hardly breathe.

Hurry, hurry, please just be over. Tanya could only hope, but even that was in vain; it went on for half a day. And when both her body and mind were flagging, finally the hands of the woman in charge stopped moving. *It's finally over.* She had nearly sighed it aloud when she suddenly heard something that made her heart freeze.

"Well, this simple outfit is good enough for the first day. Let's try some makeup!"

The first day? ... The first day?!

"Oh my gosh, your hair! Are you taking care of it properly?!"

"Huh? Umm, according to hygiene regulations—"

Her hair was cut to regulation length. In some ways, the Imperial Army was quite traditional, and this was a vestige of a rule created mainly with nobles in mind. The bizarre regulation stated that "in order to distinguish the sexes of young members of the service" or whatnot, girls who went through the academy before they had reached conscription age were to maintain shoulder-length hair. When she had looked into it, the imperative turned out to have been included mainly for the sake of noblewomen.

Sadly, the Imperial Army stuck fast to the rules, so she had to grow her hair that long, too. But Tanya could boast that her duty was performed in full. It was the perfect length—she measured it.

"Stop right there. Do you brush it?"

"Sorry, uh…"

"What kind of comb do you normally use?!"

"The standard-issue…"

There was nothing she could do. Every time she opened her mouth, the lady's expression grew more severe, and she couldn't fix it.

"Hold on. By the standard-issue, do you mean this…celluloid one?"

"Yes, that's right…"

"That's insane! We've got to teach you from square one!"

With that, she took out several combs and began to speak voluminously about each one, while Tanya stood there and felt like her mind was being physically scraped away.

...O Being X, I don't even care if it's thee this time...

If you call yourself God, then you should be able to at least fix this issue with my hair. No, I know it's impossible. I know it's impossible, but...

In her thoughts, she began bandying about absurdities that would affect her life's mission. But as her mind was about to escape reality, she was suddenly jolted back by something that looked like a branding iron.

"Umm, excuse me, what might that be...?"

"Oh? So you *are* interested in some of this, huh? I do think you would look charming with a perm. Hmm, wanna try it?"

"No, uh, er, with that iron rod?"

"Yeah, you use it to make waves, you know?"

She smiled and said she was confident in her wave-making techniques. But honestly, at the point Tanya heard that the rod would be used, all she could think about was formulating some plan of escape.

"Uhh, no thanks, er, I think it would interfere with my duties..."

"Yeah. It's too bad, but I guess we'll have to hold off on that. Then I'll at least do your makeup really nice."

"...I can't just look the way I always do?"

She knew it was a bit late to say that. She was ashamed to admit she had been overpowered, but if she wasn't able to speak up, then it would have been the undeniable truth. So she mustered her courage and asked. Would her type I dress uniform really not work?

"You look too dangerous like that. And you can talk in a gentler, more girlie way, you know. Just because you're in the army doesn't mean you have to act like a man."

"Oh, this is easier for me..."

"Oh boy, well, let's at least try this, okay? We have four days until the event, so let's do our best here, all right?"

Thus, she was shot down.

If this is how it's going to be, I'll take the battlefield. I want to go back...

How many times did she murmur that deep inside?

It went on for three days. She withstood the weirdness of the foundation brushed onto her face, the stickiness of the lipstick, the constricting corset, all of it.

…If public relations wants a dear little patriot and if that is recognized as an order by the army…then I have no choice…

Suppress yourself.
This is work. Smile, c'mon, smile.
"Hello, everyone! I'm White Silver, also known as Tanya Degurechaff!"

(Fin)

Appendixes

Mapped Outline of History

Mapped Outline of History

❶ Year 2, Part 1

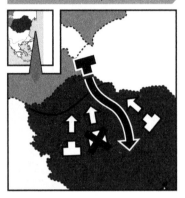

❷ Year 2, Part 2

Imperial Army Seventh Air Fleet mops up the remaining enemies.

The 203rd Aerial Mage Battalion completes its mission, returns to base.

1 The Principality of Dacia mobilizes its forces. A group of three armies near the Empire begin maneuvers and cross the border.

2 The Imperial Army's 203rd Aerial Mage Battalion rapidly deploys and secures control of the sky. With air supremacy, they devastate the command structure of the Dacian vanguard.

3 The Imperial Army grants the Seventh Air Fleet permission to engage.

4 The 203rd Aerial Mage Battalion takes advantage of the ground forces' confusion caused by the Seventh Air Fleet's attack to infiltrate the enemy capital. Later, they bomb and destroy an arms factory.

1 With the support of the Seventh Air Fleet, the Imperial Army launches its counterattack operation.

2 Imperial Army units break through the center and succeed in further disrupting the Dacian Army's communication lines.

3 The Dacian Army begins a general retreat. Due to the chaotic state of the railways, the ground troops' withdrawal is delayed. Unable to get a handle on the snowballing attrition, the main force finds their organizational collapse accelerating. The Dacian Army ultimately loses its three core armies. The Imperial Army begins pacification operations.

4 The Imperial Army's 203rd Aerial Mage Battalion is transferred to Norden.

5 Pacification goes smoothly. The Dacian capital is occupied.

Summary of the Dacian War

→The Imperial Army scored an overwhelming victory, later dubbed the "most realistic exercise maneuver," thanks to their advantages in organized movement, superior firepower, greater mobility, and absolute control of the sky.

❸Year 2, Part 3

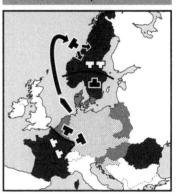

1 The 203rd Aerial Mage Battalion participates in an interception mission in Norden, engaging Entente Alliance attackers led by Lieutenant Colonel Sue.

2 The Imperial Northern Army Group conducts an amphibious landing operation with the support of the High Seas Fleet. The 203rd Aerial Mage Battalion joins the operation, parachuting in to suppress the guns defending the fjord. Following that, the army units make a successful landing supported by the fleet.

3 With its rear communication lines severed, the Entente Alliance front lines crumble. Having lost the capital, the remnants of the Entente troops retreat north and attempt to set up new defensive lines.

Mapped Outline of History

❹Year 2, Part 4

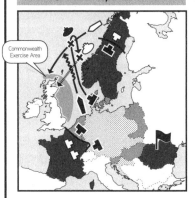

Commonwealth Exercise Area

Summary of the War in the North

→Overall, the Imperial Army succeeded in curbing the confusion caused by the sudden, major change to its war policy, properly reorganizing their lines.

Additionally, this battle established the model of using a large-scale landing maneuver in the enemy's rear to destroy communication lines, the first operation of its kind.

Based on several lessons they learned from the experience, the imperial military later conducted a joint exercise between the fleet and a mage unit.

Various issues concerning anti-ship warfare are brought up for discussion.

1 The ten councilors of the Entente Alliance launch their escape plan in order to establish a government in exile. The same day, the Commonwealth's fleet performs large-scale exercises near the Empire's blockaded waters.

2 The Imperial High Seas Fleet along with air and mage units sortie to interdict any attempted passage through the blockaded waters.

3 The 203rd Aerial Mage Battalion, assisting in the search, encounters a ship. At the same time, an imperial submarine attacks.

4 After spotting the ship, the 203rd reports contact with the submarine. On their way back to base, they receive word of a suspicious ship and go to investigate.

5 The 203rd Aerial Mage Battalion sinks a submarine of unknown nationality.

6 The Imperial Northern Army Group succeeds in occupying virtually all of the Entente Alliance territory. They continue mopping up enemy forces.

❶ Year 3, Part 1

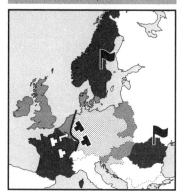

1 The 203rd Aerial Mage Battalion is transferred to the Rhine front.

2 A pro-Republic revolt in the city of Arene, located to the rear of Imperial Army frontline forces, threatens their communications. Fearing that the rebellion would cut its supply lines exactly like their forces had done in the north, imperial leadership sends in the 203rd and other units to suppress the uprising with military force.

3 The Imperial Army General Staff plans a tidying up of the Rhine lines. The purpose is to concentrate forces and put them in good order in preparation for a major counteroffensive. An information battle begins; nominally, the reason for the withdrawal is imperial anxiety about communication lines to the rear.

4 The Imperial Army conducts its reorganization, abandoning the Low Lands. The 203rd Aerial Mage Battalion performs rearguard duty during the operation.

Afterword

Before I greet you, I, Carlo Zen, declare:

The publisher known as Enterbrain actually has only one screw that's tight. On top of the title, *The Saga of Tanya the Evil*, this revised manuscript with no concern for political correctness... When they were working on my revised manuscript for Volume 1, they didn't say a word. I seriously wondered what level hero they are.

Now then, they're a bit belated, but greetings.

To those of you who bought books one and two at the same time: Nice to meet you. I appreciate you buying these two thick books. I have the feeling it's probably already too late, but...you might want to read the afterword from Volume 1 first and then come back here.

Next, to the readers of book one who picked up this book: My apologies for keeping you waiting. I personally regret it very much. I wrote in the back of the first book that the next one would be out "next spring," but I totally meant spring in the southern hemisphere (huge lie). To speak in extremes, I guess we could say the problem was Clausewitz's internal friction. And I was busy with moving and whatnot. I won't mention the name of the company, but a certain major communications infrastructure something or other had me nearly crying at the standard of their east side service. That's what they call "external friction."

In other words, Clausewitz wrote about why my book was late in *On War*. Ahh, the fog of war is scary. In conclusion, it wasn't Carlo Zen's fault.

*　　*　　*

...Uhh, I'm going to make the next volume more compact and get it to you sooner. This one is so thick I'm getting scolded to make the afterword short.

Okay, I've fulfilled my duty of accountability (I've decided), so on to a few gripes. To be blunt, it seems that you all like Grantz, or Weiss, or the middle-aged Ze-Ru duo better than Degu-san.

Please take another look at the cover. This is a light novel called *The Saga of Tanya the Evil*. It's popular among authors I know, as well as children—a light novel with a favorable reception. In other words, it's a story you can enjoy as a family.

Strangely, my editor is like, "I like when the older guys get a turn. I feel closer to them than Degu-san, so I can relax, lol," explicitly telling me to boost their presence. But I won't yield to this pressure.

So as not to turn my title, *The Saga of Tanya the Evil*, into a scam and earn society's harsh criticism, I will do my duty, even if I must resist pressure from my editor and some readers telling me, "Give us more of the cool old dudes."

Rest easy as you wait for Volume 3.

P.S. Last time I forgot to put this in. I'm peaceably extolling the virtues of peace, love, and democracy on Twitter: @sonzaix

May 2014 *Carlo Zen*

HAVE YOU BEEN TURNED ON TO LIGHT NOVELS YET?

IN STORES NOW!

SWORD ART ONLINE, VOL. 1–12
SWORD ART ONLINE, PROGRESSIVE 1–4

The chart-topping light novel series that spawned the explosively popular anime and manga adaptations!

MANGA ADAPTATION AVAILABLE NOW!

SWORD ART ONLINE © Reki Kawahara ILLUSTRATION: abec
KADOKAWA CORPORATION ASCII MEDIA WORKS

ACCEL WORLD, VOL. 1–13

Prepare to accelerate with an action-packed cyber-thriller from the bestselling author of *Sword Art Online*.

MANGA ADAPTATION AVAILABLE NOW!

ACCEL WORLD © Reki Kawahara ILLUSTRATION: HIMA
KADOKAWA CORPORATION ASCII MEDIA WORKS

SPICE AND WOLF, VOL. 1–19

A disgruntled goddess joins a traveling merchant in this light novel series that inspired the *New York Times* bestselling manga.

MANGA ADAPTATION AVAILABLE NOW!

SPICE AND WOLF © Isuna Hasekura ILLUSTRATION: Jyuu Ayakura
KADOKAWA CORPORATION ASCII MEDIA WORKS

IS IT WRONG TO TRY TO PICK UP GIRLS IN A DUNGEON?, VOL. 1–10

A would-be hero turns damsel in distress in this hilarious send-up of sword-and-sorcery tropes.

MANGA ADAPTATION AVAILABLE NOW!

Is It Wrong to Try to Pick Up Girls in a Dungeon? © Fujino Omori / SB Creative Corp.

FUJINO OMORI
ILLUSTRATION BY SUZUHITO YASUDA

ANOTHER

The spine-chilling horror novel that took Japan by storm is now available in print for the first time in English—in a gorgeous hardcover edition.

MANGA ADAPTATION AVAILABLE NOW!

Another © Yukito Ayatsuji 2009/ KADOKAWA CORPORATION, Tokyo

A CERTAIN MAGICAL INDEX, VOL. 1–14

Science and magic collide as Japan's most popular light novel franchise makes its English-language debut.

MANGA ADAPTATION AVAILABLE NOW!

A CERTAIN MAGICAL INDEX © Kazuma Kamachi
ILLUSTRATION: Kiyotaka Haimura
KADOKAWA CORPORATION ASCII MEDIA WORKS

VISIT YENPRESS.COM TO CHECK OUT ALL THE TITLES IN OUR NEW LIGHT NOVEL INITIATIVE AND...

GET YOUR YEN ON!

www.YenPress.com